D1226886

THE TEN COMMANDMENTS

Ten Short Novels of Hitler's War Against the Moral Code

THOMAS MANN · REBECCA WEST

FRANZ WERFEL · JOHN ERSKINE

BRUNO FRANK · JULES ROMAINS

ANDRÉ MAUROIS · SIGRID UNDSET

HENDRIK WILLEM VAN LOON · LOUIS BROMFIELD

Edited by ARMIN L. ROBINSON *with a*

Preface by HERMAN RAUSCHNING

Simon and Schuster NEW YORK, 1943

PUBLISHED BY SIMON AND SCHUSTER, INC.
ROCKEFELLER CENTER, 1230 SIXTH AVENUE,
NEW YORK 20, N. Y.

About the Appearance of Books in Wartime

A recent ruling by the War Production Board has curtailed the use of paper by book publishers in 1943.

In line with this ruling and in order to conserve materials and manpower, we are co-operating by:

1. Using lighter-weight paper, which reduces the bulk of our books substantially.
2. Printing books with smaller margins and with more words to each page. Result: fewer pages per book.

Slimmer and smaller books will save paper and plate metal and labor. We are sure that readers will understand the publishers' desire to co-operate as fully as possible with the objectives of the War Production Board and our government.

MANUFACTURED IN THE UNITED STATES OF AMERICA
BY AMERICAN BOOK–STRATFORD PRESS, INC., N. Y.

EDITOR'S FOREWORD

It is my hope that this book—Thomas Mann's story of the man who gave the world the Ten Commandments, and the other nine stories dealing with the men who have sought to destroy those Commandments—will help to open the eyes of those who still do not recognize what Nazism really is.

It was a privilege and a great personal satisfaction to have been able to co-operate in the final realization of this volume with Sigrid Undset, Rebecca West, Louis Bromfield, John Erskine, Bruno Frank, Thomas Mann, André Maurois, Jules Romains, Hendrik Willem van Loon, and Franz Werfel.

I am deeply grateful to these ten distinguished novelists for their enthusiastic collaboration, to Dr. Herman Rauschning for his thoughtful preface, and to Messrs. Simon and Schuster for the generous and wholehearted manner in which they made the launching of this book possible.

October 6th, 1943

ARMIN L. ROBINSON

CONTENTS

PREFACE

A CONVERSATION WITH HITLER

BY HERMAN RAUSCHNING

AT AN intimate gathering in Berlin shortly after the National Socialists' rise to power, I heard Hitler reveal himself on the most important and profound problem of our great crisis: the ethical foundation of life. What I heard proved deeply upsetting. For the first time the true face of this immense revolution of destruction unfolded itself to me.

The call "Back to nature" resounds through all the great crises of human history. To shed the burdens of civilization has been man's continuous endeavor during great transmutations. However, what the leader of the National Socialist movement sought was the deliberate destruction of the very earth whence our civilization had sprung. The great accomplishments of a long and painful history of human development were to be hurled overboard. His was no mere struggle to uproot outmoded forms in our civilization. His was a murderous assault on every form of higher human culture.

I wrote down the conversation as well and faithfully as my memory allowed. It may not be literal, word for word. But its spirit is authentic. I transmitted parts of it, in the spring of 1937, through a friend to the then Nuntius Pacelli, now Pope Pius XII. I sent excerpts to some Protestant clergymen who have been close to me. Other parts I published in my book, *The Voice of Destruction.*

The result was the same everywhere: skepticism, disagreement, and even confusion. Some of my readers held that Hitler was voicing their own ideas and desires as to humanity's maturing process. They held that I was making propaganda for Hitler.

The horrible destruction which now shakes the world makes clear to each of us today that the demoniac forces of disruption are more than mere expressions of the National Socialist's and imperialist's thirst for power. In the few pages which follow I shall give a supplemental fragment to those previously published. Only today is it becoming comprehensive. It concerns all of us, Christians, Jews, and freethinking humanists alike. It deals with the deliberately planned battle against the dignified, immortal foundation of human society; the message from Mount Sinai. Let us name it clearly and simply: Hitler's Battle Against the Ten Commandments.

By telephone Hitler had invited Albert Forster, *Gauleiter* of Danzig, and me, to spend the evening with him at the Reich Chancery. Hitler was then living on the second floor of the new Reich Chancery, which had just been completed.

We had to wait. Hitler (Goebbels was with him) was attending the performance of a new movie. When he arrived finally at a late hour we gathered in his private (at that time still), modestly furnished study. We had tea and pastries. Frau Raubal, Hitler's stepsister, a somewhat stout, matronly woman, played *Hausfrau*. I was sitting next to her, Hitler's desk at my back. Frau Magda Goebbels was seated opposite me. Hitler himself was conversing with some of his most intimate advisers. Herr Hanfstaengl ("Putzi"), then still a trusted adviser on foreign affairs, was improvising on the grand piano in the adjoining room.

Hitler had expressed himself on the new movie, and on "nationalistic" movies in general. Even the so-called experts, Hitler said, imagined that all was well as long as they chose a nationalistic, patriotic subject. He sneered at the wrong speculations on enthusiasm and patriotic fanaticism which would bring from the audiences merely negative reactions, and he developed a few basic principles as to the usage of movies as a political weapon. I did not follow the conversation in detail. Presently Hitler touched upon some important points in current politics. The *Gauleiter* of

Franconia and Bavaria had approached him because of a certain opposition in Bavaria, and they were pressing him for a decision. At that time, the institution of so-called *Reichsstatthalters* was being discussed. The conversation was carried on in low voices.

Suddenly I heard Hitler scream in his well-known manner. He was standing in front of his desk, leafing through a scrapbook with newspaper clippings about him from the time of his struggle for power. "No," Hitler yelled at Goebbels and Streicher, who were standing before him. "I am not interested. Whether 'German Christians' or Roman Catholics or God knows what kinds of Protestant sneaks, I am not interested."

"Give them an inch and they'll take a yard," Goebbels agreed. "The enthusiasm of those 'German Christians' for our movement is as big a lie as anything that has come from Protestant quarters. By misusing us for their miserable 'Away from Rome' movement, they consider themselves particularly smart."

"But don't you think we ought to support the German religious movement of Professor Hauer and others?" Julius Streicher asked.

"All this is cramped," Hitler replied contemptuously. "It is false and deceitful and without strength."

"And Chamberlain's book, *Words of Jesus*? Couldn't one cut the German churches loose from their connection with the Jewish Old Testament in the same manner?" inquired Wagner, *Gauleiter* from Munich.

"Houston Stuart Chamberlain has had the right attitude toward many of our most urgent problems," Hitler answered. "But what he has been trying to do with this 'non-Jewish' Christianity idea of his is completely nonsensical."

"Marcion already tried to separate Christianity from Judaism," Goebbels interjected. "It never worked. It couldn't possibly work."

"Historically speaking, the Christian religion is nothing but a Jewish sect. It has always been and it will always remain just that, as long as it will exist," Hitler went on.

"We don't fight only the Christian circles, we fight against

Christian ideas. They constitute the real poison in our blood," Streicher said.

"That's right. After the destruction of Judaism, the extinction of Christian slave morals must follow logically." Hitler began to pace up and down in his room. "I shall know the moment when to confront, for the sake of the German people and the world, their Asiatic slave morals with our picture of the free man, the godlike man."

"There is no difference between freemasonry and Christianity," Streicher exclaimed. "Both are the instruments of secret Jewish world domination."

"There is much more behind this," Hitler began fanatically. "It is not merely a question of Christianity and Judaism. We are fighting against the most ancient curse that humanity has brought upon itself. We are fighting against the perversion of our soundest instincts. Ah, the God of the deserts, that crazed, stupid, vengeful Asiatic despot with his powers to make laws! That slavekeeper's whip! That devilish 'Thou shalt, thou shalt!' And that stupid 'Thou shalt not.' It's got to get out of our blood, that curse from Mount Sinai! That poison with which both Jews and Christians have spoiled and soiled the free, wonderful instincts of man and lowered them to the level of doglike fright."

"The youth is on our side," Goebbels exclaimed triumphantly. "The youth of the whole world is no more interested in those old ideologies."

"The time for false considerations has ended. This is true. We no longer need to be considerate," Hitler went on. "Whatever is against nature is against life itself. That's why nations die out. They kill themselves under the curse of that 'Thou shalt' and 'Thou shalt not.'"

"Honor thy father and thy mother? No!" Goebbels interrupted. "Every boy revolts, and hates his father, and must do so to start his own life. It's an immortal law of nature."

"Thou shalt not steal? Wrong!" Hitler's voice was loud in the small room. "All life is theft."

"Thou shalt not desire thy neighbor's this and that . . . Thou shalt not commit adultery . . . Thou shalt, thou shalt not . . . what not." Goebbels laughed derisively.

"I am the Lord thy God! Who? That Asiatic tyrant? No! The day will come when I shall hold up against these commandments the tables of a new law. And history will recognize our movement as the great battle for humanity's liberation, a liberation from the curse of Mount Sinai, from the dark stammerings of nomads who could no more trust their own sound instincts, who could understand the divine only in the form of a tyrant who orders one to do the very things one doesn't like. This is what we are fighting against: the masochistic spirit of self-torment, the curse of so-called morals, idolized to protect the weak from the strong in the face of the immortal law of battle, the great law of divine nature. Against the so-called ten commandments, against them we are fighting."

THE FIRST COMMANDMENT

Thou shalt have no other gods before me

THOMAS MANN

I

THOU SHALT HAVE NO OTHER GODS BEFORE ME

A STORY BY

THOMAS MANN

HIS BIRTH was disorderly. Therefore he passionately loved order, the immutable, the bidden, and the forbidden.

Early he killed in frenzy; therefore he knew better than the inexperienced that, though killing is delectable, *having* killed is detestable; he knew you should not kill.

He was sensual, therefore he longed for the spiritual, the pure, and the holy—in a word, the *invisible*—for this alone seemed to him spiritual, holy, and pure.

Among the Midianites, a nimble tribe of shepherds and merchants strewn across the desert, to whom he had to flee from Egypt, the land of his birth, because he had killed (details in a moment), he made the acquaintance of a god whom one could not see but who saw you. This god was a mountain dweller who at the same time sat invisible on a transportable chest in a tent and there dispensed oracles by the drawing of lots. To the children of Midian this numen, called Jahwe, was one god among many; they did not bother very much about serving him. What service they undertook they did to be on the safe side, just in case. For it had occurred to them that among the gods there could possibly be a bodiless one whom one did not see, and they sacrificed to him so as not to miss anything, so as not to offend anybody, and so as to forestall any unpleasantness from any quarter.

But Moses, because of his desire for the pure and the holy, was deeply impressed by the invisibility of Jahwe; he believed that no visible god could compete in holiness with an invisible one, and he marveled that the children of Midian attached so little importance to a characteristic which seemed to him full of immeasurable implications. While he minded the sheep belonging to the brother of his Midianitic wife, he plunged himself into long, deep, and violent cogitations. He was moved by inspirations and visions which in one case even left his inner consciousness and returned to his soul as a flaming vision from without, as a precisely worded pronouncement, and as an unshirkable command. Thus he reached the conviction that Jahwe was none other than El'eljon, the Only-Highest, El ro'i, the God who sees me, He who had always been known as El Schaddai, "the God of the Mountain," El 'olām, the God of the World and the Eternities—in short, the God of Abraham, Jizchak, and Jacob, the God of the Fathers. And that meant the God of the poor, dumb, in their worship completely confused, uprooted, and enslaved tribes at home in Egypt, whose blood, from his father's side, flowed in the veins of Moses.

Full of this discovery, his soul heavy with command but trembling also with the wish to fulfill the mission, Moses ended his stay of many years with the children of Midian. He placed his wife Zipporah (a sufficiently noble woman because she was a daughter of Reuel, the priest-king of Midian, and the sister of his herd-owning son, Jethro) on a mule. He took along also his two sons, Gershom and Eliezer, and returned, traveling westward in seven day-journeys through many deserts, to the land of Egypt. That is to the lower land, the fallow country where the Nile branches out into the district called Kōs, and variously known as Goschem, Gosem, and Goshen. It was here that the tribes of his fathers lived and drudged.

Here he immediately began to communicate his great experience to his kinsfolk; he talked to them wherever he went and stood, in their huts, their grazing grounds, and their workplaces. When he spoke he had a certain way of letting his arms hang limp at his sides, while his fists shook and trembled. He informed them that the God of their Fathers was found again, that He had made himself known to him, Moscheh ben 'Amram, on the mountain

Hor in the desert Sin from a bush which burned but never burned out. This God was called Jahwe, which name is to be understood as "I am that I am, from eternity to eternity," but also as flowing air and as mighty sound. This God was inclined toward their tribe and was ready under certain conditions to enter into a covenant with them, choosing them above all other peoples. The conditions were that they would devote themselves in full exclusiveness to him and that they would form a sworn brotherhood to serve him alone in worship of the invisible, a worship without images.

Moses stormed at them and the fists on his broad wrists trembled. Yet he was not completely honest with them, and kept under cover much, indeed the essential thought, he had in mind. Fearing he might scare them off, he said nothing of the implications of invisibility, that is, its spirituality, its purity, its holiness. He preferred not to point out that as sworn servants of the invisible they would have to be a separated people, a people of the spirit, of purity and of holiness. Afraid to frighten them he kept silent. They were so miserable, so oppressed, and in their worship so confused, this kin of his father. He mistrusted them though he loved them. Yes, when he announced to them that Jahwe the Invisible was inclined toward them, he really ascribed to the God and interpreted for the God what possibly was true of the God but what certainly was true of him: for he himself was inclined to his father's kin, as the sculptor is inclined toward the shapeless lump from which he hopes to carve a high and fine figure, the work of his hands. Hence his trembling desire, hence too the great heaviness of soul which filled him directly after his departure from Midian.

He also kept back the second half of the secret; for it was a double secret. It included not only the message to his tribe of the rediscovery of their father's God and the God's inclination toward them; it included also Moses' belief that he was destined to guide them out of Egypt's house of bondage, out into the open, and through many deserts into the land of promise, the land of their fathers. That destiny was part of the mission, inseparably linked with it. God—and liberation for the return home; the Invisible—and release from foreign yoke: to him these were one and the same thought. But to the people he as yet said nothing of this second part of the mission, because he knew that one would inevitably follow from the other; also because he hoped that he himself could negotiate the release with Pharaoh, King of Egypt, with whom he had a not-too-remote connection.

Was it, however, that his speech displeased the people—for he spoke badly and haltingly and often could not find the right word—or did they divine, while he shook his trembling fists, the implications of invisibility as well as those of the covenant? Did they perceive that they were being lured toward strenuous and dangerous matters? Whatever the reason, they remained mistrustful, stiff-necked, and fearful of his storming. They ogled their Egyptian whip-masters and mumbled between their teeth:

"Why do you spout words? And what kinds of words are these you spout? Likely somebody set you up as chief or as judge over us? Well, we wouldn't know who."

That was nothing new to him. He had heard it from them once before, before he had fled to Midian.

2

His father was not his father, nor was his mother his mother. So disorderly was his birth.

One day the second daughter of the Pharaoh Ramessu was amusing herself—under the watchful eyes of the armed guard and in company of her serving maidens—in the royal garden on the Nile. There she espied a Hebrew laborer who was carrying water. She became enamored of him. He had sad eyes, he had a young beard encircling his chin, and he had strong arms, as one could clearly see when he drew the water. He worked by the sweat of his brow and had his troubles, but to Pharaoh's daughter he was the image of beauty and desire. She commanded that he be admitted to her pavilion. There she plunged her precious little hands through his sweat-drenched hair, she kissed the muscles of his arms and charmed his manhood to wakefulness, so that he took possession of her; he, the foreign slave, took possession of the child of a king. When she had had enough, she let him go. But he did not go far; after thirty paces he was slain and quickly buried, so that nothing remained of the pleasure of the Sun-Daughter.

"The poor man," said she when she heard about it. "You are always such busybodies. He would have kept quiet. He loved me." After that she became pregnant, and after nine months she gave birth in all secrecy to a boy. Her serving women placed the boy in a box fashioned of tarred reeds, and they hid the box in the bulrushes on the edge of the water. There in due time they found it and exclaimed, "O magic! A foundling, a boy from the bulrushes, an abandoned child! It is like the old tales, exactly as it happened with Sargon, whom Akki the Water Carrier found in the rushes and reared in the goodness of his heart. Such things happen all the time. What shall we do now with our find? It would be wisest if we gave it to a nursing mother, a woman of simple station who has milk to spare, so that the boy may grow up as her son and the son of her lawful husband." And they handed the child to a Hebrew woman who carried it down into the region of Goshen and there gave it to Jochebed, the wife of Amram, who belonged to the tribe of the Tolerated Ones, to the descendants of Levi. She was nursing her son Aaron and had milk to spare. Therefore, and also because once in a while and quite secretly substantial gifts arrived at her hut from sources higher up, did she rear the unclassified child in the goodness of her heart. Before the world Amram and Jochebed became his parents and Aaron became his brother. Amram possessed cattle and fields, Jochebed was the daughter of a stonemason. She did not know how she should name the questionable child. Therefore she gave him a half-Egyptian name, that is to say, the half of an Egyptian name. For the sons of the land were often called Ptach-Moses,

Amen-Moses, or Ra-Moses. They were named as sons with the names of the gods. Amram and Jochebed preferred to omit the name of the god, and called the child simply Moses. Thus he was called plain "Son." The only question was, whose son.

3

He grew up as one of the Tolerated Ones, and expressed himself in their dialect. The ancestors of this tribe had come into the land long ago at the time of the Drought. They whom Pharaoh's historians described as the "hungry Bedouins from Edom" had come with the due permission of the frontier officials. They had received pasture privileges in the district of Goshen in the lower land. Anybody who believes that they received these privileges for nothing does not know their hosts, the children of Egypt. Not only did they have to pay taxes out of their cattle, and that so heavily that it hurt, but also all who had strength were forced to do manual services at the several building operations which in a country like Egypt are always under way. Especially since Ramessu, the second of his name, had become Pharaoh in Thebes, excessive building was going on, for building was his pleasure and his royal delight. He built prodigal temples all over the land. And down in the Delta region he not only renewed and greatly improved the long-neglected canal which connected the eastern arm of the Nile with the Bitter Lakes and thus the great ocean with the corner of the Red Sea, but he also constructed two arsenal cities on the banks of the canal, called Pithom and Rameses. It was for this work that the children of the Tolerated Ones were drafted. They baked bricks and carried them and drudged in the sweat of their bodies under Egypt's cudgel.

This cudgel was hardly more than a symbol of the authority vested in Pharaoh's overseers. The workers were not unnecessarily beaten with it. They also had good food with their drudgery: much fish from the Nile, bread, beer, and beef, quite as plentiful as they needed. Nevertheless, they did not take to or care for this work, for they were nomads, full of the tradition of a free, roaming life. Labor by the hour, labor which made them sweat, was foreign and insulting to their nature. The tribes, however, were far too tenuously connected and insufficiently conscious of themselves to be able to signal their dissatisfaction to each other, or to become of one firm mind about it. Because several of their generations had lived in a transitional land, pitching their tents between the home of their fathers and the real Egypt, they were now unanchored souls, wavering in spirit and without a secure doctrine. They had forgotten much; they had half assimilated some new thoughts; and because they lacked real orientation, they did not trust their own feelings. They did not trust even the bitterness that they felt toward their bondage, because fish and beer and beef made them uncertain.

Moses, also, as the supposed son of Amram, was destined to form bricks for Pharaoh as soon as he had outgrown his boyhood. But this did not come to pass; the youth was taken away from his parents and was brought to Upper Egypt into a school, a very elegant academy where the sons of the Syrian town kings and the scions of the native nobility were educated. There was he taken, because his real mother, Pharaoh's child, who had delivered him into the bulrushes, was, though somewhat lascivious, not devoid of sentiment. She had remembered him for the sake of his buried father, the water carrier with the beard and the sad eyes. She didn't want Moses to remain with the savages, but wished him to be educated as an Egyptian and to achieve a court position. His half descent from the gods was thus to be half recognized, in silence. Clothed in white linen and with a wig on his head, Moses acquired the knowledge of stars and of countries, the art of writing and of law. Yet he was not happy among the snobs of the elegant academy, but lonely was he among them, filled with aversion toward all of Egypt's refined culture. The blood of the buried one who had been sacrificed to this culture was stronger in him than was his Egyptian portion. In his soul he sided with the poor uncertain ones at home in Goshen, who did not even have the courage of their bitterness. He sided with them against the lecherous arrogance of his mother's kin.

"What was your name again?" his comrades at the school asked him.

"I am called Moses," he answered.

"Ach-Moses or Ptach-Moses?" they asked.

"No, simply Moses," he responded.

"That's inadequate and paltry," said the snobs. And he became enraged, so that he almost wanted to kill and bury them. For he understood that with these questions they simply wished to pry into his uncertain history, which in nebulous outlines was known to everybody. He himself could hardly have known that he was the discreet result of Egyptian pleasure, if it had not been common though somewhat inexact knowledge. Pharaoh himself was as well aware of the trifling escapade of his child as was Moses of the fact that Ramessu, the master builder, was his illegitimate grandfather, and that his paternity was the result of iniquitous, lecherous, and murderous pleasure. Yes, Moses knew this, and he also knew that Pharaoh knew it. And when he thought about it he inclined his head menacingly, inclined it in the direction of Pharaoh's throne.

4

When he had lived two years among the whelps of the school in Thebes, he could stand it no longer, fled by night over the wall, and wandered home to Goshen to his father's tribe. With severe countenance he roamed among them, and one day he saw at the canal near the new buildings in Rameses how an Egyptian overseer beat with his cudgel one of the workers, who probably had been lazy or obdurate. Moses paled. With flaming eyes he challenged the Egyptian, who in short response smashed Moses' nose so that Moses all his life had a nose with a broken flattened bridge. Moses seized the cudgel from the overseer, swung it mightily, and demolished the man's skull so that he lay dead on the spot. Not even once did Moses glance about to find out if anybody had observed him. Fortunately it was a lonely place and not a soul was near. Alone he buried the murdered man; for he whom Moses had defended had instantly taken to his heels. After it was over, Moses felt that killing and burying were what he had always desired in his soul.

His flaming deed remained hidden at least from the Egyptians, who never did find out what had become of their man. A year and a day passed over the deed. Moses continued to roam among his people and to probe into their frays with a peculiar air of authority. So it happened that once he saw two slaves quarreling with each other. They were at the point of violence. "Wherefore do you quarrel and seek to strike each other?" he said to them. "Are you not miserable enough and neglected? Would it not be better for kin to side with kin, instead of baring your teeth to each other? This one is in the wrong: I saw it. Let him give in and be content; nor let the other triumph."

But as usually happens, suddenly both of them were united against him, and they said, "What business is it of yours?" Especially he who was in the wrong was extremely snappy and shouted quite loudly, "Well, this is the height of everything! Who are you that you stick your ugly nose into things that don't concern you? Ahah! You are Moscheh, son of Amram, but that means very little. Nobody really knows who you are, not even you yourself. Curious are we to learn who has appointed you master and judge over us. Perhaps you want to choke me too, as you choked the Egyptian and buried him?"

"Be quiet," whispered Moses, alarmed. And he thought, "How did this get out?" But that very day he understood that it would be no longer possible for him to remain in the country, and he fled across the frontier where the frontier had a loophole, near the muddy shallows of the Bitter Lakes. Through many deserts of the land of Sinai he wandered, and came to Midian, to the Midianites, and to their priest-king, Reuel.

5

When he returned to Egypt, fraught with his discovery and his mission, he was a man at the height of his powers, sturdy, with a sunk-in nose and prominent cheekbones, with a divided beard, eyes set far apart, and wrists that were unusually broad. He had a habit when he meditated of covering his mouth and beard with his right hand, and it was then that those broad wrists were especially noticeable. He went from hut to hut and from workplace to workplace, he shook his fists at the sides of his body and discoursed on the Invisible One, the God of the Fathers, who was ready for the covenant. Actually Moses did not speak well. His nature was halting and pent-up, and when he became excited he was apt to stammer. Nor was he master of any one language, but floundered around in three. The Aramaic Syro-Chaldee, which was the language of his father's kin and which he had learned from his parents, had been glossed over by the Egyptian which he had had to learn at school. And to this was added the Midianitic-Arabic which he had spoken so long in the desert. All of these he jumbled together.

Very helpful to him was his brother Aaron, a tall man with a black beard and with black curls at the nape of his neck. Aaron was gentle and held his large and curved eyelids piously lowered. Moses had initiated Aaron into all his beliefs and had won him over completely to the cause of the Invisible and all its implications. Because Aaron knew how to speak from under his beard fluently and unctuously, he accompanied Moses on his preaching tours and did the talking for him. Admittedly, he spoke in a somewhat palatine and oily fashion, and not nearly transportingly enough to suit Moses, so that Moses, accompanying the speech with his shaking fists, sought to put more fire into his brother's words, and sometimes would blurt helter-skelter into the oration with his own Aramaic-Egyptian-Arabic.

Aaron's wife was named Elisheba, daughter of Amminadab. She

too partook of the oath and the propaganda, and so did a younger sister of Moses and Aaron called Miriam, an inspired woman who knew how to sing and play the timbrel. Moses was especially fond of yet another disciple, a youth who devoted himself body and soul to Moses' plans, and who never left Moses' side. His real name was Hosea, son of Nun (that means "fish"), of the kin of Ephraim. Moses, however, had given him the Jahwe name, Jehoschua—Joshua for short. Joshua was erect and sinewy and curly-headed, had a prominent Adam's-apple and a clearly defined wrinkle between his brows. He carried his new name with pride, though he had his own views of the whole affair, views which were not so much religious as military. For him Jahwe, God of the Fathers, was first of all God of the fighting forces. The idea connected with the God, that is, the idea of flight from the house of bondage, was to him identical with the idea of the conquest of a new grazing ground which would belong solely to the Hebraic tribes. This was logical enough, for they had to live someplace, and nobody was going to hand them any land, promised or not, as a gift.

Joshua, young as he was, carried all the salient facts in his clear-eyed, curly head, and discussed them unceasingly with Moses, his older friend and master. Without having the means of carrying out an exact census, Joshua was able to calculate that the strength of the tribes tenting in Goshen or living in the slave cities, Pithom and Rameses, and including also the slaves who were far-flung over the country, was about twelve or thirteen thousand people. This meant that there were possibly three thousand capable of bearing arms. Later on these figures were immeasurably exaggerated, but Joshua knew them just about correctly, and was little satisfied with them. Three thousand men—that was no terror-inspiring fighting force, even if you counted on the fact that once on the way several kindred tribes roaming the desert would join them for the sake of winning new land. With such a force one could not dream up any major expeditions; with such a force it was impractical to hew one's way into the promised land. Joshua well understood that. His plan, therefore, was to seek first of all a spot in the open, a marking time and resting place, where the tribes could settle and devote themselves to the business of natural multiplication under halfway favorable circumstances. This natural growth amounted to—as Joshua knew his people—two and a half per cent per year. The youth constantly was on the lookout for such a hedged-in hatching place where they could grow further fighting forces. In his frequent consultations with Moses it appeared that Joshua saw with surprising clarity where one place in the world lay in relation to another place. He carried in his head a kind of map of all the interesting districts; he knew their dimensions measured in daytime marches, their watering places, and especially the fighting strength of their inhabitants.

Moses knew what a treasure he possessed in Joshua, knew also that he would have need of him, and loved his ardor, though he was little concerned with the immediate objectives of that ardor. Covering mouth and beard with his right hand, he listened to the strategic theories of the youth, thinking all the while of something else. For him also Jahwe meant an exodus, but not an exodus for a war of land seizure; an exodus rather for seclusion. Out in the open Moses would have all to himself his father's kin, those swaying souls confused in their beliefs, the procreating men, the nursing women, the awakening youths, the dirty-nosed children. There in the open he would be able to imbue them with the holy, invisible God, the pure and spiritual God; there he could give them this God as the center which would unite and form them, form them in his image, form them into a people different from all other peoples; a people belonging to God, denoted by the holy and the spiritual, and distinguished from all others through awe, restraint, and fear of God. That is to say that his people would hold in awe a restraining, pure, spiritual code, a code which, since the Invisible One was in truth the God of the entire world, would in the future bind and unite all peoples, but would at first be given to them alone and be their stern privilege among the heathen.

Thus was Moses' inclination toward his father's blood; it was the sculptor's inclination, and he identified it with the God's choice and the God's desire for the covenant. Because Moses believed that the education toward God must precede all other enterprises, such enterprises as the young Joshua carried in his head, and because Moses knew that such education would take time—free time out in the open—he did not mind that there was so far many a hitch to Joshua's plans, that these plans were thwarted by an insufficient number of fighters. Joshua needed time so that his people could multiply in a natural way; he also needed time so that he himself could become older, old enough to set himself up as commander in chief. Moses needed time for the work of education, which for the God's sake he desired. So they both agreed, if for different reasons.

6

In the meantime he, God's delegate, and his immediate followers, the eloquent Aaron, Elisheba, Miriam, Joshua, and a certain Caleb, who was Joshua's bosom friend, of the same age, and also a strong, simple, courageous youth—in the meantime, they were not idle, not a single day. They were busy spreading Jahwe's message and his flattering offer of alliance among their people. They continued to stoke the people's bitterness against slavery under the Egyptian cudgel, and they planted ever deeper the thought that the yoke must be thrown off through migration. Each of them did it in his own way: Moses himself through halting words and shaking fists; Aaron in unctuously flowing speech, Elisheba with persuasive chatter; Joshua and Caleb in the form of military command, in short and terse slogans; and Miriam, who was soon known as "the Prophetess," in elevated tone to the accompaniment of the timbrel. Their preaching did not fall on barren ground. The thought of allying themselves with Moses' agreeable god to become the chosen people of the Invisible One and under his and his proclaimers' banner to depart for the open —this thought took root among the tribes and began to be their uniting center. This especially because Moses promised, or at least put it forth as a hopeful possibility, that he would be able to obtain the permission for their departure from Egypt through negotiations in the highest place, so that this departure would not have to take the form of a daring uprising but of an amicable agreement. The tribes knew, if inexactly, Moses' half-Egyptian birth into the bulrushes. They knew too of his elegant education and of his ambiguous connections with the court. What used to be a cause of distrust and aversion toward him, namely the fact that he was half foreign and stood with one foot in Egypt, now became a source of confidence and lent him authority. Surely, if anybody, he was the man to stand before Pharaoh and plead their cause. And so they commissioned him to attempt to obtain their release from Ramessu, the master builder and master. They commissioned both him and his foster brother, Aaron. Moses planned to take Aaron along first because he himself could not speak fluently while Aaron could; but also because Aaron had at his disposal certain tricks with which he hoped to make an impression at court in Jahwe's honor. He could take a hooded snake and by pressing its neck make it rigid as a rod. Yet as soon as he cast this rod to the ground, it would curl up and "it became a serpent." Neither Moses nor Aaron took into account the fact that these miracles were quite well known to Pharaoh's magicians, and that they therefore could hardly serve as frightening proof of Jahwe's power.

Altogether, they did not have much luck—it may as well be mentioned beforehand—craftily as they had planned their campaign in council session with the youths Joshua and Caleb. In this council it had been decided to ask the king for permission only that the Hebrew people might assemble and voyage three days across the frontier into the desert so that they could there hold a feast of offering to the god who had called them. Then they would return to work. They did not expect, of course, that

Pharaoh would swallow such a subterfuge and really believe that they would return. It was simply a mild and polite form in which to submit their petition for emancipation. Yet the king did not thank them for it.

However, it must be counted to the credit of the brothers that at least they succeeded in getting into the Great House and before Pharaoh's throne. And that not once but again and again for tenaciously prolonged conferences. In this Moses had not promised too much to his people, for he counted on the fact that Ramessu was his secret and illegitimate grandfather, and that they both knew that each knew it. Moses had a trump card in his hand which, if it was not sufficient to achieve from the king permission for the exodus, was at least potent enough to force hearings for Moses and to grant him audience again and again with the mighty one. For he feared Moses. To be sure, a king's fear is dangerous, and Moses was playing a dangerous game. He was courageous—how very courageous and what impression he was able to make through this courage on his people, we shall soon see. It would have been easy for Ramessu to have had Moses quietly strangled and buried, so that at last really nothing would remain of his child's escapade. But the princess cherished a sentimental memory of that hour, and very obviously did not want harm to befall her bulrush boy. He stood under her protection, ungrateful as he had been for her solicitude and for all her plans of education and advancement.

Thus Moses and Aaron were able to stand before Pharaoh, even if he denied categorically the festival-vacation out into the open to which their god had supposedly summoned them. It availed nothing that Aaron spoke with unctuous logic, while Moses shook his fists passionately. It also availed nothing that Aaron changed his rod into a snake, for Pharaoh's magicians without further ado did the same thing, proving thereby that the Invisible One in whose name both of them were talking could claim no superior powers, and that Pharaoh need not listen to the voice of such a lord.

"But pestilence or the sword shall visit our people if we do not voyage three days and prepare a feast for our God," said the brothers.

The king responded, "That is not my affair. You are numerous enough, more than twelve thousand strong, and you will be able to stand some diminution, whether it be by pestilence or sword or hard work. What you, Moses and Aaron, really want is to permit slothfulness to your people, and to allow them to idle in their lawful labors. But that I cannot suffer nor permit. I have several unprecedented temples in work; furthermore I want to build a third arsenal city in addition to Pithom and Rameses. For that I need the arms of your people. I am obliged to you for your fluent recital, and you, Moses, I dismiss more or less with particular favor. But not a word more of desert vacations!"

The audience was terminated, and not only did it result in nothing good but it afterward had decidedly bad consequences. For Pharaoh, his zeal for building affronted, and annoyed because he could not very well strangle Moses to death—for otherwise his daughter would have made a scene—issued the order that the people of Goshen were to be more pressed with labor than before, and that the cudgel was not to be spared should they be dilatory; on the contrary, they should be made to slave until they fell exhausted, so that all idle thoughts of a desert festival would be driven out of them. Thus it happened. The drudgery became harder from one day to the next for the very reason that Moses and Aaron had talked to Pharaoh. For example, the straw which they needed for the glazing of bricks was no longer furnished to them. They themselves had to go into the fields to gather the stubbles, nor was the number of bricks to be delivered diminished. That number had to be reached or the cudgel danced upon their poor backs. In vain did the Hebrew foremen protest to the authorities because of the exorbitant demands. The answer was, "You are lazy, lazy are you. Therefore you cry and say, 'We want to migrate and make offerings.' The order remains: Gather the straw yourselves—and the same number of bricks."

7

For Moses and Aaron this was no small embarrassment. The foremen said to them, "There you have it. And this is all the good the pact with your god and Moses' connections have done us. Nothing have you accomplished except that you have made our savor worse before Pharaoh and his servants, and that you have given the sword into their hands for them to slaughter us."

It was difficult to answer, and Moses had heavy hours alone with the god of the thorn bush. Moses confronted the god with the fact that from the very beginning he was against this mission, and from the beginning he had implored that whomever the god wanted to send, he should not in any case send him, for he could not speak properly. But the god answered him that Aaron was eloquent. True enough, Aaron had done the speaking, but in much too oily a fashion, and it appeared how absurd it was to undertake such a cause if one had a heavy tongue and was forced to have others plead as deputy. But the god consoled Moses and meted punishment to him from his own soul. He answered Moses from his own soul that he should be ashamed of his halfheartedness. His excuses were pure affectation, for at bottom he himself had longed for the mission, because he himself was as much inclined toward his people and the forming of them as the god. Yes, it was impossible to distinguish his own inclination from the inclination of the god: it was one and the same. This inclination had driven him to the work, and he should be ashamed to be despondent at the first misadventure.

Moses let himself be persuaded, the more so as in the council with Joshua, Caleb, Aaron, and the inspired women they reached the conclusion that the greater oppression, though it did cause bad blood, was, rightly understood, not such a bad beginning. For the bad blood would form itself not only against Moses but also and especially against the Egyptians. It would make the people all the more receptive to the call of the saving God and to the idea of the exodus. Thus it did happen. Among the workers the discontent caused by straw and bricks was fomented, and the accusation that Moses had made their savor worse before Pharaoh and had only harmed them took second place to the wish that Amram's son should once again exploit his connections and once again go for them to Pharaoh.

This he did, but not with Aaron. Alone he went, not caring how haltingly he spoke. He shook his fists before the throne and demanded in stammering and plunging words permission for the exodus for the sake of the festival in the desert. Not once did he do so but a dozen times, for Pharaoh simply could not deny him admission to his throne, so excellent were Moses' connections. It came to a combat between Moses and the king, a tenacious and protracted combat, the result of which was not that the king agreed to Moses' petition and permitted the departure, but rather that one day he drove and chased the people of Goshen from his land, very glad to get rid of them. There has been much talk about this combat and the various threatening measures which were employed against the stubbornly resisting king. This talk is not entirely without basis, though it has been subjected to much ornamentation. Tradition speaks of ten plagues, one after the other, with which Jahwe smote Egypt, in order to wear down Pharaoh, while at the same time he purposely hardened Pharaoh's heart against Moses' demands, for the sake of proving his might with ever-new plagues. Blood, frogs, vermin, wild beasts, boils, pestilence, hail, locusts, darkness, and death of the first-born, these were the names of the ten plagues. And any or all of them could have happened. The question is only whether any of them, excepting the last, which has an opaque and never fully elucidated explanation, did contribute materially to the end result. Under certain circumstances the Nile takes on a blood-red coloring. Temporarily its water becomes undrinkable and the fish die. That is as likely to happen as that the frogs of the marshes multiply unnaturally or that the propagation of the constantly present lice grows to the proportions of a general affliction. There were plenty of lions left in Egypt prowling along the edge of the desert and lurking in the dried-up stream beds of the jungle. And if the number of their rapacious attacks on man and beast suddenly increased, one could very well designate that as a plague. How usual are sores and blains in the land of Egypt, and how easily uncleanliness causes cankers which fester among the people like a pestilence! The heavens there are usually blue, and therefore the rare and heavy thunderstorm makes all the deeper an impression, when the descending fire of the clouds mixes with the sharp gravel of the hail, which flails the harvest and rends the trees asunder—all this without any definite purpose. The locust is an all-too-familiar guest; against their mass advance man has invented many a repellent and barricade. Yet again and again these yield to greed, so that whole regions remain gaping in bare baldness. And he who has experienced the dismal darkling mood which a shadowed sun produces on the earth can well understand that a people spoiled by the luxury of light would give to such an eclipse the name of a plague.

With this all the reported evils are accounted for. For the tenth evil, the death of the first-born, does not properly belong among them. It represents a dubious by-product of the exodus itself, one into which it is uncomfortable to probe. Some of the others, or even all of them, if spread over a sufficient period of time, could have occurred. One need consider them as merely more or less decorative circumlocutions of the only actual pressure which Moses could use against Ramessu, namely and quite simply the fact that Pharaoh was his illegitimate grandfather and that Moses had the means to bruit this scandal abroad. The king was more than once at the point of yielding to this pressure; at least he made considerable concessions. He consented that the men depart for the feast of offering if their wives, children, and cattle remain behind. Moses did not accept this: with young and old, with sons and daughters, with sheep and cows, would they have to depart, to do justice to the feast of the Lord. So Pharaoh conceded wives and brood and excepted only the cattle, which were to remain as forfeit. But Moses asked where they were expected to find offerings to be burned and slaughtered if they lacked their cattle. Not one single hoof, he demanded, might remain behind, whereby of course it became apparent that it was not a question of a holiday but of a departure.

The hoofs resulted in a last stormy scene between His Egyptian Majesty and Jahwe's delegate. During all the negotiations Moses had shown great patience, though there was fist-shaking rage in his soul. It got to the point that Pharaoh staked all and literally showed him the door. "Out," he screamed, "and beware lest you come again into my sight. If you do, so shall you die."

Then Moses, who had just been fiercely agitated, became completely calm, and answered only, "You have spoken. I shall go and never again come into your sight." What he contemplated when he thus took leave in terrible calm was not according to his desire. But Joshua and Caleb, the youths, they liked it well.

8

This is a dark chapter, one to be voiced only in half-whispered and muffled words. A day came, or more precisely a night, a wicked vesper, when Jahwe or his destroying angel went about and smote the children of Egypt with the tenth and last plague. That is, he smote a part of them, the Egyptian element among the inhabitants of Goshen and those of the towns of Pithom and Rameses. Those huts and houses whose posts were painted with the sign of blood he omitted, passed by, and spared.

What did he do? He caused death to come, the death of the Egyptian first-born, and in doing so he may well have met halfway many a secret wish and helped many a second-born to the right which would otherwise have been denied him. One has to note the difference between Jahwe and his destroying angel. It was not Jahwe himself who went about, but his destroying angel, or more properly, a whole band of such, carefully chosen. And if one wishes to search among the many for one single apparition, there is much to point to a certain straight, youthful figure with a curly head, a prominent Adam's-apple, and a determined, wrinkled brow. He becomes the traditional type of the destroying angel, who at all times is glad when unprofitable negotiations are ended and deeds begin.

During Moses' tenacious audiences with Pharaoh, the preparations for decisive deeds had not been neglected. Moses' part in them was limited: he merely sent his wife and sons secretly to Midian to his brother-in-law, Jethro. Expecting serious trouble, Moses did not wish to be burdened with their care. Joshua, however, whose relationship to Moses was recognizably similar to the relationship of the destroying angel to Jahwe, had acted according to his nature; though he did not possess the means or as yet the prestige to get three thousand arm-bearing comrades ready for war under his command, he at least had selected a group, had armed them, exercised them, and reared them in discipline. For a beginning, a good deal could be accomplished with them.

What then occurred is shrouded in darkness—the very darkness of that certain vesper night which was supposed to be a holiday night for the slave tribes. The Egyptians assumed that these tribes wanted to have some compensation for the festival in the desert which had been denied to them, and thus had planned to hold right where they were a celebration enhanced by feasting and illumination. For it they had even borrowed gold and silver vessels from their Egyptian neighbors. Instead of this there occurred that appearance of the destroying angel, that death of the first-born, in all those dwellings unmarked with blood by the bundle of hyssop. It was a visitation which caused so great a confusion, and so sudden a revolution of legal claims and property rights, that in the next hour the way out of the land not only stood open to the people of Moses but they were actually forced on that way. Their departure could not be quick enough for the people of Egypt. Indeed, it seems as if the second-born were less zealous to avenge the death of those to whose place they succeeded than to hasten the disappearance of those who had caused their advancement.

The word of history has it that this tenth plague at last broke Pharaoh's pride so that he dismissed Moses' people from bondage. Soon enough, however, he sent after the departed ones a pursuing armed division which miraculously came to grief.

Be that as it may, it is certain that the exodus took the form of expulsion. The haste with which it happened is indicated by the fact that nobody had time to leaven his bread for the journey. The people were provided only with unleavened emergency cakes. Later Moses formed of this occurrence a memorial feast for all times. But in other respects everybody, great and small, was quite prepared for the departure. While the destroying angel went about, they sat with girded loins near their fully packed carts, their shoes already on their feet, their staffs in their hands. The gold and silver vessels which they had borrowed from the children of the land they took along.

My friends, at the departure from Egypt there was killing and there was theft. It was Moses' determined will that this should happen for the last time. How can people free themselves from uncleanliness without offering to that uncleanliness a last tribute, without soiling themselves thoroughly for the last time? Now Moses had the unformed mass, his father's kin, out in the open. He, with his sculptor's desire, believed that out in the open, out in freedom, the work of cleansing could begin.

9

The migrants, though their number was much smaller than the legend narrates, were yet numerous enough to be difficult to manage, to guide, and to provision. They were a heavy enough burden for him who had the responsibility for their fate and for their survival out in the open. The tribes chose the route which chose itself, for with good reason they wanted to avoid the Egyptian frontier fortifications, which began north of the Bitter Lakes.

The way they took led through the Salt Lake district, a district into which projects the larger, more westerly of the two arms of the Red Sea. These arms frame the Sinai peninsula. Moses knew this district because on his flight to Midian and on his return from there he had passed and repassed it. Its characteristics were better known to him than to young Joshua, who knew it only as a map he had learned by heart. Moses had seen these strange reedy shallows, which sometimes formed an open connection between the Bitter Lakes and the sea, and which at other times and under certain peculiar conditions could be traversed as dry land. If there was a strong east wind and if the sea was at low tide, the shallows permitted free passage. The fugitives found them in this condition, thanks to Jahwe's favorable disposition.

Joshua and Caleb were the ones who spread the news among the multitude that Moses, calling to God, had held his rod over the waters, had caused the waters to divide and make way for the people. Very probably Moses actually did this, and thus assisted the east wind with solemn gesture and in Jahwe's name. In any case, the faith of the people in their leader could at this moment well use confirmation, because right here it was subjected to the first heavy trial. For it was here that Pharaoh's mighty battalion, the mounted men in those grim, scythe-studded chariots all too familiar to the people, caught up with the fugitives and were within a hair's breadth of putting a bloody end to the whole pilgrimage to God.

The news of their coming, announced by Joshua's rear guard, caused extreme terror and wild despair among the people. Regret at having followed "that man Moses" immediately flared up, and that mass murmuring arose which was to occur, to Moses' grief and bitterness, at every succeeding difficulty. The women whined, the men cursed and shook their fists at the sides of their bodies as Moses himself was wont to do when he was excited.

"Were there no graves in Egypt," thus was the speech, "which we could have entered peacefully at our appointed hour if we had stayed at home?" All of a sudden Egypt was "home," that very

Egypt which used to be the foreign land of slavery. "For it had been better for us to serve the Egyptians than that we should die in the wilderness."

This Moses had to hear from a thousand throats. The cries even galled his joy in the deliverance, which when it came was overwhelming. He was "the man Moses who has led us out of Egypt"—which phrase was a paean of praise as long as everything went well. When things went badly the phrase immediately changed coloring and became a menacingly murmured reproach, a reproach never far removed from the thought of stoning.

Well, then, after a short fright everything went miraculously and shamefully well. Through God's miracle Moses stood before his people in all his greatness and was "the man who has led us out of Egypt," once again with a different connotation. The people push through the dry shallows, after them the might of the Egyptian chariots. Suddenly the wind dies down, the flood returns, and man and horse perish gurgling in the engulfing waters.

The triumph was unprecedented. Miriam the prophetess, Aaron's sister, played the timbrel and led the round dance of the women. She sang: "Praise the Lord—a wonderous deed—steed and man—he has flung them into the ocean." She had written this herself. One has to imagine it to the accompaniment of the timbrel.

The people were deeply moved. The words, "mighty, holy, terrifying, praiseworthy, and miracle-dispensing" fell incessantly from their lips, and it was unclear whether these words were meant for the divinity or for Moses, delegate of the god. For they now believed that it was Moses' rod which had drawn the drowning flood over the might of Egypt. This substitution was ever present. At those times when the people were not murmuring against him, Moses always had his troubles trying to prevent them from looking on him as God instead of as God's proclaimer.

10

At bottom this was not so ridiculous. For what Moses began to exact of those wretched people went far beyond the humanly customary, and could hardly have sprung from the brain of a mortal. They stood agape at hearing it. He immediately forbade Miriam's dance of triumph and all further jubilation over the destruction of the Egyptians. He proclaimed: Jahwe's heavenly hosts were at the point of joining in the song of victory, but the holy one had rebuked them. "How so! My creatures sink into the sea, and you want to sing?" This short and surprising pronouncement Moses spread among the people. And he added, "Thou shalt not rejoice over the fall of thine enemy, nor shall thy heart be glad over his misfortune." This was the first time he addressed the entire mob, some twelve thousand people with three thousand capable of bearing arms, with "Thou." It was a form of speech which embraced them in their entirety and at the same time designated each individual, man and woman, the aged and the child, pointing a finger against each one's breast.

"Thou shalt not emit a cry of joy over the fall of thine enemy." That was to the highest degree unnatural! But obviously this unnaturalness had some relation to the invisibility of Moses' god, who desired also to be their god. The more thinking ones among the dark-skinned mob began dimly to perceive what it meant to have allied themselves with an invisible god, and what uncomfortable and exigent matters they could expect.

The people were now in the land of Sinai, in the desert of Shur, an unlovely region which once left behind would only lead to yet another lamentable district, the desert of Paran. Why these deserts had different names is inexplicable. Barrenly they joined one another, and were both quite the same, that is, stony, waterless, and fruitless—accursed plains, dotted with dead hills, stretching for three days or four or five. It was lucky for Moses that he had fortified his reputation by impressing them with the supernatural occurrences at the shallows. For soon enough was he again "that man Moses who has led us out of Egypt," which meant "into misfortune." Loud murmurings rose to his ears. After three days the water which they had taken along gave out. Thousands thirsted, the inexorable sun above their heads, and under their feet bare disconsolateness, whether it was the desert Shur or by this time the desert Paran.

"What should we drink?" they called loudly, without consideration for the leader, who suffered because he was responsible. Gladly would he have wished that he alone had nothing to drink, that he alone would never drink again, if only he did not have to hear continually, "Why did you carry us forth out of Egypt?" To suffer alone is little torment compared to the trial of having to be responsible for such a multitude. Moses was a much-tried man, and remained so all his life, tried more than all the other people on earth.

Very soon there was nothing more to eat, for how long could the flat cakes which they had taken with them last? "What should we eat?" Now this cry arose, tearful and abusing, and Moses had heavy hours alone with God. He charged how unfair it was that God had placed all the burden of all the people on one servant alone, on Moses.

"Did I conceive all these people and give them birth," he asked, "so that you have the right to say to me, 'Carry them in your arms'? Where can I find the nourishment to give to all? They cry before me and speak, 'Give us meat that we may eat!' Alone I cannot bear the weight of so many people; it is too heavy for me. And if you demand this of me, it would be better that you strangle me to death so that I need not see their misfortune and mine."

Jahwe did not entirely leave him in the lurch. On the fifth day they espied on a high plateau a spring surrounded by trees, which incidentally was marked as the "spring Marah" on the map which Joshua carried in his head. Unfortunately, the water tasted vile, because of certain unsalutary additions. This caused bitter disappointment and far-rumbling murmurs. However, Moses, made inventive by necessity, inserted a kind of filter apparatus which held back the foul additions, if not entirely, at least largely. Thus he performed the miracle of the spring, which changed the plaints into paeans and did much to cement his reputation. The phrase, "He who has led us out of Egypt," immediately took on again a rosy glow.

A miracle occurred also with the nourishment, a miracle which at first caused exultant astonishment. It appeared that great stretches of the desert Paran were covered with a lichen which was edible. This "manna-lichen" was a sugary tomentum, round and small, looked like coriander seed and like bdellium, and was highly perishable. If one did not eat it at once, it began to smell evil. But otherwise it made quite tolerable emergency food, mashed and powdered and prepared like an ash cake. Some thought that it tasted almost like rolls with honey; others it reminded of oil cakes.

This was the first favorable judgment, which did not last. Soon, after a few days, the people became fed up with this manna and tired of staying their hunger with it. Because it was their only nourishment, they sickened of it; it made them nauseated and they complained, "We remember the fish which we got in Egypt for nothing, the squash, the cucumbers, the leeks, the onions, and the garlic. But now our souls are weary, for our eyes see nothing but manna." This, in addition of course to the question, "Why did you carry us forth out of Egypt?" Moses had to hear in pain. What he asked God was, "What shall I do with the people? They no longer want their manna. You will see, soon they shall stone me."

11

However, from such a fate he was tolerably well protected by Jehoschua, his youth, and by the able guards whom he already had called on in Goshen and who surrounded the liberator as soon as the menacing murmurs rose among the crowd. For the time being this armed guard was small and consisted only of young men, with Caleb as lieutenant. Joshua was waiting for the right occasion to set himself up as commander in chief and leader of the battle, and to bind into a regular military force under his command *all* those capable of bearing arms, all the three thousand. He knew that such an occasion was coming.

Moses owed much to the youth whom he had baptized in the name of God. Without him he would have been lost many a time. Moses was a spiritual man and his virility, though it was strong and sturdy, though it had wrists as broad as a stonemason's, was a spiritual virility, a virility turned inward, nourished and fired by God, unconscious of outer happenings, concerned only with the holy. With a kind of foolhardiness, which stood in peculiar contrast to his reflective musings when he covered mouth and beard with his hand, all Moses' thoughts and endeavors dealt only with his desire to have his father's kin alone for himself in seclusion, so that he might educate them and sculpt into God's image the amorphous mass which he loved. He was little or not at all concerned with the dangers of freedom, the difficulties of the desert, and with the question how one could safely steer such a crowd out of the desert. He did not even know precisely to what spot he must guide the people. In short, he had hardly prepared himself for practical leadership. Therefore he could be doubly glad to have Joshua at his side, who in turn admired the spiritual virility in Moses and placed his own direct, realistic, and useful virility unconditionally at his disposal.

It was thanks to him that they made planned progress through the wilderness and did not stray or perish. He determined the direction of the marches according to the stars, calculated the distances of the marches, and arranged it so that they arrived at watering places at bearable if sometimes even just bearable intervals. He it was who had found out that the round lichen was edible. In short, he looked after the reputation of the leader and master. He saw to it that when the phrase, "He who has led us out of Egypt," became a murmur, it would soon again take on a laudatory meaning. He kept the goal clearly in his head, and there he steered with the help of the stars and in accord with Moses, on the shortest route. Both of them were agreed that a first provisional goal was needed. Even if this was a temporary shelter, it would be an abode where one could live and where one could gain time. Much time had to be gained, partly (in Joshua's view) that the people multiply and furnish him as he grew older a stronger number of warriors; partly (in Moses' view) that he might lead the mass toward God and hew them into a shape that would be holy, decent, and clean. For this his soul and his wrists longed.

The goal was the oasis Kadesh. Just as the desert Shur touches the desert Paran, so does the desert Sin adjoin Paran in the south. But not on all sides and not closely. Somewhere in between lay the oasis of Kadesh. This oasis was like a precious meadow, a green refreshment amid waterless waste, with three strong springs and quite a number of smaller springs, a day's march long and half a day's march broad, covered with fresh pasture and arable ground, an enticing landscape rich in animals and in fruits and large enough to quarter and nourish a multitude like theirs.

Joshua knew of this attractive spot: it was scrupulously marked out on the map which he carried in his head. Moses too had heard something about it. But it was really Joshua who had contrived to select Kadesh as their destination. His opportunity—it lay there. It goes without saying that such a pearl as Kadesh was not without its owner. The oasis was in firm possession. Well, perhaps not too firm, Joshua hoped. To acquire it, one had to fight those who possessed it, and that was Amalek.

A part of the tribe of Amalek held Kadesh occupied and would most certainly defend it. Joshua made it clear to Moses that this meant war, that a battle between Jahwe and Amalek was inevitable, even if it resulted in eternal enmity from generation to generation. The oasis they would have to have; it was their predestined place for growth and consecration.

Moses had his reservations. In his view one of the implications of the invisible god was that one should not covet the house of one's neighbor. He said as much to the youth, but Joshua responded: Kadesh is not, strictly speaking, Amalek's house. He knew his way about not only in space but in historic pasts, and he knew that long ago—though he could not precisely say just when—Kadesh had been inhabited by Hebrew people, related ancestral blood, and that they had been dispossessed by the people of Amalek. Kadesh was Amalek's property through robbery—and one may rob a robber.

Moses doubted that, but he had his own reasons for believing that Kadesh truly was the property of Jahwe and should belong to those who were allied to him. The place bore the name of Kadesh, which means "sanctuary," not only because of its natural charm but also because it was in a certain sense a sanctuary of the Midianitic Jahwe, whom Moses had recognized as the God of the Fathers. Not far from it, toward the east and toward Edom, lay the mountain Horeb, which Moses had visited from Midian and on whose slope the god had appeared to him in the burning bush. Horeb the mountain was the dwelling place of Jahwe—at least it was one of them. His original dwelling was the mountain Sinai in that range which lay toward midday. Thus between Sinai and Horeb there was a close connection—that is, that they both were Jahwe's dwelling places. You could perhaps name one for the other, you could call Horeb Sinai. And you could call Kadesh what it was actually called because, speaking somewhat loosely, it lay at the foot of the sanctified mountain.

Therefore Moses consented to Joshua's scheme and permitted him to make his preparations for the combat with Amalek.

12

The battle took place—that is a historic fact. It was a bloody, fluctuating battle. But Israel emerged the victor. Moses had given this name Israel, which means "God makes war," to his people before the battle, to strengthen them. He had explained that it was a very old name which had slipped into oblivion. Jacob, the original father, had first won it and had thus called his kin. Now indeed it benefited Moses' people. The tribes which previously had only loosely held to each other, now that they were all called Israel, fought united under this armored name. They fought grouped in battle ranks and led by Joshua, the war-worthy youth, and Caleb, his lieutenant.

The people of Amalek had no illusions as to the meaning of the approach of the wanderers. At all times such approaches have only one meaning. Without waiting for the attack on the oasis, they burst in bulging bands into the desert, greater in number than Israel, and better armed. Amid swirling dust, amid tumult and martial cries, the battle began. It was an uneven battle, uneven also because Joshua's people were troubled by thirst and had eaten nothing but manna for many days. On the other hand, they had Joshua, the clear-seeing youth, who led their movements, and they had Moses, the man of God.

At the beginning of the engagement Moses, together with Aaron, his half brother, and Miriam, the prophetess, retired to a hill from which he could view the field of combat. Virile though he was, his duty was not to do battle. His was a priest's duty, and everyone agreed without hesitancy that that could be his only duty. With raised arms he called to the god, and voiced enflaming words, as "Arise, Jahwe, appear to the myriads, to the thousands of Israelites, so that your enemies shall scatter and those who hate you flee before your sight."

They did not flee nor did they scatter. Or if they did, they did so only in a few places and temporarily. For though Israel was made fierce by thirst and by satiety with manna, Amalek disposed of more "myriads." And, after a brief discouragement, they again and again pressed forward, at times dangerously close to the commanding hill. It clearly appeared that Israel conquered as long as Moses held up his arms in prayer to heaven. But if he let his arms sink, then Amalek was victorious. Because he could not continuously hold up his arms with his own strength, Aaron and Miriam supported him under the armpits, and even held his arms so that they might remain raised. What that means one can measure by the fact that the battle lasted from morn to evening, and in all this time Moses had to retain his painful position. Judge from that how difficult is the duty assigned to spiritual virility, up there on the hill of prayer—in truth more difficult than the duty of those who hack away below in the turmoil.

Nor was he able to perform this duty all day long. Intermittently, and for a moment only, his helpers had to let down the arms of the master. And immediately this caused much blood and affliction among Jahwe's warriors. Then the arms were again hoisted, and those below took fresh courage. What also helped to veer the battle in their favor was the strategic gift of Joshua. He was a most ingenious apprentice of war, a youth with ideas and vision. He invented maneuvers which were utterly novel and quite unprecedented, at least in the desert. He was also a commander stoical enough to be able to view with calmness the temporary loss of territory. He assembled his prize warriors, the carefully chosen destroying angels, on the right flank of the enemy, pushed against this flank determinedly, deflected it, and harried it sufficiently to be victorious in that one spot. It mattered not that the main force of Amalek had the advantage against the ranks of the Hebrews, and storming ahead gained considerable territory from them. Because of the break-through at the flank, Joshua penetrated to the rear of Amalek's force so that now they had to turn around toward him, without being able to cease fighting against the main might of Israel. And they who a moment ago had almost been vanquished now took new courage. With this the Amalekites lost their head and despaired. "Treason," they cried, "all is lost. Do not hope any longer to be victorious! Jahwe is above us, a god of unbounded malice." And with this password of despair, the warriors of Amalek let their swords sink and were overcome.

Only a few succeeded in fleeing north toward their people,

where they found refuge with the main tribe. Israel occupied the oasis Kadesh, which proved to be traversed by a broad, rushing stream, rich with nut bushes and fruit trees and filled with bees, song birds, quails, and rabbits. The children of Amalek who had been left behind in the village tents augmented the number of their own progeny; the wives of Amalek became Israel's wives and servants.

13

Moses, though his arms hurt him long afterward, was a happy man. That he remained a much tried man, tried more than all the people on earth, we shall soon see. For the time being he could well be pleased with the state of affairs. The exodus had been successful, Pharaoh's avenging might had drowned in the sea of reeds, the desert voyage was mercifully completed, and the battle for Kadesh had been won with Jahwe's help. Now Moses stood in all his greatness before his father's kin, in the esteem which springs from success, as "the man Moses who has led us out of Egypt." He needed this esteem to be able to begin his work, the work of cleansing and shaping in the sign of the Invisible One, the work of hewing, chiseling, and forming of the flesh and blood, the work for which he longed. He was happy to have this flesh and blood at last all to himself out in the open, in the oasis which bore the name "sanctuary." Here was his workplace.

He showed his people a certain mountain which lay toward the east of Kadesh behind the desert. This was Horeb, which one could also call Sinai. Two thirds of it was overgrown with bushes, but at the summit it was bare, and there was the seat of Jahwe. That this was so was plausible, for it was a peculiar mountain, distinguished among its neighbors by a cloud which never vanished and which lay like a roof on its peak. During the day this cloud looked gray, but at night it glowed. There, he told the people, on the bushy slope beneath the rocky top, Jahwe had talked to Moses from the burning thorn bush, and had charged him to lead them out of Egypt. They listened to the tale with fear and trembling. They could not as yet feel reverence or devotion. All of them, even the bearded men, shook at their knees like raffish cowards when Moses pointed to the mountain with the lasting cloud, and when he taught them that this was the dwelling of the god who was inclined toward them and who was to be their sole god. Moses, shaking his fists, scolded them because of their uncouth behavior, and endeavored to make them feel more courageous toward Jahwe, and more intimate with him, by erecting right in their midst, in Kadesh itself, a shrine in his honor.

For Jahwe had a mobile presence. This was another attribute of his invisibility. He dwelt on Sinai, he dwelt on Horeb. And hardly had the people begun to make themselves at home in the camp of the Amalekites when Moses gave him a dwelling even there. It was a tent right next to one's own tent. He called it the meeting or assembly tent, and also the tabernacle. There he housed holy objects which would serve as aids in the service of the Invisible. Most of these objects traced back to the cult of the Midianitic Jahwe as Moses remembered it. First, a kind of chest supported by poles, on which, according to Moses' explanation (and he was the man to know such things), the invisible divinity was enthroned. This chest they could take along into the field and carry before them in battle, should Amalek approach and endeavor to seek revenge. Next to this chest he kept a brass rod with a serpent's head, also called the "Brass Serpent." This rod commemorated Aaron's well-meant trick before Pharaoh, but with the additional import that it be also the rod which Moses had held over the sea of reeds to part the waters. He also kept in the tent a satchel called ephod, from which the oracle lots were drawn. These were the yes and no, the right and wrong, the good and bad, the "Urim and Thummim" judgments which were Jahwe's direct decisions in those difficult disputes which man alone could not solve.

For the most part Moses himself did the judging in Jahwe's

stead, in all kinds of controversies and contentions which arose among the people. As a matter of fact, the first thing he did in Kadesh was to erect a tribunal where on designated days he passed judgment and settled differences. There, where the strongest spring bubbled, the spring which was already called Me-Meribah, meaning "water of the law," there he pronounced his verdicts and let the holy judgment flow even as the water flowed from the earth. If one considers that there were twelve thousand five hundred souls who looked up to him alone for justice, then one can well imagine how sorely tried was he.

For all the more of them sought their rights and pressed toward his seat near the spring, as the idea of right was something utterly new to these forsaken and lost souls. Up to now they had hardly known that there was such a thing. Now they learned first that right was directly connected with the invisibility and holiness of God and stood under his protection, and second that the conception of right also included the conception of wrong. The mob could not understand this for the longest time. They thought that there, where right was dispensed, everybody had to be in the right. At first they could not and did not want to believe that a person might obtain his right through the very fact that he was judged in the wrong and had to slink away with a long face. Such a man regretted that he had not decided the matter with his adversary as he used to decide in former times, that is, with stone in fist, even if the affair might then have had a different outcome. With difficulty did this man learn from Moses that such an action was offensive to the invisibility of God, and that no one should slink away with a long face if right had declared him wrong. For right was equally beautiful and equally dignified in its holy invisibility whether it said yea or nay to a man.

Thus Moses not only had to pass judgment but to teach judgment. And greatly was he tried. He had studied law in the academy in Thebes, and knew the Egyptian law scrolls and the Codex of Hammurabi, king of the Euphrates. This knowledge helped him to a decision in many a case. For example: if an ox had gored a man or a woman to death, then that ox had to be stoned and his meat could not be eaten. But the owner of the ox was innocent except if he knew that that ox previously was wont to push with his horns and had not kept him in. Then his life was forfeit, except that he could ransom it with thirty shekels of silver. Or if somebody dug a pit and did not cover it properly, so that an ox or an ass fell into it, then the owner of that pit should make restitution in money to the other man for his loss, but the carcass should belong to the first man. Or whatever else occurred in matters of violence, mistreatment of slaves, theft and burglary, destruction of crops, arson, or abuse of confidence. In all these and a hundred other cases Moses passed judgment, leaning on the Codex of Hammurabi, and decided what was right and what wrong. But there were too many cases for but one judge, and his seat near the spring was overrun. If the master probed the various cases only halfway conscientiously, he was never finished and had to postpone much. Ever-new problems arose, and he was tried above all people.

14

Therefore, it was a stroke of great good fortune that his brother-in-law, Jethro, came from Midian to visit him in Kadesh and gave him good counsel, counsel such as the overconscientious Moses could never have found for himself. Soon after the arrival in the oasis, Moses had sent to Midian to his brother-in-law for the return of his wife Zipporah and his two sons, who had been entrusted to the safety of Jethro's tent during the Egyptian tribulations. Accommodatingly, Jethro came in person to deliver wife and sons, to embrace Moses, to look around, and to hear from him how everything had gone off.

Jethro was a corpulent sheik with a pleasant mien, with even and deft gestures, a man of the world, a paladin of a civilized, mundane, and experienced people. Received with much splendor,

Jethro put up at Moses' hut. There, not without astonishment, he learned how one of his own gods—peculiarly enough, the imageless one—had done so extraordinarily well for Moses and his people, and had, as he already knew, delivered them from Egypt's power.

"Well, who would have thought it?" he said. "Obviously this god is greater than we suspected, and what you tell me now makes me fear that we have cultivated him too negligently. I shall see to it that we shall accord him more honor in the future."

The next day public sacrifices were ordered. Moses arranged these seldom, as he had little use for a custom common to all the people in the world. Sacrifice was not essential, said he, to the Invisible One. "Not offerings do I want," spoke Jahwe, "but that ye shall listen to my voice, and that is the voice of my servant, Moses. Then shall I be your God and ye my people." Nevertheless, this once they did arrange slaughter and burnt offerings in Jahwe's honor as well as to celebrate Jethro's arrival. And again the next day, early in the morning, Moses took his brother-in-law along to the Spring of the Law so that he could attend a court session and observe how Moses sat and judged the people. And the people stood around him from morn to evening, and there was no end to it, no question of being finished.

"Now, let me ask you one thing, my honored brother-in-law," said the guest when after the session he walked home with Moses. "Why do you plague yourself like that? There you sit all alone and all the people stand around you from morn until evening. Why do you do it?"

"I have to," answered Moses. "The people come to me that I may judge one and all and show them the right of God and his laws."

"But, my good friend, how can you be so inefficient?" said Jethro. "Is that the way to govern, and is it right that the ruler should have to work himself to the bone because he does everything himself? It is a shame that you drive yourself so that you can hardly hold your head up. What is more, you lose your voice with all that judging. Nor are the people any less tired. That is no way to begin. In the future you shall not be able to transact all business yourself. Nor is this necessary—listen to my voice. If you act as the delegate of your people before God, and personally bring before him only the most important cases, those cases which concern everybody, that is all you can possibly be expected to do. As for the other cases—well, look around you," said he with easy gestures, "look around among the mob and search for respectable men, men of some standing, and place them as judges above the people. Let one of these men rule a group of a thousand, another a hundred, still another fifty and even ten, and let them all rule according to the law and tenets which you have set up. And only if it is a great matter should you be called. The lesser questions they can settle themselves; you do not even need to know about it. That is how we do it, and so shall it be easier for you. I would not today have my little paunch, nor would I even have been able to get away to visit you, if I took it into my head that I had to know about everything that is going on and if I burdened myself as you do."

"But the judges will accept gifts," answered Moses with a heavy heart, "and will declare the godless ones in the right. For gifts blind those who see and turn awry the cause of the just."

"I know that," answered Jethro, "I know it quite well. But one has to close one's eyes to that, just a little. Wherever order reigns, wherever law is spoken, wherever judgments are made, they become a little involved through gifts. Does that matter so much? Look, those who accept presents, they are ordinary folk. But the people themselves are ordinary folk; therefore they understand the ordinary and the ordinary is comfortable to the community. Moreover, if a man has been wronged because the judge of the ten has accepted gifts from his godless adversary, then let that man pursue an ordinary process of law. Let him appeal to the judge who rules over the fifty; then to the one who rules over the hundred; and, finally, to the one who rules over the thousand: that one gets the most gifts and has therefore the clearest vision. Our man will find his rights with this last judge, that is, if in the meantime the fellow has not wearied of the whole affair."

Thus did Jethro discourse with even gestures, gestures which made life easier if one but saw them. Thus did he show that he was indeed the priest-king of a civilized desert people. With a heavy heart did Moses listen and nod. His was the pliable soul of the lonely spiritual man, the man who nods his head thoughtfully at the cleverness of the world and understands that the world may well be in the right. He followed the counsel of his deft brother-in-law—it was absolutely necessary. He appointed lay judges, who, according to his tenets, let judgment flow next to the great spring and next to the smaller one. They judged the everyday cases (such as if an ass fell into the pit); only the capital cases came to Moses, the priest of God. And the greatest matters were decided by the holy oracles.

Moses no longer had his hands tied with everyday affairs; his hands were free for the larger work, the work of sculpting for which Joshua, the strategic youth, had won the workplace, Kadesh the oasis. Undoubtedly, the doctrine of right and wrong was one important example of the implications inherent in the invisible God. Yet it was only one example. Much work remained to be done. Mighty and long labor lay ahead, labor which would have to be achieved through anger and patience before the uncouth hordes could be formed into a people who would be more than the usual community to whom the ordinary was comfortable, but would be an extraordinary, a separated people and a unique monument erected to the Invisible One and dedicated to him.

15

The people soon learned what it meant to have fallen into the hands of an angrily patient workman who held himself accountable to an invisible god. They began to realize that that unnatural suggestion to omit the shout of triumph over the drowning of the enemy was but a beginning, though a portentous beginning, which already lay well within the domain of holiness and purity. It was a beginning which presupposed a certain understanding; the people would have to acquire that understanding before they could view Moses' command as anything less than unnatural.

What the mob was really like, to what degree it was the rawest of raw material and flesh and blood, lacking the most elementary conception of purity and holiness, how Moses had to begin at the beginning and teach them beginnings, that is to be deduced from the simple precepts with which he started to work and chisel and blast. Not to their comfort, certainly, for the stone does not take sides with the master but against him; to the stone the first stroke struck to form it appears as a most unnatural action.

Moses, with his wide-set eyes and his flattened nose, was always in their midst, here, there, in this and that encampment. Shaking his broad-wristed fists, he jogged, censured, chided, and churned their existence; he reproved, chastised, and cleansed, using as his touchstone the invisibility of the God Jahwe who had led them out of Egypt in order to choose them as his people and make them into a holy people, even as holy as he himself. For the time being they were nothing more than rabble, a fact which they proved by emptying their bodies simply wherever they lay. That was a disgrace and a pestilence. Ye must have a place outside the camp where ye shall go when ye need to. Do ye understand me? And take along a little scoop and dig a pit before ye sit down, and after ye have sat then shall ye cover it. For the Lord your God walks in your camp, therefore your camp must be holy. And that means clean, so that the Lord need not hold his nose and turn away from you. For holiness begins with cleanliness, which is purity in the rough, the rough beginning of all purity. Dost thou comprehend this, Ahiman, and thou, wife Naemi? The next time I want to see everybody with that scoop, or ye shall have to reckon with the destroying angel.

Thou must be clean and wash thyself often with live water for the sake of thy health. For without water there is no cleanliness or holiness, and disease is unclean. But if thou thinkest that vulgarity is healthier than clean custom, then thou art an imbecile and thou shalt be visited by jaundice, fig warts, and the boils of Egypt. If ye do not practice cleanliness, then evil black blains shall grow up in you and the seeds of pestilence shall travel from blood to blood. Learn to distinguish cleanliness from uncleanliness, or else ye shall fail before the Invisible One and ye are nothing but rabble. Therefore if a man or a woman have a cankerous sore or an evil fistule, if he suffer with rash or ulcers, then he or she shall be declared unclean and not permitted in the encampment, but shall be put outside, separated in uncleanliness even as the Lord has separated you that ye may become clean. And whatever such an one has touched, on whatever he has lain, the saddle on which he has sat, that shall be burned. But if he has become clean again in separation, then he shall count seven days to make sure that he be truly clean, then he shall bathe thoroughly in water and then may he return.

Distinguish, I say unto you, and be holy before God. For how else can ye be holy as I want you to be? Ye eat everything together without choice or daintiness, and to me who have to watch you that is an abomination. There are certain things that ye may eat and others that ye may not, for ye shall have your pride and your disgust. Those animals which have cloven hoofs and chew their cud, those ye may eat. But those which chew their cud and have undivided hoofs, like the camel, those shall be unclean to you and ye shall not eat them. Notice well: the good camel is not unclean as a living creature of God; it is merely unfit for food, as little fit as the pig, which, though it has cloven hoofs, does not chew its cud. Therefore distinguish! What creatures in the water have fins and scales, those ye may eat, but those which slither in the element without fins or scales, the entire breed of salamanders, they, though they also are from God, ye shall shun as nourishment. Among the birds disdain ye the eagle, the hawk, the osprey, the vulture, and their ilk. Furthermore, all ravens, the ostrich, the night owl, the cuckoo, the screech owl, the swan, the horned owl, the bat, the bittern, the stork, the heron, and the jay, as well as the swallow. I have forgotten the hoopoe, him ye shall also eschew. Who would eat the weasel, the mouse, the toad, or the hedgehog? Who shall be so gross as to eat the lizard, the mole, and the blindworm—in fact, anything which creeps on the earth and crawls on its belly? But ye do it, and turn your souls into loathsomeness. The one whom I shall next see eating a blindworm I shall deal with so that he will never do it again. For though one does not die from eating it, though it is not harmful, yet is it reprehensible, and much shall be reprehensible to you. Therefore ye also shall eat no carcass, for that is even harmful.

Thus did he give them precepts of nourishment and circumscribe them in matters of food, though not alone in those. He did likewise in matters of lust and love, for there too were they disorderly in rabble fashion. Ye shall not commit adultery, he told them, for marriage is a holy barrier. But do ye really know what that means: ye shall not commit adultery? It means a hundred curbs out of regard for the holiness of God. It does not mean only that thou shalt not covet the wife of your neighbor: that is the least. For though ye are living in the flesh, ye are allied in oath to Invisibility. And marriage is the essence of all purity of flesh before God's visage. Therefore thou shalt not take unto thyself a wife and her mother, to name only one example: that is not seemly. And thou shalt never and under no conditions lie with thy sister so that thou shalt see her shame and she yours. For that is incest. Not even with thine aunt shalt thou lie. That is not worthy of her nor of thyself: thou shalt shy away from it. If a woman have a sickness, then thou shalt shun her and not approach the fountain of her blood. And if something shameful should happen to a man in his sleep, then shall he be unclean until the next evening, and he shall bathe carefully in water.

I hear that thou causest thy daughter to be a whore and that thou takest whore money from her? Do this no longer, for if thou perseverest, then shall I let thee be stoned. What art thou thinking of, to sleep with a boy as well as with a woman? That is iniquity and rabble depravity. Both of you shall be put to death. But if somebody consort with an animal, be it man or woman, they shall be completely exterminated, and they and the animal choked to death.

Imagine their bewilderment over all these curbs! At first they felt life would hardly be worth living if they should observe them all. Moses struck at them with the sculptor's chisel so that the chips flew. Deadly serious was he about meting out the chastisements which he had placed on the worser transgressions. And behind his ordinances stood the young Joshua and his destroying angels.

"I am the Lord thy God," said he, risking the danger that they might in truth take him for God, "who have led thee out of Egypt and separated thee from all the peoples. Therefore shall ye separate, the clean from the unclean, and not follow in whoredom the other tribes but be holy to me. For I, thy Lord, am holy, and have separated you so that ye shall become mine. Of all the unclean actions the one most unclean is to care for any other god. For I am a jealous God. The most unclean action is to make yourself an image, be it the likeness of a man or a woman, of an ox or a hawk, a fish or a worm. In doing that ye shall become faithless to me, even if the image shall be in my likeness, and thou mightest as well sleep with thy sister or with an animal. Such an action is not far removed and soon follows quite by itself. Take care! I am among you and I see everything. Whosoever shall whore after the animal-and-death gods of Egypt, him shall I drown. I shall drive him into the desert and banish him like an outcast. And the same shall I do with him who sacrifices to the Moloch, whom I know ye still carry in your memory. If ye consume your force in its honor, I shall deem it evil, and heavily shall I deal with you. Nor shalt thou let thy son nor thy daughter walk through fire according to the stupid old custom, nor shalt thou pay attention to the flight of the birds and their cry, nor whisper with fortunetellers, destiny predictors, or augurs, nor shall ye question the dead nor practice magic in my name. If one among you is a scoundrel and takes my name in false testimony, he shall not profit by such talebearing, for I shall devour him. It is even magic and abomination to print marks on one's body, to shave one's eyebrows and make cuttings on one's face as a sign of sorrow for the dead—I shall not suffer it."

How great was their bewilderment! They were not even allowed to cut their faces in mourning, not even allowed to tattoo themselves a little bit. They realized now what was meant by the invisibility of God. It meant great privation, this business of being in league with Jahwe. But because behind Moses' prohibition stood the destroying angels, and because nobody wanted to be driven into the desert, that which he prohibited soon appeared to them to be worthy of fear. At first it was fearworthy only in relation to the punishment, but by and by the action itself took on the stamp of evil, and if they committed it they became ill at ease without even thinking of the punishment.

Bridle your hearts, he said to them, and do not cast your eyes on somebody else's possessions. If ye desire them, it soon follows that ye take them, be it through stealthy purloining, which is cowardice, or by killing the other, which is brutality. Jahwe and I do not want you either cowardly or brutal, but ye shall be in the middle between these two; that means decent. Have ye understood that much? To steal is slinking wretchedness, but to murder, be it from rage or from greed, or from greedy rage or from raging greed, that is flaming wrong, and against him who shall commit such a wrong shall I set my countenance so that he will not know where to hide himself. For he has shed blood and blood is holy awe and a deep secret, offering for my altar and atonement. Ye shall not eat blood nor any meat in the blood, for blood is mine. And he who is smeared with the blood of human beings, his heart shall sicken in cold terror and I shall drive him that he run away from himself unto the ends of the world. Say ye Amen to that.

And they said Amen, still hoping that with the ban on murder killing alone was meant. For few of them had the desire to kill, and those who did had it only occasionally. But it turned out that Jahwe gave that word as wide a meaning as he had given the word adultery and that he meant by it all sorts of things, so that "murder" and "killing" began with almost any transgression of the code. Almost every wound which one man inflicted upon another, whether through deceit or through fraud (and almost all of the people hankered a little after deceit and fraud), Jahwe considered bloodshed. They should not deal falsely with one another nor bear false witness against their neighbors, and they should use just metes, just weights, and just measures. It was to the highest degree unnatural, and for the time being it was only the natural fear of punishment which gave an aspect of naturalness to all this bidding and forbidding.

That one should honor one's father and mother as Moses demanded, that also had a wider meaning, wider than one suspected at first blush. Whosoever raised his hand against his progenitor and cursed him, well, yes, he should be done away with. But that respect should also be extended to those who merely could be your progenitors. Ye shall arise before a gray head. Ye shall cross your arms and incline your stupid head. Do ye understand me? Thus demands the decency of God. The only consolation was that since your neighbor was not permitted to kill you, you had a reasonable prospect of becoming yourself old and gray, so that the others would have to arise before you.

Finally, it appeared that old age was a symbol of what was old in general, everything which did not happen from today to tomorrow but which came from long ago: the piously traditional, the custom of the fathers. To that one had to pay the tribute of honor and awe in God. Ye shall keep my sabbaths, the day on which I led you out of Egypt, the day of the unleaven bread, and the day when I rested from the labors of my creation. Ye shall not defile my day with the sweat of your brow: I forbid it. For I have led thee out of the Egyptian house of bondage with mighty hand and with outstretched arm, where thou wert a slave and a work animal. And my day shall be the day of thy freedom, which thou shalt keep holy. Six days shalt thou be a tiller or a plowmaker or a potter or a coppersmith or a joiner. But on my day shalt thou put on clean garments and thou shalt be nothing, nothing but a human being who raises his eyes to the Invisible.

Thou wert an oppressed servant in the land of Egypt. Think of that in your behavior toward those who are strangers amongst you: for example, the children of Amalek, whom God gave into your hands. Do not oppress them. Look on them as ye look on yourself and give them equal rights, or I shall crash down upon you. For they too stand under the protection of Jahwe. In short, do not make such a stupid, arrogant distinction between thyself and the others, so that thou thinkest that thou alone art real and thou alone countest while the others are only a semblance. Ye both have life in common, and it is only an accident that thou art not he. Therefore do not love thyself alone but love him in the same way, and do unto him as thou desirest that he do unto you. Be gracious with one another and kiss the tips of your fingers when ye pass each other and bow with civility and speak the greeting, "Be hale and healthy." For it is quite as important that he be healthy as that thou be healthy. And even if it is only formal civility that we do thus and kiss your finger tips, the gesture does leave something in your heart of that which should be there for your neighbor. To that say ye Amen!

And they all said Amen.

16

Actually, that Amen did not mean very much. They only said it because Moses was the man who had led them successfully out of Egypt, who had drowned Pharaoh's chariots, and had won the battle of Kadesh. It took a long time before what he taught them and what he enjoined upon them—all those barriers, laws, and prohibitions—sank into their flesh and blood. It was a mighty piece of work which he had undertaken, the work of changing the rabble into a people dedicated to the Lord, and to a clean image which could pass muster before the Invisible. In the sweat of his brow he worked in his workplace, Kadesh. He kept his wide-set eyes on all. He chiseled, blasted, formed, and smoothed the unwilling stone with tenacious patience, with repeated forbearance and frequent forgiving, and also with flaming anger and chastising sternness. Yet often did he almost despair when once again the flesh relapsed into stubbornness and forgetfulness, when once again the people failed to use the scoop, when they ate blindworms, slept with their sisters or their animals, painted marks on themselves, crouched with fortunetellers, slunk toward theft, and killed each other. "O rabble," said he to them, "ye shall see. The Lord shall appear above you and devour you." But to the Lord himself he said, "What shall I do with this flesh and why have you withdrawn your graces from me, that you burden me with a thing I cannot bear? I would rather clean a stable untouched for years by water or spade, I would rather clear a jungle with my bare hands, and turn it into a garden, than to form for you a clean image out of them. Wherefore must I carry these people in my arms as if I had given them birth? I am but half related to them from my father's side; therefore I pray you let me enjoy my life and free me from this task. Or else strangle me rather!"

But God answered Moses out of his inner consciousness with so clear a voice that he could hear it with his ears and he fell upon his face:

"Just because you are only half related to them from the side of the buried one are you the man to form them for me and to raise them to a holy people. For if you were wholly and only one of them, then you could not see them as they are nor work upon them. Anyway, that you complain to me and wish to excuse yourself from your work is pure affectation. For you know quite well that your work is beginning to take effect. You know that you have already given them a conscience so that they are ill at ease when they do ill. Therefore do not pretend to me that you do not desire your travail. It is my desire, God's desire, which you have, and lacking it you would sicken of life as our people sickened of manna after a few days. Of course, if I decided to strangle you, then yes, then would you be rid of that desire."

The much-troubled Moses understood this, nodded his head at Jahwe's words as he lay there, and stood up once again to his travail. But now he had his problems, not only in his capacity as a sculptor of the people; trouble and grief began to creep into his family life. Anger, envy, and bickering now arose around him and there was no peace in his hut. Perhaps it was his own fault, the fault of his senses. For his senses, stirred up by overwork, hung on a Negro girl, the well-known Negro girl.

One knows that at this time he lived with an Ethiopian girl as well as with his wife Zipporah, the mother of his sons. She was a wench from the land of Kush who as a child had arrived in Egypt, had lived among the Hebrew tribes in Goshen, and had joined the exodus. Undoubtedly she had known many a man, yet Moses now chose her as the companion of his bed. She was a magnificent specimen of her type, with erect breasts, with rolling eyes, thick deep lips, to sink into which may well have been an adventure, and a skin redolent of spice. Moses doted on her mightily; she was his recreation, and he would not let go of her, though he drew upon himself the enmity of his whole house. Not only his Midianitic wife and her sons looked askance at the affair, but also and especially his half sister Miriam and his half brother Aaron. Zipporah, who possessed much of the even worldliness of her brother Jethro, got along tolerably well with her rival, particularly since the Ethiopian girl knew how to hide her feminine triumph and conducted herself most subserviently toward her. Zipporah treated the Ethiopian girl more with mockery than hate, and adopted toward Moses a light tone of irony which hid the jealousy she felt. His sons, Gershom and Eliezer, members of Joshua's dashing troop, possessed too much sense of discipline to revolt openly against their father; yet they let it be known unmistakably that they were angry and that they were ashamed of him.

Matters stood yet differently with Miriam the prophetess and Aaron the unctuous. Their hatred toward the Ethiopian mistress was more venomous than that of the others, because that hatred was the expression of a deeper and more general grudge which united them against Moses. For a long time now had they envied Moses' intimate relation with God and his spiritual mastery. That he felt himself to be God's elect worker they thought was largely conceit; they deemed themselves just as good as he, perhaps better. To each other they said, "Does the Lord talk only through Moses? Does he not also talk through us? Who is this man Moses that he has exalted himself above us?" That then was the real cause of the indignation which they manifested toward Moses' affair with the Ethiopian. And every time they noisily reproached their unfortunate brother with the passion of his nights, they soon departed into more general complaints. Soon they would be harping on the injustice which was done their fate because of Moses' elevation.

Once as the day was drawing toward an end they were in his hut, and harassed him in the way I said they were wont to harass him: the Ethiopian here and the Ethiopian there, and that he was thinking of nothing but her black breasts, and what a scandal it was, what a disgrace to his first wife Zipporah, and what exposure for himself who claimed to be a prince of God and Jahwe's sole mouthpiece on earth. . . .

"Claimed?" said he. "What God has commanded me to be I am. How ugly of you, how very ugly, that you envy my pleasure and my relaxation on the breasts of the Ethiopian. For it is no sin before God, and there is no prohibition among all the prohibitions which he gave to me which says that one may not lie with an Ethiopian. Not that I know of."

But they answered that he chose his prohibitions according to his own tastes, and quite possibly he would soon preach that it was compulsory to lie with Ethiopians. For did he not consider himself Jahwe's sole mouthpiece? The truth was that they, Miriam and Aaron, were the proper children of Amram and the grandchildren of Levi, while he, when all was said and done, was only a foundling from the bulrushes; he might learn a little humility and not insist quite so much on his Ethiopian nor ignore their displeasure quite so offhandedly. Such behavior was proof of his pride and his conceit.

"Who can help it that he is called?" answered he. "Can any man help it if he comes upon the burning thorn bush? Miriam, I have always thought highly of your prophetic gifts and never denied your accomplishments on the timbrel. . . ."

"Then why did you disallow my hymn 'Steed and Man' and why did you prohibit me from leading the round dance of the women? You pretended that God forbade his flock to triumph over the downfall of the Egyptians. That was abominable of you."

"And you, Aaron," continued the hard-pressed Moses, "you I have employed as the high priest in the tabernacle, and I have entrusted the Chest, the Ephod, and the Brass Serpent unto your care. Thus do I value you."

"That was the least that you could have done," answered Aaron. "For without my eloquence could you never have persuaded the people to the cause of Jahwe, nor won them for the exodus. Consider how awkward is your mouth! But now you call yourself the man who has led us out of Egypt! If you really valued us, if you really did not exalt yourself so arrogantly over your blood relatives, then why do you not pay heed to our words? Why do you remain deaf to our admonition that you imperil our whole tribe with your black paramour? To Zipporah, your Midianitic wife, she is a draught as bitter as gall, and you offend all of Midian with your action, so that Jethro your brother-in-law might soon declare war on us—all for the sake of your colored caprice."

"Jethro," said Moses with restraint, "is an even man of the world who well understands that Zipporah—praised be her name!—no longer can offer the necessary recreation to a highly overworked and heavily burdened man. But the skin of my Ethiopian is like cinnamon and perfume of carnation in my nostrils; all my senses long for her, and therefore I beg of you, my good friends, grant her to me."

But that they did not want to do. They screeched and demanded not only that he part from the Ethiopian and forbid her his bed, but also that he drive her into the desert without water.

Thereupon veins of anger rose on Moses' forehead and terribly did his fists begin to tremble. But before he could open his mouth to respond, a very different trembling began—Jahwe interposed and set his visage against the hardhearted brother and sister, and came to his servant's aid in a way they never forgot. Something frightful, something never before seen, now happened.

17

The foundations trembled. The earth shook, shivered, and swayed under their feet so that they could not stand upright but tottered to and fro in the hut, whose posts seemed to be shaken by giant fists. What had been firm began to waver, not only in one direction but in crooked and dizzying gyrations. It was horrible. At the same time there occurred a subterranean growling and rumbling and a sound from above and from outside like the blare of a great trumpet, followed by a droning, a thundering, and a rustling. It is very strange and peculiarly embarrassing if you are on the point of breaking out into a rage and the Lord takes the words out of your mouth and himself breaks out much more mightily than you yourself could have done it, and shakes the world where you could only have shaken your fists.

Moses was the least pale with fright, for at all times he was prepared for God. With Aaron and Miriam, who were deathly pale, he rushed out of the house. Then they saw that the earth had opened its jaws and that a great gap yawned right next to their hut. Obviously this rent had been destined for Miriam and Aaron, and had missed them only by a few yards. And they looked toward the mountain in the east behind the desert, Horeb or Sinai—but what was happening on Horeb, what was taking place on Sinai? It stood there enveloped from foot to summit in smoke and flames, and threw glowing crumbs toward heaven, with a far-off sound of fearful crackling. Streams of fire ran down its sides. Its vapor, crossed by lightning, obscured the stars above the desert, and slowly a rain of ashes began to descend upon the oasis Kadesh.

Aaron and Miriam fell upon their foreheads; the cleft destined for them had filled them with terror. This revelation of Jahwe showed them that they had gone too far and had spoken foolishly. Aaron exclaimed:

"O my master, this woman my sister has jabbered ugly words. Accept my prayer and let not the sin remain upon her, the sin with which she sinned against the man anointed by the Lord."

Miriam also screamed to Moses and spoke: "Master, it is impossible to speak more foolishly than spoke my brother Aaron. Forgive him and let not the sin remain upon him, so that God may not devour him just because he has twitted you a little about the Ethiopian."

Moses was not quite certain if Jahwe's revelation was really meant for his brother and sister and their lack of love, or if it was the call meant for him, the call for which he had waited hourly, the call that summoned him to commune with God about his people and the work of their education. But he let them suppose what they supposed and answered:

"There, you see. But take courage, children of Amram. I shall put forth a good word for you up there with God on the mountain, whither he calls me. For now you shall see, and all the people shall see, whether your brother has become unmanned by his black infatuation or if the courage of God still dwells in his heart stronger than in other hearts. To the fiery mountain shall I go, quite alone, upward to God, to hear his thoughts and to deal without fear with the fearful one, on familiar terms, far from the people, but in their cause. For a long time have I known that he wishes to brief all that I have taught you for your salvation into binding words, into an eternal condensation, that I might carry it back to you from his mountain, and that the people may possess it in the tabernacle together with the Chest, the Ephod, and the Brass Serpent. Farewell. I may perish in God's tumult, in the fire of the mountain; I have to reckon with that. But should I return, then shall I bring out of his thunder the eternal brevity, God's law."

Such was his firm resolve; whether for life or death, that had he decided. For in order to root the obdurate, always backsliding rabble in God's morality, in order to make them fear his laws, nothing was more effective than that he, bare and alone, should dare to climb up to Jahwe's terror, up the spewing mountain, and thence carry down the dictates. Then, thought he, would they observe the laws.

When the people came running from all sides to his hut, trembling at the knees, frightened by the signs and by the terrible ululations of the earth, which occurred once and twice again, though weaker, Moses forbade them their commonplace quaking and admonished them to decent composure. God called him, said he, for their sake, and he was to climb up to Jahwe, up to the summit of the mountain, and bring something back for them, with God's will. They, however, should return to their homes and should prepare for a pilgrimage. They should hold themselves clean and wash their garments and abstain from their wives, and tomorrow they should wander out from Kadesh into the desert near the mountain. There should they encamp and wait for him until he returned from the fearful interview, perhaps bringing something back for them.

And thus it happened, or at least almost thus. Moses in his fashion had only remembered to tell them to wash their garments and to abstain from their wives. Joshua, the strategic youth, had remembered what else was necessary for such an excursion; with his troop he provided the proper quantities of water and nourishment needful to the thousands in the desert. And he also established a line of communication between Kadesh and the encampment near the mountain. He left Caleb his lieutenant in Kadesh with a police detail to supervise those who could not or would not come along. When the third day had dawned and all preparations had been made, all the others set out with their carts and their slaughter animals. They journeyed toward the mountain, a journey of a day and still a half. There, at a respectable distance from Jahwe's fuming dwelling, Joshua erected an enclosure. He enjoined the people most strictly and in Moses' name not to think of climbing that mountain nor even to set foot upon it. The master alone was privileged to approach so near to God. Moreover, it was highly dangerous, and whoever touched the mountain should be stoned or pierced with the arrow. They took this command in their stride, for rabble has no desire whatever to come all too near to God. To the common man the mountain did not in the least look inviting, neither by day, when Jahwe stood upon it in a thick cloud crossed by lightning, nor certainly by night, when the cloud and the entire summit glowed.

Joshua was extremely proud of the courage of his master, who the very first day and before all the people set out on his way to the mountain, alone and on foot with his pilgrim's staff, provided only with an earthen flask, a few crusts, and some tools, an ax, a chisel, a spade, and a stylus. Very proud was the youth, and pleased at the impression which such holy intrepidity would have to make on the multitude. But anxious was he too about the man he worshiped, and he implored him not to approach too near to Jahwe and to be careful of the hot molten streams which ran down the sides of the mountain. Also, said he, he would visit Moses once or twice and look after him, so that the master would not in God's wilderness lack the simplest necessities.

18

Moses, leaning on his staff, traversed the desert, his wide-set eyes fixed on God's mountain, which was smoking like an oven and spewed forth many times. The mountain was of peculiar shape: it had fissures and veins which seemed to divide it into terraces, and which looked like upward-leading paths, though they were not paths, but simply gradations of yellow walls. On the third day, after climbing several foothills, God's delegate arrived at the bare foot of the mountain. Then he began to ascend, his fist grasping the pilgrim's staff which he set before him. He climbed without path or track many an hour, step by step, higher, always higher, toward God's nearness. He climbed as far as a human being could, for by and by the sulphurous fumes which smelled of hot metals and which filled the air choked him, and he began to cough. He arrived at the topmost fissure and terrace right underneath the summit, where he could have a wide view of the bald and wild mountain ranges on both sides, and out over the desert as far as Kadesh. Closer by he could see the people in their enclosure, far below and small.

Here the coughing Moses found a cave in the mountain wall, a cave with a projecting roof of rock which could protect him from the falling stones and the flowing broth. There he took up his abode and arranged himself to start, after a short breathing spell, the work which God had ordered from him. Under the difficult circumstances—for the metal vapors lay heavily on his breast and made even the water taste of sulphur—this work held him fast up there not less than forty days and forty nights.

But why so long? Idle question! The eternal had to be recorded, the binding word had to be briefed, God's terse moral law had to be captured and graved into the stone of the mountain, so that Moses might bring it down to the vacillating mob, to the blood of his buried father, down into the encampment where they were waiting. There it was to stand from generation to generation, unbreakable, graved also into their minds and into their flesh and blood, the quintessence of human decency.

From his inner consciousness God directed him to hew two tablets from the rock and to write upon them his dictate, five words on the one and five words on the other, together ten words.

It was no easy task to build the two tablets, to smooth them and to shape them into halfway fit receptacles of eternal brevity. For a lone man, even if he had drunk the milk of a mason's daughter, even if he had broad wrists, it was a piece of work subject to many a mishap. Of the forty days it took a quarter. But the actual writing down was a problem the solution of which could well have prolonged the number of Moses' mountain days far over forty.

For in what manner should he write? In the academy of Thebes he had learned the decorative picture writing of Egypt with all its current amendments. He had also learned the stiffly formal triangle script of Euphrates, in which the kings of the world were wont to exchange their thoughts on fragments of clay. In Midian he had become acquainted with still a third magic method of capturing meaning. This one consisted of eyes, crosses, bugs, circles, and variously formed serpentine lines. It was a method used in Sinai which had been copied with desert awkwardness from the Egyptians. Its marks, however, did not represent whole words or word pictures, but only their parts. They denoted syllables which were to be read together.

None of these three methods of fastening thought satisfied him, for the simple reason that each of them was linked to a particular language and was indigenous to that language. Moses realized perfectly well that it would never under any conditions be possible for him to set upon the stone the dictate of ten words either in Babylonian or in Egyptian language, nor yet in the jargon of the Sinai Bedouins. The words on the stone could be only in the language of his father's blood, the very dialect which they spoke and which he himself employed in his teachings. It did not matter whether they would be able to read it or not. In fact, how could they be expected to read a language which no one could as yet write? There was no magic symbol at hand to represent and hold fast their speech.

With all his soul Moses wished that there existed such a symbol, one which they could learn to read quickly, very quickly; one which children, such as they were, could learn in a few days. It followed, then, that somebody could think up and invent such a symbol in a few days, with the help of God's nearness. Yes, because it did not exist, somebody had to think up and invent this new method of writing.

What a pressing and precious task! He had not considered it in advance, had simply thought of "writing" and had not taken into account that one could not write just like that! Fired by his fervent search for symbols his people could understand, his head glowed and smoked like an oven and like the summit of the mountain. It seemed to him as if rays emerged from his head, as if horns sprang from his forehead, so great was his wishing exertion. And then a simple, illuminating idea came to him. True, he could not invent signs for all the words used by his kin, nor for the syllables from which they formed their words. Even if the vocabulary of those down in the enclosure was paltry, yet would it have required too many marks for him to build in the span of his mountain days and also for the others to learn to read quickly. Therefore he thought of something else, and horns stood upon his forehead out of pride over the flash of God's inspiration. He gathered the sounds of the language, those formed by the lips, by the tongue, by the palate, and by the throat; he put to one side the few open sounds which occurred every so often within the words, which in fact were framed by the others into words. He found that there were not too many of these framing sonant sounds—hardly twenty. If one ascribed definite signs to them, signs which everybody could alike aspirate and respirate, mumble and rumble, gabble and babble, then one could combine these signs into words and word pictures, leaving out the open sounds which followed by themselves. Thus one could form any word one liked, any word which existed, not only in the language of his father's kin, but in all languages—yes, with these signs one could even write Egyptian or Babylonian.

A flash from God. An idea with horns. An idea such as could be expected from the invisible and the spiritual one, him to whom the world belonged, him who, though he had chosen those down below as his people, was yet the Lord of all the earth. It was an idea also which was eminently fitting to the next and most pressing purpose for which and out of which it was created: the text of the tablets, the binding briefed text. This text was to be coined first and specifically for the tribe which Moses had led out of Egypt because God and he were inclined toward them. But just as with a handful of these signs all the words of all the languages of all the people could, if need be, be written, just as Jahwe was the God of all the world, so was what Moses meant to brief and write of such a nature that it could serve as fundamental precept, as the rock of human decency, to all the peoples of the earth.

Moses with his fiery head now experimented with signs loosely related to the marks of the Sinai people as he remembered them. On the wall of the mountain he graved with his stylus the lisping, popping, and smacking, the hissing and swishing, the humming and murmuring sounds. And when he had all the signs together and could distinguish them with a certain amount of assurance, lo! with them one could write the whole world, all that which occupied space and all that which occupied no space, all that was fashioned and all that was thought. In short, all.

He wrote. That is to say, he jabbed, chiseled, and hacked at the brittle stone of the tablets, those tablets which he had hewn laboriously and whose creation went hand in hand with the creation of the letters. No wonder that it took him forty days!

Joshua, his youth, came to see him several times. He brought him water and crusts, without precisely telling of his visits to the people. The people thought that Moses lived up there in God's proximity and communed with him quite alone. And Joshua deemed it strategically best to let them believe this. Therefore his visits were short and made by night.

From the dawn of the light of day above Edom to its extinction, Moses sat behind the desert and worked. One has to imagine him as he sat up there with bare shoulders, his breast covered with hair, with his powerful arms which he may have inherited from his ill-used father, with his eyes set far apart, with his flattened nose, with the divided, now graying beard—chewing his crust, now and then coughing from the metal vapors of the mountain, hammering, scraping, and polishing his tablets in the sweat of his brow. He crouched before the tablets propped against the rocky wall, and painstakingly carved the crow's-feet, then traced them with his stylus, and finally graved the omnipotent runes deep into the flatness of the stone.

On one tablet he wrote:

I, Jahwe, am thy God; thou shalt have no other gods before me.
Thou shalt not make unto thee any image.
Thou shalt not take my name in vain.
Remember my day, to keep it holy.
Honor thy father and thy mother.

And on the other tablet he wrote:

Thou shalt not murder.
Thou shalt not commit adultery.
Thou shalt not steal.
Thou shalt not harm thy neighbor by false witness.
Thou shalt not cast a covetous eye on the possession of thy neighbor.

That is what he wrote, omitting the open sounds which formed themselves. And always it seemed to him as if rays like two horns stood out from the locks of his forehead.

When Joshua came for the last time to the mountain, he remained a little longer, two whole days. For Moses was not finished with his work and they wanted to descend together. The youth admired wholeheartedly what his master had accomplished. He comforted him because a few letters were cracked and unrecognizable in spite of all the love and care which Moses had expended. Joshua assured him that this did no harm to the total impression.

The last thing that Moses did while Joshua looked on was to paint the sunken letters with his blood so that they would stand out better. No other pigment was at hand. Therefore he cut his strong arm with his stylus and smeared the trickling blood into the letters so that they glowed rosily in the stone. When the writing had dried, Moses took one tablet under each arm, gave his pilgrim's staff, with which he had ascended, to the youth, and thus they wandered down from the seat of God toward the encampment of the people near the mountain in the desert.

19

When they had arrived at a certain distance from the encampment, just within hearing distance, a noise penetrated to them, a hollow screeching. They could not account for it. It was Moses who heard it first and Joshua who mentioned it first.

"Do you hear this peculiar clatter," he asked, "this tumult, this uproar? There is something doing, I think, a brawl, a bout, or I am much mistaken. And it must be violent and general, that we hear it as far as this. If it is what I think it is, then it is good that we come."

"That we come," answered Moses, "is good in any case. But as far as I can make out, this is no scuffle and no tussle, but something like a feasting or a dance of triumph. Do you not hear the high-pitched jubilation and clash of timbrels? Joshua, how is it that they celebrate without my permission? Joshua, what has got into them? Let us hurry."

He grasped his two tablets higher under his arms and strode faster with the puzzled Joshua.

"A dance of triumph . . . a dance of triumph," he repeated uneasily and finally in open terror. For it appeared all too clearly that this was not an ordinary brawl in which one person lay on top and the other below; this was a general, united carousal. And now it was only a question of what kind of unity it was in which they thus reveled.

Even that question answered itself too soon, if indeed it need ever have been asked. The mess was horrible. As Moses and Joshua passed the high posts of the encampment they saw it in shameless unequivocalness. The people were on the loose. They had thrown off everything that Moses had laid upon them in holiness, all the morality of God. They wallowed in hair-raising relapse.

Directly behind the portals was a free space which was the assembly place. There things were happening, there they were carrying on, there they wallowed, there they celebrated their miserable liberty. Before the dance they had all stuffed themselves full. One could see that at first glance. Everywhere the place showed the traces of slaughtering and gluttony. And in whose honor had they sacrificed, slaughtered, and stuffed themselves? There it stood. In the midst of barrenness, set on a stone, set on an altar pedestal, an image, a thing made by their hands, an idolatrous mischief, a golden calf.

It was no calf, it was a bull, the real, ordinary stud bull of all the peoples of the world. A calf it is called only because it was no more than medium size, in fact rather less, and also misshapen and ludicrously fashioned; an awkward abomination, yet all too recognizable as a bull.

Around this thing a multitudinous round dance was in progress, a dozen circles of men and women, hand in hand, accompanied by timbrels and by cymbals. Heads were thrown far back, rolling eyes were upturned, knees jerked toward chins; they screeched and they roared and made crass obeisance. In different directions did the dance turn, one shameful circle turning toward the right, another toward the left. In the very center of the whirlpool, near the calf, Aaron could be seen hopping around in his long-sleeved garment which he used to wear as the guardian of the tabernacle, and which he had gathered high so that he could jig with his long, hairy legs. And Miriam led the women with her timbrel.

But this was only the round dance near the calf. Farther on what was to be expected was taking place. It is difficult to confess how far the people debased themselves. Some ate blindworms, others lay with their sisters and that publicly, in the calf's honor. Others simply squatted and emptied themselves, forgetting the scoop. Men offered their force to the calf. Somewhere someone was cuffing his own mother.

At these gruesome sights, the veins of anger swelled to bursting on Moses' forehead. His face flaming red, he cut his way through the circles of the dancers—straight to the calf, the seed, the fountain, the womb of the crime. Recognizing the master, they gaped with embarrassed grins. High up he lifted one of the tablets of the law with mighty arms, and smashed it down on the ridiculous beast, so that its legs crumbled. Once again did he strike, and with such rage that though the tablet broke into pieces, nothing but a formless mass remained of the thing. Then he swung the second tablet and gave the abomination a final blow, grinding it completely to dust. And because the second tablet remained still intact, he shattered it with a blow on the pedestal. Then he stood still with trembling fists, and deeply from his breast he groaned: "Ye rabble, ye Godforsaken! There lies what I have carried down from God, what he has written for you with his finger as your talisman against the misery of ignorance. There it lies in ruins near the fragments of your idol. And what shall I now tell my Lord so that he will not devour you?"

He saw Aaron the jumper standing near with downcast eyes, and with oily locks at the nape of his neck; he stood silent and stupid. Moses seized him by his garment, shook him, and spoke: "Where did the golden Belial come from, this excrescence, and what did the people do to you that you push them to their destruction while I am up on the mountain? Why do you yourself bray before them in their dance of debauchery?"

And Aaron answered, "O my master, let not your anger be heaped on me and on my sister. We had to give in. You know that the people are evil. They forced us. You were away so long, you remained an eternity on the mountain, so that we all thought that you would never return. Then the people gathered against me and screamed, 'Nobody knows what has become of that man Moses, who has led us out of Egypt. He shall not return. Probably the spewing mouth of the mountain has swallowed him. Arise, make us gods which shall go before us when Amalek comes. We are a people like other peoples, and want to carouse before gods which are like the gods of other peoples!' Thus they spoke, master, for if you pardon me, they thought they were rid of you. But now tell me what I could have done when they banded together against me. I asked them to break off the golden earrings from their ears. These I melted in the fire and made a form, and cast the calf as their god."

"It is not even a good likeness of a calf," interposed Moses contemptuously.

"They were in such a hurry," answered Aaron. "The very next day, that is, today, they wanted to hold their revels in honor of the sympathetic gods. Therefore I handed over to them the image as it was, a piece of work to which you ought not deny a certain amount of verisimilitude. And they rejoiced and spoke, 'These are your gods, Israel, which have led you out of Egypt.' And we built an altar and they offered burnt sacrifices and thank offerings and ate, and after that they played and danced a little."

Moses let him stand there and made his way back to the portal through the scattered circles of dancers. There with Joshua he placed himself beneath the birchen crossbeam and called with all his might:

"Who is on the Lord's side, let him come unto me."

Many came, those who were of sound heart and had not willingly joined the revels. Joshua's armed troop assembled around him.

"Ye unfortunate people," said Moses, "what have ye done, and how shall I now atone for you before Jahwe, that he shall not blot you out as an incorrigibly stiff-necked people and shall not devour you? As soon as I turn my back, ye make yourselves a golden Belial. Shame on you and on me! Do ye see these ruins—I do not mean those of the calf, let the pest take them!—I mean the others? That is the gift which I had promised you and which I have brought down to you, the eternal condensation, the rock of decency, the ten words which I, in God's nearness, wrote down in your language and wrote with my blood, with the blood of my father; with your blood did I write them. Now lies the gift in fragments."

Then many who heard this wept and there was a great crying and much nose blowing in the encampment.

"Perhaps it will be possible to replace them," said Moses. "For the Lord is patient and of infinite mercy, and forgives missteps and trespasses. But"—he thundered of a sudden, while his blood rose to his head and his veins swelled to bursting—"he lets no one go unpunished. For, says the Lord, I visit the iniquity of the fathers upon the children unto the third and fourth generation as the jealous God that I am. We shall hold court here," exclaimed Moses, "and shall order a bloody cleansing. It shall be determined who were the ringleaders who first screamed for golden gods and insolently asserted that the calf has led you out of Egypt, where I alone have done it, says the Lord. They shall all have to deal with the destroying angels, regardless of their rank or person. To death shall they be stoned and shot by the arrow, even if there are three hundred of them. And the others shall strip off their ornaments and mourn until I return—for I shall again ascend the mountain of God, and shall see what in any case I can do for you, ye stiff-necked people."

20

Moses did not attend the executions which the golden calf had made necessary. That was the business of the dashing Joshua. Moses himself was once again up on the mountain in his cave underneath the rumbling summit. While the people mourned he again remained forty days and forty nights alone among the vapors. But why so long? The answer is thus: not only because Jahwe directed him to form the tablets anew and to write down the dictate afresh—that task went more quickly because he had acquired practice and knew how to write—but also because he had to fight a long fight with the Lord before he would permit the renewal. It was a wrestling in which anger and mercy, fatigue over the work and love for the undertaking, were in turn victorious. Moses had to use much power of persuasion and many clever appeals to prevent God from declaring the covenant broken. For almost did God cast himself loose from the stiff-necked rabble, almost did he smash them as Moses in flaming anger had smashed the first tablets of the law.

"I shall not go before them," said God, "to lead them into the land of their fathers. Do not ask this of me—I cannot depend upon my patience. I am a jealous God and I flame up, and you shall see one day I shall forget myself and I shall devour them altogether."

And he proposed to Moses that he would annihilate these people, who were as miscast as the golden calf and as incorrigible. It would be impossible, said he, to raise them into a holy people, and there was nothing left but to consume Israel and rot it out. But of him, Moses, he would make a great nation and live with him in covenant. But this Moses did not want, and he said to him, "No, Lord," said he, "forgive them their sins; if not, then blot me out of the book also, for I do not wish to survive them. For my part, I wish for no other holy people but them."

And he appealed to the Lord's sense of honor and spoke: "Imagine, holy one, what is going to happen. If you kill these people as one man, then the heathen who shall hear their screams will say, 'Bah! The Lord was not able to bring the people into the land which he had promised them. He was not powerful enough. Therefore did he slaughter them in the wilderness.' Do you want that said of you by all the peoples of the world? Therefore let the power of the Lord appear great, and be lenient with the missteps of your children according to your mercy."

It was this last argument which won God and decided him toward forgiveness. With the restriction, however, that of this generation none except Joshua and Caleb should ever see the promised land. "Your children," decided the Lord, "I shall lead there. But all those who are above twenty in their age, they shall never see the land. Their bodies shall fall in the desert."

"It is well, Lord, all shall be well," answered Moses. "We shall leave it at that." For because this decision agreed with his and Joshua's purposes, he argued against it no longer. "Now let me renew the tablets," said he, "that I may take your brevity down to the human beings. After all, perhaps it was just as well that I smashed the first in my anger. There were a few misshaped letters in there. I shall now confess to you that I fleetingly thought of this when I dashed the tablets to pieces."

And again he sat, secretly nourished and succored by Joshua, and he jabbed and he chiseled, he scraped and he smoothed. Wiping his brow from time to time with the back of his hand, he wrote, hacking and graving the letters into the tablets. They came out a good deal better than the first time. Then again he painted the letters with his blood and descended, the law under his arms.

It was announced to Israel that the mourning had come to an end, and that they again might put on their ornaments, except of course the earrings: these had been used up to bad purpose. And all the people came before Moses that he might hand them what he had brought down, the message of Jahwe from the mountain, the tablets with the ten words.

"Take them, blood of our fathers," said he, "and hold them sacred in the tent of God. But what they tell ye, that hold sacred in your actions. For here is briefed what shall bind you; here is the divine condensation; here is the alpha and omega of human behavior; here is the rock of decency, which God has inscribed in lapidary writing, using my stylus. In your language did he write, but in symbols in which if need be all the languages of all the peoples could be written. For he is the Lord of all, and therefore is he the Lord of ABC, and his speech, addressed to you, Israel, is at the same time a speech for all.

"Into the stone of the mountain did I grave the ABC of human behavior, but it must be graved also into your flesh and blood, Israel. So that he who breaks but one word of the ten commandments shall tremble before his own self and before God and an icy finger shall be laid on his heart, because he has stepped out of God's confines. I know well and God knows in advance that his commandments will not be obeyed, and they will be transgressed at all times and everywhere. But at least the heart of everyone who breaks them shall turn icy, for the words are written in every man's flesh and blood and deep within himself he knows that the words are all-valid.

"But woe to the man who shall arise and speak: 'They are no longer valid.' Woe to him who teaches you: 'Arise and get rid of them! Lie, murder, rob, whore, rape, and deliver your father and mother to the knife. For this is the natural behavior of human beings and you shall praise my name because I proclaim natural license.' Woe to him who erects a calf and speaks: 'This is your god. In his honor do all of this, and whirl around the image I have fashioned in a round dance of debauchery.' He shall be mighty and powerful, he shall sit upon a golden throne, and he shall be looked up to as the wisest of all. For he knows that the inclination of the human heart is evil, even in youth. But that is about all that he will know, and he who knows only that is as stupid as the night and it would be better for him never to have been born. For he knows nothing of the covenant between God and man, a covenant that none may break, neither man nor God, for it is unbreakable. Blood shall flow in torrents because of his black stupidity, so much blood that the redness shall vanish from the cheeks of mankind. But then the people shall hew down the monster—inevitably; for they can do naught else. And the Lord says, I shall raise my foot and shall trample him into the mire, to the bottom of the earth shall I cast the blasphemer, one hundred and twelve fathoms deep. And man and beast shall describe an arc around the spot into which I have cast him; and the birds of the heavens, high in their flight, shall shun the place so that they need not fly over it. And he who shall speak his name, he shall spit toward the four corners of the earth and shall wipe his mouth and say, 'Forfend!' That the earth may again be the earth, a vale of want, yes, but not a sty of depravity. To that say ye Amen!"

And all the people said Amen.

Translated by George R. Marek

THE SECOND COMMANDMENT

Thou shalt not make
unto thee any graven image

REBECCA WEST

II

THOU SHALT NOT MAKE ANY GRAVEN IMAGE

A STORY BY

REBECCA WEST

When Elisaveta woke she rang the bell for her coffee, but Marta did not come. When she had rung again and nothing happened, she thought, "This is the third time Marta has not come this month. She is getting old, probably she will not stay with me much longer. But I will not know what to do without her, she has been with me ever since I was a little girl." Her eyes brimmed. "I am still young, but I am being left alone as if I were very old. Everybody is going away from me."

She reached out for the bottle of rose water and the pad of cotton wool she kept by her bedside to repair the damage done by the tears she shed so much more frequently than was wise in an actress. Then she picked up the script of her new part, which had fallen to the floor when she had at last dropped off to sleep, and began reading the lines to try to drive out of her mind the thought of her husband, David, who might be alive, who might not. With the Nazis there was no knowing, and no hoping.

Dropping it, she pouted the smiling defiances of an imaginary happy woman while she pulled on her dressing gown, which had to go unmended now that she lived alone, then went along the corridor, drawing back the curtains and wincing as the strong morning light fell on her tired eyes. She went to the kitchen to make the strong coffee her nerves needed before she could face the day.

"No," she murmured, "I don't want to go on a trip to Paris—not unless you can move Paris out of France, to some new, exciting country. I've been to France so often. And I don't want any diamonds. I don't want any jewels—unless you can get me some stone that's a cross between a diamond and a pearl. That I might like—though I can't be sure."

The problem was to say the lines, not as if the woman were a complete fool and meant it, or meant to be funny, but as if she were a sensible woman who was talking nonsense because the cause of her dissatisfaction was so wounding to her pride that she could not name it, yet at the same time to keep on the plane of comedy, even light comedy.

Soon, however, she ceased to say the lines. She was seduced into gentle contentment by the clean white and green paint of the kitchen and the glittering stove and pots and pans, all very bright in the spring sunshine, by the bowl of hyacinths on the dresser, by the good coffee and rye bread and butter, and, above all, by the view she saw between the checked curtains of her window.

People thought it strange of her to live so far away from the center of the town, in the most distant apartment house, right up on the heights beyond the navy dockyard. Indeed, it cost her a fortune in taxis after the theater. But it was halfway to being in paradise, looking down on the town from these windows. It might be one of the smallest capitals in Europe, beautiful Copenhagen, but it was like the seat of a king in a fairy tale. Even when she had dreamed of it as a girl in her father's parsonage at the other end of the country, pouring into the dream all she could imagine of beauty, and knowing nothing of ugliness, she had not seen it as lovely as it was.

Beneath her windows the little white houses stood on the sloping hillside among the budding lilacs with the touching, hopeful quality of a new suburb; there young people were beginning life, or old people ending lives that had been successful enough, since they were still together and had the means for comfort. All turned their faces toward the wide, high floor of the dark-blue sea, crisped now to white horses by spring winds, strewn with the hundred islands, dark with pine trees, bright with the wakening maples and birches, stretching to the white bar of the southern horizon.

At the foot of the hillside the red-roofed cottages of the old fishing village and the long, low, butter-colored buildings of the naval establishment hid all of the docks save the funnels and masts. From that the raised causeway, blue water and gentle surf on the one side, emerald salt marshes on the other, ran to the tortoise-shaped rock on which the city lay. With its gables and towers it made a shape as clear, as easy for the eye to grasp, as an intaglio on a ring. Its color was red, a soft drowsy red with nothing harsh in it, the color that some rose petals turn in potpourri. Behind it rose the pointed hills, dark with firwoods, and above them the pyramids of the snow peaks, all angular, all shapely and austerely cut yet not ungentle, like the houses and churches in the city below.

"Spring is here," thought Elisaveta. "Someday soon I will get old Sven to take me to the fisherman's pavilion on the other side of the city, where they give one those lovely prawns, just out of the water and cooked." Sven was the oldest actor in the State Theater and he had been very kind to her since David had gone, taking her about to pretty places that were not too noisy and yet were a distraction, and being patient with her when the distraction failed and she wept. She poured out another cup of coffee.

> "No," she murmured, "I don't want to go on a trip to Paris—not unless you can move Paris out of France. . . ."

Then it was that she saw what was happening. She set down her cup and saucer on the table so that the coffee spilt. She ran to the window and grasped the ledge and stared, her mouth falling open as if she were dead, as she might well soon be. The causeway was no longer dust-colored, empty save for an occasional lorry or tradesman's cart, as it always was at this hour. It was dark with a moving column of men and vehicles more brutal than lorries, monstrous even when seen from a great distance.

Crying out, she ran from the kitchen into the living room and turned on the radio. A voice, smug with successful treachery, was shouting that the city need feel no further fear, for Hitler had taken it under his protection.

Elisaveta threw herself down on the divan, sobbing and cursing and drumming with her fists on the Chinese silk coverlet. A part of her which remained calm thought wistfully, "I am not a great beauty, I am not a great actress, I am only so-so. It is not fair that I should be asked to take part in great events of history. I could have borne with misfortunes that are like myself, within a moderate compass. I could have nursed David through a long illness. I could have kept my dignity if the Director had taken a dislike to me as he did to Inga and pretended that I was old long before I really was, and made me play character parts.

"I could have gone on all my life long being patient if David and I had had a child and it had been delicate or stupid or wayward, but all this abduction and killing and tyranny, I cannot stand up to it.

"When Truda married and left the theater and it was a question who should play the leading parts, the Director said to me, 'Now, Elisaveta, this you can play and that, but not Hebbel's Judith and not Ann Whitefield. You have not the big bones, you have not the broad veins.' I wish somebody would come and say to me: 'You cannot be expected to live under Hitler. You have not the big bones, you have not the broad veins.' "

She sobbed for a little while, and then thought: "And it is all wrong. It is like having suddenly to start acting without any make-up on in the middle of the lounge at the Excelsior Hotel, or in the silk department in Lacherman's store, to have to face these tremendous events in the familiar places where one has lived all one's everyday life. It would have been better if these horrible things were happening to one in some fantastic country which one had reached only after many days' travel."

It had been at the holiday resort which everybody in the city went to in summer, which she had visited two or three times a year ever since she had become an actress, that they had taken David away. It was on the road going through the pinewoods to the lake with the overhung cliff called the Trolls' Castle, to which every family in the kingdom had at some time or other made an excursion, that the gray automobile had stopped and the four men had got out and thrown the raincoat over David's head. It was there that David had fallen to the ground and been kicked by the heaviest man in the crutch of the loins. As she heard again his scream, she prayed at one and the same time that he would come back to her again; that he had long been dead.

Then the automobile had driven off in the direction of the frontier, and she was left alone, looking about her in horror at the pinewoods she had known so long, as if they had lied to her.

There had been nobody on the road, for it was lunchtime. She had run into the woods and had found a picnic party and had stood in front of them with her hands stretched out, as if it were of them she was asking mercy, and had said: "My husband is a Jewish refugee, he is David Adler, the writer. The Nazis have come in an automobile and kidnaped him. What shall I do?"

The men and women and children had sat quite still on the grass, holding bitten slices of bread and sausage in their hands, staring at her in hostility because, though they were kind, she looked so strange, what she said was so strange. When they understood, they had gathered round her in a circle, helpless as if the sun had turned black. They looked about them at the forest as she had done, as if they were victims of a betrayal, as if they had been asked to a bridal and had found themselves at a funeral, their dress improper and an unexpected grief taking advantage of them. Their country which had always promised small delights, small comforts, small, swiftly terminated sorrows, and had kept its promise, would henceforth, now that the Nazis had come, practice such bizarre deceptions against which the mind could not forearm itself, being committed to health.

"Whom shall I turn to now?" she wondered. "Who will be strong enough, who will be a refuge in whom I can find shelter, and remember the time when everything was healthy, so that I do not go mad? I will be poor, of course. Even if I could bear to act now, they would not let David's widow play in the State Theater. Probably they will steal my savings. But that does not matter. It is seeing horrible things I will mind. My head will go. Even if it had not been David whom they took away in the automobile, even if it had been a total stranger I had never set my eyes on before, the mere sight of what happened would have shattered me. I am afraid of going mad, all alone. Who will come to save me now?"

Old Sven was too old. He had wept sometimes at the thought of the Nazis coming; now he would be utterly overcome, no shelter for her but a charge on her kindness. Besides, it was not an actor to whom one would wish to turn at this time. If there had been a great actor in the State Theater, then that would have been all right; he would have been cocreator with the greatest men whose works they had performed. He would have been wise, as they were. But there was nobody at the State Theater now who was more than an interpreter; one might as well look to a violin apart from its player for comfort in a crisis.

If one knew a great author, though he might be helpless as a child in material matters and in human relationships, and perhaps even naughty as a very naughty child, he would have wisdom. He would know what to put in the other pan to counterbalance the evil that was dragging down the scales. Because writers, if they were good, really knew something. She did not care for books and rarely read one from year's end to year's end, but she knew from the plays in which she had acted that writers were not just trying to amuse people or to make money. They were making clear a pattern in life that was there but had not been noticed by ordinary people. Often in her own life, something would happen to her that would strike her as important and strange, and yet not altogether unfamiliar; as if she had been told long ago that that was how it would be in such circumstances. Then she would remember, "But, of course, that is what the play *A Pack of Cards* was about! That was what Feierabend was trying to say. . . ."

Well, there was Egon, and there was Nils. They were certainly the greatest dramatists in the country; and some said they were among the greatest dramatists in Europe or in the world. Their plays were performed in Germany and France and England and the United States. They were wise; she had learned that over and over again. And she was so sure of their friendship that as soon as she had thought of them she stopped weeping and got up from the divan and set about dressing. As she filled her bath she wondered which of the two she liked better. She knew them equally well; she had acted in all the plays they had written during the last ten years, and each had been her lover. As she lay in the warm water she wondered which she would find the kinder friend. She had always thought of them as being, as nearly as is possible for two human beings, of exactly the same value. They were, indeed, so much alike physically that people often took them for relatives; of middle height and slim though not unsturdy, with strong blue eyes and light-brown hair and high cheekbones, they might have been fishermen from the islands constrained to an elegance unusual even in dwellers in the city. For they had beautiful clothes and shoes and gloves, all from London, much more beautiful than those worn by the shipping millionaires who could have bought them up ten times, successful though they were. They practiced their dandyism as a joke, because of its incongruity with the other characteristics they had in common; for they were alike in being grimly industrious, quietly indifferent to the opinion of the community, and able to pass at a moment's notice from life as it is lived by intellectuals to life as it is lived by sailors and farmers and timbermen. They seemed to have nothing in common with the *bourgeoisie* into which they had been born. They were a mixture of peasant and aristocrat. Of course the resemblance was not necessarily innate. They had probably developed it in the course of their lifelong friendship; for as neighbors' children they had gone to school together, they had left home together to go to Berlin University, they had worked side by side in a shipping office and had been sent to work for the firm's correspondents in London and New York at the same time.

They had both had plays produced when they were twenty-five. Fame had come to them soon and simultaneously and shortly afterwards they had married two very beautiful girls belonging to the best families in the city, girls of very much the same type, Magda and Hildegarde.

Tears came into Elisaveta's eyes as she thought how terrible the coming of the Nazis would be to Magda and Hildegarde, to whom life was entirely a matter of happiness, running up the scale from fur coats and pearls to loving husbands and perfect children. There was no consolation for the moralist in their reverse, for like Egon and Nils they had taken their good fortune with laughing modesty, as undeserved good luck and an occasion for generosity. It was just like seeing a bowl of lovely fruit overturned in the mud. "Perhaps I can do something for them," thought Elisaveta, "help them pack up if they are going to their farms up in the country."

Drying herself, she thought: "But which will be best able to help me, to make me bear it, to keep me from going mad? Egon or Nils? Which is the wiser?" She tried to remember their plays, though her mind was shocked; she did not find it so easy to grope her way back to the parts she had acted in the happier times. Egon's plays were more complete, of course. It was as if a home were shrunken to the size of a doll's house, and the front taken away. The rooms were as if flooded with soft bright light; that was the effect of the dialogue, which was always tactfully balanced, never too brilliant to divert the audience's attention from the development of the story, but never dull. One could see everything the family was doing, and with exquisite art their visible life was made to reveal their invisible life. She had often found it necessary to follow dramatists round the theater till there was an opportunity of saying: "Please, I know I am very stupid, but I would like to understand why I have to say this line in the third act?"

But Egon's characters were written in the script as plain as lifelong acquaintances; doubt was not possible. Looking back on the roles she had played for him, she saw herself in a party dress with a bodice glittering with sequins and a full skirt of white net, dancing about an attic, twitching away dark cloths that were draped over a dozen or so of these doll's houses, which had been stripped of their façades and were emitting bright light, against which the silhouettes of tiny people told the truth about themselves.

To act in Nils' plays was quite different, and perhaps not so agreeable, though one received great praise, and the audience was given over to one in a disarmed state, almost in a trance, out of which their weeping and their laughter proceeded in a natural, uncensored form. It was as if one had become a totally strange woman and walked in and out of darkness onto the lighted stage, with one's face veiled; and as if the attention of the audience became a person and crossed the footlights and tore off the veil and was at first disconcerted and then either enormously amused or enormously horrified by what it saw.

"They are both great men," Elisaveta said to herself, "but in different ways. You can't compare things that don't set out to be the same. Anyway, I am not clever, I can't judge their work."

But she had other material that she could consider. Both Egon and Nils, she remembered, had been sweet lovers, giving her much, going from her without unkindness. Though she would now have preferred that there had been nobody in her life but David, it nevertheless made her happy to remember how they had first made love to her.

Egon had come on her as she was sitting waiting for the Director in his office, which was built right on the roof of the theater and opened many windows to the sky. She had come to show the costume she was to wear in a nineteenth-century comedy: a little bonnet with a feather, a close jacket edged with dark fur, a tiny muff, a crinoline, all of which made her feel fragile and remote, the sort of woman who is cherished. Egon burst in without expecting to see her and came to a halt crying: "But how lovely you look! How lovely you are, Elisaveta!"

That was eight years before; but she still smiled with pride at the memory. She had not been a great beauty, but she had been lovely enough, she had no reason to feel sorry for herself. And she was not merely a pretty woman, she had something that would go on when she was old and ugly.

Nils taught her that. He had first noticed her one day when he had passed her in the corridor and had seen that she had been crying. He had paused, stared, looked away, and gone on, and then turned back and gripped her by the shoulders.

"Why are you crying? Little one, you must tell me why you are crying."

She had not wanted to tell him, for it was a childish matter of hurt pride, of professional vanity, and he had ceased to press her for the explanation, crying:

"Elisaveta, do you know I have never thought of you before as a human being! I've thought of you just as an actress, just as somebody who acts in my plays, but of course you're a human being, you laugh and cry, and I believe you're a wonderful human being! Elisaveta, put on your hat and come out with me, I want to talk to you, I want to learn what you are like."

He had really liked her. Ever since he had treated her with respect and interest. He evidently felt that she was one of his kind of person. To think that had often given her back her self-confidence when she had lost it.

With both of them she had been very happy; but all three of them belonged to the breed of artist to whom no love affair can mean anything unless it leads to domesticity. Love that is not a solid background for artistic achievement, that did not build a home to write in, or to come back to after the theater, might be very beautiful, but it was not worth while going to any trouble to keep it alive. Egon and she had ceased to be lovers when he went on a trip to the South Seas; Nils and she had mislaid each other when he went to the United States to produce a play and she went as guest artist to the state theaters of three neighboring countries. But ever since they had been close friends, not that they saw each other so very often, since they were all very busy, but when they met, whether at a party or café or in each other's homes, they found it difficult to separate, the two men talked so well when she was listening.

"To which of them shall I go first?" she asked herself and could not give an answer. It was pure chance that took her to Egon's house. The two men lived only a few doors from each other, at the foot of the hill in her part of the city, in a row of seventeenth-century brick houses looking onto the quay which was no longer used. It was always as quiet as a convent garden, and it was horrible to turn around the corner and find the German troops there among a crowd of townsmen, screaming and jerking at their weapons. But they were screaming dismissal. Evidently some high German dignitary had been addressing the people, for they were streaming back into their houses, their heads down, their faces blank with shame. They knew what she knew, that many of them would soon know pain and death, and that goodness would, from now on, be mocked. These people in the turd-green uniforms were those who had taken David away. Her knees gave way under her and she went to Egon's house because it was nearest.

The old servant, Johanna, was bent and weeping. Her famous lace-encrusted cap, which she made after a fashion that used to be followed by the women of the outer islands, flapped over her shaking, bluish face. With the obstinate formality of a proud servant she greeted Elisaveta as if this were an ordinary visit and there was nothing terrible about the day, and when Elisaveta spoke to her sympathetically, she asked coldly if she wanted to see Mr. Egon and announced her in proper fashion. Elisaveta clapped her hands with joy as the door opened, for they were both there. Egon and Nils.

They made a very pleasant picture, the two handsome men sitting in a room which was famous for its beauty. It ran from the front to the back of the house, and the great windows let in the lovely Scandinavian sunlight, the clean spray-washed sunlight. On the window sills there stood a line of model ships, the lovely nervous systems of their masts and riggings in silhouette, and on the walls there were pictures of the sea and portraits of old sailors and their wives. The furniture was such as the sailors and merchants of the city in the times gone past had bought for their own comfort and that of their descendants. Some had been fetched from England, because the workmanship of Chippendale and Sheraton was so well reputed. There were Persian carpets also brought in those times by the townspeople; and the floor boards had been polished with such frenzy as sailors bring to the keeping of a beloved ship. Sometimes Elisaveta had thought it a shame that the descendants of the men who had made this room had not followed the sea like their fathers, but were merely writers. But when she saw Egon and Nils sitting there, as quiet as if an end to all happiness and safety had not come, she knew that they had done better than following the sea, they had followed danger wherever it might be found.

They stood up, exclaiming with pleasure at the sight of her.

"I came here," Elisaveta said, "because—oh, first of all, because I feel frightened and I wanted some comfort and you have always been my dear friends, and secondly, because I thought you might be going away and I wondered if I could be of some help to Magda and Hildegarde, in packing or looking after the children——"

"But, Elisaveta!" they said to her, "have you forgotten?"

"Forgotten what?" she asked happily. It was lovely when they laughed at her; it was as if they were picnicking up in the mountains, or dancing in a sailors' inn at a little port.

"Have you forgotten that Magda and Hildegarde and the children all went off for a holiday in England just a month ago?" asked Nils. "Why, you came and gave all the children presents to amuse them on the journey and you waved them good-by!"

"But of course I did!" cried Elisaveta. "Oh, but how wonderful! Oh, Egon! Oh, Nils! To think that Magda and Hildegarde and all the children are safe! What a blessing!" She flung her arms around the neck of each man in turn and kissed him. Their eyes became wet; they looked down on her tenderly, as if in gratitude for speaking of what they could hardly trust themselves to speak.

Egon muttered, "Yes, as you know, now it is, comparatively speaking, all right for us."

"But how mad of me to forget that Magda and Hildegarde had gone to England!" exclaimed Elisaveta. "I actually saw them off on the boat. We stood on the quay and waved to them!" She looked at them with troubled eyes. "But you know my memory is not what it was before they took David. Oh, it's all right for parts, but about real things it is very wrong, it is as if my mind were running away from them. Hitler has begun to kill me. You will see, he will kill us all."

"No," said Egon.

"No," said Nils.

"Do you really think anything will survive him?" she asked.

"Yes," said Egon.

"Everything," said Nils.

"And in the meantime," said Egon, "he will not prevent us from drinking a toast to Magda and Hildegarde."

"No," said Nils, "not just to Magda and Hildegarde. To all our beloveds. To David as well."

Egon hesitated for a moment and Elisaveta could see what was in his methodical mind.

"No, Nils," she said. "Perhaps it is not in good order to drink to people who are alive and to people who may be dead all in the same toast. We will drink to David later. But now the toast to Magda and Hildegarde, may they be happy and well, may you all be together again before long." They drank, and she set down her glass so that she could dry her eyes. "I am not weeping because I am sad," she explained, "or frightened—though of course

I am frightened. But it is only now one realizes what people mean to one, and I have had such glorious times with Madga and Hildegarde and the children—up in the mountains in summer, and here on birthdays and on Christmas Eve. You have been lucky, getting those two—not that you don't deserve it, my dears." Her words died into her handkerchief.

They watched her tenderly, nodding. "You must come and live with one of us," said Egon.

"Yes, indeed," said Nils.

She shook her head. "No, no, hadn't you thought? I am not a nice person to be associated with. David was a Jew and I am polluted. Besides, I must stay in my home. Don't you feel that? You wouldn't either of you want to leave your houses and go somewhere else just to be safe. One has to stand by what one is. I lived in my apartment with David. I won't stop living there just because they have come."

"Yes," said Egon, "that is how it must be. One must go on living, just as one used to do, not modifying one's conduct in the least."

"Oh, my dear!" she cried. "Do nothing rash!" As the two men gently laughed, she spoke more wildly, seeing again the tallest of the four Germans kick her husband so that he fell in the dust of the road. "No, do not laugh, you are too good to be destroyed by the devils. You must stay quiet."

"No, Elisaveta," said Egon, "we cannot stay quiet. We are going on exactly as we went on before our country was invaded at three o'clock this morning."

"So that was when it happened?" sighed Elisaveta. "I have heard nothing. Did anybody resist?"

"On the frontier about three hundred of our soldiers died," he answered. "They told us that when they gathered us together on the quay. They told us that without shame, almost as if they thought it would make us respect them and like them better."

"That is why we must go on behaving just as if they were not here," said Nils, "to avenge those three hundred men."

"We must maintain the right," said Egon.

"That's not the reason that I see for standing out against them," said Nils. "The right can maintain itself. If it can't do that it isn't the right. If we all behaved like rascals and licked the swines' boots, sooner or later something would prove to the people who came after us that that had not been the way to happiness. Something would recommend honor and decency to them. I think we have got to stand out against the Germans because it is a necessary scene in this drama we are enacting.

"You see, Elisaveta, you are a distinguished actress and a distinguished woman. Egon and I are certainly good playwrights, and we have tried to be good men. None of us three has lived falsely to what we believe. What we have thought to be true we have said, what we have thought to be right we have done. This has given us power, wherever we are known, partly because people respect courage, partly because they know we have thought a little further past the point where they themselves stopped thinking. Now, because of some earlier scene in the play, at which we were not present, the Germans want that sort of power, and believe that they can take it from us as they could, and probably will, take these lovely glasses out of Egon's cupboard, the pictures off these walls, those model ships away from the windows. They think that burglars can really rob. If we go on showing that we have power, that we have an inexhaustible fount of it within ourselves, which is there because of what we are and what we do, and cannot be ceded to any other person or seized by him, then we will make the burglar doubt the efficacy of burglary, then the world will become safe for good people. Now, Egon, fill up our glasses again and let us drink to David."

He broke the stillness that fell after they had drunk the toast by saying, "Are we not fortunate, we three? For we have glory thrust upon us. Not one of us could, however weak our flesh might be, collaborate with the Germans. For you, Elisaveta, are married to David Adler, who was a Jew, and, thanks be to God,

Egon and I have never written a play that was not good for a Nazi noose around our necks."

Out on the quay there were scuffling, and some cries, and the pitter-patter of machine guns, but none of the three turned to look through the windows.

"But it is not going to be easy," said Egon.

"It is not going to be easy or difficult," said Nils. "It is going to be not so much the thing one does as the thing that life does to one."

But Elisaveta found the winter after the coming of the Nazis easier to endure than the one before. She no longer felt so empty for lack of David. It was more as if she were working her way to him. Materially, of course, life in Copenhagen was hard enough. As one who had polluted her race by marriage to a Jew, she could not see many of her friends. Old Sven, she knew, was actually frightened lest she come to see him, though he sent her loving messages. By the invention of new taxes and by levies for special purposes the Nazis took possession of the better part of every citizen's income; and this looting was carried out more thoroughly when the citizen was Jewish. She had not been extravagant, and had taken her manager's advice about investments, and consequently had fancied she would never be in want, but she would have gone hungry now if she had not been able to eat with Egon and Nils whenever she needed.

She was able to help herself by going around to the few Jewish households in the city and giving the children, who were now debarred from all but a single unsanitary school, lessons in foreign languages and elocution. That pleased her. The Jewish parents felt an inordinate concern because their children's education had been interrupted, and when she listened to their complaints she was reminded of David's intellectual greed. What with these lessons she had not much time on her hands.

Egon and Nils were still allowed to live in their houses, though their defiance of the invaders was uncompromising, but most of their servants, except the very old ones, who were now in a state of collapse, had been taken away to wait on German officers in their billets; so Elisaveta could be of real service to her two friends by sometimes helping the old women with the cooking and mending.

The great physical discomfort was cold, of course, because the Germans had taken all the fuel, but everybody was suffering that alike, and one did not feel that one was being cold because people did not like one enough to share their warmth with one.

Elisaveta might almost have described herself as happy with this new, narrow, and impoverished, but glorious way of living, had she been sure that it was going either to continue until the English won, which she thought unlikely, or to end in the simultaneous annihilation of herself and her friends. But Egon and Nils denounced the invaders and their doings not to their fellow townsmen, whom they refused to involve in their activities, but to the Nazi officials and German officers.

They constantly visited the law courts where townsmen were being tried for offenses against the invaders and afterwards they made protests to the authorities and plagued the tax collectors with complaints against irregularities. Indeed, whatever was left of legality in the country they fearlessly exploited. On days that had been kept as national festivals they went through the streets carrying flowers which they laid before the statues of great men which the city had taken pride in placing in its most beautiful squares and esplanades.

It was said that the Germans had not imprisoned Egon and Nils because of their great reputation in the United States; but it seemed certain that that slight strand of consideration would presently break under the strain they both put on it. Elisaveta did not know how she would be able to go on if the Nazis took Egon and Nils as they had taken David. Nor did she know how she would be able to go on if she saw any more horrible things. Once she started to cross the Clocktower Square on her way to a Jewish pupil and, noticing the upward stare of horror on the faces of the people about her, followed it with her own eyes to its sources, and saw six young men hanging from electric standards.

Thereafter she went about the city carefully, watching the people in front of her as she came to any public place, in case they came to a sudden halt. But one Sunday morning she forgot her carefulness. She was hurrying down to Egon's house to help Johanna cook a goose which some peasant had smuggled down to the city under his coat as a gift to the man who, as was known all over the country, was keeping the habit of its freedom alive. Egon had asked some of his friends to share it, and Nils was going to send along some of the last of his French wine. Wrapped in a big cloak she had once worn in a historical play and bought afterwards because it was so becoming, she turned the corner of the quay where Egon and Nils lived, with her head down, butting the February winds. She was thinking what good things they would be able to cook for days to come with the goose fat, when she heard a yelled word of command, raised her eyes, and had just time to cover her ears against the sound of the shots. Ten young men, some of them blindfolded, were standing at the end of the quay, where the little light tower was. At the other was a party of soldiers with raised rifles. The ten young men all fell forward on their faces. Near her was another crowd of young men, surrounded by soldiers, who prodded them with bayonets to make them look at the ten figures lying face downwards on the cobbles. She ran to Egon's house and brought the knocker down rattling on the door until Johanna opened it.

They sat together, the two women, talking about how they should cook the goose, in the great airy kitchen, which looked out on a little garden where in summertime tall roses bloomed between the dark savory kitchen herbs. Now the roses were sticks tied up in sacking, and the herbs were stumps level with the ground, and a light miserable snow was falling.

Suddenly old Johanna burst into tears. "Yes, I know," said Elisaveta, "it was terrible, it was terrible; however, one must go on."

When the goose was in the oven Elisaveta went up into Egon's study. It was right at the top of the tall house, just below the attics. He was sitting at the window, looking out at the angry sea and the distant pine-black islands. His desk was littered with sheets of manuscript covered with unfinished paragraphs, thrown down in a disorder usually alien to him, and when he greeted her he was careful not to turn his face toward her. She went and stood beside him, looking out at the dark skies and the darker waters.

"Did you see it?" he asked.

"Yes," she said, "I walked straight into it. Why was it done? Who were they?"

"Just ten young men of all sorts who had not seemed amenable," he answered. "The beasts read out their offenses, but it was all very vague. I didn't recognize them all. There was the son of an orchestra conductor, and the son of the Greek professor up at the University, and Dr. Brand's son, and the boy who used to serve ice-cream sodas in the pastry cook's by the Cathedral. And there was old Sven's nephew."

"Oh, poor old Sven!" she wept. "But, Egon, such children!"

"Such children," he agreed. It came back to her, what she had seen: the ten bodies lying lumpishly like amateur actors practicing a fall, on the familiar, pretty cobbles, the crowd of boys looking at their dead comrades with eyes that did not dare grow bright with rage and pride, that were like the eyes of defeated old men.

"Do you mind if I cry?" she asked Egon.

"I am crying," he said.

They sat silent for a time.

"I am trying to think out something that Nils and I are going to write together," he told her. "Something in quite a new style for us. Much more concentrated, much more impressive. It will have to tell stupid and wicked people what their stupidity and wickedness are, in quite a few words."

"It is to be about this?" she asked.

"Yes," he said.

"Oh, be careful," she mourned, "be careful!"

"We are being careful to do what we must do at the right time for the sake of our city," he said.

It was in her mind to cry out, "But then what will become of me?" That would have been, however, wholly disgraceful.

"I hope," he said, "you have not brought trouble on yourself by associating with us. You must certainly not come near us tomorrow or the day after."

They were silent for a moment, and then he muttered a phrase, repeated it, repeated it again, and then broke off with an exclamation of annoyance. "It won't do," he said. "It's not the sort of thing I'm used to doing, and, anyway, it's very difficult in our language. It would be easier in English or in French."

"I do so admire you for knowing what you want to say," she said. "To be so certain of what should be said you must see quite clearly the meaning of this event, how it fits into the scheme of the universe. That's what I don't know, and I feel lost for want of knowledge."

"I don't quite understand you," he said. "Whatever Nils and I know, you know it better. There's nobody with greater moral sensitiveness than yourself. I can't imagine you doing a dishonorable or cruel action."

"You speak too well of me," she said, "and, anyway, I am not the keeper of my own conscience. My father and my mother taught me that certain things were wrong, and I have always feared to do them and feared the people who did them. Also the other way of behaving is more happy and cheerful. There is really no choice between them for a sensible person. But, indeed, there I often fail. You would be surprised if you knew how horrid I am. But this is not what I mean. You have some knowledge about the universe which I have not got. That is shown by the fact that you are going to write something about what they did to the boys on the quay this morning which is going to explain it to people, which is going to move them to do something. I wish you would tell me what it is." Her tears broke out, but she spoke through them. "Because it would make me able to bear what happened to those ten boys, it would make me able to bear what happened to David. You must tell me, Egon, because I cannot go on like this, seeing evil lording it everywhere, seeing good and wise and pleasant people done to death. What does it mean? Why is God doing this to us?"

Egon said slowly, his eyes looking far out to sea, "The problem isn't easy to formulate, but one knows where one is, I think. There are certain things in life which are beautiful. If there is a God they would please Him. If there is no God they would still represent ultimate values. That is proved by our assumption that they would please Him, for if He does not exist He is the embodiment of our dreams of what is highest. So one must give one's life to preserving these values, to letting love, and justice, and truth have their way with men."

She twisted her fingers in and out, acting her perplexity. "But the boys on the quay were innocent."

"Certainly."

"But they are dead. Nothing will make them live again. What is there in existence that makes that right?"

"We must pit ourselves against those who killed them."

"But that will not give them back their lives. It won't bring David home to me."

"If there is a God," said Egon, "then we shall all of us live again, and you shall be reunited with David. If there is not a God, then it will still be well with us. It is well with the boys on the quay because they died on the side of virtue. It will be well with you and me and Nils because we too kept our integrity. You must try to remember, Elisaveta, that defeat such as Europe has suffered at the hands of the Nazis is not of real importance. You cannot reverse the meaning of an abstract noun by an event on the material plane. Love and justice and truth remain what they were before Hitler came to power, and we are participants in their unchangeable glory. Forgive me," he added shyly, "if I sound priggish, but I am a writer of comedies and it is not my trade to write expressions of faith. But that, my dear, is what I believe."

"It is a very beautiful belief," said Elisaveta. She crossed her knees and swung her foot backwards and forwards, staring at it. It came into her head how much she had disliked Rome. She had liked the country outside it, she had enjoyed eating at wayside inns under vine pergolas and going to see the waterfall at Tivoli; but she had hated those great columns which were everywhere, either lying about on the ground or standing up in quite insufficient numbers to make a comfortable building. She saw love and justice and truth as just such columns.

"You have comforted me greatly, Egon," she said. But the feeling of bleakness in her bosom was so absolute that she got to her feet, anxious to go somewhere where she need not think of this desolate faith and see the dreary winter sea. "I must go down and baste the goose now."

She would have been glad if Johanna had wanted her help; but the old woman was querulous and asked it to be remembered by all parties concerned that she had been cooking geese long before anybody else in the house was born. So Elisaveta wandered into the great sitting room on the ground floor, where the ships were, and the pictures of great sailors and their wives. There the table had been laid for the lunch party, and at the sight of the gleaming table silver, it occurred to her that the rest of the silver in the room, the candlesticks and the French winetasters which were used as ash trays, was less bright. So she went to Johanna and asked if she should polish it, and Johanna said that she might, so she sat down by the fire, which was larger than usual, for Egon and Nils had been saving up their fuel for the party, with a candlestick on her lap and a soft cloth in her hand and a saucer full of polish. She was busy rubbing away and crying her eyes out when Nils came in with a basketful of decanters in each hand.

He set them carefully down on the floor and went over to her and knelt before her. When she covered her wet face with her hands he took them in his own and made her look at him.

"Were you thinking of David?" he asked. "Or of what happened today?"

"Of neither," she sobbed, "of the world. Of life. Oh, Nils, it is all so dreary."

"So dreary?" he repeated. "Do you mean what we are going through, the lack of food, the darkness, the cold, those brutes? Dear heart, it will not last forever."

"That is not the point," she cried, "for even if it goes, even if it does not come back in our lifetime, it will come back some time. History is full of suffering. And I have asked Egon what it all means, and he tells me it has no meaning except that love and justice and truth are beautiful things, and that we must serve them always, and that if there is a God, he will let us into heaven as a reward for our service, and if there is not we will have the satisfaction of having done the right thing. And it is so dreary. It is like going to school forever. Nils, it is so dreary!" She put down the candlestick on the floor and wept into the crook of his arm.

"Hush," said Nils, "hush. That is what Egon thinks; and it has taken him a long way. There is obviously much in his creed, because the way it has taken him is all in the opposite direction from barbarism. But I do not think like Egon."

She drew back from him and looked into his face. "What is your belief?"

He was disconcerted. "My belief," he said, "my belief . . . why, Elisaveta, it is written behind all my plays, as yours was written behind all your performances. I do not know how to put it into words directly. But I must try . . ." Abruptly he lifted her out of the chair and held her by the shoulders, facing him. "Run away and put on your cloak. There's no use merely talking about these things. They must be made visible. We of the theater know that. I'll take you somewhere where you'll see what I mean. I intended to go there anyhow, and finding you has made me forget it. Hurry, or we will be late."

"Where are we going?" she asked in the hall, as he wrapped the cloak around her.

"If I told you," he said, "it would not be true, the words would give you a false picture of what we are about to do."

The day was so harsh that when they got outside the door they ducked as if they had been shot at, and Elisaveta moaned. But he said, "It is not far," and he took her up one of the steep alleys leading off the quayside.

"But this only leads to the St. Sebastian Place," she said, "and there is nothing there but the church."

"Trust me, trust me," he said, "and hurry, hurry, we must hurry." When they came to the square he guided her straight across it to the church, but she hung back.

"But surely we are not going to church. I cannot go to church, I am an unbeliever, I have not been to a service for many years."

But he said, "Hurry, hurry, this is such a service as there has never been before, and as for unbelief there is more to be said on that subject than we used to think."

And indeed the old red church, which was not large but very noble, having been built at the time when the fishermen were simple yet rich, held such a gathering as she could not have conceived coming together in real life. All the people in the village were listening to the service, all the people she had known for many years, and they all looked changed as by a long illness. She could not have imagined such a uniformity of appearance save as the result of make-up under common instructions. Yet they did not look weak. On the contrary, a strong pulse seemed beating through them, and in the eyes they turned to the altar there was a fervor as if there was great acting about, and they were all exalted by it, as often happens in a theater when a genius is playing. But it was not the pastor who was that genius, for he was in the same state as his flock, and had he been among them he would have been undistinguishable from them. He, like they, seemed astonished by the words of the service as they left his mouth. They seemed to linger in the air before him that spoke them and those that listened to them, like the spray that rises from a great waterfall and hovers as if considering the greatness of the leap and slowly rejoins the stream below.

Elisaveta did not wonder why this talk of God and man and giving His only son should have moved her deeply, for it had nothing to do with her troubles; it was impossible to work out from it any way of regarding what had happened to David as anything but an undeserved suffering. But sometimes a play whose total effect was true was made up of lines that, taken by themselves, carried no great significance. Certainly the total effect of the service was true. As she stood among the pale and anguished but not passive people she felt her courage like an eagle in her breast, she felt herself capable of going on tunneling until the earth crumbled and she was with David.

"Go forward now," whispered Nils, as the worshipers went forward to the communion table.

"I have not fasted," she murmured.

"What happened this morning is like a fast for all of us," he said. "Let us go forward."

They had to stand a long time, for almost everybody in the village had come to take communion. When at last Elisaveta came to the pastor and brought down her lips to the chalice, the meaning of her act escaped her. She wondered, as the wine passed her lips, why Nils had made her do this thing, but when she stood erect again, and passed on, the action achieved, she would have liked to utter a high clear cry of relief. But she was doubtful lest she had done an unreasonable thing, lest she had been, as men say, hysterical.

Out in the street, she turned to Nils and looked at him in question. He drew her to him and kissed her on the lips. There were many people standing about, but even those who were gazing at them with interest, remembering that in other times this man and this woman had been the embodiment of romance and art, did not look offended or even startled. The kiss was grave, it was a part of that terrible day.

"But why did you make me go there?" she asked. "Why did you make me take communion? I tell you, I have long been an unbeliever. And God did nothing to save David."

"Why did we all go there today?" he said. "All but Egon, who does not think as we think. We went to keep faith with someone who is hidden from us because he is at the end of time. Someone to whom we have promised that though man is born in ignorance of the meaning of life, in ignorance of his own nature and the nature of the universe, and though his environment perpetually tempts him to remain in this ignorance, he shall come to understanding. That someone may be man himself, or it may be God. I do not know. My ignorance on that point is part of the ignorance we have promised to dispel."

"But how do you know?" she asked. "How do you know we made that promise?"

"Idiot, idiot!" he cried laughing and pressing her arm against his body as they hurried down the alley. "I know we made it because I find myself keeping it. What have I done all my life but write and write and worry out a little more of the truth than was known before? And if I had stopped doing that, if I had retired on what I made, and had lived here in my fine house on the quay and sailed my boat among the islands and gone up to the mountains when it was time for the snow or the flowers, I would have felt and you would have felt, and all the world would have felt, that I was guilty of a breach of faith. And you, too, if you had left the stage, then too we would have felt that a vow had been broken."

"Oh," she said, smiling faintly, "how could anything I do matter?"

"In each of your performances you told us something of what a woman is, and that is something we do not yet know. We do not fully know what a woman is, we do not fully know what a man is, we are working in the dark even when we try to train and discipline ourselves, which we must do before we start out to explore the universe. You did a great thing for the people who saw you, and you must not forget it, for without that you cannot understand what you are or what you meant to David. You are a wonderful and important person, Elisaveta."

"But I cannot play the great parts," she murmured.

"Idiot, idiot!" he cried again, "you filled out the parts which the author had not known how to write completely. But we are talking too much about ourselves, we artists cannot get off the subject. That is right in a way. I would never have written if I had not been the kind of child that runs about all day saying, 'See what I've done,' you would never have acted if you hadn't been the kind of child that runs about all day saying, 'Look at me.' But what I tell you about, this vow, is not special to us because we are artists. All the world takes it and keeps it or breaks it. There are fishermen, there are shipwrights, there are industrialists, there are politicians, about whom we feel, 'So! That man is showing the world what it is to go out to sea for fish, to build a boat, to handle machinery, to govern the state,' and there are housewives about whom we feel, 'There is a woman showing the world how to be a man's mate and bear children,' all showing how a human being can bear himself under such a destiny. Then there is a feeling amongst all that it is well, that the harvest has been brought in. But there are other men and women who never master a craft, whose lives never take on recognizable form before the eyes of the world. They die without learning anything or teaching anything, and we have the feeling not only of loss but of resentment, as if they had not played their part in a common enterprise. All this must mean something, it must relate to something in the future. So I go to church, though I am not certain that Jesus was in fact the Son of God, and I take communion with Him, because I know what I promise has relation to what he demanded of men, and I do not think He can find my action offensive, for I am willing to give my life, which is all I have, to keep my promise. And I am sure I was right, for I felt happy doing it. Didn't you, Elisaveta?"

"Yes, I did," she said. "But I wish I could see what was happening more plainly."

"But this is not a plain matter," he said. "We have been put in a ridiculous position by Providence, let us admit it. We find ourselves acting in the second act of a play, and trying to do justice to our parts, without any recollection of the first act, and no knowledge of what the third act is to be. There is nothing to do but to guess, and use the guesses of other men whom we recognize as likely to have guessed well. And one can do it, one can get through. Why are you not dead, seeing what happened to David?"

"That surprises me too," she said, nodding.

"I tell you, there is something afoot, it is not merely a question of maintaining standards which already exist; of preserving love and justice and truth. It is a question of finding out something, of discovering what we ourselves are, what God is, and what the two, mankind and God, are to make together.

"Why, that is the reason the Nazis are wrong. It is not just that they come into this country, which is ours and not theirs, and that they kill us and put us in prison and take away our food. That would be justified, if they could achieve any respectable end by doing it. But they cannot. It interferes with the keeping of the promise.

"It is the duty of mankind to understand the universe. We need, as people say when there is a lot of work to be done, every pair of hands. And no man can say for another what is his best way of increasing his understanding.

"We must all follow our own path to reality. And that is what Nazism will not let us do. It puts this man here and that man there, and it takes no heed if each says: 'But from this place my eyes can see nothing.' And it will not listen when men who are in places where they can see tell us what they have seen. If what they have seen is of any moment, the Nazis will choke their voices in their throats, lest the new things they have discovered should weaken the Nazis' claim to govern. They wish to repudiate the promise, they want to disappoint the person who is waiting for us at the end of time. They wish to make the world a dead planet. We who rebel against the Nazis are keeping it bright. Elisaveta, did your mother and my mother ever think we should do anything as wonderful as this? As keeping a star alight?"

"I think that is what they hoped," said Elisaveta, "but we did not think their hopes would come true."

They had turned the corner and were on the quay, which was still commanded by the death of the young men. There were many of the townspeople standing about looking toward the place where they had died. It was still guarded by German soldiers, looking gross and trivial in their health.

They ran into the house and she picked up the candlestick off the floor where she had left it, and sat down and went on with her polishing. Nils went over to the basketful of decanters he had set down and clicked his tongue with annoyance.

"This room is not warm enough for wine," he said. "See, we will have to put it close to the fire. Chambertin it is, to drink with the goose. A man's food, a man's drink." As he bent over the hearth he looked up at Elisaveta, "All the same, it will be difficult, you know, before the end. For me certainly, for you probably, if you are not careful."

"I have always taken the coffee as it comes out of the pot," she said, "strong or weak. I am not boasting of the strength of my character, it is probably a sign of weakness."

"That is not what I mean," said Nils. "Now what I believe comforts us, but it may fail us when we are in very great pain."

"Oh, perhaps," she said.

Presently she went out to help Johanna with serving the goose. When she returned, Egon had come down from his study and the room was full of guests. They were all old friends of hers. There was the Director of the State Theater, and two other dramatists, and the leading actor, and the editor of the newspaper, with their wives. All were haggard as if after prolonged weeping, but they were gay.

"What a lovely color you have, Elisaveta," said the Director, handing her a glass of spirits.

"Yes," said the editor's wife, "and we know it's all natural. We have no cosmetics now. Tell us, Elisaveta, how is it done?"

"Bending over an oven!" laughed Elisaveta.

"But none of us have anything to put in our ovens," said the Director, "so that raises another question."

They were poor jokes, these people would have been ashamed to make them in the old days. But they served. Everybody moved through warmth, they spoke and held their heads as if the Director still had the theater he had spent his life in making, as if the actor and the dramatists could still fill the loving and attentive air of the theater with what in their breasts longed to be out there; as if the editor's office were not given over to his enemies; as if the wives were sure that none would come to their houses by night in lorries.

There was a great ohing and ahing when the goose was brought in, and much laughter when Nils told them they could eat up Egon's bird with an easy conscience, and not think guiltily of those they had left at home, for he also was a dramatist and a peasant had brought him a goose too, and he had had it cooked, so that each guest could take away a slice or two for his family. And there was a great deal of joking about the affinity between geese and dramatists.

Then when the wine was poured out, the men had much amusement in guessing the vintage, which was easy, and then the year, which was more difficult, while the women mocked them for their solemnity over what, after all, was meant to be swallowed.

It was at that point in the meal when the door was flung open and the Nazi major came in. He stood on the threshold and stared at them. Egon and Nils rose to their feet, but with quick movements of their hands bade the others remain seated.

"Heil Hitler!" said the major.

There was a silence. They all thought of the dead boys and felt ashamed as they murmured *"Heil Hitler!"* but it was not worth suffering for such a little thing.

"Who are these people," the major asked Egon, "and why are they here?"

"They are my friends," said Egon. "They are here to have their Sunday dinner with me, as they often did before you and your people invaded our country." He indicated the spread table, his guests, with their fine heads, the delicate glasses holding wine, the polished silver candlesticks. "This is how we lived before you came."

The major did not answer for a moment. He looked about him with a steady, absorbed gaze as if he were trying to take away what he saw with his eyes. Then he shouted: "I have come to warn you that if you have gathered together in protest against today's disciplinary action, you do so at your peril. In the past we have been too gentle with your people, you intellectuals who refuse to collaborate with the New Order. But after today there will be no more forbearance."

His voice stopped suddenly. His hungry eyes, his pale, angry, resolute, and perplexed eyes stared ahead of him. The guests stirred on their chairs. The Director licked his dry lips and put out his hand for his glass, but stopped when it was halfway to his lips, fearing to offend the intruder. He looked as if he were about to propose a toast, and the editor picked up his glass and held it likewise, and murmured so softly that only those who sat about the table could hear it: "To the ten young men." Then all the other guests raised their glasses and Egon and Nils too bent down and found theirs.

The gentle movement, which seemed concerted and yet surely could not have been, startled the major. "Stand up!" he cried, as if in fear. "Stand up!" They all stood up. More than ever they looked simply like people drinking a toast, not like threatened people, nor yet like defiant people.

It was the actor's wife, her whispered words merely a faint pulse of sound not to be heard save by stretched senses, who said again, "To our ten young men." They all raised their glasses to their lips, halting them before their breasts according to the custom of their country.

"What are you doing? What are you doing?" shouted the major, striding into the room.

Egon explained wearily, "My friends were about to drink a toast. When you told them to stand up, they naturally continued."

"To whom is the toast?" shouted the major.

"To some other friends," said Egon. "You must excuse us, Major. This was a great city for friendship before you came."

Rage flamed in the major's face. "Why do such people as you continually reproach us? We came here to protect you from the British, we came here to bring you prosperity by giving you full rights in the New Order. And we are your brothers, our people and your people are Nordic Aryans."

Around the table all stood with their heads down, looking at the heeltaps of their toast.

"We have discovered the way of living which is right for mankind," cried the major, "and we are trying to share our discovery with you, and you will not accept the gift."

Around the table all shifted from foot to foot, still looking down at their glasses.

"But tomorrow," cried the major, his voice rising, "it shall be different."

The door crashed behind him. At the table all sat down again. They laughed, as people do who see somebody behaving in a way which betokens him their inferior, but who are not naturally unkind. Nevertheless, there was a chill wonder in the center of their laughter, for they knew that tomorrow it would indeed be different, perhaps by the considerable difference that lies between life and death.

"Thanks be to God," said the editor's wife, who had two chins and was as plump as a pigeon, "he did not stay so long that the gravy grew cold," and she polished her plate with a crust. The others broke into affectionate jeers and teasing, then Elisaveta told them there was something else to come, and there were many exclamations of surprise, the party forming again into what it had been, but harder, more impregnable.

When she and Johanna brought in the sweet they had made the day before of bottled fruit and sago flour, the sweet which was the unvalued standby in Copenhagen before the Germans came and took everything away, they clapped and cheered so that it was heard outside on the quay; and they were not sure that there were not some soldiers among those who came and peered through the windows. But they did not turn their heads to look.

"That German," said Nils, taking his seat after he had been around the table pouring out some sweet French wine to drink with the fruit pudding, "said that he and his kind had discovered the way of living that is right for mankind. That means they believe they could draw a picture of God's mind, and another picture of man's mind. What blasphemy! For we know almost nothing."

Egon put down his spoon and fork. "I am not with you there. I think we can draw a picture of God's mind, and it is not like the picture that he drew, and the Major is wrong and we are right."

"No," said Nils, "that is why it was written in the Tables of the Law, 'Thou shalt not make unto thee any graven image or any likeness of anything that is in heaven above, or that is in the water under the earth.' "

"But I have read the reason for that commandment somewhere," said one of the guests, "and it was an attempt of the Jewish priesthood in the time of Moses to shepherd the faithful away from the competitive religions of the day, which practiced an attractive form of idolatry."

"Yes, yes, that was the reason in the first place," said Nils, "but it has survived, like the rest of the commandments, because Moses had an eternal mind, and his thoughts have meaning upon meaning on which the centuries have hardly time enough to ponder. For me that commandment means that man must never pretend to have accomplished that task which will be unfinished so long as he himself exists. He was set upon earth in order that he may acquaint himself with reality, which is an impossible task, since reality creates itself anew as fast as the learner learns. It cannot be achieved until the end of the earth, the death of the stars; and until then a man lies if he says that he has learned his lesson and can make a graven image of anything that is in heaven above, or that is in the earth beneath, or that is in the water under the earth. Little sketches we can make, but that is all, and they are worthless unless we know that they are worthless, that we as yet lack the knowledge to make them true images. It seems to me that a man's work is dead and a man's soul is ideas, if he does not make this admission that all sacred truth is still veiled, for this relationship between us and a mystery is what constitutes life. Why need we go on living if all is known? Why do we love life so if it is not that it enchants us with its magnificence of undisclosed secrets?"

Egon said, "I would not agree with you. One wants to live because life is agreeable!"

"Today," said Nils, "I have a good opportunity of pointing out to you that quite often it is not."

Egon smiled and shrugged his shoulders. "And as for man's mind, we know enough to say we know all."

"Yes," said someone, "since Freud has shown us the way we are justified in saying we know all."

"I feel," said Nils, "that our experience during the last few months has transcended all the experience of our previous lives."

"What you mean," said Egon, "is that we have adhered to our principles, and that we have been happy in doing so."

"No," said Nils, "I have thought thoughts and felt passions which were unknown to me before. I have learned many things about my own nature which had before been hidden from me."

Some of the guests said, "Yes, I know what you mean," and one said: "No, one is what one always has been," and the others were silent.

"Yes," said Nils, "one is always what one has always been, and what one always will be. But what is that? And how extraordinary it is that we should be here at all on this earth, which spins about in space, incommunicado, knowing nothing of other stars or of the limits of space! And how extraordinary it is that being alive makes other things, trees and flowers and fish! And how extraordinary it is that anything should exist at all! I thought these things when I was a little boy, and then I was distracted by immediate problems. Now they come back to me, and I remember the words of the Bible—'for I speak of a mystery.'"

"But Saint Paul used them when he was speaking of marriage," said one of the dramatists, smiling, "and there is nothing more ordinary than marriage."

"There you prove my case," said Nils, "for there is nothing more ordinary than marriage, yet it is a mystery."

A stir ran about the table, and they all smiled, a troubled and reflective smile. Some of the husbands and wives were happy, some were not.

"No," said Egon firmly, "it is something very reasonable. Reasonable and beautiful."

One or two of the guests laughed aloud, the rest were silent. The editor's wife wiped her mouth and said, "Are not all marriages happy since the Germans came? A stick is something to lean on, whether it is straight or crooked."

"Yes, yes," said the guests, nodding their heads.

"Then there is something mysterious about marriage," said Nils, "as mysterious as the action of the molecules that make a stick solid and not liquid."

"Oh, you mean mysterious in that sense," said Egon.

Nils' hands made an exasperated flutter and Elisaveta rose and pushed back her chair, saying, "And now I must go out to the kitchen, for our hosts are giving us coffee, real coffee and some real milk!" At which the company clapped their hands, and the editor said, "Ah, they have sold themselves to the Nazis. You can see. There's everything here."

When all the guests had gone home they called in Johanna and thanked her for preparing the feast. Elisaveta stood up, stretched herself and yawned, looking at herself in a mirror. She was still slender, it would be years before she looked old. "Oh, dear, I would have liked that party to go on forever," she said. "It was fun. But now I must go and help Johanna wash the dishes."

"And we must go upstairs and get on with our piece of work," said Egon. "Have you thought of anything, Nils?"

"Yes, I have it all in my head," said Nils.

"Then we had better go upstairs at once," said Egon. "The printers will be here early this evening."

"I will say good-by now," said Elisaveta, "so that I won't disturb you when I have finished. Good-by, dear Egon and dear Nils. And thank you for all the good food and all the good wine, and the lovely gay party. It . . ."

She had been about to say that it had made them forget what was happening outside, but that was not true. The gaiety of the party had existed inside the terror of the day, enfolded by it.

"Elisaveta," said Egon, "we must say good-by. A real good-by. You must not come back here. It will not be safe."

"Please do as we say, Elisaveta," said Nils. "It would be a heavy burden on us if we were to bring suffering on you. And you must be here when David comes back."

She thought, "But I am going to David. Why should he come back here, where there will be nothing?" But in order not to burden them, she opened her arms to them and raised her face for their kisses.

"Good-by, Elisaveta," they said.

"Good-by, my dear, dear friends," she answered. She stood in the hall and watched the two men go up the wide, wooden stairs and bending over the banisters of the landing to kiss their hands to her before they passed out of sight, and then went to wash the dishes.

That evening she burned everything in her apartment which she did not want to fall into the hands of strangers. She made up her best silver spoon and china into brown-paper parcels and marked them with the names of her closest friends, and left them with her neighbors. She burned all of David's letters quite without regret, for she felt she would not need them much longer. Then she went to bed and slept well, and woke up early the next morning. She emptied all her little stock of sugar into her cup of coffee and had it sticky-sweet, as she liked it but had never dared have it for fear of growing fat.

She dressed with care, choosing her warmest clothes. Then she went out into the lifting darkness and took the way down to the fishing village. As she was hurrying through the square which marked where the village and the new suburb met, her eye was caught by a patch of white on the wall of a house, which had not been there the night before. Shuddering in the morning cold, she stood in front of it and waited till the light should be clear enough for her to read it. Some passers-by joined her. When the patch could be seen for what it was, some moved away, others raised a defiant cheer. She read it with excitement that brought her heels off the ground, that set her bobbing up and down like a dancer waiting for her solo to begin.

It was a manifesto, signed by Egon and Nils, telling how the people in the city looked upon the killing of the ten young men the day before. It said that they considered the Germans common burglars for invading their country; it said they knew the German story that they had come only to forestall the English was a stupid lie; it said that they regarded the murder of the ten young men on the previous day not as an impressive display of power, but as the kind of idiot brutality that burglars might show to householders whom they had bound and gagged.

It said that the people of the city did not respect the Germans because they had conquered them; a feat that an organized band of gorillas could have achieved. They despised the Germans as undermen who had interrupted the normal course of life toward greater good will and understanding because they were unable to take part in it. The people in the city, the manifesto said, had many faults; they were often shamefully petty and mean. But they had tried to make their city a glory to the earth.

Generation by generation they had had more and more recourse to the kindnesses of science, they had listened more attentively to art, they had felt greater charity toward children and the unfortunate, they had been juster masters of themselves and more willing servants of their fellows and had asked more urgently what purpose their lives should fulfill. And they had availed themselves gratefully of such happiness as had existed since the beginning of the world.

Now the Germans were trying to cancel this achievement, they were trying to blot out the city and make it as if people had never come out of the forest centuries ago and built huts on the seashore and carved boats out of tree trunks. They had blotted out freedom, they had blotted out virtue, they had made time meaningless. But those who wanted to be meaningless were likely to be successful; what was nonsense was soon forgotten. An idiot's babble was not remembered. The Germans would perish.

Elisaveta wished David were standing beside her reading it. He would have appreciated it. It was written in a style that was peculiar to this city. A man born there who read this while far away, without signatures, would have said to himself, "This was written by one of the townsfolk." But it would have been understood anywhere in the world. It reminded those who might have forgotten what life was like before the Germans came, and what it had been like afterwards.

It reminded those who might have forgotten what the difference is between good and evil. It set down in black and white what the city had been, and what the Germans were.

"How I would have liked to speak that from the stage!" thought

Elisaveta, and she turned away and hurried off, as to a rehearsal. She went to Egon's house, not from the quay but by the back door, for fear that Egon would try to turn her away, and be distressed by her resistance. It was the day when the family washing was done, so she helped Johanna collect the linens. A great deal had been used the day before.

Then there came a thunder on the door, and Johanna went to open it. She came back, saying, "They have come!"

Elisaveta kissed her and thanked her for all she had done for her in the years she had come to the house, and then went out of the kitchen.

In the living room Egon and Nils were standing face to face with a group of soldiers, one of whom was reading something aloud to them. When she came in, a soldier said, "Yes, this is the woman who is always with them. We have orders to arrest her also." Nothing could have been more convenient. She had feared she would have to strike one of them before they would take her.

She and Egon and Nils looked at each other and laughed, full of the joy that had visited them every now and then during the last few days. But at the same time they swayed on their feet, sick and dizzy with fear. For now began the pain and torture.

They were in prison for some weeks, and were frequently taken before a kind of judge and questioned about a conspiracy which did not exist. As their answers were necessarily unsatisfactory, they were always beaten after these inquiries. During this time they did not see each other, but one night at the end of three weeks they were all brought into the hall of the prison and were then taken to the railway station and put on a train that went through the darkness in an easterly direction. It was pleasant to be together again, but the guards would not let them talk much.

Elisaveta was at first ashamed of letting Egon and Nils see her as she was. Her hair had become lank and greasy, her face powder had been taken from her, and of course she was not properly clean. But they did not seem to mind, and they were dirty and unshaven.

In the morning they got out at a railway junction on a plain and they were made to sit all day and to lie all night in a small room with stone floors where the railwaymen filled their lamps. The air stank with oil and it was very cold. They had to sleep on pallets laid on the stone floor. But now they were over the frontier and the railwaymen spoke a foreign language, so that they felt as if they were a stage nearer the end of their journey, which would be the extremity of foreignness.

In the night Egon said to Elisaveta, "Did you think our manifesto was all right? People who read it would remember how things were, wouldn't they?"

"You did not think it was too long, did you?" asked Nils.

It was just like a first night in the old days. Before the guard could tell her to shut up, she said, "No, not a word too long. I said to myself as I read it, 'I would do anything to speak that from a stage.' "

The next day, toward noon, they heard a train puff in and shortly afterwards they were taken out on to the platform. The train was made up of cattle trucks. They had been looted from France, for they had *8 chevaux, 40 hommes* painted on them. But when the guards led them up to a truck and slid back the doors, they saw more than forty human beings inside. There were men, women, and children, all strange in appearance. Their skins were yellow and greasy, their black hair was screwed up into tight verminous curls, in their eyes black irises swam in oily yellow whites, and they stank.

As the door opened they cried out in terrible squawking voices, "Let us empty the bucket, let us empty the bucket!" and they pointed to a bucket in the corner, standing in an overflow of excrement. One of them by a clumsy touch upset the bucket and it streamed to the open door where Egon and Nils and Elisaveta were standing. They shrank back, but the guards pressed them in, jeering at them, "You chose to be with the Jews, you shall go with them to Poland and you shall see what fine friends they have."

They had to pass over the spilt excrement to enter the truck.

The door slammed behind them and they looked about at the filthy and lousy people, smiling insincerely and thinking, "Perhaps Hitler was right about the Jews after all." But an elderly man, his face red with insect bites where his beard met the smooth skin, put out a hot and slimy hand and pulled at Elisaveta's skirt and said, "I cannot see you, lady and gentlemen, because the brutes have broken my glasses, but this I know, you do not smell. And it makes me remember that once I did not smell, that in those days I despised people who smelled. Do not despise us, lady and gentlemen, for till we got on this train, we did not smell. I was a lawyer, most of the people here were superior workmen, and we used to be clean and have clean homes. But we have been three weeks coming across Germany in this train. So do not despise us. It will not be just, if you despise us."

"No," said Elisaveta, "we are artistic people and so not much in the way of despising people. And in any case, I am the wife of a Jew."

"For God's sake," said Nils, "do not think we despise you. We respect you and we need your help. For the joy that sustains me against the Germans comes and goes. And now it has gone from me."

"Let us tell each other who we were," said Egon, "and who we shall be again."

For a time the Jews found relief in recalling their names, and where they had lived, and in what comfort, and which of their kin had been unusual in talent. But soon they fell silent, for they were cold and hungry and tired and sick, very sick. There was one man who seemed to be near death; he sat with his eyes closed and never spoke.

When night came, they found there was no room to lie down straight, but Egon and Nils and Elisaveta were able to huddle into a heap. Their bodies ached, and presently the tears began to stream down Elisaveta's face.

"What is it, little one?" asked Egon.

"What is it, darling?" asked Nils.

She blubbered like a child, "Things are crawling over me."

The two men burst out laughing and hugged her, saying, "Poor little Elisaveta," and it seemed no shame to her.

In the middle of the night she awoke and smelled the stench of the degraded animals around her who had been people, and shuddered with horror because that was what the Nazis would make of her also. But Nils felt her shudders and drew her close to him, and she saw that his face was shining.

"That joy," he whispered, "it goes away, but it comes back."

"Yes," whispered Egon, "one cannot be anything but proud of being here." They listened to the roll of the carriage wheels and the snoring of the people around them, and ecstasy flowered in them. "We will not always be happy like this," Nils warned her. "One must keep on remembering that. It goes away, though it comes back."

During the morning, toward noon, there were a grinding noise and an upheaval. Everybody shrieked. When there was stillness again they found they were piled up on the wall of the truck which was opposite the door. The truck had been tilted on its side. Some of the metal stanchions had freed themselves and were sticking out dangerously. Some of the people at the bottom of the pile were quite still. Egon had injured his left arm and shoulder. There was blood trickling down Nils' brow. Elisaveta's body had been bruised. After a little, guards came and opened the door, which was now above them, and helped them to get out. They found themselves on a vast, unbroken plain, covered with light snow. Many people were screaming. The guards told them to go over and sit on an embankment that marked an irrigation ditch, about two hundred yards from the railway track.

"Come on," cried Elisaveta to Egon and Nils, when she found herself on the ground, happy as she had been all her life when she found herself starting to do a new thing. But they answered only faintly, and she perceived that their injuries were not like hers. She found herself crying, as she still did when she woke from a bad dream: "David, David!"

She turned to the guards and told them that her friends were ill, but remembered, before their faces told her so, that they were pitiless. There was nothing to do but guide Egon and Nils to the embankment. But long before they got there she saw that Egon could not go any farther.

"Can we carry him together?" she said to Nils. But Nils did not hear her. He looked at her with the blue, blue eyes of a fisherman from the isles, and she saw that he too had nearly gone from her. "Go on to the embankment," she said to him. "Sit down with the others and I will come to you."

Egon had sunk on his knees. She laid him flat on his back, hoping that he was only faint. "What is wrong with you, my little child?" she asked. As she spoke, she noticed that his eyes were immense and pellucid as a child's.

He said, "Under my arm."

She could not look for a second, for a spurt of light had caught her eye and she had to see what was happening to the train. It had been derailed and flame was passing from the engine, where it had already died, and there was a ghost of smoke haunting a pile of twisted metal along the whole long line of trucks. The telegraph pole had been brought down and the broken wires were like twisted fingers pointing to the sky. Then her mind returned to Egon. She put her hand under his armpit and found that blood was pouring down inside his waistcoat. One of the metal stanchions had struck him and cut a vein.

A guard was passing, clubbing some Jews before him. She cried out: "Among these Jews, there may be a doctor. Find him. This man is dying. He is a great man." The guard looked at her with empty eyes, that made nonsense of the fact that there are Jews who are clever and not animals to the extent of being doctors, that Egon was a great man. Again she cried, not from habit, but out of a desire that a miracle would happen, "David, David!" But in this place there was no one to bear Elisaveta's part but Elisaveta. She put her hand under her dress and tore her chemise away from its shoulder straps, rolled it into a pad and put it against his wound, set her knee to it and pressed.

"Elisaveta," said Egon, "I regret nothing. I have served the ideals of love and justice and truth."

"My little one," said Elisaveta, "my sweet one." The pad against her knee was wet. Egon's face was becoming white, blue white.

"I have done what is right," he said faintly.

"And more than that," said Elisaveta. But she knew as she spoke that he was about to die.

"What is right," he repeated more faintly still.

"My baby, my little baby," said Elisaveta; and before she had ended, he was dead.

She stood up and looked about her. The train was now wholly consumed by fire; the guards were beating toward the embankment such of the Jews as were old or so infirm as not to have already accomplished the passage. On the white snow all human beings were like small, black flies. She scanned the horizon and saw no farmstead save one that might be six or seven miles away. The Jews would not be able to walk so far; she herself doubted if, after her less exhausting imprisonment, she still had the strength to do it. She remembered that this was a country of vast estates. It might well be, now that the electric wires had gone, that it would be many hours before help reached them. The cold was so extreme that it ran in a network of fire through her body. Most probably she, and everybody she saw before her, would before very long be dead of exposure.

She looked down on the calm and noble face of Egon, from which life had in this little time completely departed. Then she looked up at the gray sky, across which an army of violet-blue clouds was riding.

"So this is where doing what is right leads me," she said to herself. "This is the reward of serving love and justice and truth. One dies on a snowy plain under an empty sky."

She knelt down beside Egon and tried to say a prayer, but her friend was gone; she might as well have been praying beside a cod laid out on a fishmonger's slab. She said, "And it is just Egon's word against the Germans. Love against hatred, justice against tyranny, truth against lies." Under this sky it seemed uncertain that a wise man would take one side rather than the other. She stood up and walked away. Even if there had not been Nils to look after, she would not have stayed with him. He was dead, he had gone away; and it seemed as if David was gone away too, farther than she could go to find him.

There were many people lying on the embankment, moaning and crying out against the pain of injuries and the searching cold. The lawyer whose face was red with insect bites was walking up and down at the foot of the embankment, calling out in mockery: "Hail, Jesus Christ, King of the Jews."

She found Nils stretched out between two children who were nuzzling against him for the sake of the warmth of his body. The blood was still running down his brows, and she bound it with what was left of her chemise. He smiled, but his eyes were set on the sky above him, and he said, "Thank you, Anna." Now she was entirely alone. Nobody in the world was thinking of her.

"I am thirsty," he said later.

She melted a little snow in her hand and propped his head up while she poured the water into his mouth. But his eyes sought the sky again and his head tilted back, and the water dribbled down his chin.

"Nils, Nils," she said, "keep your chin down or your cannot drink." But she spoke halfheartedly, because she liked to watch him looking up so eagerly. It made her heart live again.

"I have had enough water," he said, "and I want to look at the sky. I am watching a great battle."

She sat back on her heels and watched the clouds ride above

her. The cold was torturing her, but the sustaining joy had returned.

"No," said Nils, and shut his eyes. "It is no use. One cannot see the battle. The sky is too small a frame."

But every now and then he opened his eyes and looked up at the sky, until the dusk came, and the snow began to fall.

THE THIRD COMMANDMENT

Thou shalt not take
the name of the Lord
thy God in vain

FRANZ WERFEL

III

THOU SHALT NOT TAKE THE NAME OF THE LORD THY GOD IN VAIN

A STORY BY

FRANZ WERFEL

HE TOLD me the story himself. He was a short, sturdy redhead with a coarse complexion and the heavy hands of a peasant. His eyes, dark green, were usually downcast; but sometimes they would flash fire, giving a boyish, defiant air to this man of forty, who had evidently had some hard knocks from life.

Looking at him, you would never have supposed he was a Catholic priest. He wore neither ecclesiastical collar nor black habit, but a gray suit of the kind affected by German tourists, with shorts and Tirolean socks that exposed the knees and ankles. When I first saw him, in Paris, the suit was already quite threadbare. In America, two years later, it had by no means improved.

We had met briefly in Paris. Although I took an immediate liking to his looks and manner, we did not become really acquainted. For I had been warned against Chaplain Ottokar Felix.

Mistrust is one of the most poisonous plants that flourish in the dark shadows of political exile. Every *émigré* mistrusts every other, and if he could he would even suspect himself, for his spirit is in turmoil; it has no home.

Who is this Austrian chaplain? people asked. Why did he leave the country? Nobody knows anything about him. He had taken no part in the fight against the Nazis, either by word or by deed. The Austrian clergy made peace with them after the *Anschluss*. Suppose this wonderful priest in his Tirolean socks is an emissary of the Party, sent to spy on us. How did he get across the frontier? By the way, somebody saw him recently in the Rue de Lille. The German Embassy is in the Rue de Lille. . . .

I thought all this chatter sheer nonsense, yet still I avoided him. But when he suddenly appeared in my room at Hunter's Hotel in St. Louis, I felt an unexpected pleasure. This occurred in the late fall of 1941. The evening before, I had given a lecture on "The Crisis of Modern Man," trying to show that the deepest cause of our misery was our loss of faith in God.

Chaplain Felix, who had been in the audience, said a few kind words about my efforts, and told me I was on the right path, but that it would lead me still deeper into the mystery of our modern despairs.

He looked pale, tired, underfed. But when I asked, with the idea of helping him, how he was getting along, he dismissed the question with an abrupt gesture. He had all he needed, he said. During our two or three encounters in Paris, too, he had declined to talk about himself or his affairs.

We were discussing perfectly general subjects, therefore, when suddenly I remembered the suspicion of him that the refugees had expressed in France. As I looked at the man now, it seemed to me more irrelevant than ever. Yet I could not help myself: against my will and against the dictates of my feelings I asked what had driven him from home.

He turned his honest, weather-beaten face and looked squarely at me. His freckles and coarse complexion almost seemed like pockmarks; his bristly red hair topped a low but attractively wrinkled forehead. His eyes, which had no lashes, sat deep in their sockets. That made them disturbing when they gleamed.

"I'm grateful to you," said the chaplain, "for asking me about something so far back and not about something like the concentration camps that I escaped from in France, or how I slipped through the heart of the German lines, or about the bypaths in the Pyrenees—about the various adventures that every one of us, after all, has had."

"Why are you grateful?"

He was silent some time before answering.

"Well, because I've been thinking all day about Aladar Fuerst. . . . Your lecture had something to do with it."

Seeing my bewilderment, he smiled indulgently: "There was a fine man for you, a good man, Dr. Aladar Fuerst. And he was the first to fall before the enemy, the enemy of the world, in this great war that's going on. Nobody knows about this first casualty, and he will never get a medal for dying a hero's death. But he did more than just get killed in the war."

"What war are you talking about? When Austria was swallowed up, in 1938, there wasn't any war——"

"Oh, you'll see in a minute," the chaplain nodded, "the war began then. Ever since yesterday I've been wanting to entrust this forgotten story to you, that is, to put it in your hands. You understand?"

"What story?" I asked.

The chaplain's hand shaded his weak eyes against the bright afternoon sunshine that poured in through the window overlooking the big park in St. Louis.

"It's the story of a Jew who did not want to take the name of the Lord in vain," Felix said rather softly, and added a few seconds later: "It's the true story of the profaned and reconsecrated cross."

2

Father Ottokar Felix had the parish of Parndorf, a market village in the northern Burgenland between a range of wooded hills and the long, reedy lake of Neusiedl. The Burgenland—the name "Castle Country" comes from the many medieval castles crowning its southwestern heights—is the newest, poorest, and in many ways the most remarkable province of Austria. Before the First World War it belonged to Hungary, which was forced by the peace treaty to surrender it to neighboring Austria. It is a typical border region, where Hungary, Slovakia, Yugoslavia, and Austria all meet. Accordingly, its inhabitants are a rather motley group. Hungarian landowners, Austrian peasants, Slovak harvest hands, Jewish traders, Croat artisans, gypsies, and finally the nondescript stock of the Kumans, who were swept westward by the Turkish invasions in the seventeenth century.

Parndorf itself, with its ring-shaped market place, its goose pond, and the low thatched roofs crowned with storks' nests, is one of the more dismal villages of the region. Its almost Asiatic melancholy contrasts sharply with the large graciousness of the Austrian countryside. These hamlets give no hint that Vienna and the lofty Alps lie close at hand. The boundary between East and West seems to cut through them like a razor.

Parndorf's sole importance is that it lies on the main line between Vienna and Budapest. The shiny cars of the great express trains connecting Orient and Occident go roaring past its tiny station—a world-wide distinction that has not fallen to the lot of the chief towns in the province.

Why Ottokar Felix was transferred from the Viennese workmen's suburb of Jedlesee, where he was chaplain at the main church, to the God-forsaken village of Parndorf, I do not know. As the transfer took place in 1934, after the distressing battles between the Vienna workmen and the federal troops—everyone remembers that historic stage on the road to collapse—I think it not unlikely that the chaplain was compromised in the eyes of his superiors by his support of the Socialists, and underwent a sort of punitive banishment. He gave no hint of this, and I felt shy about pumping him.

The Jews had a small congregation in Parndorf, perhaps ten families, totaling thirty or forty people. There were similar congregations in every county and hamlet of the long, narrow Burgenland, in Eisenstadt and Mattersdorf, the big cities, in Kittsee and Petronell, the so-called Three Corners where Hungary, Czechoslovakia, and Austria meet, and in Rechnitz, far down in the south, on the border of the kingdom of Yugoslavia. Most of these congregations consisted of a few old families, related or intermarried all over the country. Everywhere you found the same names—

Kopf, Zopf, Roth, Wolf, Fuerst. Next to the millionaire Wolf family in Eisenstadt, the Fuersts were the most distinguished, though in quite a different way. They had never acquired large property, but as early as the seventeenth century had produced a line of rabbis and scholars who played an important part in the peculiar intellectual history of the ghetto.

The Burgenland Jews were proud of two things: their learned men and their roots in the country. For in contrast with other Jewish communities, they had long since forgotten the curse of wandering and homelessness. They had never immigrated from Russia and Poland or from Moravia and Hungary; they boasted that they had always been in the country, except for a few who had moved from neighboring Styria into this freer boundary region, along with the persecuted Protestants, at the time of the Reformation.

The prominent Fuerst family came from the very Parndorf to which an unkind fate had banished Chaplain Ottokar Felix. Here too lived Dr. Aladar Fuerst, a man in his thirties, married but a few years, the father of three children. The youngest, a boy, was exactly three weeks old on the Black Friday when Austrian liberty was murdered. Aladar Fuerst must have been a visionary and fond of solitude; though a doctor of philosophy and law, a graduate of the celebrated Hebrew Seminar at Breslau, a man of the world who had lived in various European capitals, he could think of nothing better than to come back to the thatched roofs of his native village, bury himself in his choice library, and fill the office of country rabbi for Parndorf and a few neighboring congregations. He held services in a tiny, ancient synagogue, and gave religious instruction to the Jewish children at various neighboring schools.

In such a little place the chaplain and the young rabbi met almost daily as a matter of course. And in view of the delicate similarity and dissimilarity between their two offices, it was equally a matter of course that for a long time they confined themselves to a courteous salutation in passing.

A wedding, to which Dr. Aladar Fuerst was also invited, brought about their first conversation of any length. Afterward Fuerst paid a call on the priest, which was immediately returned. The rabbi invited the cleric to dinner. Regular, though sedate and formal, social intercourse followed.

Presumably, something more than a difference in religion raised a barrier between Felix and Fuerst. Even free spirits find it hard to overcome a strangeness centuries deep and an ancient mutual mistrust. Nevertheless, as he admitted to me, the Christian priest quickly became fond of the Jewish rabbi. He was profoundly astonished, not so much by his intellectual friend's brilliance and wide reading (which did not greatly concern him as a practical man), as by something else.

Whenever he had had dealings with a son of the house of Jacob, he had always read in the man's eyes a lurking hostility, even a painfully concealed horror inspired by the anointed priest of a once-implacable church, and this had set narrow limits to any conversation. Fuerst was conspicuously different. He was amazingly at home in every department of Catholic theology, and seemed to take great pleasure in displaying his knowledge. He quoted Paul, Thomas, Saint Bonaventure, and Newman more expertly than a harassed village chaplain could have done.

The priest believed he was right in thinking that something more than vanity had caused Aladar Fuerst to go so far in overcoming his fathers' wariness of Christ, as ancient as it was natural after their endless sufferings. Yet at the same time he had not departed even a step from his own faith.

Felix quoted one remark by the rabbi that moved him deeply. It was spoken during a conversation about the Mission to the Jews, a delicate subject that not he but Fuerst had introduced with quite alarming outspokenness.

"I can't see, Your Reverence," the rabbi had said, "why the Church is so interested in baptizing the Jews. Can it be content with winning perhaps two or three real converts among a hundred weak renegades or climbers? Besides, what would happen if all the

Jews in the world were to accept baptism? Israel would disappear. And with it the last actual, physical witness to divine Revelation would vanish from the earth. The Holy Scriptures, not only the Old but the New Testament, would become an empty, insubstantial legend like any myth of the ancient Egyptians or Greeks. Doesn't the Church see the terrible danger—and particularly at a moment of complete breakup like this?

"We belong together, Your Reverence, but we are not one entity. The Epistle to the Romans, as you must know better than I, says that fellowship of Christ is founded upon Israel. I am convinced that Israel will survive as long as the Church survives, but also that the Church is bound to fall if Israel falls."

"What makes you think that?" asked the chaplain.

"The sufferings we have gone through down to this very day," replied the rabbi. "Or do you think God would have allowed us to endure so much and so long, for so many thousands of years, all for nothing?"

3

On Austria's Black Friday, the eleventh day of March, when the inconceivable happened, Chaplain Ottokar Felix was sitting in his living room. It was seven o'clock at night. An hour before, he had heard Chancellor Schuschnigg's farewell words spoken in a leaden voice over the radio, "We must yield to superior force," and then, "God keep Austria," and then a great silence, and the strains of Haydn, solemn and heart-rending. Felix had turned off the radio and sat motionless beside it. His rusty, paralyzed mind futilely turned over the question of how he must behave in the catastrophe that had come so suddenly upon the unhappy country.

Then the door opened, and Dr. Aladar Fuerst came into the room. He had not waited for the housekeeper to announce him. He wore a Prince Albert coat; the Sabbath, of course, had already begun. His thin face, with its dark eyes behind long lashes and its sparse black side whiskers, was a few shades paler than usual.

"Forgive me, Your Reverence," he began rather breathlessly, "for bursting in on you like this. We had already begun the holy day, and I've only just——"

"I should say it was events that broke the Sabbath," the priest remarked, as if to help him out. He pushed forward the armchair for his unexpected guest, who, however, declined to sit down.

"I need your advice, Your Reverence. You see, here's what I expect; I was so trusting, and now . . . Had you heard that young Schoch is in the neighborhood, has been for a week? It was all arranged long ago. Schoch is the Storm Leader of the S.A. here. He's drummed up the whole crew, the farmer boys, the laborers from the cartridge factory, the unemployed; they're all getting drunk in the tavern, threatening to kill all the Jews this very night."

"I'll go straight to old Schoch," said the chaplain; "the rascal is still afraid of his father——"

This was not true, and Felix himself knew perfectly well that it was not the son who was in mortal terror of the father, but the father of the son. He only said this because he could think of no better way to calm Fuerst.

Old Schoch was the richest winegrower in the neighborhood and a good Catholic. But he had had decidedly bad luck with his youngest son, young Peterl. At least so far. The biography of Peter Schoch had its charms. A strikingly good-looking lad at seventeen, he had got one of his father's servant girls with child—which is far from a sin according to the local view—but then he had threatened the girl and the child with violence and had broken open her trunk and stolen all her savings.

Old Schoch, who doted most idiotically on his youngest son, this time flew into a rage (as he had not done over the lad's earlier pranks), primarily because the unsavory tale had leaked out. With the help of his older sons he first thrashed Peter soundly, and then sent him to the forestry school in the city of Leoben. (In addition to their vineyards, the Schochs also had timberlands.)

But as the handsome ne'er-do-well had spent six full years in the first grade of primary school, and could hardly read and write even yet, he promptly failed the entrance examinations at Leoben, which any first-class logger could pass with ease. Far from sending word of his defeat home, Peter stayed in the bustling town, which he liked much better than dismal Parndorf, and threw away a lot of money that he managed to extract from his parent for his alleged studies.

In quieter times Peter Schoch's career would certainly have come to a bad end. But in these memorable days the "Movement," handsomely supported in all neighboring countries by the Third Reich, came to his rescue. It was the Movement's custom, with far-seeing wisdom, to secure such ne'er-do-wells to itself. It knew by experience that an aversion for the alphabet and regular employment almost invariably brought with it a talent for reckless rowdyism. And for the first blow to break the resistance of the Austrian people, nothing was more urgently needed than a body of determined rowdies.

A not inconsiderable share of the favor with which certain Party chieftains regarded Peter arose from his golden-blond hair, his slim figure, his stubby little face. In contrast to the bald pates, pot bellies, and limping legs of the leaders, he was a glorious embodiment of racial doctrines and of the perfect Nordic man. Photographers did honor to him almost daily, and many copies of his pictures adorned the files of the German race bureaus.

And thus it was that the son of the rich Parndorf winegrower became an "irregular." The Munich Party funds gave him so large a subsidy that he played the part of Croesus among his peers. A few foolhardy misdeeds on behalf of the Party made his name known, and when he finally went to prison for some months as a saboteur and bomb thrower, he had at last advanced to the ranks of the martyrs who were "delivered from shame and misery" after the Berchtesgaden meeting and the collapse of the Austrian government. This, in brief, is the story of Peter Schoch, whose mere name was enough to make Dr. Aladar Fuerst—and others, too—turn pale with horror.

The rabbi at last sat down. The chaplain handed him a small glass of brandy. "We mustn't begin by expecting the very worst," he said.

"Why mustn't we?" asked Fuerst, lifting his head with a jerk. "Perhaps we should . . . Listen, Your Reverence," he went on tensely after a while, "a train leaves for the Hungarian frontier in an hour. Oughtn't we—I mean the whole family—though of course my poor wife has only been up for three days . . . What shall I do, Your Reverence? Give me your advice—I do need it."

Father Ottokar Felix then did something for which he has never forgiven himself. Instead of shrugging his shoulders, instead of saying, I don't know what's best, he gave his advice, definite counsel, and it was bad. But at such moments who can tell whether he is advising well or ill?

"Are you really going to throw everything overboard in such a hurry, my dear Dr. Fuerst?" said the chaplain, unfortunately comparing his own situation with the doctor's. "We don't even know about the new government yet. Who can tell—in Austria everything may turn out differently from what we think. Why don't you wait and see for a few days?"

At these words Aladar Fuerst heaved a sigh of relief. "I do thank you for your advice. I'm sure you're right; Austrians are not Germans, and I'm a good patriot. It would be terribly hard for me to leave our house. Within the memory of man, my family has always lived here; our tombstones in the cemetery go back to the Middle Ages, and when I left the outside world I deliberately chose to return to Parndorf. Perhaps . . ."

The chaplain accompanied him out into the clear, starlit night.

"I'll look in to see how you're doing tomorrow," he said as they parted.

But Aladar Fuerst said, uneasily shaking hands with Felix: "There's only one thing I'm afraid of, Father Felix. I'm afraid people like us have grown too soft, and won't have the old strength and fortitude of our fathers under persecution. Good night."

4

At nine o'clock the following morning—just when Chaplain Ottokar Felix was considering how far his Sunday sermon might go in attacking the victors—a sound of tumult and shouting penetrated his closed study window. Instantly he rushed outdoors, hatless and coatless. The Market Ring was filled with a crowd even bigger than the one that usually assembled for market days or church festivals. Expecting something interesting, they had poured in from the hamlets of the desolate Parndorf Heath, and even from the remote shore villages of the great reedy lake—peasants, farm laborers and girls, workmen from the cartridge and sugar factories of the neighborhood, and in addition a crowd of the unemployed who were no longer getting government relief and who usually supplied the most turbulence at any riot.

The center of this mob was a detachment of Brown Shirts lined up in ranks, all of them already wearing swastika armbands on their left arms. They were drawn up opposite Parndorf's most imposing building. It was probably not fitting that the Fuerst family should own this edifice, one of the few in the village with two stories and a mansard roof. However, one could hardly hold Aladar Fuerst responsible for the fact that his grandfather, in the happy days, fifty years ago, had been incautious or presumptuous enough to build this metropolitan house amid a world of wretched thatched huts.

On the ground floor, at the sides of the archway to the courtyard, were two large shops, the Town Bakery of David Kopf and the Grocery and General Store of Samuel Roth's son. The proprietors of these shops, their wives, sons, daughters, relatives, and assistants, were standing in a tight little knot outside the gateway; in their midst was Rabbi Aladar, the only one who held his head really high. In contrast with the night before, he did not seem crushed. Peter Schoch, the commander of the present military engagement, had taken up his post as the antagonist of this symbol of forlorn hope. Obviously delighted, he held an automatic rifle in the bend of his arm, the barrel pointing at Aladar Fuerst. Beside Schoch stood a scrubby little man with a pinched, witch's face that looked as if it could be distended or collapsed at will like an accordion. The man wore a pair of steel spectacles on his nose and a red cap on his head, for he was Ignaz Inbichler, the Parndorf stationmaster.

When Chaplain Felix arrived, Peter Schoch was just finishing a pungent harangue. Its intonation, at once deeply injured and bitingly scornful, reproduced to the life the radio speeches of the great Party deities.

"German men and women! It is insufferable for our fellow Germans to receive their daily bread from the hands of a Jewish bakery. How that would delight the international Jews, to go on poisoning our innocent children with his matzos! Those days are past, because this is a historic moment. In the name of the German people's community I declare Kopf's bakery Aryanized. Fellow German Ladislaus Tschitschevitzky takes authority in his place. *Sieg Heil!*"

Peter Schoch spoke in a labored newspaper idiom mingled with naked, vulgar dialect. The Brown Shirts bellowed the *Sieg Heils* after him, keeping time. The crowd remained oddly silent, apparently filled with unconcerned curiosity.

Now the man with the red cap took the floor. This obscure frontier village differed not a whit from Berlin: the two basic aspects of the National Socialist Party were both present. Schoch represented utter heroism; Inbichler stood for the twinkling-eyed diplomacy that pats the victim artlessly on the back as heroism rips his stomach open.

And so Inbichler, the stationmaster, addressed the little handful before the gate: "Gentlemen! Everything will proceed in order. There will be no uncontrolled action. Everything will take place according to regulation. Germanism is organization. Not a hair of your heads will be touched. You have only to sign a form certifying that you are turning over your trash to us quite voluntarily and will leave German soil at once. If any inmate of this house should be found here after five o'clock this afternoon, he would have no one but himself to blame for the disagreeable, I may say *very* disagreeable, consequences. Even I could then do nothing for him. . . . There are only two ways to solve the Jewish question. In the infinite kindness of his heart, our Leader had chosen the second way."

The chaplain realized that by interfering he not only could accomplish nothing, but would endanger himself to no purpose. He therefore raced home and excitedly telephoned the police, the county authorities, and finally the provincial government at Eisenstadt.

Everywhere he got the same evasive answer. With the best will in the world, they said, nothing could be done against the dubious elements momentarily in control of the streets. They were Party members, and the Party was getting its orders direct from Berlin. The voices on the telephone shook with the most grievous discomfort. Undoubtedly all the lines were tapped, and the officials dared not speak openly.

Losing no time, Father Felix hurried to see a well-known local landowner, and in his car was roaring toward Eisenstadt within half an hour. There, at the capital, he went from pillar to post, finally winding up with the Apostolic Administrator of the Burgenland. He was the ecclesiastical head of the province, a Monsignor So-and-so.

The placid prelate received him with darkly unctuous suspicion. Since the supreme ecclesiastical authority, His Eminence the Cardinal Archbishop of Vienna, he said, had chosen to meet the new temporal power (which, according to dogma, must after all derive from God) in a spirit of confidence, he himself could only recommend an obedient emulation of this attitude to the provincial clergy. He was well aware, he said, of what was going on today in the villages of the country, but he strongly urged that there be no interference on behalf of the expelled Jews. No doubt these occurrences merited condemnation, but they were in no way within the province of the parish priests.

Folding his hands, the prelate concluded: "We will pray for the Jews, but in other respects we must keep constantly before our eyes the fact that all authority derives from God."

"Even if the Lord puts Satan in authority, Monsignor?" asked the chaplain a trifle rebelliously.

"Even then," said Monsignor, with a heart for any compromise.

On his way home the chaplain leaned more and more toward accepting the decision of the cardinal and the prelate as a wise one. There were things more important to protect than a few robbed and expelled Jews. The Church itself stood in danger. Would it not be best to lie low and stay home for the next few days, perform the Sunday offices without a sermon, and guard against all friction?

Probably he would have yielded to this impulse if Aladar Fuerst's words had not kept running through his head: "I am convinced that Israel will survive as long as the Church survives, but also that the Church is bound to fall if Israel falls."

5

When Chaplain Felix arrived at the Market Ring in Parndorf, the church clock was just striking three. The two trucks belonging to Moritz Zopf's trucking concern were standing in front of the Fuerst house. Furnishings, beds, cupboards, tables, chairs were being carried out of the bakery, the shop, and the courtyard driveway and stowed in one of the trucks. Stationmaster Inbichler was scrutinizing each piece with shortsighted intentness and the conscientious zeal of a good customs inspector, for the exiles were not allowed an ash try or a box of matches without his approval. And, in fact, he put aside for himself any article that took his fancy, shrouding the appropriation with a muttered incantation that sounded something like "German national property." The Brown Shirts had stacked their rifles and were lounging about, smoking. Schoch and his staff were at the inn, where Peter had been presiding for several hours over a lavish banquet to which the mayor and other Parndorf notables had rushed with fawning haste.

There was no wind, and a peculiar milky vapor hung over the village. The group of outcasts had grown considerably, numbering more than thirty souls. Chaplain Felix was surprised to see them all busily scuttling about, running a hundred senseless errands, and moved apparently more by insectlike unrest than by any purposeful plan. The children in the group watched the bustle excitedly, but they were eager, not frightened. All of them, however, looked as if they had been up all night; they were like shadows stirred by a gusty wind of destiny imperceptible to Christians even as it blew across the market place.

Felix went into Rabbi Aladar's house. The young mother, a delicate, bright-eyed woman from the Rhineland, scarcely risen from childbed, was working breathlessly. Her white forehead under the parted brown hair was deeply furrowed with exertion. She was standing amid a mountain of bed and table linen and underwear, trying vainly to cram all of it into an already overcrowded traveling hamper. Now and then she looked up. Her eyes shone moistly with weakness and bewilderment. From the next room came the peaceful chatter of children and an occasional insistent squall of an infant.

The chaplain found Aladar Fuerst in front of his bookcases, which filled all four walls of the big living room from floor to ceiling. A few hundred volumes that he had picked out from the many thousands rose in tottering piles at his feet. He held a book in his hand and was reading, reading raptly, with a ghost of a smile on his face. He seemed to have completely forgotten reality. The spectacle of this Jew reading with absorption amid the collapse of his world deeply impressed the chaplain, as he emphasized to me.

"Your Reverence Dr. Fuerst," he said, "unfortunately I gave you bad advice. The fact that that advice is tormenting my conscience is no help to you or to me, either. Luckily you have a Hungarian passport. Perhaps the Lord means better by you and yours than by us. It would not be the first time He has brought to safety the people in which He manifested Himself, when He seemed to be punishing it."

Dr. Aladar Fuerst gave the priest a long, remote look, which moved and disturbed him so much that he turned to and helped carry down the favorite books chosen to go.

An hour later everyone was ready. Inbichler had kept the best property of the exiles, the more valuable furniture, all the silver, all the women's jewelry, and whatever money and securities he could lay hands on; for all those who were being banished, Fuerst included, were stripped to their shirts and subjected to a thorough search. The rabbi took this ignominious proceeding, aggravated by derisive remarks from the Brown Shirts, with such absent-minded equanimity that Felix was almost annoyed at him. I'd be hitting about me, he thought. The only thing that Inbichler passed uninspected, with a gesture of disdain, was the books.

But since, as Inbichler had said, everything had to "proceed in order," and "Germanism was organization," he made out a careful receipt for each article he was keeping. This raised naked robbery to the level of law and governmental action, making it all the sweeter to the robber.

Peter Schoch, having taken his seat beside the driver of the first truck, began blowing the horn furiously. It was four o'clock. Night would fall within two hours at latest.

The Brown Shirts kicked and cuffed their victims into the first truck, where they tumbled against one another, and then had to sit on the floor. Now at last the small children began to be uncomfortable, and a few of them started crying. The closely packed spectators remained deathly silent, and from their curious faces there was no telling whether they approved or condemned what was going on. Schoch's men were getting their motorcycles ready.

At this Chaplain Ottokar Felix stepped up sharply to Ignaz

Inbichler. "Chief," he said, "I do not know whether you are acting under official orders, and if so, whose. But I will point out to you that if you are acting on your own authority, you will be held responsible, tomorrow, the next day, someday, in one way or another. It is a well-known fact that these people have lived here for centuries, and no one has ever had cause to complain of them. Things may be different in Vienna and the big cities, but not here. You have given them a bad fright, Chief; I think that's punishment and revenge enough. Let it go at that, and we can all wait for the legal settlement of the Jewish question."

The pinched man with the accordion face sucked luxuriously at his cigarette and blew a cloud of smoke in the priest's face. "Don't be impatient, Your Reverence," he cooed sweetly, "everyone will have his turn. Our black-coated friends might very well come next. That idea had already occurred to me. However, if you're so fond of the Jew swine, you can go right with them."

"So I will," said the chaplain, leaping into the truck. He had no idea what had brought him to this perilous resolution. And indeed it was not a resolution at all. It was an action apparently not caused by his own will.

The Jews stared at him incredulously. Mrs. Fuerst was the only one sitting on a chair, which had been put into the truck for her. She was holding the baby in her arms, while her husband tried to quiet the second child, a tiny girl. The chaplain took the rabbi's eldest, a four-year-old boy, in his lap and began to joke with him.

The motor whirred. The powerful truck started off with a bounce, for the road was full of deep holes. The second car followed. The Brown Shirts' motorcycles came chattering after.

6

They went bumping along the rough country road that follows the big lake, though it is not visible from there. This road leads to a desolate boundary station on the Hungarian frontier. Why the main route to the important frontier town of Hegyeshalom had not been chosen remained Peter Schoch's own spiteful secret. In the first truck, jammed with roughly shaken people, no one said a word. When Chaplain Ottokar Felix tried to encourage the outcasts, they all listened to him with the strained, watery eyes of deaf-mutes. The tremendous quarries of Rust must have been passed by the time twilight fell, and with it, from the reedy lake, drifted one of the thick, choking fogs which the people of the region so superstitiously dread.

Schoch halted the column. The Brown Shirts got off their motorcycles. A curt command: "Everybody out! Unload! The trucks go back."

Through the steam from some witch's caldron in which the daylight had trickled away, the storm troopers rushed at the second truck. Bureaus, sideboards, cupboards, cherished household furnishings, boxes of china and kitchenware went flying through the air into the muddy road, where they smashed to the accompaniment of scornful laughter. The women let out a woebegone cry.

The chaplain, absolutely beside himself, grabbed Schoch by the wrist. "What does this mean? Are you crazy?"

With his fist, Schoch landed a blow on the priest's chest that sent him staggering. "I'll have you before communion, you damned incense-swinger," he laughed.

Next the rabbi's books followed the ruined household goods. Aladar Fuerst came running up, his arms outspread. But when Felix stooped to pick up at least a few of the volumes, Rabbi Aladar made a gesture of resignation that seemed to the chaplain positively grotesque in its Jewishness. "What's lost is better lost," he intoned to himself, with his slender head on his right shoulder.

"Left of the road," Peter Schoch commanded in echoing tones. "Forward march!"

Those who hesitated, old and young, were driven into the open fields by the Brown Shirts. None might lag. No consideration was given the old people or the children, either. If a few of the Jew brats pegged out on the forced march, so much the better. These were outcasts completely beyond the law, people protected by no state on earth, for the governments of England, France, and America had, after all, not only made no vigorous protest, but had hastened to announce that they would sagely refrain from interfering in another country's domestic affairs. Not only the governing circles of the Party, but even the simplest Party sympathizer, knew that the English Prime Minister, Mr. Chamberlain, along with his adherents, was covertly a friend and regarded the fight against Jewish Bolshevism (represented in Parndorf by Aladar Fuerst) with tacit approval. When but here and now would there be another such opportunity, right in Europe and in this effete age, for the primitively heroic and, furthermore, legitimate sport of a real, ready-made man hunt? It was enough to stir your blood, with a rousing hip-hurrah! The eager hunters rocked with laughter at the Jewish shadows panting before them in the fog.

The fog began to grow black. Suddenly the chaplain felt himself wading ankle-deep, then almost knee-deep, in ice-cold water. They had reached the wet swamps that fringe the lake near Moerbisch. Ottokar Felix picked up the four-year-old, whom he had been leading by the hand. Now he carried the child on his left arm, and with his free hand helped the young mother who was mechanically dragging herself and the infant along.

I remember that Felix stopped at this point in his story. The gray eyes in that coarse-skinned face stared at me.

I made use of the pause to ask: "What were you thinking in the swamps of Moerbisch, Chaplain?"

"I don't know what I was thinking," he replied, "probably nothing at all. But now I think mankind must keep incessantly punishing itself. It is bound to, quite logically, for the sin of lovelessness that has brought about all our misery, that makes it keep on growing piece by piece."

7

It was almost a miracle that after this "short cut" they got out of the swamp comparatively quickly and regained the road. It was a still greater miracle that no one had been injured or lost. At nightfall it grew bitterly cold, and the fog lifted. Yonder glowed the lights of Moerbisch. Everyone started to run. Beyond the last houses of Moerbisch lay the longed-for frontier. Home, but yesterday the familiar scene of an accustomed life, was already a strange inferno, looked back to with horror.

The night was very dark. An icy wind blew in gusts. The flag of the conqueror was already flying from the Austrian customhouse. But when the old frontier guard, who had not yet been relieved, caught sight of Peter Schoch with his Brown Shirts and their victims, they vanished from the scene as swiftly as if the bog had swallowed them up. The road to the Hungarian boundary station lay open, not a hundred yards away.

Aladar Fuerst gathered up the exiles' passports. Most of them, his own included, were Hungarian papers, since a good many Burgenlanders had for various reasons retained their original Hungarian citizenship, notwithstanding the treaties of Trianon and Saint-Germain. No doubt the Magyar frontier would be open without question at least to all those whose papers were in order. That was no more than simple law and justice.

Rabbi Aladar, with the bundle of passports in his hand, went over to the Hungarian customhouse. The chaplain silently accompanied him. Peter Schoch followed them at a shambling gait, whistling cheerfully.

The functionary in the office never even glanced at the passports. "Have you gentlemen had permission from the Royal Hungarian Consulate General in Vienna, please?" he asked with the greatest courtesy.

Aladar Fuerst's lips turned white. "What permission, for goodness' sake?"

"By an ordinance of ten o'clock this morning, the frontier may not be crossed except by permission of the Consulate General."

"But this is quite impossible," stammered Fuerst. "We knew nothing about it, and would not have been allowed to get such permission, anyway. After all, we were given six hours' notice, under threat of death."

"I'm very sorry," said the immigration officer, shrugging his shoulders, "but I can't do anything about it. You gentlemen will have to show the permission of the Consulate General."

Peter Schoch stepped up and slapped the "forms" on the table by which the exiles affirmed, over their own signatures, that they proposed to leave the country voluntarily and without compulsion.

"Go fetch your commander," said the chaplain in a tone that made the young official stand up and comply without remonstrance. Ten minutes later he was back with a slender, grizzled officer who had obviously, by the look of him, served in the old, glorious army. He took the passports in his hand like a pack of cards and ruffled them nervously.

The chaplain tackled him sharply: "Major, I am a witness that these people were looted down to the skin a few hours ago, and hounded through the swamp to the frontier as if they were worse than animals. Dr. Fuerst is a Hungarian subject, and so are many of the others, as you can see by the passports. There is no ordinance among civilized people that can refuse entry to these citizens in search of protection."

"Now, now, Father," said the officer, looking at Felix with dark, bitter eyes, "there are all kinds of things among civilized people . . ." He added coldly, "I have to follow regulations."

"There aren't many of us," pleaded Aladar Fuerst. "Most of us have relatives somewhere in Hungary. We shan't be a burden on the state."

The major pushed away the pack of passports with a gesture of revulsion. He did not deign to glance at any of those present, neither Fuerst nor Felix nor Schoch. After frowning thoughtfully, he said rather roughly, "You go on back across the border and wait."

It was only when the chaplain looked at him, aghast, that he muttered: "I'll telephone to Sopron, to the Obergespan."

8

There was an open space in front of the Austrian customhouse. To the left the road went off toward the reedy shores of the lake; to the right it vanished among vineyards. Using their motorcycle headlights, the Brown Shirts had turned this space into a sort of lighted stage. They rounded up the old men in this circle of light, and were amusing themselves after the fashion of the German concentration camps by making them do rapid knee bends and other gymnastics: "Up! Down! One! Two!" After a time eighty-year-old David Kopf, the baker's father, collapsed with a heart attack. The chaplain was very nearly ready to join the ranks of those being tormented and share their humiliation. But he knew all too well that he would merely have called forth the asinine laughter and scorn of the victors drunk with their triumph.

One thought kept running through his mind: "These lucky ones are driven to sin, while these unlucky ones do penance. Which, then, are lucky and which unlucky?"

A crowd of spectators had gathered around, people from Moerbisch and soldiers from the Hungarian frontier post. They did not conceal their horror and fury. Felix heard a noncommissioned officer spit and say savagely to his neighbor, "If I had to go through anything like that, I'd kill myself, and my whole family too, on the spot."

An hour later an auto arrived, bringing the Obergespan (the Hungarian provincial governor). Sopron, the capital of the neighboring county, was but a few miles from the frontier. The local potentate was a fat, amiable gentleman, with the elastic grace too often favored by corpulent dignitaries. His face was turkey red, his mustache snow white, and he was visibly perspiring in spite of the glacial cold. Stepping with easy nonchalance into the focused glare of the headlights and jovially beckoning everyone close, he planted his fists on his hips, setting off his bulging figure to better advantage, and rocked to and fro on his toes like a cavalryman.

"Now, now, good people, what's all this?" he began in fatherly tones, addressing himself to the exiles. "I can't overstep legal enactments. I'm only an administrative organ. I'm responsible to the Ministry of the Interior at Budapest. Hungary is a constitutional state, and a Christian one, certainly. But *ultra posse nemo teneatur.* I can't create a precedent. Why, after all? If I let you across the border today, others will come tomorrow on the strength of it, tomorrow and the day after and maybe for months. That would be a fine how-do-you-do—surely you can see that yourselves. Hungary is a country with its arms and legs cut off, and it has almost a million Israelite citizens, and it has innumerable unemployed, and really now . . . I'm sure you understand what I mean, don't you? Well, then! Now do go on back home, all of you, and don't make trouble for me. Personally I'm very sorry I can't do anything for you."

The Obergespan had spoken like a kindly old gentleman trying to induce naughty children to give up some prank and go home at once. He had addressed his speech to the wrong audience, giving only an occasional uncomfortable glance at the armed Brown Shirts.

Then Peter Schoch broke the deep stillness. "Sooner than let 'em go home we'll knock off the whole lot."

And everyone realized that the storm leader's words were no empty threat. At first Aladar Fuerst tried to explain calmly to the Obergespan that it was the middle of the night, and quite out of the question to let infants, small children, a woman barely risen from childbed, and a number of sick old people spend the night at large (if you could call it) in the open air, in the midst of nothingness. Here, in neither one country nor the other, was after all true nothingness. His voice was not beseeching, but weary, the voice of a man who knows that no plea and no appeal to reason will do any good.

But the chaplain's voice now was imploring. He begged the official in the name of Christ to shelter the outcasts beyond the frontier at least for one night, because they would not be taken in at Moerbisch or any other Austrian town, and the murderous threats of the armed gang were meant in deadly earnest.

The Obergespan rocked busily on his toes, and wiped away the sweat. "But, Reverend Father," he complained in almost wounded tones, "why must you make my situation more difficult than it already is, you of all people? Do you think I'm not human? Once and for all, the government has closed the frontier. I regret it extremely."

By way of consolation the Obergespan thereupon had his chauffeur distribute to the women and children some provisions he had brought from Sopron. It may have been chance or it may have been part of his character that they consisted mostly of the stick candy sold on street corners.

The grizzled major stood the whole time not saying a word, surveying the tips of his boots. Finally the Obergespan drew him and the chaplain aside. They walked back and forth in the road between the two customhouses.

"I've just thought of something," the Obergespan began. "It may be a way out that will satisfy His Reverence. But I mustn't know anything about it, understand, Major?"

Thereupon he unfolded his plan. The major was to let "the company" apparently cross the frontier, but to smuggle them back to Austria during the night, preferably on one of the flat barges that traveled on the lake. This would satisfy both the law and the dictates of humanity.

The major halted and drew himself up. "Your Excellency has only to wink, and I will evade the law in the present case. But I am a family man myself, and I will not be a party to the outright massacre of women and children; and they will be massacred if we take them in and then put them out again."

"Just as you please, my dear fellow; it was only an idea," smiled the Obergespan, deeply offended, and got into his car without noticing the chaplain's upraised hands.

9

The night had brightened somewhat. A very white quarter moon had risen, seeming to sharpen the cold. In the near-by vineyards a hut used by the vintagers for shelter from wind and weather during the season stood out against the blackness. Aladar Fuerst took his exhausted wife and children to it. The chaplain carried the four-year-old, who had fallen asleep in his arms, into the hut. Meanwhile the major had sent straw ticks and blankets from the Hungarian frontier garrison and distributed bread and coffee. He also ordered his men to put up two tents for the exiles, one for the men and one for the women. The Brown Shirts looked on these preparations with extreme disfavor, but dared not prevent them, since they were being made by an armed foreign power whose friendship was for the moment still needed.

The chaplain withstood the temptation to go to Moerbisch and ask a night's lodging of the parish priest. Aladar Fuerst had tried to persuade him, saying that nothing more could happen till morning. But Felix was physically tough, and an uncomfortable night meant little to him.

He had asked and received from the major a large bottle of milk for Fuerst's children. But as he was approaching the hut with this gift, a quick blast on a horn sounded from the open space, and a sharp command rang out in Schoch's piercing voice: "Assembly! All men fall in!"

The shadows that had just lain down to sleep in and around the tents staggered to their feet and assembled, hollow-eyed, in the glaring beams of the headlights. Aladar Fuerst came last, with Felix behind him. While some of the older men were groaning as if awakened from deep sleep, Rabbi Aladar now had a gentle, dreamy look.

Peter Schoch marched solemnly toward him, very slowly, his small eyes squinting voluptuously, his mouth twisting with great promise. The Brown Shirts laughed at the top of their voices. This was sure to be the great treat, one well worth staying up several nights for. Storm Leader Peterl was famous for his brilliant and comical notions. He stood blond and straight before Fuerst now, towering high above the small figure of the rabbi. In his right hand he held a wooden swastika, a simple cross that he had abstracted from a pauper's grave in the Moerbisch churchyard and had hastily transformed into the symbol of victory by nailing on short arms. No doubt it had been made specially for the sport he had in mind. There were no swastikas in the country yet, and in this predicament Schoch had had the happy notion of taking the Christian adornment from the sunken grave mound of some forgotten soul.

He raised this strangely macabre swastika high above his head like a Crusader. "Jew swine and garlic-eater," he cried, his voice showing plainly how much he was enjoying himself, "you're the rabbi, hey? Are you the rabbi?"

No answer.

"You're the rabbi with curls and caftan, jumping around in front of the Ark of the Covenant on the Shabbos, invoking your great Jehovah—is that right, Ikeymatzo Crappamoe?"

The motorcyclists roared, delighted beyond measure at this parodied Hebrew. Fuerst stood silent, almost inattentive.

"You're the rabbi who kisses your Ark on the Shabbos, hey?"

No answer.

At this Schoch gave Aladar Fuerst such a blow in the stomach with his left fist that Fuerst fell to his knees. Then he turned to the Brown Shirts. "Nobody can say we don't treat you right. Jew swine, I am allowing you the honor of kissing the symbol of the exalted Germanic race with your dirty mug. Appeal to your great Jehovah. And our horse-collared friend there can sing *Kyrie eleison* for accompaniment."

Aladar Fuerst, still on his knees, quietly took the swastika held out to him by Schoch, who now fell back a step. At first he held it irresolutely in his hands, this rude, crumbling cross from the grave of the unknown dead, smelling of damp spring earth. During those tense seconds Ottokar prayed that Fuerst would do nothing rash, but would kiss the swastika.

Instead something utterly unexpected happened.

The chaplain interrupted his story; these were his actual words: "A Jewish rabbi did what I, a priest of Christ, ought to have done. He restored the profaned cross."

Aladar Fuerst's eyes were half closed; he seemed to be acting as if sunk in some distant dream, and his motions were not quick, but reflective. One after another he broke off the loosely attached strips that made the cross a swastika. But as the wood had suffered from wind and weather, one end of the rotten cross arm snapped off; it became evident that the retransformed cross had been damaged and was no longer quite what it had been.

There was dead silence. No one attempted to stop him as he raptly destroyed the triumphant symbol. Peter Schoch and his men did not seem to understand what the action signified. For more than a minute they stood helpless, not knowing what to do. A smile hovered on Rabbi Aladar's face, which was turned toward the chaplain standing beside him. And he handed Felix the cross as if it were something belonging to the priest, not to himself. Chaplain Felix took it in his right hand. In his left he still carried the milk bottle.

Just then someone in the ranks of the Brown Shirts cried: "Jew swine, can't you hear that the Hungarian wants you over there? Run, Jew swine, run!"

Sure enough. Aladar Fuerst staggered to his feet, looked around, breathed heavily, saw the group of Hungarian soldiers under the distant lights of the other customhouse, to which they had withdrawn. He hesitated for a moment and then began to bound wildly toward Hungary, toward life.

Too late! There was a shot. Then another. And then the rattle of automatic rifles. Fuerst did not get twenty steps. The Brown Shirts jumped at him where he fell and trampled him with their hobnailed boots as if to stamp him into the ground.

On the far side, Magyar words of command snapped like whips. With leveled bayonets, Hungarian frontier guards, quivering with rage and spoiling for a fight, advanced on the murderers. The major took the lead, pistol in hand.

Seeing this, Schoch and his men left their victim where he was, whirled about, swung themselves on their motorcycles, and faded away with a bad smell of exhaust gas. For it lay not only in the genius of their Party policy but in the nature of their murdering courage always to know within a hairbreadth how far they could go without endangering the great cause.

The wounded man was carried into the Hungarian customhouse and stretched out on one of the benches. He was unconscious. A doctor summoned by the major soon arrived. He found a spinal injury and two shots through the lungs. There were also several broken ribs and severe contusions.

The chaplain tried to look after Mrs. Fuerst, who had lost her voice and the power of speech. She crouched wide-eyed beside her husband, despairingly moving her lips without a sound. The thin, piercing cries of the infant cut through the room. Its mother was incapable of giving it the breast.

Toward morning Aladar Fuerst, Rabbi of Parndorf, passed away. Before the end he opened his great, dark eyes. They sought the eyes of the Chaplain of Parndorf; their expression was quiet, very remote, and not dissatisfied.

By his death Aladar Fuerst saved his congregation. The major defied government orders and risked his own livelihood by allowing women, children, and old men to cross the border. They were taken to Sopron. Nine men in the prime of life remained behind. The major advised them to head northward. He had heard a report, he said, that the Czechoslovak frontier had been opened to fugitives. Let them trust in God, and look for some sort of vehicle beyond the reedy lake.

10

"And you, Father?" I asked.

"And I?" repeated Ottokar Felix absently. Then he reached for his hat. "This story wasn't about me. But since you're interested, obviously I couldn't go back to Parndorf. So I went along with the nine other men, and got across the Slovak frontier at an unguarded point. We swam a river. Since then I have been roaming from land to land with the children of Israel."

We went out of Hunter's Hotel into the street. The sun was setting gloriously behind the huge park. It was Friday evening, and a pleasant hour of the day. People were going home. The traffic was heavy; four lines of cars made no headway in the street. The women were very lovely with their bare, gleaming hair. Their laughing voices embroidered the blanket of sound. America was all peace and contentment.

"Look," said Felix, blinking at the passing scene. "Just look at all these kindly people, well fed, well dressed, good-tempered. These innocents don't realize that they have long since been involved in the war—the first war in their history that has really been a question of whether to be or not to be. They don't realize that Peter Schoch is upon them, perhaps among them. Many of these men are going to fall in battle. They will go out to defend the decent life and liberty of their nation. But there's much more at stake than freedom and a decent life; there's the desecrated cross without which the night will engulf us. And only God knows whether it will be granted to the whole world to do what Aladar Fuerst, the little Jew, did with his feeble hands."

THE FOURTH COMMANDMENT

Remember the sabbath day,
to keep it holy

JOHN ERSKINE

IV

REMEMBER THE SABBATH DAY, TO KEEP IT HOLY

A STORY BY

JOHN ERSKINE

WHEN the Kaiser said there must be war, the news traveled up the hillside to the Ehrlich farm, and Karl was mildly stirred, much more perplexed. He was then fifteen years old. There had always been wars, of course; the schoolbooks said so, and his father sometimes talked about his own march against the French, which was a glorious adventure, brief and decisive. But his father couldn't remember why France had to be invaded, and now even the Kaiser, wiser than any Ehrlich, neglected to explain what mischief England had been up to. Someone had shot an Austrian prince—and war was declared on England. Certainly it was wrong to kill Austrian princes, but on occasion they shot themselves, without English aid, and the assassin now was a Serb. Here was a puzzle. He would ask Heinrich about it—Heinrich Braun, his best friend.

Heinrich, the shoemaker's son, lived in the village, the only circumstance about him which Karl did not admire. A home should be on the land, if possible on high land, so that you could see far. A true home would have growing things around it, and cows with their calves grazing, and pigs grunting, and geese waddling. There would be plowing, planting, reaping—cycles of work and love. Cattle and horses come to their barns not merely from habit, partly also through affection. What more could a man want for himself? Over the Ehrlich fireplace hung a motto, cut in wood —*My Home Is My World.*

Heinrich, down in the village, had his world, but it was not his home. He lived in ideas. His dark eyes looked always for what was not there. He smiled easily, but ridicule more often than admiration lighted up his thin dark face. In their first days at school together Karl heard the teacher refer to Heinrich, in irritation, as one of these child radicals. Heinrich bothered the teacher with awkward questions, more awkward as he grew older. Karl was a bit terror-stricken the day Heinrich challenged the teacher outright. The order-loving pedagogue, safe in his platitudes, referred to the Valhalla legends as mythology, and Heinrich wanted to know if anything should be called a myth which happens daily under our eyes, and the schoolmaster, to be crushing, asked what parallels to the goings-on of the gods had come under Heinrich's observation, and Heinrich gave instances, hitherto unpublished, from recent village history, and the teacher requested him to hold his malicious tongue. Heinrich might have stopped there but he had his audience fascinated, and what orator can deny himself a climax? In humbleness of manner he asked why those like himself and the teacher, who sought and imparted truth, should be afraid of it. For this sally he was severely disciplined.

Karl inclined toward the schoolmaster but he admired Heinrich. He wished to live nowhere but on the hill farm, yet he could see this advantage in the village, that where neighbors were, as it seemed to him, huddled together, they met often and talked much, and men and women who talk enough are well informed—or if their information is wishful rather than sound, it surely is ample. Heinrich's facility he envied; his own tongue, he knew, was slow.

Perhaps because he was but fifteen or slightly older, it did not occur to him to ask Elizabeth what she thought of the war cloud, though she had been his comrade and Heinrich's through school. Now that they helped their fathers at home she was still their companion, sought out by both of them on holidays or whenever a free hour could be seized. She was the postmaster's daughter, and Heinrich had the best of it, living close by. He had glimpses of her through the day and evening walks while Karl was busy with the cows on the hill, he was in and out of her father's house, and now and then an errand brought her to the cobbler's shop. She resembled Karl in her large health, her blue-eyed serenity, her talent for silence, but though she listened willingly she could at times speak out. Heinrich knew she had a brain and respected it. But he would have gone along with Karl in the belief, a conviction of instinct, that a woman's opinion about war is unimportant.

Yet it was Elizabeth's opinion that he remembered. That evening he finished his milking task and hurried down to the shoemaker's shop. All day the young men of the village had been leaving to join their regiments or to begin their training, and only the middle-aged remained. Half a dozen of them crowded the small room where Heinrich and his father worked at their benches by lamplight. The onlookers talked in low tones. He came in unnoticed.

"So late tonight, Heinrich?"

"Why not? It is war. In war men think of their boots."

Karl looked at the group, who to him seemed old. Were they preparing already for their turn?

Heinrich, looking up, laughed at the frank, bewildered face.

"What makes you solemn? War is good business. Should it last, the English and Father and I will be millionaires."

The older men disapproved. "Heinrich," said his father, "you are not serious. It is now time to be serious."

Karl was shocked by Heinrich's words, not because their tone was light but because they might be true. He already had a farmer's distrust of the men in great cities who, as he understood, manipulate the world's business. They might contrive a war if they saw profit in it. He wished Heinrich had said the English alone would make money from slaughter, but if the bloodstain was even now on their own village, no wonder Shoemaker Braun disliked any mention of it.

He went from the shop to Elizabeth's house, not for discussion but for comfort. When Elizabeth was near it was easy to be cheerful. At the moment Postmaster Wilhelm Hoffer was lecturing his daughter. She stood on the other side of the lamp table where he sat. Papers lay spread out before him, and his hand waved a pen as he talked.

"Come in, Karl—no, you do not intrude. I tell Elizabeth she must now be a woman and manage by herself, but that she has done since her mother died. Yet I was here, going and coming—until now she was not altogether alone."

"Postmaster, is this war for you too?"

"That's what I ask!" cried Elizabeth. "Why should Father go? He is too valuable here. Besides, they have not asked for him yet. Father dear, the Kaiser knows you wouldn't be dangerous to the enemy."

"Daughter, those who exercise authority accept also an obligation. I must set an example. Older men can sort letters and sell stamps. When the Kaiser is less busy I shall ask to be relieved."

"Father, you will be killed—you are so absent-minded!"

He shook his head. "I must do my part."

Karl took a deep breath and cleared his throat. "Postmaster, I do not understand this war. What does it mean?"

"Death!" said Elizabeth quietly. "War means death."

"To our enemies," corrected her father. "We will say no more about it. I have work to do."

For a while Karl talked with Elizabeth by starlight, waiting for Heinrich to be finished with his work. When he came at last, Karl lost no time.

"What is this war about?"

"I told you—it's for business. There's not enough for England and for us, therefore Carthage must be destroyed, as the schoolmaster used to say. Too bad! The English are excellent people. They make good shoes."

"But the Kaiser cannot be the tool of the greedy! He would not, just for money, send us to be killed!"

Heinrich laughed, but he lowered his voice. "Listen, Karl—a king is like an actor. He'd rather play a good part than a bad one, but some kind of part he must have, and once he accepts it, he believes it's the best part, and no one else can do it so well. He'll leave the stage only when he's encouraged to go by ancient vegetables."

"But, Heinrich, you talk treason!"

"Well—sometimes the truth is called that."

Those days in 1914 taught Karl to see the rift between himself and this friend of his own age, whose mind seemed too old. An earthquake engulfed the world, but Heinrich looked on as from a distance or a height, declining to be involved. Shoemaker Braun was right—it was the moment to be serious; Postmaster Hoffer was right—a man should be loyal. Unless Heinrich took care he would soon be unpopular.

Yet he continued to comment on the universe, and the universe let him go unpunished. That had always been Heinrich's luck—once he was out of the schoolmaster's reach. The villagers knew the boy would talk, and from habit they expected to listen. Some of them perhaps would have said the same things, could they have found courage and the right words. Elizabeth, Karl grieved to observe, never opposed Heinrich, never argued with him, urged nothing in defense of the Kaiser, applauded no uniform, was roused by no flag-waving. Unless Elizabeth took care, Karl Ehrlich would discontinue his admiration, sharp though the pang would be.

In school, because she spoke seldom, he had felt a closer sympathy between them than between her and Heinrich. Now that he was older he liked to think—in fact, he took for granted—there was more than sympathy between them. In a few years he would ask her to marry him, and there was no doubt what her answer would be. A year ago, in late summer, he asked for a kiss, and ever since her cool lips, her clear eyes, haunted him. How soft lips could be! How deep her eyes were, when you held her close! She made him think—it seemed to him a noble comparison—of his father's farm, the rich soil, mother earth—of the night sky, the stars and the moon, always nearer to a meadow than they could possibly be to a village street. He had trusted her nature. She would love him—Heinrich, otherwise unpredictable, would remain their friend.

This happy confidence, shaken in the first war days, was restored in part the Sunday after mobilization. Pastor Groff, as all the world knew, was sadly put out that the village warriors should be torn away before he could fortify them with one of his sermons. Meditating on what he would have said, he decided to say it anyway. When his congregation, therefore, gathered that morning in the little church, they knew that the subject of the discourse would be, "With What Armor Shall We Be Armed?" The pastor's housekeeper had communicated the title to her intimates. The question, they agreed, was an excellent one, and appropriate. The answer would perhaps be drawn from the sixth chapter of St. Paul's letter to the Ephesians. But the housekeeper neglected to report the text, which at first hearing seemed to point away from the theme of armament. There could be no mistake, however. Pastor Groff, up in his pulpit, announced it firmly:

"Remember the sabbath day, to keep it holy."

Karl, seated with his parents, glanced at Heinrich across the aisle—and thought of Elizabeth, with the postmaster, several pews in front. In church Heinrich kept his face straight, but he would have a blistering opinion about this advice, which not only had missed the train but also was impossible for soldiers to follow. How could an army on the march observe the Sabbath? Elizabeth might neglect this obvious point; for her no good counsel would arrive too late, since she would apply it strictly to her father, who was still, as Heinrich would say, grooming for the conflict.

But before long the sermon gripped him. Pastor Groff, though a little wordy and formal, was digging into the truth. "What is it," he asked, "to keep the Sabbath holy? It is to cease from secular toil, to lay aside so far as we can all thoughts and all activities which concern earthly things; it is to frequent the House of God for prayer and praise; it is, in short, to give one day, one undivided day, to Him who gives us all our days. This is the commandment. In this literal sense it is our duty to keep it.

"But if the commandment meant only this, in humbleness before God I should believe and should teach you that something more is required. This law, as Moses brought it down from the Mount, is both negative and positive. On the negative side it is specific—we are to do no work on the seventh day, our son is to do no work, our daughter is to do no work, our manservant is to do no work, our maidservant is to do no work, our cattle are to do no work, the stranger within our gates is to do no work. On the positive side we are merely told to keep the Sabbath day holy—an order which seems to leave much to our discretion.

"But our Heavenly Father, having bestowed upon us at least a measure of common sense, expects us to use it. The negative directions for the most part we interpret freely, after the example of our Saviour. We cook our meals on the Sabbath, we wash the dishes and make the beds and put the house to rights. Those neighbors who were called away in our defense may at this hour be toiling harder with hand and brain than ever on weekdays at home. We doubt not that God understands.

"But the other side of the commandment they need not, and surely they do not, neglect. Though they cannot set apart twenty-four hours, they use the day to serve what they hold sacred—their families, their homes, their fatherland.

"I believe there is a Sabbath of place as well as of time. This room in which we now are, this village, this whole landscape, are seen at this moment by our absent ones. What the remembered vision means to them, who shall say? Some farm on these hills, some brookside in the valley, a shop, or a doorway, or a bend of the road, may recall the very place, the very moment, the prophet was seen coming from Sinai, from the presence of Jehovah, with the skin of his face shining. To each of us one supreme experience is given—at least one; that is his Sabbath day; he who does not keep it holy is a lost soul."

Karl listened as to a revelation. Pastor Groff told him little about the war but much about himself. For him this morning would be sacred. No longer would he be disturbed by Heinrich's bright thoughts, since they touched only the surface, like the negative items in the commandment. What if a mean person here and there did indeed make money out of war? If his country had seemed to him noble, then noble his country was, he dare not think otherwise; who would have any faith at all if he began to distrust his own generous perceptions? He saw a parallel to his love for Elizabeth; if a man finds beauty and goodness in a woman, then beautiful and good she is, and those who hint she isn't are simply not in love. He felt sorry for Heinrich, now that he understood him; Heinrich had as yet no Sabbath to keep.

This new philosophy of his, obviously, was not for public discussion, but he spoke to Heinrich and Elizabeth about the sermon, as soon as the service was over and they had a moment together, strolling down the village street. Elizabeth thought the pastor had spoken wisely but had said little new. Of course everyone held something sacred. She couldn't see that the pastor had given encouragement to laxness; evidently he expected them to attend church as usual.

Karl was startled that words which roused him had seemed tame to her. He was even more astonished when Heinrich voted the sermon one of the best the village was likely at any time to hear. For once, he declared, the preacher had come near to saying something, and if here and there he fell back on worn formulas, it was of small consequence compared with his manly effort to wriggle free. The Sabbath may be a place as well as a time—that was an idea! He himself was so constituted that he couldn't worship God more on one day than on another, and he doubted the correctness of the statement that God rested on the seventh day; the earth even on Sunday kept spinning on its axis, the planets continued in their orbits, and he didn't believe they traveled on momentum. But the sacredness of a place he could understand. God is everywhere, but we are not; if ever our eyes are opened, it must be in some infinitesimal portion of the universe, the corner or niche which is ours. But even the smallest place, if we find a vision there, will be Sabbath enough.

Karl remembered those early days, I repeat, as the time when he and Heinrich were often together yet as often growing apart, Heinrich being habitually frivolous, only on occasion profound. In some things they would never be far apart; their roots would always draw life from the same ground. But Karl was deep-rooted and would remain so. Heinrich would pull himself up, move around, try something new.

2

In the second year of the war Postmaster Hoffer had his wish and joined the troops. To his regret he functioned, not with the first line, but in the Commissary. Yet his work, as he wrote his daughter, was less sheltered than one might suppose. His share of peril, he confessed, was satisfying. One of the storerooms under his control was blown to matchwood by a shell the other day, only an hour after he had left it. Elizabeth turned very white when she read this.

She now had a neighbor in the house, an elderly widow, whom the postmaster, thoughtful to the last, selected to cure loneliness. The widow was present in person but she had lost her hearing. Out of courtesy Elizabeth shouted at her for a while, then from the same motive learned to live with her in silence. After all, there was little change in her habits; she had always known solitude. Her father wasn't deaf but he was preoccupied, and as a minor government official he couldn't be interrupted.

In the third year Heinrich was called, the wild talker, who with green temerity had indicated to all who would listen the absurdity and the shabbiness of war, of this war among others. Karl was not the only friend who feared that the Kaiser, having overheard Heinrich, sent him into battle somewhat before his time, by way of teaching him a lesson. But Heinrich went cheerfully, bore himself well in the training camp and soon in the trenches, and before the winter was half over became a corporal. When Karl warned him by letter to keep a watch on his tongue, he wrote home that having learned to dodge or parry the strokes of village critics, he had strong hope to escape both the firing squad of his superiors and the bayonets of the foe.

With Heinrich gone, Karl had Elizabeth to himself. He tried not to realize his good fortune in selfish terms, but it was pleasant to finish the day's work on the farm, goaded by no rivalry—to go down the hillside at last and find her alone—under the widow's eye, to be sure, but likely to have no other caller.

They talked of the war, of course. She spoke chiefly of her father, he of Heinrich. It was out of affection that he spoke of his friend, now that the friend was gone; he had always respected or envied the brilliance he himself lacked. Why Elizabeth had so little to say of Heinrich was a mystery. Perhaps she had outgrown his reckless ways, perhaps she found his knifelike wit too sharp for the present sadness of the world. If this were her reason for silence Karl could see merit in it; he wanted her—and what lover ever deplored sincerely a rival's downfall? But when he spoke of Heinrich Elizabeth's face had a light in it which did not seem hostile. Heinrich might be dangerous still.

Of course, Elizabeth was under a strain; she probably had no comfortable time of it at home, with her father gone and the widow installed, with food scarce and housekeeping more and more difficult. If she became, young though she was, slightly eccentric, Karl could excuse her; there was no longer any youth for anyone—those with the fewest years were aging in an unnatural way. On Saturdays and Sundays he would take Elizabeth for a walk, when the weather was favorable, not that the farm didn't give him walking enough, and it was three miles down to the village, but the fresh air and the exercise might strengthen her nerves. They walked always on bright days for a few minutes after Pastor Groff dismissed his flock.

Early in May, 1917—on May 4, to be precise—he suggested that they take the river path, the flower-bordered trail along the brook. Even in spring it was only a brook, but the village liked to call it a river. Elizabeth loved its windings, its diminutive waterfalls, its shaded pools; at one bend she always paused for what she called a "breathing spell," not because she would be out of breath but because the view up and down the stream was from that point expansive, and when she saw it her spirits lifted. On this May morning he thought it might please her to go where they had often walked with Heinrich, but Elizabeth developed a sudden unwillingness to look at the river, least of all to visit the "breathing spell," and when he argued with her she led him back to her father's garden, and shortly sent him home to the farm.

She was very young, remember, and he was only a boy—not a particularly clever boy. Heinrich too, though busy at his soldiering, was not yet, by the calendar, a man. But they ripened overfast, all three, from the gentlest of childhoods to a middle age storm-swept and heroic or, if you prefer, diabolical. Perhaps their end was as simple as their beginning; it needs to be told simply, if events which almost defy interpretation are to be clear.

Shortly after that May morning in 1917, when Elizabeth declined to walk by the brook, Karl was summoned to the training camp. In the final months of disaster and retreat he saw hard service but came through, as he would have said, unscathed. Heinrich would have said as much of himself. But the war did things to both. Heinrich was changed, certainly, but perhaps only as time in any circumstances would have brought out the character of which in boyhood he gave hints. With Karl the change went deep.

He resented in war two things, the women and the killing. No question but his resentment touched the heart of the matter; take sex and slaughter out of war, and little remains. He was born, we repeat, for a simple life—to love landscape, to love music so long as it was not very good, except that he would have liked Schubert—to admire art, especially the mediocre kind, and in any medium to admire platitudes, which is not entirely a bad thing, since a platitude is likely to be true. What he lacked in taste he would make up for in loyalty. He would be a credit to his fatherland. He would remember to keep his Sabbaths holy.

That seemed his destiny, before the war. In the training camp, however, he met for the first time large numbers of his own sex, in excellent health, with their impulses no longer tamed by social pressures. From the common talk he took the impression that most men think the usefulness of women is impersonal, one woman being essentially like another. He thought of Elizabeth, was shocked by what he heard and saw, and continued the way of life he would have followed at home, yet the most disturbing allies of the devil, he admitted to himself, were the girls who waylaid you whenever you stepped out of the camp—who, in fact, besieged the place. They did not consider themselves victims of masculine selfishness, nor did it seem appropriate to call them shameless hussies; they bore themselves with cheerful confidence, as though they were patriots, engaging for the moment in the most civilized kind of social work. Evidently they had taken to heart the formula of generous citizenship—to every man according to his needs. If they did not serve their country directly, they did what they could for those who for their country would die.

They did not occupy all of Karl's thoughts; the drill sergeant also had his attention. He learned the current manual of arms, he learned to use a rifle and a machine gun, and he learned how to kill a man with a bayonet. The bayonet exercise horrified him. To stab a stuffed dummy was bad enough, once your imagination was roused, but how would it be in actual fighting? The dummy had no face, no voice; you couldn't know whether it hurt the dummy to be killed. Karl wondered whether his first victim would shriek or groan or call on God. He did not fear for himself; he had the faith which has sustained all soldiers since the beginning of time—he, of course, would come out of it all right.

It needed only a week or so of fighting to make him think again of women. No one had told him this weird effect of mortal danger, that if it does not paralyze you it will redouble your faculties, sharpen your senses, put color into the universe. Facing death in battle, he observed, resembled going to a village fire; why did all fires occur on starry nights, under placid moons? How did your ears manage to catch the slightest crackle of the blaze? In battle, where he might well expect death, Karl learned what it is to be alive—and when his regiment was relieved, sent back to recuperate, he discovered the part of himself which had slept. In the small town near which he and his comrades reposed, the first sight of a girl was too much for him and his philosophy; fighting had roused in him what could not be controlled. Later he hated himself, but there were other battles and other girls, and less and less self-reproach. He accepted his world and became a cynic. To say that war made a man of him is to hide an inner loss. He was aware of it himself. Elizabeth had said, innocently wise, that war is death.

On the other hand, he could now use the bayonet without a pang. The enemy had a bayonet too, or a knife, or a gun; it was your life or his, and the choice when suddenly presented turned out to be easy. Karl was a great soldier, his officers reported—a born killer. He was astonished at this reputation but not inclined to protest against it. The memory of the girls, a very wholesale memory, troubled him, but no ghosts disturbed his sleep. He was doing his duty; the fellows he stopped on the bayonet blade were doing theirs. War was war.

But Elizabeth would not enjoy hearing of the bloodshed, still less of the girls. The thought of Elizabeth, he liked to reflect, was his Sabbath; the fact which he contrived not to face was that he had learned to keep his Sabbath apart from the rest of his days.

As it happened, he was the first home, five weeks before Heinrich. Elizabeth still had her widow. The postmaster would have returned before Karl had he not been what he considered a war casualty. Having maintained vigilance against shells and bombs, he became absent-minded again with the signing of the Armistice, and got himself run down by a truck.

So Karl once more had his chance to talk with Elizabeth alone. She was a woman now, wiser, more confident than when he went away, and far more self-contained. The village had suffered its share of wounds—she had watched the sorrow come down, cloud upon cloud. War was a tragedy—but it was over now, and she was for putting it out of mind as quickly as possible.

"But we cannot forget. It has done things to us!"

"Words will undo nothing, Karl. It's foolish to look back."

"But to go on as we were is impossible. The world changes fast."

"I hope so. I believe we should change it faster."

"Elizabeth, I wish it would stay as it was!"

She looked at him a moment. "It must be that you yourself have changed greatly, if you fear change so much."

"I didn't say I feared it."

She shook her head. "That is what your words said to me. Karl, have you lost something of your old self?"

The question was all kindness. She must have learned to recognize unhappy souls—he knew she was reaching her hand to him, and if he had then spoken of the women and of the killing and of his inner confusion, they might have moved forward to a new understanding. But he couldn't be frank.

"I think I am more my old self than I ever was! So I shall remain, please God!"

He prophesied correctly but not quite as he intended, rather as if to expand the truth in Elizabeth's remark, that those who yearn too fervently for an unchanging world have themselves ceased to be what they were. In the effort to recover himself he transformed instincts of natural piety into reasoned grounds for harsh criticism. The step from criticism to fanaticism is neither large nor hard.

He began at home, with his parents, while they were still aglow with thankfulness for his return. Hans Ehrlich, the father, had counted on three boys to take over the farm, but two had died in infancy, and when Karl, the remaining hope, was called to the war, the old man felt the blow as notice served by heaven that there should be no more Ehrlichs in the world. Now that the son who had seemed lost was alive again, Hans blamed himself for lack of faith and made up for it by an increase of hope and charity. No matter how much had gone wrong, the times would be set right again, now that Karl was home. There was, to be sure, no money in the land, food could be raised but not sold, since the hungry had nothing to pay with; honest trade had come to a stop everywhere, in the village as in the towns, workmen could not be hired, the soil could not be cultivated, the cattle starved unless they went to the slaughterhouse. But Hans Ehrlich refused to be discouraged now; Karl and he could look after a cow or two, a few pigs, chickens, geese—and rabbits were never few. There is a blessing in the soil, he liked to say, when he sat down with Karl and Mother Ehrlich to their thick warm soup.

In other days this wisdom would have been enough for Karl, but now he regretted that his father accepted with little protest things as they were, so obviously not as they had been. The world was slipping into misery, and it would slip faster unless it were rescued and restored. He said as much.

"Karl," his father would reply, "leave something to God."

Such willingness to cast the burden on the Lord was in an excellent tradition, but Karl found it depressing.

"We should stir ourselves," he told his father one day while they were cleaning out the cowshed. They had been up that morning at five.

"Stir ourselves, son?"

"We should organize."

Hans Ehrlich laughed. "Organize what?"

"We should plan together—all the farms, the village, all the villages. We should——"

"Co-operatives are not everywhere an advantage, son."

"This would be more than a co-operative—it would reach further. The men in the regiment spoke of it. Why should an army be organized and not——"

"Karl, the army was well organized, but we lost the war. Some of us do not wish to be all the time in the army."

"But could we not unite, plan together, buy and sell for each other——"

"There are many still who would not like that."

"They should be compelled to accept what is best!"

"Compelled? How?"

Karl had not yet thought so far.

"I should not care for it myself," said his father. "Before we knew it we should be taking orders. That is good for an army but it is not good for a farm. Everywhere the soil is different and so is the weather."

"Yet we may come to it."

"I hope not in my time, son. I am too old for such ideas."

Karl fell silent. What was he arguing for? It was his father who had not changed—who still loved the old ways.

His parents had never engaged so much of his attention—never, he was glad to believe, so much of his affection. He discovered that they were interesting to talk to, that they were both set in their ways, but that they both were surprisingly tolerant—on many questions too much so, he feared. His father's thin, weathered face was stubborn but kind—at moments wistfully kind. His little mother, short and stout, drew her thinning hair back so that the set of her firm lips was exaggerated in her moon-shaped countenance; but when she laughed her eyes twinkled, and there was a revelation of the mischief in her, the zest for living, which hard work and many years could not quell. Like her husband she would go her way, but she was willing that others should go theirs.

Karl, in his search for the life which had been, resumed his churchgoing, and bowed himself in the old pew, between his father and his mother, saying with them the ancient prayers which forever need to be said, confessing those ancient sins which mankind sees to it are renewed daily, like the manna from heaven. Here surely, at such moments, he might have found his ancient world. But there were always Pastor Groff's sermons to spoil the morning. The good man's liberalism had become slightly offensive. His charity had extended itself by degrees over such a multitude of sins that the difference between sinner and saved had become, Karl felt, imperceptible. The village would perhaps be better off if the pastor would stop drawing the teeth from the Law from Sinai.

Yet Mother Ehrlich disagreed. The pastor, she insisted, was a good man, a man of God, exemplary in his own life, and humbly imitating his Master's gentleness toward the weak. It was her habit to speak of sinners as weak. She could even find excuses for other women—a rare generosity. When Karl spoke, for example, of the village girls as having grown overbold, she took up a vigorous cudgel for them. Not even Pastor Groff had enjoyed from her so warm a defense. From now on, she pointed out, there would be many girls and not many boys, and in a tolerable world women were entitled to a man apiece. God inspired the Scriptures but it was a male, undoubtedly, who wrote the inspiration down. It is not good for man to be alone—for man, mark you! Why not tell the other side of it, too? Those village girls, now—if their eyes inquired of every youth who came down the street, if they confessed a hunger which should have been reserved for a proper lover—think how many lovers were sleeping under strange sod, planted in rows wholesale.

Karl was so moved by his mother's outburst that he mentioned it to Elizabeth, but again he fell short of complete frankness. Neither to her nor to his mother did he give the true reason why the bold village girls offended him. He was careful not to say that their eyes recalled the women who followed the army, who had hunted him—or whom he had hunted. What he told Elizabeth was that he hardly recognized his mother, her ideas were so changed, and Elizabeth's reply was this—that Mother Ehrlich had probably thought this way always, that her thoughts were those of every woman, that a woman has the right to speak out, to ask for what she needs, even to ask for love.

He wondered if she were telling him to propose. Since she held such ideas, exceeding his mother's in audacity, he wondered if she had been exchanging letters with Heinrich.

Heinrich was home at last, the same sharp thinker and bright talker but with a new capacity for happiness. Karl marveled that such a gift should be brought back from war. The three friends began to spend evenings together, always at Elizabeth's house, of course, and Heinrich as of old did the talking. Karl listened with a new interest. The familiar recklessness of tone was what one first heard, but after a moment there was an unexpected seriousness. The two friends could at last agree; the war had taught them both the same truths. Heinrich wanted a return to habits sane and tried, but he feared an excessive conservatism. "When a country goes to war," he said, "the rulers must find a powerful motive for killing off their own people as well as the enemy. All wars, therefore, begin in self-defense. When the troops go far, however, carrying the fight into the other fellow's country, then the war must be in defense of the other fellow in spite of himself, it must be in defense of culture, of world civilization. So long as a war succeeds, its motive is international, but when you're defeated it's quite another story. You are disappointed, disillusioned, embarrassed, shamed. You keep repeating to yourself, 'Nobody loves me!' For comfort you turn to your happy past, in your misery exaggerating the happiness. Your own country, best of all lands, all the greater in defeat! That is nonsense, of course; it's the dangerous kind of nationalism. We're to be nationalistic, Karl, in a crazy way, from now on."

So far so good, but Heinrich added a disturbing sentence—"All we are waiting for is a Messiah."

Well, wasn't that just what they were waiting for? Karl detected here the old cynicism; Heinrich was scoffing. But a leader was just what they needed, an organization and a leader.

At home he gave his parents a somewhat expurgated report of the new Heinrich, stressing the improvements and avoiding the other things. Heinrich, he said in effect, had always been brilliant; now he was solid.

"Before long, I suppose," said Mother Ehrlich, "he will marry."

Heinrich married? Heinrich?

Mother Ehrlich replied to his bewilderment. "He will marry Elizabeth. How comes it that you don't know? You I thought he would have told. In the village it is no secret."

"But—he has been away!"

Mother Ehrlich laughed. "As if she wouldn't settle it before he went! That girl was always a woman."

He was not crushed—he was confounded. He stood for a moment without a thought, but also without pain. Heinrich would marry Elizabeth? Those words meant nothing. His mind ceased to be paralyzed. His mother listened to gossip. The village would soon learn the truth, that Elizabeth would marry Karl Ehrlich. He would lose no time. If Heinrich married her—he would no longer be able to think of her with affection, which was absurd. Also, he would feel very unfriendly toward Heinrich. He must speak to Heinrich before he saw her. If Heinrich had really thought of marrying her, he would have spoken first to his best friend, would he not?

He stopped at the shop early that evening and persuaded Heinrich to leave his work for a stroll. It was dull walking in the village—why not go a mile down the main road? Heinrich's good spirits were remarkable that day. Karl told him so.

"You are one person, my friend, who has not been too sadly changed. You are improved, if I may say so; to what you were is added now a mellowness."

"We are growing up, Karl. The first signs of ripeness should begin to show."

"Elizabeth also has improved. I am the only one who, I fear, has not progressed."

"Absurd! You've progressed as much as is good for you!"

Karl edged into his theme. "When I think of Elizabeth, I am humble. I am very fond of her, Heinrich."

"She is fond of you."

"Has it not seemed to you, Heinrich, that her character, always charming, has gained in strength? She is now an individual."

He was embarrassed and therefore stiff; he despised himself for his awkwardness. Heinrich laughed. "I never thought she wasn't an individual."

Karl forgot what he had planned to say next. "She will make a good wife," he blurted.

"I am sure she will," answered Heinrich quietly. Karl decided to skip all preliminaries and come to the point.

"I intend to marry her. You are my best friend. I wished you to know."

Heinrich stopped in the road to look at him. "You mean—you have spoken to her?"

"Not yet."

"Ah! I did not see how it could be."

They walked on a few steps, mechanically. It was Karl this time who stopped and turned.

"Why did you think it could not be?"

"Because I asked her yesterday, and she said yes. From her letters I knew she would—and she knew I would ask her. We have belonged to each other for a long time. Karl! This must not hurt you! I will not let it hurt you! We are always friends, are we not?"

"I would have spoken to her sooner," said Karl, "if I had had money. A man should be able to care for his wife."

"Karl, you're taking this too hard! You'll find the right woman—there're plenty of them. This sort of thing was bound to happen. It might have been the other way, you know——"

"I expected it to be the other way! It should have been!"

"We've walked far enough for one day," said Heinrich, turning back toward the village. "I am sorry for you, but I have done you no wrong. You needn't reproach me—I refuse to feel guilty!"

"You are right, of course," said Karl, suddenly cold and formal. "Forgive my hasty words! I congratulate you. I congratulate Elizabeth."

Heinrich took him by the arm. "I'm awfully sorry, old friend!"

For a moment or two they walked in silence.

"It's funny," said Heinrich, "I proposed to Elizabeth when she was twelve years old. She rejected me with vigor. We were walking along the brook, and we sat down on one of those rocks at the 'breathing spell.' You remember the place?"

"I remember it."

"She was a cute little thing that day. She said she was too young to hear such proposals, and, anyway, I should speak to her father for permission."

Again they walked without a word.

"You remember that sermon of the parson's, about keeping a Sabbath?"

Karl corrected him. "Keeping *the* Sabbath."

"No, he didn't say it that way—he taught me then to keep holy not only the Lord's day but all the places and moments which to me are sacred. I learned then the importance of knowing what deserves to be kept holy. It helped out in the war. You know what I mean, don't you? It must have happened to you too."

Karl envied him, almost to the point of hatred.

"When I came home," his friend went on, "I began to drop into the church at the lunch hour, always when no one else was there. I suppose you've done the same thing. The building is unnaturally still—mystic—all silence and emptiness. Yesterday I slipped into the last pew. Elizabeth came in and sat beside me. What all-seeing goodness provided that she should come? We said nothing. Suddenly, from the same impulse, we knelt and prayed. When we rose and came out, we were engaged—married—whatever the word is, when two are fused into one soul."

"And you had said nothing to her?"

"What was the need?"

They were in the village now, and Karl nerved himself for the moment when he must take farewell of the girl he had, only half an hour ago, declared he would marry. A farewell of some sort this meeting would be, and he knew it would be hard, but he did not foresee the kind of hurt he was to suffer. When Elizabeth's eyes met Heinrich's, he saw at last, by the light in her face, what his mother had guessed long ago. He saw also that he had been stupid even to hope for Elizabeth, if Heinrich wanted her. It was terrible to feel he was surrendering too quickly; it was twice terrible to realize that, being himself, he could do nothing else.

"Elizabeth, I wish you the greatest happiness. You and Heinrich."

She glanced at Heinrich with quick reproach, as though a precious secret had been made common by sharing. Karl hated her for that look, hated them both for leaving him out of their lives. No, he didn't hate, he never could hate them; he resented the truth about himself, that he was weak and second-rate. A man had a right to feel resentment, hadn't he? Resentment, not hatred, and against bad luck or injustice in general, not against Heinrich. Heinrich and he had been as brothers. A man shouldn't hate his brother.

3

Karl began life, then, a beaten man, reconciled to his inferiority, or at least willing to be reconciled. Ten years later he still lived on the hillside. His father was feeble, his mother was dead. He could have sold the farm, but he said it was his duty to stay. He might have said he was afraid to try any way of life but that to which he was born and in the place of his birth. He had become a little unsociable, yet he would have been uncomfortable among strangers. To balance his timidity he was stubborn. When his neighbors in the village had occasion to describe his character, they said he was very admirable—which is a low order of praise, meaning that his faults didn't show but it was difficult to like him. The cause of this difficulty they could not explain; he led a correct life, he supported deserving causes, he gave to the poor, he showed himself regularly in church.

He had not married. The neighborly verdict, by and large, was that he had an antipathy to women, but a minority opinion, inclined to sentiment, held that he had a weakness for women and in his time had known many, and one of them he had loved, but she wouldn't have him. The object of this baffled passion was named. In fact, several names were offered. The memory of the village, with passing time, was becoming uncertain.

Heinrich in the third year of his happy marriage moved to a large city in the north. He explained this uprooting by his need of mental stimulus, a little more daily argument than the village provided, but he was thinking of Elizabeth, as everyone knew. She deserved, his love told him, a larger scene. So they withdrew from Karl's world, but he wrote to them with a fierce kind of regularity, as though determined not to let them escape. At intervals Heinrich returned to see his father, and always he would climb the hillside for a word with Karl. Sometimes Elizabeth was able to come with him, but not often. Gradually the visits fell into a pattern, a ritual rather than a routine; Heinrich kept his Sabbaths, as Karl knew. At least two visits yearly. On one visit he would stand for a moment at the brook, at the "breathing spell"; on the other he would go to the church at noon and sit in the rear pew.

He fascinated Karl. Such mawkishness, when wrath and strong dreams were stirring! In a town not far off—no city but quite a town—the organization was forming, that union of patriots which he had foreseen. He was not, then, so stupid after all! Perhaps it would be his turn, now that marriage had softened Heinrich into ridiculous sentimentality. Heinrich in his married condition would be too prudent to join the organization. There was a risk —it took courage. Karl began to hold up his head. His father had said some people would not approve of the union, and his father was right. The government did not like it at all. Karl joined, and met his fellow patriots—or, as the timid would say, his fellow conspirators—in secret. Their purpose was so simple and so right that Karl marveled at the perversity which tried to stop them. They would restore to the fatherland what had been torn or stolen from it—the self-respect, the respect of other lands, the leadership in culture, the old and beloved folkways, and of course some territory, but that was less important.

The organization spread fast, as he had said it would. It roused hope in those who despaired of ordinary leaders, it promised a way out from the long shadow of defeat, it called youth to a crusade, and since youth at the moment had little to do, youth went crusading. How wise of the organization, Karl reflected, to call on youth! Though he was no longer young, he knew by experience what a cure for self-distrust is the discovery that one is needed.

After sunset one evening, in the twilight, two of his fellow patriots from the village in the next valley appeared suddenly out of the dusk as he finished his chores. They laughed at the start they gave him.

"You must have a bad conscience, Karl. Confess! What have you been doing?"

Now that he knew who they were, he was flattered that they had looked for him in his home. Two of them at once! Except for the organization gatherings he couldn't say he was well acquainted with them, but he liked their manner, it was so sure and firm.

"Karl, you have a view from your hill! What a sweep! But it's a large farm—you try to work it alone?"

"Alone now, since there are no men and my father is very old."

They glanced quickly up at the windows of the house.

"My father," continued Karl, "is now stone-deaf."

They turned to him again, a little sheepishly. "Our leader warns us, as you know, to be careful. He has reason to fear spies among us. They will be hunted down, but meanwhile we must not talk where others will overhear."

"It is a pity," said Karl, "we are not the army. A spy in the army is shot."

The two men stood motionless, blotted out by the night, only shoulders and heads showing against the sky.

"Karl Ehrlich," said one of them, "you are to be the leader for this district. You will report to me—I will see that you have the necessary instructions."

Responding to the crisp tone, Karl from old habit saluted.

"For the present," said the military voice, "your rank will not be publicly defined, but in case of open conflict your duties will be those of a lieutenant."

An officer! If there should be another war, he would go as an officer! Karl Ehrlich straightened his shoulders. Here was justice at last—they had sought him out, they put confidence in him! He was not stupid!

"Lieutenant Ehrlich," said the voice, "have you a pistol?"

"A rifle, not a pistol."

In the darkness a gun was thrust into his hand. "You may need this. Keep it out of sight. Here are cartridges—enough for the present."

"But what am I to do?"

The other two laughed. "Didn't you express a wish," said the military voice, "to shoot spies?"

"That, I should like," said Karl cheerfully.

"You will do what you are told, whether you like it or not. Be clear on that point, Lieutenant Ehrlich! Good night to you."

They left him in a daze of exaltation. He was now a strong man—he would show them he was stronger than they thought.

Some months later Heinrich came to the village on one of his pilgrimages, and before departing again to the city he climbed the hill to see his friend. He brought with him more gossip than usual—Elizabeth would have another child—workmen were better paid in the large towns but they were more restless—everyone nowadays was restless.

"Karl," he said abruptly, "you belong to the organization. Don't look scared, man—I know you do. I belong to it, too."

"The membership," said Karl, "is a secret!"

"Not our membership, not between you and me, is it? I thought you'd be glad to know I was in."

"I am glad you are one of us," said Karl. "There is naturally a branch in your city. No wise man will stay out."

"That is probably so. What's your opinion of the Leader?"

"The Leader?" Karl was shocked. "We do not discuss the Leader."

"Why shouldn't we—that is, you and I? He has a great mind—or he has reliable instincts. I haven't decided which. But it's too bad he hasn't a heart."

Karl stared. "But you just said you have joined us! You cannot talk like that! It is not permitted!"

Heinrich laughed in the old way. "When I said I joined, I meant I came in. I didn't mean I parked my soul outside."

Karl's face darkened. "But you understood that hostile criticism is not welcome. You have the choice of being absolutely loyal or of——"

"If I can't be loyal," said Heinrich, "if I'm convinced I can't stay in, I'll resign."

"No!" Karl was firm. "You will not resign!"

"Well, I'm only thinking about it as yet, but if that's what I decide, don't try to persuade me. After all, what disturbs me is personal—others may not feel as I do. I heard the Leader say we must put out of memory the false teaching which enslaved our childhood—we must give our complete allegiance to the new truth. That rather touched me, Karl. What truth is new? You and I wanted the old truth to come back."

"He is right," said Karl. "Our minds and hearts should be wiped clean. For us there is only the Leader, and a new world."

Heinrich looked at him. "Don't be crazy! There is no new world, there is no new gravitation, there is no new light, there is no new darkness. He wants some new commandments—that was what I couldn't stomach. He can't make progress, he says, until the famous ten are done away with! Well——"

He looked down the hillside, toward the village. "Karl, you remember about keeping the Sabbath? If the Leader can't succeed without robbing me of a few memories, of a few glimpses of truth——"

"In your allegiance," said Karl, "am I to understand that you put your visits to the brook and the church, those sacred memories of yours, rather ahead of the Leader?"

Heinrich laughed. "Are you saying it's my duty to care more for him than for Elizabeth?"

Karl glared at him. "If we have reason to suspect you, there'll be no more visits to the brook and the church."

"If he thinks he can keep me away, let him try!"

When Karl next attended the organization, he was gratified by the salutes of his juniors. Already they had been informed that he was an officer. He was gratified also to learn that the next meeting would be held in an empty barn, where unobserved they would do some twilight drilling. That was the reason, he could see, why they made him a lieutenant. They needed a framework of veterans to take charge of enthusiastic but inexperienced youth. And he was further gratified by the attention he received from one of those who had come at dusk to the farm—the one with the military voice.

"You find that gun satisfactory?"

"I haven't used it, Captain."

"But you should. You should practice a little, every day. I meant to speak of it the other evening. I should have asked you then if the gun balanced the way you like."

"Captain, I am more familiar with a rifle."

"Ah, yes—to be sure. Well, practice a little and I'll stop by when I can, to show you some points."

He said it casually, as though it were indeed through thoughtlessness that the revolver had been entrusted to a man who didn't know how to use it. Karl was gratified that his acquaintance with the weapon was taken for granted, as though he had always carried sidearms. He startled the hillside by firing at a wall behind the barn, so that even his father thought he heard something, and small boys came up from the village to see who was making the noise. Karl was proud to be watched by admiring eyes, so long as his cartridges held out. The captain came from his valley, as he had promised, once or twice a week, always with a pocketful of fresh cartridges and interested in the condition of the gun, whether it was properly cleaned and oiled. Karl looked forward to these calls. Having now a place in the world, he acquired confidence, and being confident he became happier, more generous.

On one visit the captain asked whether he knew Heinrich Braun, who formerly resided in the village. The question was abrupt but it was put without emphasis; apparently the captain had just happened to think of it.

"He is a friend of mine."

"Do you ever see him?"

"Only when he returns here."

"How often is that?"

The voice was becoming military again. Karl hesitated to speak of Heinrich's cult of the "breathing spell" and the church pew. After all, they were Heinrich's business.

"Your answer," said the military voice, "is important to the organization. You must conceal nothing."

"Captain, he comes at least twice a year."

"For the purpose of talking with you?"

"He has another errand, but afterwards he comes here for a moment."

"He is a member of the organization."

Karl was on the point of saying he knew it, but checked himself. "He will be a good man for us, Captain."

"What is that errand of his?"

Against his will Karl obeyed the tone of command. "He has a wife—he is deeply sentimental, though he pretends not to be—there are two anniversaries, moments of his courtship——"

"He comes all this way just to drink his wife's health?"

"Captain, for him those anniversaries are sacred."

The captain laughed, as one who can no longer be astonished by human queerness. Apparently his curiosity about Heinrich was at an end.

But when he called again he returned to the theme, and in a darker tone. He had just examined the pistol and found it as it should be. Karl wondered why a pistol must be examined so much.

"This friend of yours—Heinrich Braun."

"Yes, Captain?"

"Did he take your girl from you?"

"He married Elizabeth," said Karl feebly. "She was the postmaster's daughter."

"But you wanted to marry her yourself."

Karl had nothing to say.

"Is he then your friend?"

"Now he is—at one time he was not."

The captain looked him through and through. "I'm afraid he's a traitor. I'm not sure, but that's what I believe. If he's a traitor, he must be shot. You said so, if I remember."

Karl was chilled to the bone.

"I wait for your comment, Lieutenant."

"He should be shot—if he is guilty."

"Would you shoot him?"

Karl thought hard—then cleared his husky throat. "If he deserves it, then it should happen to him, but I am not sure I could do it."

"Well, if there is doubt, you won't be asked. I may be wrong, anyway." He handed back the pistol, deliberately. "You are now on trial. He is a clever fellow. If you gave him the smallest hint, he might escape us."

After that conversation, Karl had something to think of. When he said that he was friendly to Heinrich, he meant that there had been a change since he had risen to rank and since Heinrich had joined. So far as he knew, Heinrich was not a lieutenant. But if Heinrich, after their plain talk, chose to imperil the cause, he need expect no friendship, no mercy. In the new world there would be small room for the favored or the lucky.

When next the organization met for their drill, the captain

made a little speech which Karl felt was aimed at him. There was serious disaffection in the ranks, not among their group but in places uncomfortably near, and the Leader had requested that loyal members should hear plain words. The lukewarm and the treacherous must be eliminated. It was not their primary mission but it might become their duty to serve as executioners. Strong action, which seemed the only course in self-preservation, would probably lead to an open clash with the unsympathetic authorities. The members were urged to keep their equipment in condition for instant use. Target practice would be arranged on remote and solitary properties. Secrecy, of course, was more important than ever.

Karl was aware of some inconsistency here. There had been no secrecy about his pistol practice; his farm was not remote, and the village boys had come up to watch his prowess. Besides, the captain was becoming too military, too like the old army; he apparently expected to have all the ideas, to announce them, and to receive nothing but brainless obedience. Karl, being himself an officer, wished to contribute more than that. He asked the captain if some of the others, a few who lived fairly near, might not use his barnyard wall for their rifle exercise. The captain turned icy and declared the idea altogether unwise. Slightly nettled, Karl asked why the organization should risk the names of assassins when treacherous members could be removed as innocently as apples from a tree. The captain's face warmed.

"And what is your method, Lieutenant?"

"Accident, Captain. Let them die by an accident. Or let it be a private quarrel, which does not concern the organization."

The captain's face took on a queer look—a very strange look, indeed. "Lieutenant," he said, "you have a future."

Within a fortnight he stopped at the farm, this time late in the evening, and Karl asked him into the kitchen, where there was a lamp. On the point of accepting a chair, the man glanced warily at the staircase.

"Your father?"

"He is in his room. As I told you, he cannot hear."

The captain sat down. "How goes the pistol practice?"

Karl brought his gun from the kitchen chest. "Again I need cartridges."

The captain broke it, squinted through the barrel toward the lamp flame, emptied the mechanism on the table.

"You keep it clean, certainly. I wish these boys we have were half as thorough."

"I'll assemble it," said Karl, reaching across the table. The captain slowly put the gun together himself. Apparently he did not hear the offer.

"That idea of yours, Lieutenant, proves admirable. I feared it would involve a strategy too complicated, but our first two cases fortunately were simple. The city branch to which your friend belongs has suffered two shocking losses. One member, a station-master, slipped under a passing train. Another, a young surgeon, committed suicide at night in a dark street. He cut his wrists with one of his own instruments. A third member is suspected, but all he has done about it, so far, is to run away."

The blood pounded in Karl's forehead. "Heinrich?"

The captain nodded.

Also, he slipped the gun into his pocket, unnoticed. Karl's brain was in a turmoil. Loyalty to Heinrich, love of Elizabeth, respect for whatever another man kept holy or for what to himself had once been sacred—all withered and vanished as in a furnace, where the writing on paper lasts for a second after the paper is consumed. For so brief a second lasted his better self. Then he faced his mortal foe, bayonet to bayonet, his life or the other man's. Heinrich must die—or Karl Ehrlich, if he weakened. Nothing for it now but to aim straight, lean your weight on it, drive home. He felt no hesitation, no regret, rather a sense of liberation. He was free now to be as strong as in most of his life he had been weak. He could take charge of this affair.

"You have no clue to his whereabouts, Captain?"

"None. We depend now upon you."

"He will come to this village next Tuesday. It is one of his anniversaries."

"But surely he won't put himself in obvious danger!"

"Captain, on this anniversary he visits a bend in the brook. He will come. I know him."

"If he really does——"

"I will wait for him at the brookside, Captain! He will drown by accident!"

"Hold on to yourself, Ehrlich! You're going wild. You look like a crazy man!"

"Captain, I am sane, I assure you."

"I don't know about that. You propose to drown him. The brook is shallow as a dishpan. I suppose you will hold him under till he quiets down, then you'll stand gaping at your work till the villagers pounce on you! Where's that touch of accident, to sweeten it up?"

Karl rubbed his forehead. "I need time to think this through."

"You've already thought it through—you don't realize how well. He doesn't have to go to the brook in broad daylight, does he? The anniversary would be just as tender after dark, and this time safer, wouldn't you say?"

Karl couldn't think of an answer. "He always comes to talk here afterward," he said aimlessly.

The captain laughed. "Well, sentiment is sentiment. Now, here are your orders—on Tuesday go about your work as usual, but don't set foot off this farm till I tell you."

"Very well, Captain."

There was a noise on the stair. Old Hans Ehrlich, fresh from his bed, was creeping down. The captain sprang up, one hand in his pocket.

"Karl," said his father, in the shaking ghost of a voice, "something is wrong. Look around the place before you come to bed. I know something is amiss."

Karl hurried up the staircase and shouted into his ear. "Go to bed, Father—nothing is wrong. Come on, I'll help you up."

"Eh? What was that you said?"

He turned the old man around, got him to his room, hurried back. "His eyes were on me," he reassured the captain. "He's half blind, anyway. He didn't see you."

"You're quite sure?"

"Quite."

"You have your orders for Tuesday?"

"Yes, Captain."

Till Tuesday! It was tedious waiting. Conscience gave him no pang—he merely wondered how the captain would work it out, the accidental part of it. He lost faith in the captain's ability to plan when he realized the gun had been carried off absent-mindedly. Even if his father had scared the visitor, the gun should have been remembered. But he was to see the captain on Tuesday; he would ask for the gun then.

Obeying orders, he stayed on the farm—in fact, clung to the house all day. At dusk old Hans was lifted up the stairs to his room. Karl lighted the lamp. The strain of waiting was terrible. He began to lose hope.

Without a knock the captain entered and shut the door quickly.

"Turn that lamp down!"

Karl turned it down.

"They are coming up the hill. They will be here at once."

"Who, Captain?"

"Listen to your orders! When you let them in, turn the lamp up again, as high as you can get it. I'll slip to the top of the stair, to keep your restless parent from interfering. They won't see me. Put them on the far side of the table where I can see them."

"You mean Heinrich?"

"There are more than we bargained for. Too late to turn back. We'll go through with it."

They heard voices and, in a few seconds, footsteps. The captain was at the top of the stairs.

"My pistol, Captain!"

"You won't need it till later."

When the knock came and he opened the door, Elizabeth left the support of Heinrich's arm, to step forward with her hands outstretched.

"Karl—true friend—you have saved us!"

Heinrich had said she was to have another child. She was near her time.

"Sit down, both of you—on the other side—the chairs are more comfortable."

"Karl dear, what a terrible day! He would come here for one of his memories——"

"More than a memory," struck in Heinrich, with something of the old spirit. "And I told you to stay home."

Elizabeth leaned forward. "He's fleeing for his life, Karl. I had to be with him."

Heinrich laughed. "She's timid about her irreplaceable husband, like all good wives. I left town, Karl, till our bright boys recover from a brain storm."

"But you know they are following you, Heinrich!"

"My dear," said he, "you are safe." From an inside pocket he took a gun and laid it on the table before him. The sight of it had neither surprise nor terror for Elizabeth.

"I knew we were safe at least for this night when we got Karl's message."

Karl tried to think. "My what?"

"The message the boy whispered, at the brook."

"What boy?"

Heinrich's fingers moved toward his gun. "He said you had sent him, Karl—we were to come here—for the sake of old times——"

In the small kitchen the captain's pistol was deafening. Elizabeth shrieked. The pistol spoke again. The captain came down the stairs, without haste.

"We are indebted to you, Lieutenant. The accident practically arranges itself. You both loved her. The rival who loses must have his revenge. They exasperated you, coming to your house. Your target practice has been conscientious—and public. My pistol—yours—it should be in your hand—has two empty shells. This pistol—his—should have one——"

Old Hans Ehrlich was awakened by what seemed an explosion. He thought he heard a scream and another loud noise, but he wasn't sure. He got his door open in time to hear a third shot, and then, oddly enough, the front door slammed. He was sure of that because it shook the stair tread under his bare feet.

Three quiet figures were stretched on the kitchen floor, a woman and two men. Each of the men grasped in his right hand a gun.

THE FIFTH COMMANDMENT

Honor thy father
and thy mother

BRUNO FRANK

V

HONOR THY FATHER AND THY MOTHER

A STORY BY

BRUNO FRANK

BARBARA piled the neat little farewell gifts into the basket of her bicycle, put the bouquet of fresh-cut flowers on top, and set out to look for Heinrich. She looked in the streets of the small town, then out among the ripening fields, and finally up in the forest, in the clearing which she knew had always been his favorite spot.

But she did not find him. It seemed almost as if he were eluding her, even today, the day of his return to the front. As she started out again, it occurred to her that she had spent the best part of her short span of years in search of Heinrich. Slowly, listlessly, not really hoping any longer, she pedaled on.

Her bicycle was a handsome machine, obviously brand-new. The frame was blue and white like the June sky overhead, the hubs and spokes gleamed in the sunlight, and the reflector in the back sparkled like a giant ruby.

Her father had brought the bicycle back with him recently from Holland; Barbara's brothers and her mother received one apiece just like hers, each in a different color, gay and bright and shining. In the conquered countries gifts like these were dirt cheap—for Germans; the power of the Reichswehr and the power of the reichsmark swept along side by side. Everything, of course, was purchased in orderly fashion—none of it was booty. "Looters will be shot on the spot," her father had once declared. And his word was law. For Obersturmbannführer Erwin Bretschneider was ordained, by virtue of his position, to be a powerful reflection of the Führer's infallibility.

So Barbara and her mother, their consciences clear and untroubled, went about as living symbols of the might of German geopolitics: in homespun spring coats from Austria, in gay blouses from Serbia, in shoes from Bohemia, in stockings from Lyon, and, in winter, in fur caps from Poland. Their handbags were decorated with runic patterns from Norway. For Obersturmbannführer Bretschneider had official business in all these countries. He never spent more than a few days at home, and then orders would already be in his pocket to take a plane to Oslo, Sofia, Paris, or Brussels.

Barbara had circled the little town on her bicycle and arrived at the station. It was not at all impossible that Heinrich was already on his train, without having bothered to say good-by to her.

The waiting room and the platform swarmed with soldiers. There was something in the air again. Barbara had heard people say that with the Balkans and Greece already conquered, according to schedule, it was now Russia's turn. England, as everybody knew, was tottering, completely stunned and stupefied by the blows of the Luftwaffe. Obviously, this was the moment to turn east. People, it was true, did not dance in the streets, or shout, "On to Moscow! To Moscow!" They just said, "This time it's Moscow," much as a peasant would speak of a section of new land for his day's plowing. As soon as Russia was taken care of, England would be put out of its misery, and then the Reich would proceed across the sea to finish its foreordained task of world conquest. It would be silly—in fact, childish—to worry about things like that ahead of time.

She looked among the waiting soldiers, but did not find Heinrich. Then, as she pushed her bicycle out of the station, she suddenly came face to face with her father.

Herr Bretschneider was sitting in an open Mercedes, his adjutant beside him. He wore his black uniform, the silver skull-and-bones glittering on his visored cap.

"I'm glad you're here," her father said. He took off his pince-nez, brought it in front of his small, round mouth, and breathed on each spotlessly clear surface. Then he carefully rubbed the glasses against the fine black cloth of his sleeve.

"Go home and tell your mother and grandmother that I didn't have time to say good-by. I'm taking the twelve-o'clock plane on official business."

"I can't go home now," said Barbara. "I have to go out to the villages."

In the Bretschneider household "going out to the villages" meant going the rounds of the neighboring peasants, foraging for butter, eggs, lard, or cheese. Less important families were liable to severe punishment for such black-market purchases.

"To the villages, then," Herr Bretschneider said, his glasses still in his hand. Perhaps he only took them off so that he would not see that flower-decked basket with its packages. He never really liked to see too much, particularly when it concerned his family. He could be conveniently blind upon occasion. It particularly pleased him to be small of stature, and thus relieved of the necessity of looking taller men in the eye. As a criminologist, he held no brief for staring a suspect down. One could rely on a man's intuition, his sense of touch and smell, his memory, his reasoning, and his routine. Those were enough.

There was nothing military in Bretschneider's appearance. The Obersturmbannführer—the rank was equivalent to that of a lieutenant colonel—had a pale-gray, soft, flabby face, with the sensitive features of a romantic bureaucrat. He had a profound passion for his work, for a few domestic animals, for the beauty of the human body, and for the Party. He hated noises of all kinds—shooting, cursing, even a loud answer were enough to disturb him intensely. "Must we have that?" he would ask on such occasions, smoldering with fury. His hands were very small, white, and delicate—quite feminine, in fact. He liked to look at them when he was going through his papers, which contained accounts of incredible gruesomeness.

"You couldn't possibly go home, then?" he asked quietly. "Must you go out to the villages *right now?*"

"Yes, right now, right this minute!" Barbara shouted excitedly.

"You don't have to shout like that. I just wanted to let Mother and Grandmother know . . ."

"They don't get upset any more when you go away. Are you flying to Russia?"

He smiled vaguely. He knew—and Barbara sensed that he knew—what it was she really wanted to find out. She was not in the least interested in where *he* was going.

"Of course they don't get upset any more," he agreed calmly. "It's only that this time I might be away longer than usual. So I'll just say good-by to you, daughter. See that you always do your duty!"

He took off his pince-nez and breathed on it once more. For he happened to glance at the flower-decked basket again, and also at his daughter's almost-sixteen-year-old breasts bursting under the confinement of her embroidered Serbian blouse.

"Well—behave yourself! And make yourself useful. Try to think of other things besides eating. You look exceptionally well fed to me."

The adjutant beside him laughed dutifully, but the Obersturmbannführer's face remained grave.

He ceremoniously pulled on his fine Italian gloves.

"Remember—make yourself useful!" he repeated, and looked away from Barbara's gleaming white throat with distaste. Then he raised his arm negligently in the Party salute, and appeared to have completely forgotten her.

Barbara's face flushed. She glanced at the station clock, got on her bicycle, and started off in the direction from which she had come. She decided to try just once more.

At the edge of the forest stood a small chapel with a statue of the Holy Virgin before it. Barbara had never paid any attention to it before. Neither in school nor at home had it ever been hinted to her that there was anything more to such a figure than a piece of clay, some fading colors, and a bit of flaking silver-and-gold leaf.

Today she stopped in front of it. She took her flowers, which were really meant for Heinrich, and put them at the feet of the Madonna. It was shocking behavior for the daughter of the Obersturmbannführer. She did not even know why she did it—whether to plead for Heinrich's safe return from the front or simply to ask that she find him in the forest clearing.

She was an attractive child; pretty according to the new Germany's race-conscious standards of feminine beauty. She was blonde, with narrow cheekbones and light-blue eyes. Though not tall, she was well proportioned, her young body sport-hardened and vigorous, with firm shoulders, arms, and breasts. She was perhaps a little strained by her duties and by the drilling she had to undergo as a member of the "Bund of German Girls" and also as the daughter of an important family. But she gave herself no airs and was fundamentally pleasant and friendly.

She was well liked in the little town. Which was nothing short of a miracle, because her family was quite thoroughly hated, envied, and feared—feared most of all. The townspeople tried to persuade each other that the Obersturmbannführer and his two sons were a source of pride and honor to the community so they themselves would not seem quite so pitiful as they really were.

Barbara was liked not because anyone detected a tendency toward revolt in her. That was, in fact, quite out of the question. From earliest childhood she had been exposed to nothing but the ideology of the new Germany. Her father had belonged to various patriotic organizations long before the Third Reich came into power—in fact, when he was still a student in the gymnasium. Then, while yet almost a boy, he had joined the National Socialists. So Barbara spoke and thought only the approved—and the permissible—words and thoughts, just as children in all countries say and think only the things they hear from their parents and their teachers. She had learned her lessons well: German Language, German History, German Geopolitics, German Race Theory. And it never occurred to her to think anything but that

—this is how it is, this is what must be done, this is important, otherwise they would not teach it to me.

She knew that in no other country were things so perfect as in Germany, and that only after the Germans arrived could things be improved in the other lands of the earth. She knew that the inhabitants of a number of neighboring countries had been ordained by fate to become Germany's slaves, and she had no objections. The important thing was that Heinrich and herself and the children that would someday be born to them should belong to the masters and not to the slaves.

When Fräulein Mittelmann, instructor in Race Theory, called her at least once a week "a perfect example of the Nordic-Germanic master race," she was as modestly pleased as a child who is praised for good behavior. She served as a race exhibit to the class. They took the dimensions of her face, and examined the structure of her body and her extremities. It was all pretty boring, and sometimes Barbara could not help yawning, or she would giggle when some of the girls, during these anthropological researches, engaged in a little secret tickling. But since it was her duty, she would stand obediently before her ungainly teacher, in her "eugenic clothes," which consisted of a pair of shorts and a sheer net blouse.

She found everything that went on about her perfectly natural. It never occurred to her, for instance, to object in the slightest when a year ago her class took action against Herr Ebbinghaus, the history teacher. During a discussion of the Treaty of Versailles, this Ebbinghaus had been guilty of incredible objectivity; he had had the effrontery to point out that, when the Führer undertook to free Germany from the yoke of that shameful document, none of its decrees were in force any longer. Such willful deception could not remain unpunished. The class had unanimously denounced Herr Ebbinghaus. He had subsequently disappeared from the school, and no one ever heard from him again.

Such things happened every day. And they naturally did not stop short of the family. Barbara knew a half-dozen girls in her class who had reported their fathers or mothers or both because they had heard critical opinions expressed at the dinner table, or because their parents were guilty of secret trafficking with Jews or Socialists or other enemies.

The guilty parents were put in concentration camps. The families were ruined. But that could not be helped. Barbara knew where the solemn duty of German youth lay. German youth was but an instrument in the hands of the Führer for the reconstruction of the future. German boys and girls were his tools. All other considerations were relegated to the background.

She herself was naturally above such inner conflicts, above them as few children had the good fortune to be. Her family, particularly her father, represented the political ideology of the Führer in its purest form.

Barbara had other things on her mind.

She pushed her bicycle past the chapel, up along the forest path toward the clearing, slowly, not really hoping any more. But then she saw him, lying in the shade.

He was sprawled out on his back in his brand-new uniform. His eyes were shut.

She leaned her bike against a tree, tiptoed up to him, and began to muss up his thick, black hair. He paid no attention.

"Dead?" she asked.

Heinrich nodded.

She listened to his heart, just over the Iron Cross on his breast.

"It's still beating, though."

"Not much longer. It's coming."

"What's coming?"

"We're marching on Moscow. And we're singing: 'Give me then your pale white hand, hand, hand, For we're marching, for we're marching, westward now to Engelland.' There's a Russian waiting on the roof of the Kremlin—he raises his gun to his shoulder, and shoots me straight through the heart."

"And he hits me," she said. "Because I, Barbara Bretschneider, am in there."

"Where'd you get such ideas? You're not in there."

"Oh, I'm not? Well, then, who is? That lousy Germaine, perhaps, in the Rue Saint-Honoré?"

"Perhaps."

"Or that Fietje in Antwerp with her wooden shoes?"

"Possibly."

"Or that Marushka or Morazka, or whatever her name is, that you fished out of the Struma River?"

Heinrich grabbed her by the arms, hurting them.

"Nobody's in it—they're not, and you're not."

"Let me go!" she shouted angrily, trying to free herself from his grip.

"And there's nothing inside your heart, either," he went on, "or inside any other heart in Germany. This isn't a country for hearts. And when I kiss you like this, then I'm kissing you *without* my heart, just as I've kissed all those Germaines and Fietjes."

He pressed her to him and kissed her wildly.

"Not that it gives me any particular pleasure," he burst out. "What is there to such a baby mouth, with all of *Festung* Europe full of ripe women ready and eager to welcome German soldiers?"

Using all her might, she finally freed herself.

"Now you're being hateful—I can't stand you when you're being hateful!"

She knew and feared these outbreaks of somber cynicism in him, and her eyes filled with tears. She grabbed him by the shoulders, shaking him as though she wanted to bring him to his senses.

"Heinrich, this is our last day together! Why do you act this way?"

"Because I just can't stand you, that's all."

She suddenly became very quiet, straightened her dress, and sat down on the green moss.

"Yes, you say that as if it were a joke. But it's true. You really can't stand me. I've been running after you ever since I was eight years old. No—don't interrupt! I have to come out with it some time."

She looked at him gravely.

"You were always the best in everything in the Hitler *Jugend.* They all looked up to you. And if it hadn't been for your family you would have gone to the Führer School, perhaps even to the Braunschweiger Academy. I admit I ran after you. But when I tried to talk to you at night in the *Jugendheim,* you pushed me away."

"Of course. Why should the future Führer, Heinrich Keller, bother with an eight-year-old snit?"

"All right. Then why did you change all of a sudden? Why did you become so charming and sweet overnight?"

"Obviously," he said, "because in the meantime you had turned into a ripe young woman of nine."

"Because you wanted something from me! I've suspected it all along."

"Right," he said simply, looking at her. "I wanted something."

"I've suspected something else too, Heinrich. You aren't really a good German, the way you ought to be, and you aren't really a good soldier, and you weren't even a good Hitler Youth—deep inside, you weren't! You've been putting on an act, you've been putting on an act for our benefit—even today, in the middle of the war, you're putting on a comedy. Because your heart, Heinrich, certainly isn't 'empty.' It's just that the right things aren't in it. No Barbara, nor even a Fietje or a Germaine, has room in your heart—because there's a man in it."

"Naturally," he agreed with a scornful smile, raising his arm. "*Heil* our . . ."

"You know very well whom I mean! And because that man was in a concentration camp at the time—you suddenly started to be nice to me."

"Ah?"

"Yes. Because you wanted my mother to put in a good word for him. You worked away at it like a mouse gnawing at a net until your lion was free again. Then as soon as you got what you wanted, that was the end of your feverish industry in the Hitler *Jugend.*

And now, ever since the war started, you've been saying the strangest things . . ."

"And I pay no attention to you again. Right you are, Barbara. The only thing worrying me is how to get away from you. Listen—I'll tell you a secret: the reason I did everything to persuade Chamberlain and Daladier to attack our beloved fatherland was so that I could be sent to Poland—as far away from you as possible. If you look at it that way, the whole history of the world becomes quite simple."

She laughed a little, and put her arms around his neck.

"Must we fight all the time?" she said tenderly.

"You're right. We're wasting time."

He took her in his arms for an endless kiss.

"Heinrich," she whispered as soon as she caught her breath, "you know that I don't care for anything in the whole wide world—all I really want is you. We'll be married as soon as you're back from Moscow. Then I'll be fit and we'll have children—racially perfect children."

"Stop talking nonsense!"

"Why is it nonsense?"

"Forget about it—all that business about marriage and your racially perfect children. If I ever do come back, then we can kiss each other again, Barbara. And one day perhaps even more. But you couldn't marry the son of a man who spent six years in a concentration camp."

"What do I care about that!" she snapped angrily. "What difference does it make to me what your father committed!"

"I've already told you that my father 'committed' nothing."

"Heinrich—people don't spend six years in camp for nothing."

He sat up straight and looked at her gravely.

"Now, you listen to me! I don't want to hear you talk about my father as if he were a criminal. He was the greatest man in town when he was the rector of the old gymnasium. All the men your father's age used to sit at his feet, and whatever they knew they learned from him. And now—it's shameful the way he has to grub and scrape, peddling postage stamps. I send him all I can out of my pay, and I still don't know how he manages to keep from starving."

"Perhaps," said Barbara, "the seven dwarfs leave a little package in front of his door once in a while."

"So it was you," he said, looking away from her. His cheeks were burning. After a while he went on more quietly.

"Nobody knows how long this thing in the east is going to last, or if we're ever going to get back. That's why I want to tell you what my father 'committed.' For a whole decade he watched the struggle between the National Socialists and the Leftists. Finally he couldn't stand it any longer, and at the next election he ran for office on a democratic platform. That was just before the New Order took over. You couldn't call him cautious, not my father! He made bitter, caustic speeches, attacking not only National Socialism in general, but also the Führer in person—the way Demosthenes attacked Philip—but you wouldn't understand about ancient Greeks like that."

"I certainly wouldn't, thank heaven. But I do understand this much—your father did 'commit' something. If he really was as great a man as you say, then he must have known perfectly well that only the Führer could save Germany."

"Possibly," said Heinrich. "Perhaps he really understood the ancient Greeks and their politics better than he did the times he lived in. But the National Socialists certainly didn't make it any easier for him to understand. They murdered his best friend."

"Who was that?"

Heinrich did not reply at once. He hugged his knees, his eyes staring into the green of the forest.

"A relative of yours," he said finally.

"Of mine?"

"The Obersturmbannführer's father. Your grandfather Bretschneider."

"But he died on the battlefield."

"He did?"

"At Verdun. Grandmother told me herself."

"Your grandmother is a frightened old lady who is even more afraid of her own son than the rest of the people in this town are —and that's saying a lot. She tells you what your father orders her to say. No, Barbara. Your grandfather died years after the war."

"But where could he have died? With one of the Free Corps? In Oberschlesien? In the Ruhr valley?"

"Right here! Not two miles away from here he was tried by the *Feme,* the secret court, and they beat him to death right then and there. It was gang murder, to put it plainly."

"But why?" Barbara asked, staring before her.

"Yes, why! Why is a man murdered by that unholy inquisition? Because he once belonged to the Party and because he quit." He looked at her evenly. "And it was my father who made him quit."

"Your father. That's great!"

"Great or not—both of them paid for it, those two intellectuals. Your grandfather was fished out of the lake near the Marheineke estate, his skull bashed in."

"I swam in it yesterday," she said with a shudder.

"And then, when the Party came to power eleven years later, they got even with my father, that vicious criminal. So now you know, my darling, why he is so deep in my heart."

They were quiet for a long time.

"Let's not talk about it again, ever," Barbara finally said, her voice hoarse and heavy.

"Very well. We're just spoiling our last day together. Who knows how long I'll be away this time."

She looked at him anxiously. "Are you sure it's the Reds this time?"

"Positive."

"Why should that take a long time, Heinrich? Poland took sixteen days, France six weeks, Yugoslavia three days, Greece not much longer. Let's say this time it'll take as long as the others put together—July, August, September—in October you'll be in Moscow."

"Stop crying. A German girl doesn't cry!" Frau Bretschneider kept reminding Barbara in the weeks that followed. But the harshness with which she spoke did not sound quite genuine. It had a mechanical, unconvincing ring.

"Stop crying, you fool! There's no crying in Germany," said her younger brother, Heinz-Dieter, with the derisive harshness befitting his position. As a recognized member of the Hitler *Jugend,* he stood far above his sister in the Party hierarchy. He was a gangling, sharp-featured boy, whom nobody ever saw laughing. Since the beginning of the new offensive he was constantly sent on all sorts of secret missions which kept him out of town and away from home and school for days on end.

"Don't be such a baby," her grandmother would say to her gently. "Girls simply don't cry any more in Germany."

All of them were right, of course. No one in Germany had any reason to cry. Everything was going smoothly and according to schedule on the new front. After the border was crossed, the enemy showed immediate signs of disintegration and collapse; two weeks later he was calling on his last reserves, and soon the situation was so out of hand that the Soviet military leaders did not even know where their own front lines were. This state of affairs continued through the lovely, crisp days of September. By the tenth of October, the battle in the east was as good as finished; by the twelfth, the annihilation of the Red Army was an accomplished fact—so that by the fourteenth, fifteenth, and sixteenth of October things in the east could be relied on to take care of themselves.

It was strange, therefore, and rather annoying, that with so much land for Germans to conquer there was so little to eat. Ever since the beginning of the new campaign, food had suddenly become very scarce, and even an eminent family like the Bretschneiders had a hard time obtaining their necessities in the village black markets. This created a double problem for Barbara.

For the authorities had seen to it that Franz Keller, the former rector and present postage-stamp peddler, was always waited on last in the food stores. He would go away just as empty-handed as the few Jews and other such creatures who had, incredibly enough, managed to continue some sort of existence in the town. Herr Keller was so carefully watched that Barbara no longer dared to place her packages in front of his door herself; instead she sent them through an old town character named Stiemel. Stiemel had once been a Social Democrat, but now was a sort of superannuated errand boy for the Party.

Once a week, on her way to school, she would secretly meet the old man at the edge of town. They met where the main street ran into the express highway connecting the small town with Nuremberg in one direction and with Leipzig in the other.

It was early in the morning, scarcely daylight. A November wind was whipping away at the torn decorations of the triumphal arch which had been somewhat prematurely erected on this spot at the time of the French collapse, when everyone expected England to come to its senses and make peace with the new Germany. But England did not make peace, and the soldiers did not return home to march through the triumphal arch. And now the November rain was pouring across its grandiose inscription, weeping red and brown and silver tears down its face.

Barbara waited in her long, warm coat and sturdy shoes, with the Polish fur cap on her head. Under her arm she held her brief case, with the parcel of food for the outcast inside it. Stiemel was late. Trucks full of workingmen on their way to the country went past her. The men called out to her coarsely. When the old man finally came, she slipped the package to him and pressed some money in his hand.

"Listen," she whispered, as though someone might overhear her, even out here, "ask the rector if *he* heard anything from Heinrich. Tell him I didn't get a line since August. And be sure you're here again next Thursday!"

She came home from school every day, her hopes mingled with fears. Maybe the mailman had brought a letter from Heinrich. Or maybe one day he would bring back one of her own letters, with the envelope marked "Killed in Action." Letters like that were arriving often now.

She did not know that, before leaving, her father had had two conversations that had a direct bearing on her correspondence with Heinrich. One was with the postmaster and the other with the local chief of the censorship bureau. The Obersturmbannführer of the Gestapo expressed a wish which, under the circumstances, was an order. He asked that the letters between his daughter and the son of Franz Keller, the former convict, be held back, in the unlikely event that the eastern campaign might last beyond the month of August. The letters were to be delivered to his secretary, who would call for them from Headquarters from time to time.

The Bretschneider home was in a charming wooded section near the railroad embankment. It had once belonged to a Jewish manufacturer who made a hobby of collecting French impressionists. He was the only person in town who thought them beautiful. After his home, his factory, and all his worldly goods were confiscated, he was granted permission to take his decadent paintings abroad with him. It was later learned that the paintings were incredibly valuable, and the official who was—perhaps not unbribed—responsible for such regrettable laxity was subsequently given a thorough tongue lashing.

The Obersturmbannführer obtained the house from the state through a transaction which was more a token payment than an actual purchase. It had actually been confiscated from the art-loving manufacturer with this end in view. Where the Van Goghs and Pissarros had once hung, the walls were now bedecked with framed copies of *Mein Kampf* surrounded with antlers and buffalo horns. These had been bought in dozen lots, since the dreaded Gestapo chief had a deep antipathy to hunting.

He made other changes too. The gallery, which had been decorated in the Italian style, was redone in dark, heavy oak paneling. It was now his study, and its huge dimensions recalled Mussolini's famous audience chamber in the Palazzo Venezia. To anyone entering the room, the outlines of the great man were vague in the distance, and if the caller felt thoroughly intimidated, made an ass of himself, and, if possible, tripped once or twice in the deep, soft folds of the carpet as he made his way toward the desk, the Obersturmbannführer considered the arrangement successful.

Herr Bretschneider profoundly disliked daylight. He felt comfortable only when he could convince himself that it was really evening or night, preferably a dark midnight. He had a thick row of firs planted outside, along the entire length of the room, so that electric lights had to be on all the time. The Obersturmbannführer, his adjutant, and his secretary did all their work by artificial light, at three desks placed at right angles to each other.

At this time, during Bretschneider's official absence, all the drawers of these desks, as well as the built-in files around them, were carefully locked. A large safe was concealed behind the central panel of the long wall, and that, too, was always kept locked. The secretary would occasionally come down from Headquarters, and at such times he had access to all these secrets. The keys were on a chain which he buried in his innermost pocket—and probably even took to bed with him.

During the months her father was away, no one in the family ever entered the gloomy study except Barbara. She came because in front of the oaken panel which concealed the safe there stood a radio.

It was a powerful long- and short-wave set which could tune in any station in the world. Listening to foreign broadcasts was punishable by death in the Third Reich. This, of course, did not apply to a high officer of the Gestapo, such as Herr Bretschneider; in fact, one of his duties was to keep his ears to the ground. Barbara could tune in on London, Sydney, or New York with equal ease and clarity. Although she understood a little English, she was not in the least interested in the broadcasts emanating from the Anglo-Saxon world. What kept her, for hours on end, tense with anticipation and anxiety in front of the polished cabinet were the German-language broadcasts from Soviet Russia.

She both feared and hoped that one day she would hear Heinrich Keller's name over the radio. She did not really believe that it would happen, but it was not impossible, since one of the tricks of Russian propaganda was to pick individual cases for their broadcasts. "Inhabitants of the city of Gotha," they would say, "the infantry battalion which was once stationed in your city has been completely annihilated." Or they might say, "Bürgermeister Struve of the town of Bitterfeld, the last of your three sons has today given his life for your Führer." Once—she had not heard it herself, but she knew about it—her father and her elder brother were also mentioned, as two particularly vicious beasts who had been tried and condemned to death by Moscow. She would often wake up in the middle of the night, haunted by the fear of missing the crucial moment, and would slip, barefooted, into the study. Out in the night, she could hear the endless lines of freight trains rolling toward the east. And at any moment a calm voice might say over the radio:

"Barbara Bretschneider, daughter of Obersturmbannführer Bretschneider, today we found your letters on the mangled corpse of your sweetheart, Heinrich Keller." Or: "Your gravely wounded fiancé, Heinrich Keller, has been deliriously calling your name for days." Or—oh, wondrous hope: "Your fiancé, Heinrich Keller, was one of the nine thousand captured by the Red Army this week. He sends you his love and assures you that he receives good treatment in Soviet captivity."

That was the way Barbara thought it would sound, though the chances were one in a million. But the radio never told her what had happened to him.

Actually he was shot down by a machine-gun bullet during the fighting in the Ukraine. The bullet passed right through him, two inches above his navel. But he lived. Because he had enough strength left to open the package of crystallized sulfa preparation and to sprinkle his wound with the miraculous healing powder. A little later, at the German field dressing station, they gave him a similar drug to drink in great quantities of water. Three days later his condition was so improved that he was put on a comfortable hospital train and shipped off to Rumania.

But Barbara listened in vain. She did not know that right there beside her, inside the safe, were all the letters she had written to Heinrich, carefully bundled, tied and sealed, and marked in the secretary's handwriting, "Private—Highly Confidential." All of them were there, and so were his letters to her. There was no talk of kissing, of "running after" one another, of other women, in these letters of hers. They were desperate calls of love and longing, the gropings of one lost in loneliness, and made honest and sincere by the imminence of death. There they were, stifling behind the oak-covered steel wall, a foot away from her desperately straining ear.

Herr Bretschneider had never been away from home so long. Finally, toward the end of February, 1942, he returned home. He wore two new, very high decorations, had been promoted to "Standartenführer," and obtained a ten-day furlough on the basis of this advancement.

The "coldest Russian winter in centuries," as the German papers called it, had not bothered him too much. He usually performed his duties in well-heated rooms, and when, upon occasion, he had to be outdoors, he bundled himself in a warm fur coat. Nevertheless, a noticeable change had come over him. His small, soft hands, holding his knife and fork at the table, trembled slightly. Also his vocal cords appeared to be functioning under difficulty, so that his voice, though not exactly hoarse, sounded heavy and lifeless. The women of the household could not help noticing these symptoms. But Barbara was the only one to notice a more subtle change in her father. For she was an intelligent, observant child, in spite of the fact that everything in her upbringing was designed to prevent her from thinking.

From her father's sparing remarks about the war and politics, Barbara was unable to discern any real concern over the fact that the Soviet armies had so completely upset the plans of the Führer and his General Staff, and that all of the Führer's basic designs were utterly destroyed.

And she heard quite right. Naturally her father was too intelligent not to recognize the dangers Germany faced. The entrance of the United States into the war, particularly, was not to be lightly dismissed. But like so many other men who had witnessed the dizzy rise of that man, Herr Bretschneider was unable to suppress an inner delight that, at long last, something had happened to stop that astronomical ascent. It was an illogical attitude to take, since his own interests were inextricably interwoven with the Führer's. Yet there it was.

Of course, none of this kept him from performing his official and patriotic duties with the greatest zeal. He had, during the past three years, in various European countries—most recently in the Ukraine—ordered the execution of more than fifty thousand people.

His personal sensitiveness was, however, not affected in the slightest, and he was looking forward with painfully mixed emotions to the forthcoming interview with his daughter. On the fourth day after his arrival he had ordered her to appear before him in his study.

Adjutant Schilling opened the door for Barbara and withdrew. She walked slowly, reluctantly, toward her barely visible father, her eyes not on him, but on the life-size photograph of the Führer. It hung in the middle of the wall over his head, flanked right and left by buffalo horns. She did not trip on the soft carpet and held herself well as she halted in front of his desk.

Herr Bretschneider did not begin to talk at once. He occasionally glanced down at his small hands, trembling slightly as they played with a broken bayonet tip. For although his nervous system abhorred any loud act of violence in his presence, or shooting, or even hunting, he took a keen and knowing interest in weapons and in all sorts of military booty. His desk was full of them.

"You know, of course," he finally began, his heavy voice weighted with sentimental overtones, "that our fatherland demands the sacrifice of a great many human lives in this war. Our losses must be replaced by our women, and by you young girls. Your country is counting on you. You understand that, my child, don't you?"

"I understand," said Barbara.

"You have reached the prescribed age, and you fulfill the requirements. The Führer, the Party, and the fatherland expect you now to become a mother."

"Very well, Father," said Barbara politely.

Herr Bretschneider put down the bayonet tip and picked up a round disk which looked like the face of an alarm clock. A Russian booby trap had been hidden behind that disk, and its explosion had taken a German life which would have to be replaced by Barbara.

"I expected no other answer from my daughter. You may discuss the details with your mother."

And he nodded, indicating that for him the interview was ended.

"I prefer to discuss these 'details' with you," said Barbara. "You see, to me these details are the only things that matter."

Herr Bretschneider screwed up his face, as though he were suffering from neuralgia.

"Very well, if you insist. In a few days, while I am still home, you're going to marry my friend and fellow Party member, Paul Runze. You know him well. He is a Party member of the highest standing, in charge of carrot and sugar distribution for this region. He's a wealthy man. Yesterday he asked for your hand for the third time."

"Did he?" said Barbara. "I have to tell you, Father, that this doesn't interest me in the slightest. I am not going to marry the renowned Party member, Herr Runze. I am going to marry Heinrich Keller."

Once more Herr Bretschneider looked as if he had seen enough of his daughter. He took off his pince-nez, breathed on the lenses, wiped them clean, then put them down on his desk with a decisive gesture.

"That's just like you," he pronounced. "I return home after months of nerve-racking service, and my daughter's greeting is not, 'How are you, Father?' but: 'Have you heard anything of this—what's his name—Heinrich Keller?' I'm not likely to forget that soon."

"I said hello to you, Father, and I kissed you," Barbara said very softly. "Only then did I ask whether you happened to know where Heinrich was stationed."

"My child, as you know, there are many millions of German soldiers at the front. How many millions is a military secret. I couldn't possibly keep track of every private, or noncom, or whatever he is. And it so happens I don't even know this particular fellow. I do recall, however, that his father is a prisoner in a concentration camp."

"His father *was* in a camp," she corrected him.

"Right. I remember he was freed before his time at the instigation of my three ladies. Well, then, this Heinrich has obviously not written to you for some time. Which leads us to the probability that he has found himself another sweetheart, in a place like Odessa or Kiev, which are full of delightful girls—or perhaps he's been killed in action."

Barbara choked back a sob. Herr Bretschneider raised his head.

"I hope you aren't crying," he said quietly, sharply, and for the first time his voice had the tone with which he pronounced his death sentences. "A German girl doesn't cry."

Barbara quickly rubbed her index finger along the side of her nose.

"I am not crying, Father. I just have a cold. A German girl may have a cold. And furthermore, if a German girl has faithfully served her Führer and the Party at all times, and if she has been outstanding in the performance of her duties, then she certainly doesn't have to marry Herr Paul Runze."

"Oh, she doesn't!" said Herr Bretschneider, his face turning red with anger, something which seldom happened to him.

"No, she doesn't," said Barbara. "That sort of thing is no longer tolerated. We young National Socialists do not permit ourselves to be peddled off by the older generation. The man I want is a good soldier. He received a promotion after every campaign, and he came back from battle with the Iron Cross, First Class. None of my letters have come back marked 'Killed in Action,' so I have reason to believe that he is well, and that when he returns he will give me racially perfect children, better ones than Herr Runze ever could, with his pig's face and his swollen lips. If you try to force me to marry him, I'll know what to do. I'll write to the State Youth Führer in Berlin and also to the Bureau of Health. Then we'll see what happens!"

She was waiting for his reply, braced for battle. But the battle did not materialize. The Standartenführer did not raise his voice to remind his daughter of the dictates of the fifth commandment. Nothing was so emphatically, so furiously, denied by the new state, nothing was so violently stamped out of the heart of German youth as filial devotion. The schools and Party organizations deliberately fashioned the youth of the nation into a mortal weapon against an older generation which had its roots in a different ideology, and which was therefore not to be relied upon. "Honor thy father and thy mother"—to the ears of German boys and girls the words had a feeble-minded, idiotic, in fact, a treasonable quality. Today's commandment was: "Honor thy Führer and thy state, and sacrifice to them thy parents. Spy upon them, for they are suspect, watch them, threaten them. Report them—that is not only permitted; it is thy duty. Deliver them unto bondage, to the lash of the gaoler, or unto the hangman. Thou canst not, if it serves thy Party and thy state, commit an injustice to thy father and thy mother."

The grotesque irony of this situation was that the threatened father himself personified the Party and the state. Report him? Appeal against him to a machine wherein he was an important cog? In his time, Herr Bretschneider had obeyed to the letter the National Socialist commandment regarding his filial duties. There was in his past a very dark chapter—a very bright one from the point of view of the new morality—which really had started him on his career.

He did not answer his daughter. He seemed to have forgotten her presence. He had put on his pince-nez again, and he was soon engrossed in the tremendous facts contained in the documents before him.

His leave came to an end on the appointed day. Only his wife was on hand to see him off. Barbara was in school, and the younger son was off on one of those secret missions which were occupying more and more of his time.

The Mercedes stood in front of the house, and Adjutant Schilling was holding the door open. Herr Bretschneider came out of the house and stopped on top of the stairs.

"Oh, yes," he said casually, "and if Barbara doesn't want to, she naturally doesn't have to marry my good friend, Runze. I don't believe in forcing my daughter into her own happiness."

He brushed his wife's cheek lightly in something resembling a kiss, pulled on his no-longer-new Italian gloves, marched stiffly down the stairs without looking back, and drove off.

A few weeks later Herr Bretschneider's secretary came down from Headquarters. He busied himself for two days in the study and, just before his departure, gave Barbara a note from his chief.

It opened with the salutation, "Dear daughter," and closed with the words "Your loving father," but the rest of it was written in the cold, dry tone in which he gave orders to his subordinates. Barbara, the note said, was to present herself on such and such a date at a designated office in Berlin, where she would be given further orders. She was to take along clothing and other necessities for a stay of three months' duration.

Neither her mother nor her grandmother had any idea what the whole thing was about. They assumed that because of her excellent schoolwork Barbara had probably been selected for some special course of study. And they thought no more about it. After all, children belonged more to the state than to their family. It was not enough to be resigned to this change; it was supposed to be welcomed with pride and joy.

As for Barbara herself, she had no objections. She was glad at a chance to get out of the dark and dreary house. Particularly to get away from the radio, for it had become an obsession. If there was any place where she could hear about Heinrich, it certainly was Berlin, the nerve center of war information.

She had a long talk with old Stiemel, her messenger, before she left, and he proved unexpectedly helpful and understanding. Then she packed cheerfully and left cheerfully.

•

Herr Bretschneider and his adjutant drove up before a hospital deep in the mountains of Transylvania. It was in the middle of a forest, high above the cascading waters of the Prahova River. The place was near the Castle Sinaia, which had been the summer residence of the King of Rumania before he made his escape.

Herr Bretschneider was announced. The head of the hospital, Dr. Gaukelmann, met him in the hall and led him into his study. In civilian life the doctor had been chief of the surgical division of the State Hospital in Breslau. He was a large, heavy-set man with the vast face of an elephant, from which two tiny, gray eyes blinked wisely and distrustfully behind his tremendous nose.

From the very first moment Herr Bretschneider was certain that Dr. Gaukelmann was an idiot. Idiots were always wasting his time.

The doctor was carrying on at great length about the great advances in his science. "Basically," he declared, "these preparations are simply sulfa derivatives, with the addition of carbon, nitrogen, and oxygen in various proportions. By means of these we are able to save a great deal of valuable blood—German blood."

It sounded as if he meant this as a personal compliment to the

Standartenführer, and Herr Bretschneider acknowledged it rather impatiently.

"So is the enemy, unfortunately," he interjected.

The doctor stared ahead of him blankly, like a puzzled elephant. "I beg your pardon?" he finally said.

"So is the enemy, unfortunately," Herr Bretschneider repeated, rather sharply.

He usually let people finish what they had to say. But this scientific cretin was getting on his nerves. And in order to annoy the doctor, he proceeded to address him by his civilian title—a vexation for any German in uniform.

"I mean, Herr Professor," he went on, "that these new healing devices of yours carry their own dangers with them. I can visualize a future when our National Socialist state will have to support a veritable horde of unfit man power. They will have to be fed, housed, and paid for—who knows how long. The case of this Heinrich Keller is typical."

"Really—typical of what?" Dr. Gaukelmann asked with irritating stupidity.

"Typical of this, that we are otherwise employing a great deal of thought and energy toward ensuring ourselves a racially perfect generation in the future. Unfit human material of all ages is relentlessly eliminated—a benefit both to the state *and* to the material. And yet when it comes to our poor, long-suffering soldiers who have magnificently fulfilled their duty on the field of battle—we deprive them of this benefit."

"But they don't suffer!" cried Dr. Gaukelmann with eagerness. "And since Herr Standartenführer evinces a special interest in the case of Lieutenant Keller—that particular patient doesn't suffer at all. He's now on the way to recovery. Fortunately he had the strength, immediately after receiving his wound, to apply the preparation himself. Later we naturally were still faced with the possibility of peritonitis, but I'm now definitely able to reassure you, Herr Standartenführer: our patient is completely out of danger."

Herr Bretschneider stared at the elephant face with disgust.

"*My* patient is the state! Do you understand, Herr Professor? And my patient would only then be out of danger if you had sufficient patriotic and scientific courage to give that poor fellow with his stomach wound something that would put him thoroughly to sleep—a hefty dose of pantopon, for example. Thereby *my* patient would be spared many years of suffering."

Dr. Gaukelmann stared blankly at the broad white surface of the table before him.

"May I be permitted to remark, Herr Standartenführer, that in a few months Lieutenant Keller will be fit for front-line duty and furthermore that he will also be fit to marry and bring healthy children into the world—for the Führer and for our country."

Herr Bretschneider gave up. He snapped the catch of his left glove shut with unusual vehemence, snapped it open again, and shut it once more. Then he turned to go, without another word.

Dr. Gaukelmann whipped the door open for him and bowed obsequiously. Then he looked after the stiffly departing figure, and his face wore an expression of strange amusement. The doctor's fat, flabby stomach was secretly heaving, as though suppressing a laugh or a sob.

Adjutant Schilling was waiting outside in the Mercedes. He no longer looked like a man of twenty-eight, but like a man of fifty. He had dozed off over the secret reports lying on his knees. They drove off in the direction of Bucharest.

"Schilling," Herr Bretschneider was saying as the car sped along, "I tell you it's hopeless! Here we've been educating these people for ten years. And what's the result? Professor Dr. Gaukelmann from Breslau! Our young people may be insolent, but at least they understand what it's all about. The older generation is a pack of idiots. Here we went and chased the Jewish competition for these doctors out of the Reich. And what thanks do we get? They complain about having to work eighteen hours a day and that they're liable to fall asleep at the operating table." The Standartenführer looked as though every single bone in his body were aching. "My dear Schilling . . ."

The adjutant pulled himself together. "Yes, Herr Standartenführer?" He was forcing himself to keep his eyes open.

"Schilling—in the course of my duties I have made certain psychological observations. I always know. I don't need to see. I can sense the sort of look on their faces when my back is turned. I tell you—the Führer in his darkest hours is right: it's no use trying to do anything with the Germans. Superiority of German blood! It was a terrific idea. And it did wonders for us. But now it's turned sour. Schilling—you're not listening to me! You're sleeping with your eyes open! And with my secret report to the Reichsführer of the S.S. on your lap! That's typical. Henschke—driver!—are you asleep, too? No answer! Asleep at the wheel. They're all asleep, just like Gaukelmann. . . ."

Meanwhile, immediately after this visit, Heinrich Keller disappeared from the hospital, no one knew where. He was swallowed up by the seething mass of Balkan humanity. And Dr. Gaukelmann's days in the clear mountain air of the Rumanian forest were also numbered. A week later he was transferred to a hospital for contagious diseases in Poland. And there was little prospect of his ever going back unharmed to Breslau.

In the fall of 1942 Barbara returned home. When she was asked where she had been, she would only answer: "In the east." What had she learned? "A lot of things." How was the food? "Better than here."

Her mother did not question her much. She was very busy—her hands were full. Every day brought new cares to German families. And in addition to everything else, her husband's eminent position was constantly piling additional duties on Frau Bretschneider's shoulders. There were already clearsighted men in the Party who thought the day not far distant when German wives and girls would have to bear arms against the internal enemy, against those whose enthusiasm showed signs of waning.

Grandmother Bretschneider was overjoyed at her granddaughter's return. In fact, she looked upon it as a deliverance. True, there never had been a really close relationship between them; such a thing was inconceivable between a child of the Third Reich and a relic from the past. But Barbara had always been more friendly to her than the other members of the family, and her grandmother was pitifully grateful for this friendship.

During the last few months the old lady had suffered a great deal at the hands of her grandson, Heinz-Dieter. The Hitler Youth found a constant source of entertainment in treating her as though she were a "suspicious character." He spied upon her and searched her room in her presence, as though she were thin air. He examined her bed, her clothes, her linen, and left everything a shambles. He "confiscated under higher orders" her beautiful, ancient Lutheran Bible, her prize possession. Later he tossed it back to her with the remark that, as a special favor, she was permitted to keep the book until further notice.

One day at the dinner table he suddenly came out with the pronouncement that the old and senile should be looked upon as dangerous criminals who ought to be eliminated—after all, weren't they robbing the younger members of the state of food and clothing? There was no reason why death by gas in the "Hitler Chamber" should be reserved only for feeble-minded children, and not for the widows of certain men who, during their lifetime, were weak-minded enough to be in close friendship with inmates of concentration camps. This sort of thing was repeated with variations. Young Heinz-Dieter, with those sharp features that never smiled, was full of ideas.

But Barbara's home-coming turned out to be a disappointment for the old lady. Her granddaughter no longer paid any attention to her. She no longer paid attention to anything or anybody, for that matter. She just moped. She spent hours in front of the radio again—but not to listen to the Russians. This time she tuned in on dance music, preferably Viennese waltzes. Occasionally she would get up on her feet and go into a few hesitating dance steps on the soft carpet, as though she were trying to recall something half forgotten. But she would tire of it soon, and return to her place to listen lazily to the languorous melodies.

She scarcely opened her mouth. Like her brother Heinz-Dieter, she seemed to have forgotten how to laugh and smile.

"Barbara, don't you want to do something?" her mother would ask occasionally.

"No thank you. Others are doing quite enough."

"But our country asks all of us to do something."

"I've already done enough for our country."

Her mother was puzzled that no one paid any official attention to Barbara. No German girl these days, no matter how prominent her family was, could stay out of at least a half-dozen organizations. But not a soul paid any attention to Barbara. She no longer attended school, and her work at the "Bund of German Girls" seemed at an end. It was as if she were dead, as far as German officialdom was concerned.

Barbara had become perhaps even more lovely than before. Her shoulders, her arms, her breasts were fairly bursting with health. But in contrast to all this ripe roundness, her features were beginning to become sharp, and the cobalt blue of her eyes seemed hard and lifeless. When she started out for a walk, her steps would be lithe and supple for a while, then suddenly her grace would be gone, and she would just drag herself along. Somewhere out in the fields, or up in the forest, she would sink down on a rock or on a tree stump. She would break off a twig and beat the ground before her mechanically, until the dust rose from the earth and enveloped her.

Or she would walk on the streets, the bedraggled fur cap on her blonde head, her hands deep in the pockets of her neglected coat. She greeted no one and spoke to no one. When she met her former schoolmates she looked right past them. One Sunday noon in a quiet side street she bumped into old Stiemel, her former messenger. He stopped, took off his cap, and bowed his gray head deep before her as though he were a beggar asking for alms.

"What's the matter, Fräulein? Did you forget about our old rector?"

She did not answer. She walked around him and past him as though she had never seen him.

She came home late for dinner. Her father and her elder brother, Eberhard, had arrived unexpectedly and were at the dinner table.

No one stood up to greet her. And this time Barbara did not have any questions to ask her father. Herr Bretschneider reached his hand out to her negligently, and went on talking. Eberhard, in the green uniform of the Waffen S.S., stared at his sister with a dark, uneasy grin.

This Waffen S.S. was a newly created wartime unit of the Party, whose function at the front usually came only after a stronghold had been taken by the troops of the regular army. Then this elite guard would step into action, tear through the streets of the town with banners flying, gather those inhabitants who had been guilty of resistance, and hang them on the most prominent window ledges and balconies of the main street. Because of this the Waffen S.S. was better clothed and fed and higher paid than the fighting men of the army. Barbara's brother was a picture of well-being.

The Standartenführer, on the other hand, seemed to have definitely aged. His hands were fluttering away quite out of control. But he pretended to be in the best of moods and in great high spirits. Contrary to his custom, he spoke at length about the war and about politics; and, for the first time, he went into boastful stories and predictions of victories to come.

The summer offensive had been a "total victory." Total victory —Herr Bretschneider kept repeating these two magic words on which millions of Germans had been getting drunk for a decade. Their Führer and Commander in Chief had, during the summer and fall, chased the Russians deep into the Caucasus—and farther north to Stalingrad, which was as good as in German hands now. Aside from a slight setback in Africa, where the famous Field Marshal and desert fox had abandoned a piece of worthless land to the enemy for tactical reasons, the German position was excellent.

Herr Bretschneider left no doubt that before next summer the Russians were really done for. And as for the Anglo-Saxons, a blind man could see that they had absolutely no intentions of engaging in serious conflict. They were getting more and more used to the idea of the peace that Greater Germany was striving for. Never did the future look rosier.

Neither her father nor her brothers said a word to Barbara during dinner. Toward the end of the meal she stood up, went into the adjoining study, turned on the radio and tuned in on Vienna, which came through with one of its sweet waltzes.

When she came back, the men of the family were alone, drinking their beer and smoking their cigars. Herr Bretschneider was talking shop, his fingers in a didactic semicircle.

"As a rule," he was saying, accompanied by a lilting waltz, "I am not present at the executions. But if I happen to be, I can't help observing how much the male body gains in beauty through hanging. By that I don't mean the twist in the neck. That is not an aesthetic improvement. It looks like the result of a toothache, with the pain causing the head to twist. But from the shoulders down to the toes, the whole body takes on a slim sort of elegance, particularly around the hips, especially when the corpse is allowed to dangle for a few days. You must have noticed that, Eberhard."

Eberhard declared that he hadn't noticed it. But he felt that he should add something to this cultural discussion. In Rostov, he said, the Waffen S.S. had gone to considerable pains. "On one side of the street we hanged only men, and on the other side only women. They were all hanging at the same level—straight as an arrow. But a thing like that takes time."

Heinz-Dieter was listening with bright, shining eyes. None of them paid any attention to the fact that Barbara was sitting at the table again. Besides, their stories scarcely penetrated her consciousness.

The waltz was cut short in the middle of a chord. Herr Bretschneider raised his head.

"Go on in, Eberhard, and see what the announcer has to say."

Such interruptions usually meant that important announcements were to be made. News of victories were always introduced by a fanfare. But this time there was no fanfare. Eberhard came right back.

"The Yanks seem to have landed in North Africa. Unpleasant situation for our Conqueror of Egypt."

He appeared to find the whole thing amusing. But Herr Bretschneider's hands were fluttering wildly. At that moment the telephone rang. Three telegrams arrived during the next hour. Herr Bretschneider and his green-uniformed son left home that very evening.

Two old men stood whispering on the stairway of a house on the outskirts of town. It was a January day in the year 1943. The faces of the two old men were as dull and dreary as everything around them—the dilapidated stairs, the damp, pea-soup-colored walls, the dust-caked windows under the gable.

"And, Stiemel, were you able to transmit your message clearly and distinctly?"

"But I'm telling you, Herr Rector. I met her this morning for the second time, in the Naumburger Strasse. I took my cap off, and said, 'We've finally had word, Fräulein! He's alive and well.' "

"And she didn't react to that?"

"She just stared at me. I thought she didn't understand me, *that* was how she looked at me. Sort of dark and angry."

"And then she said *that?*"

"Yes."

"Let me hear it again, Stiemel, exactly as she said it!"

"She said: 'Really? But a lot of others are alive, too!' "

"And then she went away?"

"Turned around and walked off."

"Without another word?"

Stiemel shook his head. He stepped closer and whispered in the other's ear.

"Herr Rector, she's found another this summer. That's the way they all are now."

Someone was coming up the stairs. The rector slid through his half-open door. Stiemel pulled the visor of his cap over his eyes and ran downstairs.

"So, you're really alive."

"You don't seem to be happy about it."

"Were you wounded?"

"Yes."

"Where?"

"Through the stomach."

"Are you well again?"

"Fit for front-line duty."

"You've become an officer."

"I've been trained for desert fighting. Africa probably."

"That's fine. Congratulations."

They were sitting opposite one another in their old place, each on the angular stump of a freshly felled tree. Where the forest once stood was now a sea of stumps. The wood was needed in the factories, for heating, for building trenches.

The afternoon sky was faded and dull; there was no snow on the ground. It was a tepid winter, wretched and miserable—it got on people's nerves more than good, biting, frosty weather.

"So you're really alive," she said once again, poking away with a twig at the roots underfoot. "I thought it was a trick. I thought your clique was trying to trip me up with it."

"My clique?"

"That messenger. Your father. All those people."

"I know—you didn't do anything for Father any more."

She did not answer, just stared stubbornly ahead of her.

"I see. They've got you, then."

"Yes, I've had my education."

"That's why there weren't any letters?"

Barbara looked Heinrich in the face for the first time.

"There were plenty of letters. But you had your pretty Ukrainian girls, of course. I hear they're very blonde, blonder than I am."

He looked at her gravely.

"You say there were plenty of letters. Did you really write me letters?"

"It's been so very long ago," she said vaguely.

Heinrich thought for a moment. Then he nodded his head as if he had just had a suspicion confirmed.

"Did *you* write to me?" she asked softly.

"Who, me? Not a line."

"You see," she said, "you've always been like that. It's a pity I wasted so much time on you."

"Yes," said Heinrich. "It's a pity. It's a pity that such a high Gestapo official had it in for me. He wanted to stuff me with pantopon, that great man. He just didn't suceed, that's all."

"Who didn't?"

"Your father."

"You mean, my father wanted to have you killed?"

Heinrich nodded pleasantly.

"Well, perhaps Father was right. You're more dangerous than the others. You hide behind an officer's uniform, and underneath it you're really a traitor."

"Do you want to see me dead now, Barbara?" he asked.

She stood up. "I hope you'll be happy, Heinrich. But I don't want to have anything more to do with you."

"Sit down!" he said sharply, commandingly.

"If the lieutenant insists."

And she sat down.

"You're going to have a baby!"

Barbara's dull eyes were following the movements of a bullfinch as it pecked away at the dead leaves on the ground.

"Are you married?" Heinrich asked.

She shook her head.

"Will you tell me with whom you've fallen so desperately in love that you couldn't even wait until after the wedding?"

Barbara laughed. "You obviously know nothing about our methods of feminine education."

"No."

"People don't 'fall in love' any more. Personal feelings have nothing to do with the matter." Barbara had memorized the words just as she had memorized her dance steps. "Our duty is to have children to give our Führer, and to have them with anyone who has been selected as best fitted for the purpose."

"Best fitted. Of course I, with my stomach wound, couldn't possibly be that."

"No, you couldn't. You with your stomach wound, and your father, and your old messenger, and your whole secret infamy!"

Heinrich paid no attention to Barbara's words, and put his hands on her shoulders.

"Now you are going to tell me everything just as it happened. I have to know everything. It's important. They took you east—to Poland—to a stud farm."

"You may call it a stud farm, if you want to be vulgar. But please take your hands off my shoulders—they disgust me."

He let his arms fall to his sides.

"Tell me," he said.

"Well—at first I had no idea what it was all about. We were very well treated. Not even Americans have the kind of food we got there. And dancing lessons, and riding lessons, and then they mixed something in the food that was supposed to make us wild. A lot of beautiful girls. And handsome boys, at least a hundred of them. Not only Germans, boys from all countries, picked for their Nordic appearance. But I still don't know what it was all about. The blond boys didn't mean anything to me. I don't need any blonds, I thought, I'm blonde enough myself. When one came the first night, I fought him off. And the second one, too. Then for weeks on end they continued my education. One has no right to insist on any one individual, particularly not to one who's been rejected by the Party. Selecting the father of one's children is not a question of taste. That's the way it used to be in the dark days of the Weimar Republic. Finally, after a great deal of education, I understood. They sent another boy and I didn't fight that one. But I didn't get a child from him. Then there was another one, but I didn't get a child from that one either. So they sent me for an examination. The doctor was a nice fellow; he always had his little jokes. He made some minor adjustment, and then it worked. The girls usually stay and have their children right there. But Father gave them different orders, and as soon as they were certain, they sent me home."

"In what month are you?"

"The third."

"Come," said Heinrich, "let's get up. It doesn't do you any good to be sitting here."

Barbara stood up, listlessly, obediently. They walked toward the city, side by side, hardly speaking, like good friends or like an old married couple.

"I've received my education, too," said Heinrich.

Barbara was looking at the slate roofs of the houses on the outskirts of town, glimmering in the oppressive air.

"It wasn't like mine," she said tonelessly.

"No—but I've also learned in *my* education that it isn't a question of the individual!"

"Isn't it?"

"The individual must never act on his own initiative alone. If the individual goes into action too soon, he is lost."

"He is lost? To whom?"

"To the cause."

"What cause?"

Heinrich stopped.

"To the one that is growing stronger and stronger every day, in Berlin and Hamburg and Prague, in Amsterdam, in Paris, and in Belgrade, and in a hundred other cities. So. And now you can go and report me if you like. Then they'll shoot me tomorrow morning."

"My father was right all the time. Marrying a man like you is impossible."

Heinrich was paying no attention. He looked as though he were tasting something good.

"Yes, I think I will, anyway," he said slowly. "I think I'm going to shoot that mad dog today—myself!"

"And I think it'll be best if we part here, Heinrich. I have nothing to say to you. I don't want to see you any more."

"But I still have something to say to you."

"All right."

"I want to kiss you."

She turned her face away from him. "That shows how depraved you are. You want to kiss me in spite of everything."

"I know that. I'm always depraved and heartless when I want to kiss you."

She laughed for a second—as she used to laugh in the old days. For a single moment, no longer, she looked at him with the old enchantment in her light-blue eyes. Then it was night again.

"There's no sense to that any more. Kisses only disgust me, particularly yours. Good-by, Heinrich, I won't see you any more."

"I'm going to walk you home."

"Inside?" Barbara asked with irony. "You've never been there. Do you want to shoot him? He isn't even in town."

"I'll walk you home, anyway."

"You don't have to worry about shooting the mad dog, as you called him. Someone else took care of that for you."

Heinrich stared at her. "Is your father dead?" he asked.

"Wounded, I think."

"Wounded—how?"

"I don't know—I'm not interested. My mother received a telegram. And then she went away. He's lying hurt someplace. But I'm not interested."

They were at the garden of her house.

"I've learned to dance pretty well over there," she said. "I'll show you a few steps if you come inside."

"I'll come some other time."

"You won't. Good-by."

"Good-by."

The rest of the day, and the three that followed, passed quietly. She sat around the house, listened to her music, knitted a little, or leafed through a magazine. She went to bed early, and sank into profound sleep, as though she had been doing hard physical labor. Her room was on the second floor, far from her father's study.

On the fourth night, toward morning, she thought she heard people banging doors and moving furniture about. But she did not awaken completely and sank back into her deep sleep.

She came down late for breakfast. The dining-room table was not set. There was a note on it in the ungainly handwriting of the cook: "I'm gone," it said.

The door to the study stood open. She glanced inside and walked in slowly.

The imposing room was a shambles. The filing cabinets and the drawers of the three desks stood wide open. The soft carpet was strewn with papers, with newspaper clippings, with empty document folders. The place had been thoroughly, ruthlessly ransacked.

A large envelope marked "Private—Highly Confidential" was lying on the floor in front of the radio. It was ripped open, the strings torn, its seals broken. And above it, the oak-covered door of the safe stood ajar.

Barbara never knew about the safe. She saw piles of letters strewn about inside. One of them was on the ledge. She took it in her hand and recognized her own handwriting. She let it drop, picked up another, and read:

Barbara beloved,

A soldier needs bread, soup, tobacco, warm quarters, but nothing half as much as letters from the one he loves. The men around me have little bread, wretched soup, scarcely any tobacco, and never any warm quarters, but they do get mail.

Heinrich Keller is the only one who doesn't. He hasn't had any since last August, not even for Christmas, he hasn't had any for five long months . . .

Her knees gave in. She sank down in front of the radio cabinet where she had spent days and nights vainly hoping, fearing—while right there beside her, inside those steel walls, their love was being choked to death.

She sat like that for a long time, clutching the letter in her hand. She did not cry. This was beyond tears.

She heard two voices in the distance. They came from beyond the dining room. The voices did not immediately penetrate her consciousness. They were the voices of Heinrich and of Grandmother Bretschneider.

Barbara stood up, the letter still in her hand.

"But I'm telling you," she heard, "she isn't home. Go away, Herr Keller, I beg of you!"

"I know she's here," said Heinrich, coming into the dining room. Then he saw Barbara through the open door.

"Herr Keller," the old lady whispered behind him, "this is terrible! If someone should come!"

"Who should come, Grandmother?" said Barbara quietly.

"Heinz-Dieter! He'll report me."

"Heinz-Dieter is gone, and so is the cook." She pointed to the note lying on the table.

With that she turned from her grandmother as though everything had been settled. And she held the letter out to Heinrich.

He glanced at it briefly.

"Was this here in the house?"

"Right here, Heinrich. All of them. It would take a month to read them all. You know, Heinrich, you were right after all—he ought to be shot." She staggered a little. "I'd better sit down. I don't feel so well."

They sat down beside each other.

"In heaven's name!" the old lady whimpered. "This is impossible!" But she sat down herself.

"And what in the world are you two talking about? Who must be shot?"

"I know," said Barbara, with a sickly smile, "we mustn't have thoughts like that. Your old Bible God is against it."

Heinrich put his hand over hers.

"It would only be in the family tradition, Frau Bretschneider. And Barbara would really have better reason to do it than your son had that time."

"I don't understand a word you say."

"You understand me very well! Your son informed on his father and brought him before the secret court. Your son murdered his own father."

"That isn't true!"

"It's true he didn't do it with his own hands. As far as I know, he let his friend and fellow Party member, Paul Runze, do that part of the job."

"Runze," Barbara repeated quietly. Heinrich glanced at her. But she said nothing more.

He was quiet a moment, and looked at Frau Bretschneider.

"There's nothing unusual in that today. Today it's the plain and simple duty of children to spy on their parents and grandparents, to set traps for them, to inform on them and ruin them. Children don't think anything of it any more. But in '24—before they came into power—things were still different. To deliver one's own father to the executioner in those days was still considered the peak of Party loyalty and Party discipline. Your son set an outstanding example with his action. I believe it was the start of his brilliant career. 'Honor thy father and thy mother that thy days may be long upon the earth. . . .' "

"He must be destroyed," said Barbara rigidly.

"There isn't much left to destroy any more."

"Have you seen him?"

"I've seen him. I had to go to the station. I'm leaving town tonight." He glanced at Barbara. "He's lying there in the station."

"Then he might be here any minute! Herr Keller—if he should see you here!"

Heinrich shook his head.

"He won't ever see anyone again."

And then he told them. He told them with some reservations, for, no matter how evil the man was, this was his mother.

Bretschneider, lying prone on a bench in the stationmaster's office, was scarcely more than a ball of gauze on top of a large roll of bandages. His wife was at his side, waiting for an ambulance to bring him home. But ambulances were very much in demand these days.

"Is he conscious, Herr Keller?"

"That depends," said Heinrich. "He is conscious. But his consciousness is not the same."

He told them no more about it. He could still hear that hysterical howling coming out of that bandaged ball—and the voice was not Bretschneider's. It was the Führer's voice, a precise, mechanical imitation—a wild jumble of phrases from his speeches. The people at the station jammed against the glass door, pushed and shoved and trampled on each other, and refused to go away.

They knew what had happened to him. The soldiers and officers who came on the same train had gone into great detail about it. Heinrich repeated what he had heard—with reservations.

The naked truth was that Herr Bretschneider had been so badly shot up that he was stone-blind and raving mad.

He was traveling with his adjutant, Schilling, on the road from Minsk to Mohilev, a considerable distance from the front. On a spot where the road turns sharply and runs down to the Drut River, his car was fired upon from both sides at once, with hand grenades and a machine gun.

The adjutant was killed instantly. Herr Bretschneider was shot through the nose and temple, and also wounded in the spine. The chauffeur, who was uninjured, drove on at a furious speed until he reached the next occupied village.

The Standartenführer's face was a bloody, eyeless lump of flesh. His body was completely inert and paralyzed. At the hospital there was no need to anesthetize him. His horribly changed voice started its raucous imitation as he was lying on the operating table. Fury and invective spouted like pollution out of the bloody hole that had once been his mouth.

The doctors and attendants dared not look at one another. Later they gave him pantopon, a great deal of pantopon—but, in consideration of his high rank, they did not quite give him enough to put an end to that stream of blasphemy. He kept at it whenever he was conscious.

Bretschneider's superior, Brigadeführer Tetzlaff, arrived from Vitebsk. He took one look at what was left of the man, listened to his ravings for a minute, and the matter was settled. The wounded man held too important a post to permit it to remain vacant even for a week. His successor, with Bretschneider's secretary, was to fly to Germany immediately. Not a single document of importance was to be left in the vicinity of this jabbering wreck.

Barbara nodded. "They certainly took care of that in a hurry. They were here last night." She nodded toward the open door.

There was a noise outside. Heavy steps, the steps of men carrying something, were heard from the corridor. And over this came the hoarse rattle—like the infuriated howl of a rabid dog—of the voice whose rantings had first lured a people into slavery and madness, and then forced the whole world into a bloody holocaust.

"*Volksgenossän und Volksgenossinnän*—we have been struggling for fourteen long years. The Jewish yoke has been broken. National Socialist Germany . . ."

Now the slow tread of the stretcher-bearers sounded on the stairs going up to the bedrooms.

"*Volksgenossän und Volksgenossinnän,* I have ordered my fellow Party member, Göring, to create an aerial armada. The plutocrats, the Bolsheviks . . ."

The men were now walking overhead. They set down their burden. Then two doors were heard to close.

The old lady put her arms on the table and dropped her head in her arms. A knot of gray hair came undone and hung beside her.

"Come outside, Barbara," said Heinrich, getting up. "I want to tell you something."

They left the house through a side door, crossed the garden, and walked through a wooden gate. It was not cold, and clouds hung low and gray.

The railroad tracks ran past the spot, and a narrow, neglected path led between the embankment and the garden fence. No one ever walked here. Heinrich put his arms around her, and she did not resist him. He stopped after a few steps.

"You must forget all that," he said. "It's all behind you now. It never really happened."

Barbara said nothing. Then: "Must you leave tonight?" she asked.

"Yes. I have orders to leave for Rome. Then probably Tunis. But you're coming with me."

She stared at him.

"Listen to me, Barbara! I'll make it short. The train leaves at eight-ten. It's a troop train, but I found out it's going to have one car for civilians. Be prompt! It's only stopping for four minutes."

He took some papers from the breast pocket of his uniform.

"Here's your travel permit and your ticket, and here's your exit visa. All made out in your name—all in perfect order."

"How did you get these?"

"Oh," he said, "there's really nothing to it. Part of our 'education.'" He held two documents up against the light. "This one is yours, and this one is mine. See if you can tell the difference."

He arranged the papers carefully, and put three of them into her hand.

"Naturally, you're not to speak a word to me on the train! You don't know me at all. You'll best not leave your compartment at all. We'll meet at the station in Rome."

"But, Heinrich, what am I going to do in Rome?"

"You're not going to stay in Rome. There's a small suburb called Genzano that's supposed to be very nice. A lady named Ziegler runs a boardinghouse out there. A fervent National Socialist, this Frau Ziegler, almost as fervent as I am. While I'm in Rome I'll be able to drive out there on a motorcycle. There's a lovely garden and peace and quiet and sunshine. You'll stay there until the British or the Americans arrive, or until the war is over some other way. And," he said softly, "the baby will be born there."

Barbara stood with her arms limp at her sides, the three pieces of paper in her hand.

"Heinrich," she whispered, "do you really want me, after all that's happened?"

He took her gently in his arms.

"What sort of man would I be—if I blamed you for what these swine had done?"

He drew her to him and put his lips upon hers.

She cried out as if she had been mortally wounded and pushed him so hard that he staggered.

"I can't kiss any more, Heinrich, I can't! Everything disgusts me so—myself and this thing in my body. They've soiled and ruined my blood forever, I know it."

"Please don't," he said quietly. "It's going to be all right. You'll see! It'll pass. Everything will be all right once you're under that blue sky, at peace with the world. I'll wait, Barbara! Don't be afraid."

She nodded vaguely.

"I'm not afraid any more," she said.

"And now you better go in, or they'll miss you. Pack only bare necessities. And don't forget the time: ten minutes past eight. It's marked on the ticket. There's another train leaving just before ours, but it goes only as far as Munich. Be sure you get the right train!"

"Yes, Heinrich, I'll be sure."

It was a very long train. Heinrich was standing in front of the last coach, to which he had been assigned. He was straining for a glimpse of Barbara, though without much hope of seeing her. Three remote, dim lamps were all that illuminated the entire station, and the place was packed with soldiers getting on and off trains.

The train whistled, and it was already moving when Heinrich finally jumped on. He had to push his way through the crowded corridor.

The train was circling the town, which lay dark and quiet in the night. Suddenly it jerked to a lurching, sickening stop, throwing everyone violently forward. The cars rumbled and clattered wildly as they bumped against each other.

Heinrich's forehead was smacked hard against the windowpane.

"God damn it!" he thought furiously. "A lot of good this'll do her in her condition! I hope she was sitting already."

He looked out the window and recognized the place. They were just above the Bretschneider garden, right where he and Barbara were standing a few hours ago.

He walked to his compartment, found a vacant place, and made himself comfortable.

Up front, a few hundred feet away, some men were standing around the locomotive. The engineer and his stoker were gesticulating and shouting at one another. Two men were on their hands and knees, looking under the wheels with a flashlight. The engineer and the stoker kneeled down also, and suddenly they were quiet.

The horrible sight was removed. The engineer and the stoker returned to their places. Slowly the train to Rome started to move again. Its axles cried out in a piercing groan—there was no grease to soothe them.

THE SIXTH COMMANDMENT

Thou shalt not kill

JULES ROMAINS

VI

THOU SHALT NOT KILL

A STORY BY

JULES ROMAINS

WALTER KUNHARDT, the son of an innkeeper in a small town in Saxony, was born in the closing years of the nineteenth century. The inn was not high-class, but it was well kept and brought in money. It consisted of a score of rooms which accommodated not only transients but also a small number of minor clerks and skilled factory workers. The principal source of profit was the bar adjoining the inn—a large room, divided in two by an incomplete partition. Half of the room contained the rows of bottles and the bar. It was here that Kunhardt's father spent most of his time. The other half, since it was somewhat less public, was well suited to private meetings.

A good many out-of-towners visited the bar, but in general its clientele consisted of workers and employees—members of the Social Democratic Party, some of them Party functionaries and some of them union functionaries. In spite of its small size, the town was an industrial center and therefore a good field of activity for the Social Democrats and the unions. Kunhardt's inn was located in the vicinity of the two largest factories. In the beginning, some militant Socialists had taken lodgings there. They attracted other comrades. Little by little the bar became a habitual rendezvous for this particular group. They met at the bar for general conversation, but more serious discussions between the local officers of the Party and the heads of the unions took place in the other half of the room. Indeed, debates which afterwards had more or less serious consequences—even subversive talk—took place over the pots of beer. Here, too, national leaders of the Party or Reichstag deputies were occasionally received. And in their honor the beer was replaced by slender bottles of white wine.

The innkeeper seldom left the bar except to inspect the kitchen. Soon, however, he was aided by his son Walter, especially in the evening when the boy had finished his homework and the customers were most numerous. Walter often had to attend to the people in the other room. On important occasions he would even stay there all evening, standing in a corner like a headwaiter ready to receive orders. Even without trying to, he began to listen to the talk that went on. Ideas to which he was at first indifferent, which he scarcely understood, filtered into his mind. Like a parrot, he could have retailed a Socialist speech to his friends. But, little by little, the ideas began to acquire meaning; they awakened his feelings and captured his imagination. Walter Kunhardt became a Social Democrat as naturally as one breathes. The world and the future appeared to him full of great red banners floating on waves of the International. The heroes who appealed to his fancy were those whose names he heard spoken with respect by the habitués of the bar. One day Bebel himself, while passing through the town, took part in one of the committee meetings in the back room. Walter had the honor of listening to him, of approaching him and receiving an order from his lips.

The elder Kunhardt certainly did nothing to encourage his son in this direction. He was a prudent and well-balanced man. On principle he favored the government. He did not feel the need of taking part in politics and he considered all agitation bad for business. But he could not help having a certain consideration for the Social Democrats whom he saw in his house every day, or even a certain sympathy, since they formed the nucleus of his clientele. And, besides, they were mostly decently dressed men who did not get drunk, who paid regularly and greeted him politely. At one time the police visited him to see about organizing a system of espionage upon the meetings and discussions in the bar. He stated that nothing went on in his house or was said which was at all dangerous to law and order. Finally, to get rid of his visitors he promised to inform them if he overheard any alarming talk. But Kunhardt's indulgence for advanced ideas stopped there.

2

The innkeeper felt that he had amassed a respectable little fortune. He therefore considered it natural that his eldest son, at least, should ascend to a social position superior to his own. Walter showed himself a brilliant scholar in elementary school and, when his teachers advised preparing the young man for the university, his father was quite willing to have him attend a secondary school in a near-by town. A few years later Walter was matriculated as a student in the University of Leipzig.

Walter was generous by nature and intensely loved poetry, music, and sentimental reflection. He soon convinced himself that the best thing possible for him would be a career as a university professor. He selected two branches of knowledge: philosophy and romance languages, one of which he would eventually choose after he had definitely oriented himself.

Leipzig at that time was one of the most liberal universities—even considered a hotbed of advanced ideas. Doubtless the old student guilds were only open to young men from wealthy families of reactionary sentiments, but outside these guilds a large number of students did not hesitate to profess left or extreme left sympathies and even to form groups in which they stimulated each other's enthusiasm. Several professors showed in their teaching that they held similar opinions. Some of the younger ones were not afraid to attend these student meetings in the evening, at which times the most reckless theories were supported.

In this milieu Walter Kunhardt soon found both a pleasant atmosphere and two or three very intimate friends. The closest of these friends was Wilhelm Rosenkranz, the son of a doctor and of Jewish descent. The family lived in Leipzig. Although the family had been converted for two generations on his father's side and one on the mother's, he never thought of hiding its origin. The doctor's wife spoke freely of her grandfather, who had been a rabbi at Chemnitz. Walter Kunhardt never thought of being disturbed by such details, which seemed to him no more striking than being born blond or brunette. If he had happened to learn that his own great-grandfather had also been a Jew from Chemnitz he would have been equally untroubled by it and not even especially interested.

He had a strong affection for Wilhelm and spent evenings with him in interminable discussion. They had many tastes in common. Wilhelm was also preparing for a university career and, after taking his doctor's degree, expected to specialize in romance languages. He had an idealistic love for France and Italy. Walter criticized him for being only feebly Socialist, for cherishing internationalism as a vague sentiment. He made efforts to provide him with a doctrine.

Walter was received by Wilhelm's parents. He fell in love with his friend's younger sister, Ulrica. They were too young for there to be any question of marriage, but Walter had permission to take the girl walking occasionally. Walter hardly dared to speak openly of his affection, and his love-making consisted of reciting poems as they walked under the trees that lined the lanes, particularly Heine's poems, which they both especially admired.

The man whose influence affected Walter Kunhardt most deeply at Leipzig was Kreusch. Hermann Kreusch, a well-known historian of philosophy, had held a chair at the university for many years. His colleagues and many of the students considered him eccentric, a Bohemian with a touch of genius, and his digressions were habitually forgiven. He paid little attention to his courses. Sometimes he let himself go and touched on all sorts of subjects, using extremely free language. Instead of trying to attract students to enlarge his audience, he enjoyed snubbing them, especially when they came of reactionary families, whether Prussian or Bavarian. On the other hand, when he singled out certain persons, he made them his friends and shared all his thoughts with them.

Born at Trieste of Württemberg parents, Kreusch retained a love for the Mediterranean civilization. He never concealed his distaste for the Prussian spirit, militarism, and everything concerned with it. When he spoke of Frederick II, Bismarck, or the Prussian General Staff, he resembled a medieval preacher resigned to soiling his lips with the names of Satan and Beelzebub. He admired the Italians and the Chinese, he said, because they hated war. He also made a cult of Tolstoy and went almost as far in renouncing murder and violence.

Kreusch was fond of saying, "The first thing which separated man from the animals was the invention of speech. The second thing was not the discovery of fire and the malleability of metals but the possession of that extraordinary formula: *Thou shalt not kill.* At that point man turned his back on thousands of centuries of animalism. Since then man has had a sure way of knowing whether the laws and political regimes which are offered him, the kind of civilization toward which he is moving, represent a step forward in the direction of humanity or a regression toward primitive animalism. All he has to do is ask himself: 'Does this improve the chances of this formula or does it diminish them?' " Kreusch said this with so much intensity that Walter and Wilhelm, who was also his pupil, felt that they were confronted with one of the higher verities.

Wilhelm asked him: "But in certain circumstances, even though we are urged to do things directly contrary to the pacifistic principle, can we condemn these actions absolutely as Tolstoy would have, or make a direct refusal? For instance, suppose it were a question of preventing a criminal act or defending one's country when it is attacked?"

Kreusch replied: "There is always a way of telling. If you can *in all sincerity* translate the order given you or the order which you give thus: 'We are required to break the commandment which forbids us to take life. But it is clear that in bowing to necessity we deplore this with our whole hearts, and our essential aim, even in doing this. continues to be promoting upon this earth the triumph of the commandment *Thou shalt not kill.*' If, on the contrary, you cannot so translate the order without laughing or shrugging your shoulders, then you are acting in a bad cause."

Walter objected: "But can one always judge as clearly as that? When, for example, the authorities or those in power require the breaking of this commandment, isn't it easy for them to deceive us, to make us believe it necessary and that the principle still remains valid, when actually the motive is hatred, cruelty, greed, and the spirit of conquest and domination?"

Kreusch looked Walter and Wilhelm in the eyes for a long time and said with a trace of irony: "No . . . man's conscience can see through these lies very clearly when it takes the trouble. When it doesn't see clearly, it's intentional; conscience has become an accomplice. Then let the blood which he is willing to spill cry out against man and may he be accursed through all the centuries!"

3

Walter Kunhardt was nearing the end of his studies when the war of 1914 broke out. He had never received any military instruction and in the ordinary course of things, thanks to university deferment, would not have been called up before a year or two.

Walter naturally thought that mobilization would soon reach him. It was not so. A first examination deferred him in 1915 for lack of physical development. A second examination confirmed this decision nine months later. The reason given no doubt had some truth in it. But perhaps Walter benefited from certain official recommendations to conserve students as long as possible. Thus he escaped until the year of Verdun. He was not inducted until 1917, was trained with relative slowness, and really did not take part in the war until the last period. Indeed, he was never engaged in action at the front. He saw instead repercussions of front-line actions which were becoming disastrous. He was present during the dislocation of the German war machine. He was aware of the weakening of discipline, the disorganization of the supply service, the murmurs of the soldiers. One evening at a halting place when he had had nothing to eat, he used the ink that was left in his fountain pen to write in big letters on the inside of his canvas duffelbag: *Thou shalt not kill.* This final phase of the war, though it did not often expose him to danger, filled him with horror and disgust, for along the road lay massacre and destruction. His only consolation was that circumstances had relieved him of the duty of killing.

When he took off his uniform—without quite knowing how he had attained the rank of sergeant—he told himself that one thing was certain: he would never put it on again.

4

Walter plunged anew into his studies, secretly desiring to bury himself in them. He was already a doctor of philosophy, but finally deciding to specialize, like his friend Rosenkranz, in romance languages, he wished to round out his scholarship in this field. He would have liked to spend long periods in France and Italy, but since the times were rather unfavorable, he contented himself with going to Berlin. There he became the assistant of the celebrated Haxner, a teacher of romance philology.

Haxner had a daughter, Frederika, who was neither pretty nor ugly. Walter convinced himself that he was in love—just enough so that he could believe his desire to become Haxner's son-in-law was dictated by his emotions. He had never forgotten Ulrica Rosenkranz; but he had long since ceased to yearn for her, and she had become absorbed in other affairs of the heart.

Walter married the professor's daughter and found himself very intimately connected with his father-in-law's work, the private life of the family, and the intellectual circle in which its members moved.

In this circle he imbibed, not scorn for politics but indifference to them. Haxner, who in his way was a great soul, with broad and courageous attitudes toward his own science, had a habit of saying: "Politics don't concern us; we have no training in this field. One of the verities we are most sure of is that in any field only experts can be successful. Not only does the tyro waste his time, but he's actually a pest!" The word he used was coarser and more forceful.

In the beginning Walter remarked that, although he was quite ready to admit *he* was not an expert, he was not sure who was. Experience showed that fools, ignoramuses, and rascals had seized power in the past and had interfered in the management of most difficult affairs. Did not honest, intelligent, and educated people have the right to put their oar in, at least to find out what was going on?

Walter only dared to make timid suggestions, and when Haxner took the trouble to answer it was evident that he would have been satisfied if, for the administration of the government, there were something equivalent to the General Staff of the army. And did Haxner offer to give advice to the General Staff? Was he wrong in having confidence in these eminent specialists? He dismissed such useless discussions to return to subjects that vitally interested him, such as the "law of the evolution of the conditional in Latin languages," which he was always bringing up since he believed he had discovered it.

The words "General Staff" produced a spasm of moral anguish in Walter. He saw suddenly Kreusch's Beethovenlike head and his ironically clairvoyant smile. He heard Kreusch's voice again and the tone he used for the words "General Staff." Walter Kunhardt had a sort of hallucination. In the mental penumbra which developed, there appeared in front of him a vague image of one of those Biblical walls on which warnings are written. And what was written, or rather suggested, like a sign half seen in a fog, was *Thou shalt not kill.* But was it something different—something entirely different? . . . Perhaps, O God! perhaps . . . For a couple of letters seemed to have been extinguished in this luminous announcement. A negative takes up so little space—and no one knows better than a philologist what changes occur when a little negative begins to weaken.

Indeed, during this period Walter lived in a kind of general intimidation. When his spirit ventured in certain directions formerly familiar to him he experienced an almost magical touch of paralysis. The strange thing was that he felt no discomfort or, rather, did not know if he ought to feel discomfort.

One day Haxner learned that a teaching position was open at the University of Marburg and advised his son-in-law to apply for it. "The level of scholarship in romance languages is fairly high at Marburg. You will begin to make a reputation for yourself. Young people from the best families in Germany study there. The town is charming. Frederika will be delighted with it."

5

The matter was easily arranged, and the young couple settled at Marburg. Haxner had told the truth. Marburg and its surroundings had a romantic charm. Sometimes it was like being in a medieval tale (conveniently adapted for the modern reader); sometimes it was like being on a holiday tour (especially recommended for lovers and young married couples).

The atmosphere of the university itself seemed particularly designed to disconcert the son of a Saxony innkeeper who had respectfully taken orders from Bebel and the Social Democrats—or, for that matter, even a former Leipzig student. A number of the students at Marburg actually belonged to the aristocracy. Junkers from Brandenburg, Pomerania, and East Prussia traditionally sent their sons there and some of them, in response to a surprisingly modern impulse, even went as far as sending their daughters. The spirit of Marburg, its general tone and reputation, made things perfectly safe.

The university was, of course, a stronghold of select and haughty student guilds. There was other evidence of the cult of archaic traditions. From the beginning Walter was astonished at the number of slashed faces he met in the university corridors and in the streets—sometimes five or six a minute on one street. It was evident from their gauze dressings or crossed strips of adhesive that the scars were quite recent. For the custom of dueling, considered in so many other places a barbaric survival and rather a burlesque, was still highly honored at Marburg. What a change after Berlin or Leipzig! Happily, the department of romance languages was not rich in slashed faces. Walter noticed only one doubtful one in the class assembled in front of him.

This did not mean that his students were uncharacteristic. Most of them, he soon learned, came of rich families or of distinguished parents. Some of them were of the old nobility. The attitude of his students gave him no cause for complaint. In the beginning, considering the composition of the student body, he was prepared for differences of opinion. "They'll try to haze me," he said to himself. "They'll discover tendencies in my teaching or implications in my words which they won't like. They'll pretend to be scandalized. No doubt they'll discover my background. They'll find out that I served beer to Bebel and the Social Democrat *canaille*. I shall have to get over some rough spots."

Nothing like this happened. They listened to him courteously, almost indifferently. The work he gave out was performed correctly, and no one took advantage of it to slip in any suggestion of opposition. They did not respond enthusiastically, of course, but what he noticed on their faces often seemed like a good-natured desire to understand.

Walter was puzzled. He said to himself: "They accept my teaching because they consider me qualified to carry on my profession. They are completely indifferent to my private opinions. They respect me as a professor. They have no more interest in what I might be, aside from the professor, than they would have in the *Weltanschauung* of the agent in the Marburg railway station."

Since this annoyed him a little, he made a point of revealing his personal opinions, on one pretext or another. In the program of his courses he had announced the study of certain French classic writers. As examples to explain and comment upon, he chose texts from Voltaire, Rousseau, and Hugo most likely to scandalize the offspring of Junkers. He even underlined perfectly obvious comparisons. His auditors showed signs of amusement, condescended to laugh now and then, but did not react in any other way.

Walter felt a new enthusiasm for the ideas of his youth. He looked up quotations from his former reading which used to move him, which had seemed to him to express the higher truths. Some of them he copied out on strips of paper in handsome gothic letters and then, returning to a habit characteristic of his people, stuck them on the walls of his study, above his worktable. In the middle, in the largest letters, he placed: *Thou shalt not kill.*

He finished off this sententious decorative scheme with several portraits, among them Tolstoy's. And since it was the year of the Locarno Pact, in a corner of the room he nailed up the photos of Briand and Stresemann, slanted toward each other and attached by one fastener at the bottom.

He wished to remind himself that he had not changed at heart. He also did not mind giving visitors a chance to learn the sort of man he was.

Frederika, when she saw this arrangement, did not seem especially happy about it. She refrained, however, from making any comment. What Walter awaited with the deepest interest was the reaction of his students.

They came often enough to his house to ask advice or to request his help in overcoming some difficulty in their work. While talking in his usual tone of voice to the first ones who visited him after the arrangement of his slogans and portraits, he did not fail to watch very closely for the shock they were sure to receive.

It must have been a very slight shock indeed, for it was quite imperceptible.

Walter Kunhardt continued to correspond with his old comrade and dear friend, Wilhelm Rosenkranz. With the unconscious bashfulness of men devoted to serious tasks, they always waited until they had some professional matter to discuss before writing. Two years before, Rosenkranz had obtained a modest enough position at the University of Leipzig, where he was already attracting attention. He warmly urged Walter to come and join him at their dear old university, where there was plenty of room for all sorts of talents and where he would be joyfully received. (Rosenkranz had made sure of this by a friendly investigation and, as soon as Walter agreed to it, began an intensive campaign in his favor.)

6

The great event in Kunhardt's life was the arrival of the Frenchman Pierre Camus and his subsequent stay in Marburg at the end of 1926.

Pierre Camus was just one year older than Walter. He was a university graduate who had taught for some time in secondary schools, German being his specialty. He planned to obtain a chair in a good university in the French provinces, and while waiting for it wished to spend more time in Germany. He had accepted the position of lecturer in French at the University of Marburg, which, considering his degrees, might seem a rather modest situation, but he was above such trivialities. He knew the big German cities of the north; he wanted to know something of the ancient and romantic Germany and to work and roam about at leisure. Not having enough money to cover his own expenses and, what was more, preferring university contacts to solitude, he decided that Marburg was a good place to be and that the position of lecturer, with its mild advantages and light duties, was better than nothing.

Kunhardt and Camus became friends very rapidly. For the German this friendship became something more intimate and precious than an ordinary relationship. Walter needed gaiety, and his new friend furnished it abundantly and at regular intervals. Walter, though he loved his country deeply, in spite of himself had certain secret doubts in the bottom of his heart concerning Germany's destiny. Pierre Camus gave him serenity, not because he avoided problems, but because he dragged them forth from obscure and tormented regions of the spirit and flooded them with good humor and good sense.

Pierre Camus had served during almost the whole war and had no liking for imperialist Germany and Prussian militarism. He was not unaware that the German soul was full of dangerous forces quite aside from any political regime. But he owed a good part of his development to Germany and had spent years in intimate study of its great men, so he continued to love it in spite of its faults, as members of a family exert themselves to love an ungrateful child.

He expressed these sentiments to Walter Kunhardt without any embarrassment. For instance, he said to him: "Germany has spent her time losing the position which she deserves. Since the Middle Ages she has done nothing but commit political errors. She is always trying to find out who her main enemy is. And her main enemy is herself. Yes, the German people is a kind of violent fellow who is very gifted but who always ends by being thrown out of the house because he makes his comrades hate him." He added: "Germany's misfortunes will be over on the day that she realizes no one has anything against her. She will gain much more through confidence and friendship than by periodic attacks of fury."

When he entered the Kunhardts' little house—where he was to become a familiar guest—Pierre Camus saw the panel of portraits and mottoes above the worktable. He read, *sotto voce,* the central inscription: *Thou shalt not kill.* He smiled faintly, very faintly, and without irony or malice. It was a smile of benevolence, a smile which said: "It's all very well. . . . We don't expect so much. The important thing is that it should last."

But when Pierre Camus tried to ask more concrete questions,

when he said to Walter, "Haven't you observed certain serious symptoms? Aren't your republicans too self-effacing and too timid, on the one hand, and, on the other, haven't you got too many extremists and fanatical rabble-rousers? You know how readily your people respond to that kind of agitation. Don't you think the time has come for the thousands and thousands of honest people who think as you do to speak out more loudly and to rescue a republic that has nothing to be ashamed of?" Walter's answers were deceptive, not because they were insincere, but because they came from a soul unused to certain responsibilities, frightened at the idea of assuming them, and full of a premonition of failure.

"I get the feeling," Camus said to himself, "that I am talking to a minor who does not yet take an interest in the affairs of adults, or to the subject of an absolute monarch who considers the lofty aims of government to be way above his head."

One day Kunhardt's conscience was painfully put to the test. Pierre Camus had been at Marburg for some months. He saw Walter every day and they had long walks and long talks together. The Frenchman had come to the point of confiding all his personal affairs and of speaking quite freely about French life, public and private. Above all, they both considered preserving good relations between France and Germany a most sacred cause, and Camus made it his duty to point out any tendency in his country which might be dangerous to the aim they both had so much at heart. "How," he said to himself, "can I hope to persuade this excellent German to look conditions in his own country in the face if I do not set him a good example with regard to affairs in my own?" Several times he stated: "The duty of the friends of peace is to watch over their own governments. It's the best way of avoiding new catastrophes."

And Walter seemed to approve.

But one day Walter was told that the rector of the university wished to see him. This personage received him with a rather mysterious solemnity. He held out a folded note and said in a quiet voice:

"You will learn the contents of this when you are alone. I believe I know what is in it. I don't have to tell you that it is a confidential matter. The fact that instead of its being mailed to you it comes to you by my hand is sufficient proof of that. . . . You will have to spend some time away from Marburg. . . . Try to find a plausible reason, such as something connected with your family. That is what we will give out. Even your students must not know the real reason."

When he returned home, Walter opened the note. It was a call to a four-week period of military instruction. Across the left-hand corner of the paper was the notation "strictly confidential." The details of the order made it clear that this period of training concerned the reserve forces. The action was flatly in contradiction to Germany's international commitments. It was therefore not surprising that he received it secretly.

Walter did not ask himself whether he ought to obey. Even to pose the question would have required an almost Tolstoyan heroism which Walter dared not even consider in actual life.

With a cheerful smile he told Pierre Camus that an urgent family matter was calling him to a certain part of Hanover and would keep him there several weeks. Camus, who had never heard him mention any members of his family in Hanover nor had noticed any previous sign of preoccupation in his friend, listened with a polite smile. Then Walter began to embroider his story. He provided his family in Hanover with intricate difficulties and enlarged on the inconveniences of the trip, details he invented very badly since he had the imagination neither of a novelist nor an adulterous woman. Pierre Camus' silence, barely colored by a smile or broken by a monosyllable, said very clearly: "Why do you make so much trouble for yourself, my good friend? I don't ask you to."

Walter returned from his training period with a first lieutenancy and the secret conviction that the General Staff, while waiting for the authority to rearm the Reich, was trying, by extensive and secret activities, to keep the cadres of the old army in good order in preparation for a future one. An ironical situation less than two years after the Locarno Pact and while the policy of European reconciliation was in full swing.

But, however ironical the situation and productive of philosophical reflections, Walter refrained from confiding in his friend. He described the views around Hanover with unnecessary zeal and also the boredom of family meetings with the lawyer.

It was precisely when Kunhardt returned that Adolf Hitler was first mentioned in talk between the two friends.

"Who is this Adolf Hitler?" Pierre Camus asked. "What do you think of him? I don't know why we've never talked about him. Anyway, while you were away, since I lacked your company, I strolled about and chatted with the students much more. . . . It seems to me that this Hitler begins to make a lot of noise and inflame a good many minds."

Even before he thought the question over, Kunhardt had a confused notion that he must defend and protect. Yes, without realizing it, Walter Kunhardt's first reaction was to "protect" Adolf Hitler. (He would have been surprised, perhaps scandalized, if anyone had told him so.)

"Oh!" he said in a detached voice, "he begins to make a noise, it's true. But that's all it is. No one really takes him seriously. The reactionaries, Hugenberg and the Stahlhelm, who are the ones to be really feared, use him like a puppet to amuse the crowd. He'll crawl back into his hole as quickly as he has come out of it. And if his effect on the masses counterbalances the actions of the Communists, which are rather alarming, he won't have done any harm."

"Hm! . . . My talks with the students," Camus said, "gave me a different impression. Aside from his clownish antics, Hitler seems to have done a serious job. Several of your students spoke to me about his ideas without laughing at all. . . . However, I should like to believe that he has absolutely no chance with the great majority of reasonable people."

7

Pierre Camus left Marburg after a semester and wrote several friendly letters to Kunhardt. Then one day Kunhardt received the following from his great friend, Professor Wilhelm Rosenkranz:

> Success at last, my dear friend! And I hope you, yourself, are not going to negate all the good work. I have finally beaten down the last resistance. The Council is only waiting for you to make an official application. There is a chair ready for you. . . . To quiet those who maintained that your work and mine would be in a certain sense a duplication, I have offered to turn over certain material from my program to you. Don't let it trouble you. We shall have plenty of time to arrange things between us. . . .

Thus Walter Kunhardt became a professor at the University of Leipzig and had the pleasure of returning there, where he had formerly been a student, as a teacher of considerable prestige. His pleasure, however, did not remain long undiluted. He soon perceived that contacts were not established between him and his students, their relationships being limited to details of the work. He tried to understand them, but most of the young people remained completely incomprehensible to him. Certainly the moral gulf between him and his classes was no greater than at Marburg, but at Marburg the thing was not surprising: he had even expected worse. At Leipzig, in his old university, in Saxony, which he flattered himself he knew by heart, this impression of failure became very depressing.

He confided in Rosenkranz. His friend. trying to hide a certain embarrassment, said: "You notice it more because you have just come. . . . Of course the atmosphere is not what it used to be. But you'll see, one gets used to it."

Kunhardt tried to get used to it, at the same time making efforts to pierce the barrier between himself and his students. In his courses he found pretexts for digressions and discussions of general ideas. The attitude of his students seemed to say: "There he goes, riding his hobby again. Does he think we're going to waste our time in discussions with him?"

He tried to entice them to his house for friendly chats. Either they avoided it, preferring to meet somewhere else and listen to the words of God knows what teachers, or else they were merely reticent. On the wall above his desk, as at Marburg, Kunhardt had once more nailed up the slogans and the portraits. The sixth commandment was faithfully installed in the middle. Only the twin photos of Briand and Stresemann were missing, doubtless because they no longer had current significance.

The students who came to see him did stop to look at the slogans. They did not behave exactly like those of Marburg. They opened their eyes very wide as if they were aware of something curious, an incongruity which they really had not expected. Then a sort of jeering smile appeared on their faces, a smile tinged with scornful indulgence. But they refrained from any comment.

"They act as though I were a survival of a bygone epoch, as though I were a fossil," Kunhardt said to himself sadly and bitterly. . . .

It was during these years that Hitler was coming into power. The signs of his ascendancy multiplied on all sides. One had only to read the newspapers, to pass through the streets in which processions were marching. One had only to see the number of swastikas increasing on walls, in buttonholes, on the breasts of young girls. One had only to overhear student conversations in corridors, to catch certain murmurs which sometimes traversed a classroom. Walter Kunhardt tried not to notice all of this. He learned to walk through life staring straight in front of him, his ears voluntarily stopped up. His mental hobby was "thinking of something else." He worked as much as possible. In his leisure moments he read historical novels or detective stories, but felt in a state of siege, and his inner tension did not cease.

Even Rosenkranz avoided speaking of these painful subjects. Among Kunhardt's other colleagues only one, Boehlen, was openly pro-Hitler. Walter felt a perverse curiosity about this Boehlen. How could a cultivated man be a Nazi—even, people said, an ardent Nazi? Boehlen, seeing an opportunity to propagandize, asked nothing better than to explain himself. Each time he cited some provocative or absurd article of Nazi doctrine, he used to add, "These are ideas which must not be interpreted literally or approached with our usual point of view. They have a dynamic value."

Boehlen lent Kunhardt a copy of *Mein Kampf*, which the other had not yet read.

"Of course," Boehlen said with a smile which disclaimed all fanaticism and invited his questioner to share a flatteringly superior intellectual attitude, "you must take some things and discard others. Hitler is a necessary and only semi-intelligent instrument of the German national consciousness. His theories on war have the value of symbolic images. He, himself, a former soldier and victim of the war, is actually deeply concerned with peace."

Walter Kunhardt, while reading *Mein Kampf*, had somewhat the reactions of a well-brought-up adolescent looking into a very obscene book. He was continually disgusted and indignant; he wanted to throw the book away. But he did not throw it away. In certain instinctive levels he felt agreeably stimulated and a sort of evil dizziness filled his head, a drunken relaxation which he did not at all mind.

In 1932, during the International Exposition at Leipzig, Walter had Pierre Camus, now a teacher at Lille, invited to give three lectures at the university. They had continued to correspond. Walter had had news of his friend's marriage, then the birth of a child. Perhaps he hoped this visit would give him a respite from his growing moral tension. Perhaps he was obeying still more obscure feelings.

Their meeting was cordial. But Camus was not slow in bringing the conversation around to the "lightninglike development" of Hitlerism, which worried him as it did so many other Frenchmen.

"Do you remember what I said to you four or five years ago? You maintained that the danger wasn't serious, that Hitler was only a puppet. In six months this puppet is liable to be master of Germany. You're going to have persecution of the Jews, suppression of all liberties. You're going to see your country rolling in the direction of a war of revenge."

"But, you see," Kunhardt said cautiously, "this situation is very difficult to appraise from the outside. The unjust treatment of Germany by the Allies has given Hitler his best arguments. As for the Jewish question, there are things I can't say to my friend Rosenkranz that I can say to you. Don't forget that at Berlin, for example, three quarters of the lawyers and doctors are Jews . . . and in the theater, the press, and even the university, the lack of proportion is almost shocking. . . . Anyway, Hitler will not succeed. The movement has already reached its peak. The reaction is about to set in. Even if by some fluke he should be victorious, don't think that would mean war. What are the refrains of the Nazi propaganda? 'Peace with honor,' 'Peace and equal rights.' Don't criticize the German people too much for listening to these refrains with pleasure. They have suffered so much!"

Pierre Camus looked at him with a faint smile, tinged with disillusionment, with ironic clairvoyance: a smile that Hermann Kreusch had once worn.

"God grant you are right!" he said. "If everybody in Germany, including Hitler, wants peace, there is little likelihood that it will be disturbed." Then he added in another tone: "Now I'm not surprised that Hitler's rise has been so rapid, if people like you, who ought to offer him the most violent and unshakable resistance, are talking this way."

Their later meetings were marked by a lack of frankness.

8

In the months following Pierre Camus' visit, the situation grew rapidly worse. The Nazi tide rose everywhere. Even by closing one's eyes and ears it was impossible to avoid being obsessed by it. The students affiliated to the Party, now more and more numerous, flaunted it even in their academic activities. They became insolent. Hitler himself, though not yet in complete control, soon would be. Old Hindenburg would not long stand between him and absolute power.

Walter Kunhardt, whose teaching had already gradually changed (he tried not to admit it), no longer hesitated taking deliberate precautions. He dropped every digression or allusion from his courses which might seem suspicious to a Nazi. In the middle of semester he made changes in the authors to be discussed, in order to get rid of certain dangerous texts. He began to live in terror of his students. As he talked he never ceased watching the ones he feared most.

He allowed himself to be seen more often with Boehlen and by the questions he asked showed that he took a serious interest in Nazi doctrines. He did not dare to break with his old comrade, Rosenkranz, but with the help of his wife, Frederika, he managed to weaken their relationship. And Rosenkranz, who felt anti-Semitic passions gathering about him, made the job easier by shutting himself up at home on the pretext of having work to do.

One day a petition was brought to Kunhardt for his signature. It came from several of the university professors who had used all their remaining courage in order to take this step. It was couched in the most respectful—one might almost say the most humble—terms. They requested the authorities not to apply the anti-Semitic measures, which had just been announced, indiscriminately to the universities. They pointed out that despite their Jewish origins certain people had rendered eminent service to German science and could do so in future.

Walter spent several hours in front of his worktable, asking himself if he should sign. Before him were the portraits and the slogans. He told himself: "I am certainly not a coward. Who could say that, in view of these slogans which have become terribly compromising and which, in spite of Frederika's hints, I have not removed—and shall not remove?"

He spent a whole sleepless night trying to make up his mind. He had not spoken to his wife about the petition, in order to spare himself advice he could imagine only too well.

In the morning he signed the petition and returned it himself to one of the first signers, his eyes ringed from lack of sleep. His lips were cold and his heart beat painfully.

Some weeks later he was alone in his study, facing his slogans. He had no courses that day and had not been away from his desk.

It was almost night. The lamp with the reflector lit up the papers on his desk. In the hall the telephone had rung several times, but there had been no one on the line.

During the day he had heard distant echoes from the town, and the maid, when she returned from shopping, had said: "There are people in the streets making a fuss—students."

But such incidents had become so frequent that they no longer attracted attention. Hardly a day passed that young Nazis, students or otherwise, did not get up a procession with banners, songs, and shouting.

Suddenly the maid came into the room, holding a letter. "Someone just brought this. It wasn't the postman. It was a boy."

The professor's name was written on the envelope in ink and in a hasty, almost unrecognizable handwriting.

He opened the note. The message was penciled:

My dear Walter,

For some hours I have been besieged in my house by a howling mob of young people, many of whom are our students. They are shouting "Death to the Jews!" They threaten to break the windows and set the house on fire. I telephoned the police. They have practically sent me about my business. They asked me if anything were broken or set on fire. I said that they had broken one or two windows with stones and that they were howling for my death but hadn't actually killed us yet. I telephoned the university. With a great deal of difficulty I got in touch with one of the provosts, who said that if the police would not interfere it was very difficult for him to do anything. He told me to be calm and not to provoke them! As if I had any intention of provoking them! I felt more like weeping when I saw the faces of my students—students whom I know so well, whom I've taught as well as I know how, whom I've been fond of! As it gets dark the crowd seems to be getting larger. I am afraid that they will work themselves up and, when night comes, actually carry out their threats. My poor children are in a state of indescribable terror. I tried to telephone you two or three times, but the line was never free. It even seemed to me that it was deliberately put out of order. Then I wrote you. In the name of our long friendship, I beg you to hurry. Only you can protect us. Our students respect you. They will listen if you speak to them. Please come to me, dear Walter. Just now I hear them shouting more loudly than ever.

WILHELM ROSENKRANZ

Walter, letter in hand, remained several minutes in a kind of stupor. His thoughts whirled. Then he got up, moving like a sleepwalker.

He stuffed the letter into the bottom of one of his inside pockets. Then he got his hat and went out of the house, walking on tiptoe and softly closing doors. He did not know what he was going to do.

Rosenkranz' house was ten minutes' walk from his own. Shortly before one reached it, there was slight inclination in the street, leading into a small open circle. The house in which Rosenkranz lived was situated on the other side of the circle, on the corner formed by the cross street which cut in from the left.

Walter moved rather quickly, keeping in the shadows. Since it was a residential quarter, there were no stores and almost no people passed by. There were only a few street lights, and the trees cut off a good part of the illumination.

The nearer he came to the circle, the more clearly Walter heard muttering and shouts. He moved all the more carefully. Sometimes he slipped along the walls, sometimes he kept in a series of shadows and, before crossing a lighted spot, looked in every direction.

When he reached the circle he realized that, thanks to the low angle of the sun and the grilled fence of the property on the corner, he could have a very good view of Rosenkranz' house without showing himself prematurely. "Let's see what's going on first," he said to himself. Consequently he posted himself at the little wall surmounted by the grille and began to watch, sometimes by looking into the street, sometimes by peering through the bars.

The circle, having four street lamps, was better lighted than the street. Walter saw a small crowd clearly illuminated. Some of the young people were standing in groups of three or four on the pavement in the open circle. Many were sitting in rows on the edge of the sidewalk. Others were clinging to the grille surrounding Rosenkranz' garden. Others had climbed onto the neighboring walls and leaned against the ironwork. Altogether they numbered no more than a hundred. Some wore the Nazi uniform and probably had no connection with the university, but the majority seemed to be students, some recognizable by their caps, others by their general bearing. Without really seeing their faces, Kunhardt thought he could identify a good number of his own students, most of whom also had classes with Rosenkranz.

Every now and then one of the crowd would shout, and other voices would join in and amplify it until it became a furious clamor, or snatches of song would be chanted in chorus or by one voice. Above all, the young people gave the impression of waiting for something. Exactly what were they waiting for? The windows of the house were dark. Not a sign of life came from the Rosenkranzes. It was easy to imagine them hidden away in some inner room, the trembling children holding back their sobs.

"They won't kill them," Kunhardt said to himself as he tried feverishly to reassure himself. "They'll go on braying like that for a while, then they'll get tired. They'll go home. It's only an exaggerated form of hazing. The provost was right. The thing to do is not to provoke them. If I intervened I would irritate them. . . . Yes, that would be quite inept."

He heard more violent shouts, then a noise of glass breaking, followed by a general uproar. Someone had just thrown a stone through one of the windows. Kunhardt began to be terribly worried. Many of the young people sitting on the edge of the sidewalk had got up. Was it the beginning of a general assault?

"What am I to do?" Kunhardt asked himself, flattened against the grille, his collar up to his ears. "What am I to do? . . . If I could only do something!"

Then he began to breathe easily again. The uproar, instead of growing worse, gradually subsided.

"It was nothing! . . . They'll stop there! . . . Above all, don't provoke them!"

Ten minutes later Walter slipped into his own house like a thief.

The following morning when he entered his classroom, in which the students were already assembled, murmuring and a long-continued trampling of feet greeted him. At first he stopped and grew pale. However, the traditional significance of things had not changed. The trampling of feet and the murmuring had been familiar to him for many years. It was the students' way of saying "Bravo!" It meant approval. And their faces confirmed it. There was no hostility in them.

When the class was over he met Boehlen and got the explanation from him:

Professor Rosenkranz, having had his house besieged until midnight without any sign of letup, decided to escape with his family. He slipped out of his house, carrying several bundles and followed by his wife and children. Though they left the garden by a gate which opened on a little alley, they were noticed. The besiegers threw stones at them, and the professor had been rather badly wounded on the forehead. It was believed that the Rosenkranz family had succeeded in reaching the station. Doubtless they had gone to seek shelter far from Leipzig until the agitation died down.

On the other hand, it was known (by what means?) that Rosenkranz had sent to his friend Kunhardt for help and that Professor Kunhardt had refused to respond. He had, as the students said, "scornfully brushed off the Jew." The students were very pleased, and to congratulate him for this honorable action they had greeted him that morning with the murmured ovation and the trampling of feet.

While listening to these reports, which he neither denied nor confirmed as far as they applied to him, Walter felt an ignoble mixture of shame and sense of security. Then he remembered the inscriptions on his wall and trembled a little.

Less than a week later, after having been away from home all day, he went to his study, lit the lamp on his table, and looked at the wall above it. The sentence *Thou shalt not kill* had been added to. On a strip of paper the same width and in the same kind of lettering was written, *even vermin?* Upset and excited, he went to his wife. Who had been in his study while he was out?

"Three of your students," said Mrs. Kunhardt, "came a little more than an hour ago. They didn't tell me their names, but I knew their faces. They wanted to know if you would be back soon. I said I thought so, without knowing just when. They asked permission to wait in your study. They left after about half an hour."

"Come and see what they did."

The expression on Frederika's face indicated that she was not particularly indignant about the lesson the students had given their professor. It rather seemed to say: "Does he want to go on exposing himself to similar insults? Will he go on flying in the face of danger?"

Alone, that night, Walter Kunhardt took the inscriptions down from his wall, one by one. He made them into a little package and put it into a drawer, which he locked with a key. After some hesitation the portraits followed. He felt like a poor man who, after a disaster, follows the dead bodies of his family to the cemetery all alone.

9

From hearing others repeat it and from repeating it to himself Walter Kunhardt had convinced himself that Hitler clung tenaciously to peace and that with prophetic intuition, behind his calculated outbursts of fury, he was following a tremendously skillful policy; that, piece by piece, all German claims would be satisfied without spilling blood. It was, of course, true that blood was spilled internally from time to time: the regime was harsh; beaten Jews cried out. But with practice one succeeded in closing one's ears, and there was plenty of opportunity for practice.

The Munich agreement delighted Kunhardt. The sharper the crisis, the more convincing the demonstration. The Führer's methods were fully justified. Walter, whose heart had stood still for a moment, was so delighted that he had a little dinner of celebration at his house for friends and colleagues. At the end of the meal, Walter, drunk on German champagne, rose and suggested a toast: "I am not sure that God exists but I am sure that our Führer has been sent by God!"

In the beginning of September, 1939, the aims of this gift of God became more serious. Kunhardt, now a captain in the reserves, was immediately mobilized, being attached to a section of the General Staff. At first he spent two weeks in Görlitz, in Silesia. His superior officer was a certain Colonel Struder, who had the physique and the joviality of a butcher. He had proved himself, when times had been difficult, as a storm trooper and, during one of the great purges, had been transferred to the regular army. His lack of education and the brutality of his manners had not hindered his advancement. Though one could easily imagine him at the head of a regiment of shock troops, what was he doing in a section of the General Staff? It was whispered that his job consisted chiefly in spying. He did not hesitate to mock the old-style Prussian officers of more or less aristocratic birth and impeccable grooming who seemed to look at the Nazi regime through a monocle. "We know them!" Struder cried. "The purges haven't cleaned everything up. We have our eyes on them." When he was drunk, which was often, he added, beating on the table: "Even a general, you understand, take it from me, I'll bump him off like anyone else if he doesn't toe the mark!"

Or he would turn to Kunhardt, chuckling and winking his heavy eyelid. "The reservists . . . yes . . . there's all kinds among them. We have to watch out, especially the ones over forty. . . . Yes, there's all kinds, former Communist filth, former Social Democrat garbage, former Jew lovers." He went on chuckling: "Even among the officers. . . . But they'd better look out. We have ways of knowing. We won't miss."

Walter Kunhardt listened with smiles of agreement and secret writhings in his vitals. "Perhaps he has something on me," he thought. "Am I being singled out?"

News from Poland was decisive and good. "It'll be over in two weeks," Struder said to Kunhardt. "You see, France and England have made a pretense of anger. They had to save face. Then in two weeks, the Führer will turn to Chamberlain and Daladier and say to them: 'Now, let's talk. You're not going to bother me about Poland any more because Poland doesn't exist. Don't behave like idiots!' They'll have to scratch their heads a little for form's sake. You know, in those wretched countries they have to take their crappy parliaments into account, they have to have some sort of face-saving hot air for the parliaments. But don't worry, you'll eat your Christmas goose at home probably without even being under fire."

Walter asked nothing better than to believe it. He thought sometimes of the slogans locked in his drawer at home. "If only we have such luck," he thought. "If only the war can be got over with when it's just begun, without there having to be any question of killing! . . ."

One morning Struder said to Kunhardt: "We're going."

"But where, Colonel?" Walter turned pale.

"To Poland, by God. But don't get upset. Our troops have already been in Warsaw for several days. There's nothing but a little clean-up job left to finish in the east. The only trouble is that these Russian bastards, on the pretext of helping us, look as though they're going to occupy a piece of Poland. And what are we going to do there? About what we're doing here, I think—which is practically nothing. But just the same, you see this war of a few weeks is good training for the army. The more units that have contact with the front or with the terrain just behind the front, the better it will be. I know, too, that they want the General Staff to look the terrain over where our troops have made their lightning advance. We'll have planes at our disposal to go joy-riding over the battlefields—if you can call them battlefields. What we are most likely to see are long trails of rusty iron from west to east—that will be what's left of the Polish army after our Panzer divisions squashed it. Even from the point of view of satisfying our curiosity it will be a nice trip."

"I shall look at the trails of rusty iron since it's necessary," Kunhardt said to himself. "I'll try not to think too much about the squashing. Anyway, it lasted such a short time! The loss of life, even on the other side, can't have been very great."

The trip to Warsaw was a disappointment, for it took place almost entirely at night by railroad. Walter dozed in the car and reflected: "I'll wager when we get there we'll find things restored to normal. We must give our army credit for being as effective at rebuilding as at destroying. The poor Poles! . . . The lesson must have been hard, but they needed it."

Warsaw's appearance unfortunately didn't suggest quite that nuance of paternal severity. Great sections of the city lay in ruins.

Fires were still smoking. Palaces and public buildings were nothing but limestone walls. Worst of all, there were corpses, corpses in every corner, blocking the sidewalk or filling the gutters or piled against trees like heaps of sand: corpses of soldiers and civilians, with stinking, marbled flesh. One got the impression that the industrious German army had overdone its task of reconstruction and re-establishment of normal life.

How difficult it was to have comfortable thoughts while walking along these streets! A poisonous brew close to delirium began to be distilled in Walter's mind. He almost believed that this indiscreet exhibition of smoking ruins and marbled corpses had been organized by his own private demons. As he walked, he imagined a species of pocket Mephistopheles, agile as acrobats, climbing in the trees along the avenue, making horrible faces, and, just to defy him, hanging banners from one branch to another reading: *Thou shalt not kill.* And other demons even slyer were perching on his shoulder and whispering in his ear: "Hermann Kreusch's golden rule, you remember it, don't you? Look how well it applies here. Isn't it clear that it's just a minor infraction of the rule which doesn't harm the basic principle? You can't help seeing that the killers have done good in spite of themselves and that the principle still reigns in their hearts."

He surprised himself by saying aloud: "But I didn't kill! Look! . . . It wasn't I!" Unhappily, this statement did not quiet his conscience.

10

The next morning the jovial Struder said to him: "Hey! Good news! Get ready! We're going up in a plane. A fine four-seater reconnaissance plane. There'll be us two, the pilot, and the gunner. Don't make a face! We don't have to fling ourselves on the rear guard of the enemy. It'll just be a picnic. I had trouble enough getting hold of the plane. They need the machines so badly. But I wanted to see what was going on. We're going to fly due east over the plains where the debris of the Polish army is still in flight. There are other things besides the army; the roads are full of people running for their lives on foot and in wagons, the rich ones in their cars, even big shots. I don't have to tell you that's worth seeing!"

They took off at ten o'clock in the morning.

"What a swell machine!" Struder cried. "Fit for a general. It's almost as quiet as a passenger plane. We can talk without using these contraptions if we yell a little. I like it better. Can you hear me, Lieutenant?"

"Quite well, Colonel."

"What about you, Captain Kunhardt?"

"I can hear you all right, Colonel. I can't hear the Lieutenant so well."

"It doesn't matter. You haven't anything particular to say to each other."

Struder was sitting at the left behind the pilot; Kunhardt a little behind Struder and to the right. The machine-gunner was farther back, near the end of the tail.

"Colonel," said the pilot, turning a little, "I'd better not fly very high. You can see better . . ."

"Yes, of course. . . . There's no danger of their firing at us?"

"Who? The Poles? That depends on the direction you pick, Colonel. In the north and the northeast there's still fighting. Some Polish units are resisting. We can't avoid being fired on if we fly low. . . . They haven't much chance of hitting. But still, once is enough."

"What about the refugees? All the ones running like hell across the plains? In what direction will we find most of them?"

"Toward the southwest, Colonel. They're headed more or less toward the Rumanian frontier—those that are headed anywhere."

"Fine, that's where we'll go!" Struder said as if it were a matter of high strategy. He went on speaking for the benefit of both Kunhardt and the lieutenant: "We're not on any particular mission, you know. If we fly in the direction of the battle we might get in the way of our comrades. We'll go to the southwest."

They flew for some time without seeing anything worth noticing. Far from being choked with refugees, the whole plain seemed dead. Then two carts were seen on a crossroad; after that, on the highway itself, two or three rustic-looking vehicles.

"What a nuisance!" Struder cried. "We got here too late. They've all run out some days ago and they're way off by now. . . . What a nuisance! We won't see anything. It's idiotic." And he chewed his thumbnail disgustedly.

To comfort him, the pilot twice pointed out black heaps of rubbish on the right-hand side of the road.

"What's that?" Struder asked crossly.

"Cars that have been set on fire. Probably hit by bullets from planes. Perhaps the occupants are still inside."

The face that Struder made showed that he was not a child to be amused by toys. Did anyone think that one or two miserable stage props would do for the Great Flight of the Poles?

"It's idiotic," he repeated. "We should have come last week! God damn it, God damn it!"

After two hours of flying, Struder let out a yell of anticipation: "Say, Lieutenant, over there, what's that?"

"Refugees."

"Are you sure? Swing over to the right so that we can see better."

A few irregularly distributed flyspecks began to appear on the highway. In spots they formed clumps. They hardly moved.

"At last!" Struder cried. "We're catching up with them. Keep going! Keep going!"

The empty spaces on the road became shorter. The black flyspecks were squeezed closer together. It was evident that within a kilometer the highway would be packed. In addition, the approach of the plane produced a curious transformation: the clumps seemed animated by an internal convulsion. Then the plain was spotted here and there with flyspecks, and when there was a near-by wood, trails of black dots were developing between the road and the wood. From the height of the plane these movements seemed so slow that they were noticeable only from the slight change in the pattern on the ground.

"They're afraid of us," Kunhardt was thinking. And he looked with a certain anxiety at Struder, who was delighted.

"Keep going! Keep going!" Struder yelled at the pilot.

After a few minutes the first cars became visible. They too were fleeing eastward, and their flight was more noticeable. In their way, they too reacted to the presence of the plane. Some speeded up, others slowed down. One halted by a little piece of woods, and brownish flyspecks issued from it and slowly moved in the direction of the trees.

"Try making a half circle," Struder shouted, stamping with joy. "Steer any way you please, make circles or something. . . . We want to fire on them."

He turned back toward the tail. "Hey, gunner! Take a shot at them!"

As the gunner didn't seem to hear, Struder yelled at Kunhardt as loud as he could: "Tell him to shoot at them, right away! Come on, what are you waiting for?"

Kunhardt was pale as death. He opened his trembling lips. When he tried to move his neck it seemed paralyzed. But the gunner had heard.

"What shall I fire on, Colonel?"

"What the devil! On the ones running away from their car. . . . Lieutenant, can you hear me? Fix it so that the gunner has the woods and the highway back of us within range. . . . I can see the telephone is better for giving orders. . . . Kunhardt, tell the gunner to fire at the people running away from the car, before they get to the woods, for Christ's sake! And let him try to set the car on fire! That would be fun! And then let him enfilade the highway! Let's go! Let's go! All he has to do is bang away. The position of the plane is fine. Jesus Christ, Kunhardt, repeat my orders!"

Struder, his face red and his eyes popping, was swinging about in his seat, yelling toward the front and the rear, addressing the pilot, Kunhardt, and the gunner. Kunhardt finally obeyed. He leaned back until his head was near the gunner's and in the despairing, toneless howl of a drowning man repeated the orders.

The machine gun began to rattle.

11

Struder and Kunhardt returned to Görlitz at the beginning of November. There they passed a relatively quiet winter. Kunhardt was occupied in writing very careful reports concerning French papers and periodicals sent him in bundles from Berlin. Then he had to make French translations of various texts, whose destination was not at first apparent, in as easy and natural a style as possible. They were mostly a kind of proclamation or appeal which sometimes seemed to be addressed to the troops, sometimes to the civilian population. The tone was varied, running from friendly exhortation to the most terrible threats, including seizure and execution of hostages. Walter, a little disturbed, went on translating, trying at all times to keep the style easy and natural.

This sort of life continued until the invasion of Denmark. Kunhardt, with a group of his comrades, headed by Struder, was sent there.

Then came the crushing defeat of France. Walter Kunhardt was moved by it. He had a fondness for France and things French. He had always hoped for friendship between France and Germany. But from his point of view, like that of so many Germans, the conditions of this friendship were that France would do nothing "against the interest of Germany." He never asked himself if this formula, in spite of its modest air, was not likely to take on a more and more ironic significance. For, in the first place, it had been a question of doing nothing "against the interest of Germany" when Germany tried to make a comeback after her defeat and to rid herself of her treaty obligations. Then it had been a question of doing nothing "against the interest of Germany" when she yearned for "room to expand" and when she annexed Austria, took over Czechoslovakia, and dismembered Poland.

More than once at his desk in Copenhagen, Kunhardt thought of his friend Pierre Camus. In all this misery, what had happened to him? The last time he had had news from him was in October, 1938. In his satisfaction at the Munich Pact Walter had written to Pierre to tell him how glad he was that war had been avoided between their two peoples. The Frenchman had answered lukewarmly and a little dubiously. "Of course I prefer this to war," he had said, "provided that your country knows when to stop." And he had added: "I now have a seven-year-old daughter and a boy of four. Unlike some, I don't have to fear that mobilization will take my children from me (when my son is grown up I certainly hope that the present European madness will be over), but I am not anxious for them to undergo the horrors that such a conflict will let loose." Pierre Camus had also informed him that he had just been appointed professor in the Department of Literature of Caen.

In the beginning of the spring of 1941 the section to which Captain Kunhardt was still attached was sent to occupied France, under the command of the jovial Struder. But then it was broken up. While Struder and others set out for Brittany, Kunhardt was made a member of the garrison of Chaumont.

Kunhardt had read many descriptions in the German press of the impeccable behavior of the troops occupying France, of the excellent reception given them by the people (now delivered from the English yoke), and of the open and friendly relations soon established between the victors and the vanquished. He was therefore quite anxious to see for himself. He was about to have an excellent opportunity, for his new position, attached to the commandancy of the town, consisted almost entirely of administration and police work.

He was not too disappointed by the situation at Chaumont. The commandant was a well-mannered person, a lukewarm Nazi, and entirely without ferocity. The troops behaved well. True, the measures they had to carry out were close to confiscation or even pillage, but everything was formally correct. The population was well behaved, too. Its attitude was extremely cold, however, and bore no resemblance to the touching descriptions in the German papers. "My God," Kunhardt said to himself, "after all, these people have many bitter things to put up with and also material privation. We can't expect them to give us three cheers."

Some months later he learned that Struder had been transferred from Rennes to Caen, as head of the administration and the police, and had requested several of his former subordinates, including Kunhardt.

Kunhardt, who hated Struder, was not at all pleased at getting into his clutches again. On the other hand, Caen was where Pierre Camus lived, and by chance they might meet. It was only a chance, for Camus might be a prisoner of war or have moved. Kunhardt had no doubt that the meeting, if it took place, would be agreeable to both of them.

12

Pierre Camus was having lunch with his wife and two children. To tell the truth, the ceremony was more important than the actual food. By a curious mischance, Normandy, the land of plenty, which had formerly fed many other sections, including England, was no longer able to feed its own inhabitants. This was not so mysterious. A glance at the station with the trains loaded for Germany was enough to explain it.

Pierre Camus was not anxious to talk today. He was absorbed in thought, looking in turn at his wife, his daughter, his son, even at the little white dog with curly hair that the children were allowed to seat between them on a chair at the table. He was reflecting that for a civilized man to be hungry every day from morning to night was a humiliating state of affairs. "Suppose someone had told me in the past that a time would come when I would stop in the middle of my lecture to think that I was hungry—or that I would awaken in the night to think that I was hungry—or that I would even be hungry in my dreams!"

But today he was hungrier than usual. Perhaps it was a caprice of his body, which for a long time had been demanding a series of imaginary meals. Perhaps it was the fault of the season, the cool, clear days that awakened the drowsiest appetite.

The maid brought to the table a dish that had exhausted the ingenuity of her mistress and herself. It was the result of hours of standing in line at the stores, of saving scraps. A brownish sauce hid the contents: a few wretched morsels of inferior meat, some old bread crusts, a handful of dry beans, the stump of a turnip.

As he looked at the steaming dish set upon the table, Pierre Camus felt himself fall prey to the madness of starvation. He said to himself: "I could take all that. I am the strongest. No one here could stop me. And afterward I would stop being hungry. Oh, how good it would be! It would be a wonderful feeling. It would be worth anything."

For a moment he played with the idea. "I have only to stretch out my hand, to pull the dish toward me, to dump everything in my plate. And then just put my head down and eat."

He smiled sadly; he looked at the two children and the little dog with white curly hair, sitting so virtuously between them.

"Look at him, he's only a little dog and yet he wouldn't think of such a thing. He's hungry, too. His nostrils are trembling pitiably. And yet when the children have their share on their plates, right next to him, nothing in the world would make him grab for it. He will wait until given his tiny portion. . . . Has he a stronger character than I? Is he more civilized than I? . . . After all, that's what civilization is."

Pierre Camus smiled again, pushed the dish toward his wife, and said gently: "Serve yourself, my dear. Serve the children. We mustn't forget poor Bob, who's wriggling on his chair and trying not to groan. . . . I see you have worked miracles, Madeleine, and you, too, my poor darling."

The meal over, Pierre Camus sat smoking his daily cigarette. Madeleine, the maid, came back into the room.

"A German officer wants to talk to the master."

"A German officer?" Camus frowned.

"Let's hope," his wife said, "that this won't be something disagreeable. It seems that a real brute, a Colonel Struder, has come to take command."

"Go and ask him," Camus said to Madeleine, "what he wants to see me about."

The maid returned.

"He says it is just a personal visit, that he used to know the master. Oh, he speaks French very well. He told me his name. Wait a minute. Professor Coun . . . Coun . . ."

"Kunhardt?"

"Yes, that sounds like it."

"Kunhardt?" cried Mrs. Camus. "That professor you knew at Leipzig?"

"Yes."

"What is he doing here?"

"I have no idea. Haven't you noticed that for some time we've been meeting a great many Germans in our country?"

"Are you going to receive him?"

"It's hard to do anything else."

Mrs. Camus wrung her hands nervously. "Would you rather I stayed? If he's come to trouble you, to threaten you, I'd like to be with you."

"What are you worrying about? He's inoffensive enough. . . . No, it would be better if I received him alone. . . . Madeleine, will you take him into my study, and tell him I'm coming?"

Pierre Camus did not offer his hand, he only indicated a chair with a movement of his head.

"Don't you recognize me?" Kunhardt said timidly, smiling as he sat down.

"Of course." The Frenchman's face did not change.

Kunhardt remained silent for a moment, seeking words.

"You must realize that I can put myself in your place. . . . We meet under unfortunate conditions . . . after having been good friends for so many years. But neither of us counts for anything in what has happened."

Pierre Camus laughed faintly.

"Will you tell me," he said slowly, trying not to allow any emotion to creep into his words, "what you have done to prevent Germany from falling into the hands of her present masters? Or what you have done to stop them when they threatened Germany and all of Europe with war? And what you have done since the war to disassociate yourself from actions which your conscience must certainly consider to be crimes?"

Walter smiled unhappily. He tried to combat his inner discomfort by a feeling of pitying indulgence.

"This is not the time to discuss all that," he said. "There are so many things to be said. . . . Believe me, this war between our two peoples has wounded me beyond anything. Up to the last minute I hoped it could be avoided, that France would not declare it, preferring to negotiate again."

"Allowing Poland to be crushed? You don't flatter France."

"Well, what's past is past. We aren't at war any more."

"You think so?"

"Not you and I. Peace would have been signed long ago and I'm sure it would have been an honorable peace, if only France and Germany . . . Even the occupation . . . Oh! we try to make it as easy as possible, except for . . . unavoidable frictions . . . but I perfectly understand that it is very painful for you. Why, the occupation wouldn't even have been necessary, at least to this extent, except for the obstinacy of the English in carrying on the struggle."

"It seems to me I've already read that somewhere," the Frenchman said.

Kunhardt opened his eyes wide with discouragement. He sighed and was silent. In his left hand he held his officer's cap. With his right hand he tapped his uniformed knee.

"At any rate," he went on, "it's the future that counts. Germany only wants to make friends with France. Don't you think that it is to our mutual advantage to collaborate?"

Camus barely smiled and replied quietly.

"I was going to tell you that it would be contrary to the principles for which we fought and also dishonorable. These are words which can still have a meaning for us but which would seem ridiculous to you."

"To me? Why so?"

"Naturally to you! . . . Honor, principles, great moral laws are things you write on strips of paper to decorate walls with, aren't they? . . . But when things get serious . . . No! Let's speak of our interests, let's talk facts. Some people would say France would be wrong in siding with Germany because once Germany is victorious she will keep her in a miserable and humiliating position. All very well, but such reasoning is fundamentally worthless. I prefer to say brutally that it's to France's interest to side with the victor."

"Well?" said the other, growing pale.

"Well, between us two I am quite sure that Germany will lose this war—as she did the other."

"How can you say that?"

"I wouldn't have said it six or eight months ago. But the situation has changed."

"How can you say that?" the captain repeated. "Our victory is indisputable. It has already taken place. We have only to consolidate it."

"You are speaking as a combatant. But listen. Who understood the situation most clearly in the last war? Those who were neutral. And we in France are neutral, aren't we?"

Kunhardt seemed scandalized and overwhelmed by turns.

"Are you saying what you really think?" he cried.

"Of course." And for the first time Camus' smile was almost

friendly. "Do you remember our former conversations? I told you that Germany always brought about her own ruin. This time she has begun again. Yes, in the beginning it was doubtful, but now," he nodded his head confidentially, "she is lost."

Kunhardt stood up, looking quite haggard. He didn't know what to do except to say foolishly, between two sighs, "And you, an old friend of Germany, speak this way?"

"I don't see that sentimentality can change anything. Since I was a friend of Germany, I have been hurt more than other people. Those who expected the worst of her have a certain satisfaction in their misery. But we who tried not to see her faults too clearly, who tried to believe in her a little—how can you add to our disappointment and bitterness!"

13

Walter Kunhardt had been at Caen for three months, without visiting Pierre Camus again. He had seen him only once, under very difficult circumstances.

Struder kept the population under close surveillance, being especially avid in hunting down those who listened to British broadcasts. Each morning his myrmidons brought him lists of people who had been reported or caught in the act. One day Struder called Kunhardt in and, pointing to a name on the list, said: "Do you know that name?"

"But . . ."

"Don't deny it. You've known him very well for a long time. You even went to visit him a few days after your arrival here."

"I didn't think there was any harm in it, Colonel. We've always been urged to cultivate good relations locally whenever possible."

"You could have told me about it. But that's not the question. This gentleman has been pointed out to me as one who listens to the British radio. You are to call him in. You are to receive him yourself. You will tell him first that his set is confiscated—that's the minimum. You will then tell him that we could and should lock him up, but out of regard for you, who will answer for him in the future, we are letting him go free. Only, he will be under special surveillance and, of course, considering his position, will be one of the people we shall take as hostage if the attitude of the population becomes unco-operative. . . . Tell him all that."

Kunhardt called in Pierre Camus and, not daring to look at him, transmitted the colonel's message.

But one morning when Kunhardt entered Struder's office, he saw the colonel in a state of apoplectic fury.

"Ah, there you are! . . . Good. Do you know what happened last night? Well, one of our noncommissioned officers has been assassinated right in the street. Stabbed twice in the back with a dagger. Oh, those cowards! Those sons of bitches! Sergeant Waldegg—he was part of the detachment that watched for people listening to the radio. Of course, no one knows who's guilty. I'm going to pick out ten hostages from the lists we've already drawn up. I shall choose particularly those who have an objectionable attitude or who have listened to the British radio. This is to let you know that your Professor Camus will head the group. I could ask for authority from those higher up to have them shot, and it would be granted immediately. But I'm human, I'm a decent fellow. I'm going to shut them up inside the buildings of the little stud farm near the town gates. It's very easy to turn into a prison and also very easy to watch. Anyway, we may have other needs for it presently. I appoint you commander of the establishment. I'll give you the number of men you'll need. No one can say that in appointing you I've chosen a brute, an executioner. . . . You'll have very respectable lodgings. I know the place. . . . I want to show the systematic benevolence which the German authorities would like us to use up to the end."

"But, Colonel, isn't there any way of discovering the guilty ones?"

"Bah, there isn't the slightest clue. No one will give them up. Even if we do find them, having ten hostages on hand is an excellent precaution. For, of course, I intend to announce publicly that the lives of the ten hostages will answer for those of our men. In case of another assault, they'll immediately be shot. I shall have the necessary authorization when the time comes. And these aren't empty threats. Up to now I've shown pity. But this will be the last time."

Walter Kunhardt screwed up his courage to ask Struder not to give him this post.

"I don't have any of the necessary qualities. I should be more useful somewhere else."

"What!" cried Struder, fixing him with a ferocious stare. "I'm giving you a proof of special consideration! And you're flinching? Do you want me to believe that you serve the Reich and the Führer against your will and that you're still secretly in sympathy with the Social Democrat, Jewish, Communist crooks? And at this moment when our fatherland is attacked on all sides, when our armies in the east have to hold the front against the Soviets?"

Kunhardt made no more objections.

14

When Captain Kunhardt took over, he called his men in and said: "We would rather serve our German fatherland on the field of battle, but we are here to carry out a task and we will do so with firmness. We must keep very close watch and not allow any disobedience on the part of the prisoners and no communication with anyone outside. But at the same time you must not forget that these men are not actually criminals. On the contrary, they are honorable men who are kept here to answer for the cowardly assaults which others may commit. You must treat them humanely and take their unhappy position into account. I shall punish disobedient prisoners but I shall also punish any cruelty suffered at your hands."

This speech comforted him. He needed comfort. "After all," he said to himself, "perhaps it's better for me to have this position than someone else. It's not pleasant for me, but the prisoners will benefit. I shall spare them any additional suffering. Struder can't force me to torture them. If necessary, I shall stand on the honor of a German officer."

Nevertheless, Kunhardt led a very melancholy life in the improvised concentration camp. One of his chief preoccupations was avoiding Pierre Camus. On the first day and the second he really wanted to call him in. A hundred times he ran over a little speech he would make to him: "You think that I have something to do with the misfortune which has overtaken you. Actually I have done all I could to shield you. Anyway, my presence here—and God knows I didn't wish to be here—should give you some feeling of security. Tell me if there is anything you want. Your quarters are not too bad, are they? I'll do anything I can. Would you like to send a message to your wife?"

But the first day he did not dare to call him in, nor the second. And then it was too late: the little speech would have been difficult to deliver and thoroughly unconvincing. What had restrained the captain was a mixture of fears: fear of what Struder might think if he found out (and he found out everything), a general fear which had been the daily bread of Germans for years, and, above all, fear of Pierre Camus himself, fear of having to face him while making the little speech.

The ten hostages had been lodged in three rooms, four prisoners in each of two rooms and only two in the third. Kunhardt had taken care that Camus was placed in the third room and had given him a companion he felt would be agreeable to him: a young lawyer who was considered one of the most distinguished men of the town. The rest of the prisoners consisted of another lawyer, a doctor, a druggist, an industrialist, two municipal councilors, and two merchants.

Kunhardt, in order to avoid Pierre Camus, had to keep away from any place where the prisoners were allowed. And since he could not exercise any personal supervision he was obliged to act through his subordinate, Sergeant Heilman, who was fortunately neither stupid nor cruel.

"Is everything all right?" he kept asking Heilman. "Do they make any complaints? Report everything to me. I don't appear because I don't wish to weaken my authority, but of course if any of them wish to speak to me personally, let me know immediately and I will see what can be done. I particularly want to know if Pierre Camus has asked for anything. Does he ask you about me?"

Then alone at his table, where a few books lay beside the official documents, facing a wall covered with faded paper upon which he could easily imagine portraits and slogans, he sometimes said to himself: "I am *their* prisoner."

It was barely eight o'clock in the morning. The telephone bell rang, and Kunhardt picked up the receiver.

"This is Colonel Struder. Just to let you know that I'll be with you in twenty minutes. Something very serious has come up."

After twenty minutes of great anxiety Kunhardt saw Struder entering.

"Lieutenant Buchholz was just attacked last night by 'French patriots,' as the underground papers call them. A dangerous wound. He may die. Of course, the ones who did it have disappeared. But we have clues. We know that there were three, two of them students in the Department of Literature and by an unfortunate coincidence pupils of your Professor Camus. I'm looking for them. Up to now we've lost the trail. In any case, I'm going to make an example. We must spread a salutary sense of fear . . . and strike immediately in order to create a stronger impression. Whether we catch the culprits today or not, I'm going to have three of the hostages shot tomorrow morning. Of course, one of them will be Professor Camus, who is quite likely an accomplice. Then I'll grant an eight-day reprieve. If we haven't caught the ones responsible by then, we shoot the other seven hostages."

"But you said . . . Colonel . . . tomorrow morning in any case . . . But suppose the guilty ones are caught by then, wouldn't it be a terrible thing to . . . It seems to me the population will be more angry than afraid."

"I have good reason to believe that they won't be caught."

"And why Professor Camus in particular? He's been carefully watched since he was brought here. He hasn't had any connection with the guilty ones. I can guarantee it."

For half an hour Kunhardt begged and argued as best he could. Struder ended by saying:

"We'll wait till this evening. If by luck the three murderers are caught . . . well, I'll think it over—even though I don't feel like weakening at present."

Kunhardt did not leave his study all day. He hardly dared to look out of the window. He was indeed a prisoner. And the thoughts that came to him during his imprisonment were hardly pleasant.

At seven o'clock he could hold out no longer and called the Colonel on the phone.

"I was going to call you," Struder said. "I have news of the three assassins. They reached the coast during the night. At dawn they set sail in a boat that was either stolen or lent to them. That's the result of our investigation. They must have escaped to England. It seems that they have been talking of joining de Gaulle for some time. It also appears that your famous professor hasn't hesitated to advise his students to leave the country and to do their duty where they can. I have proof that last month two of his students left for the same destination. So the situation is clear cut. Prepare to carry out the execution tomorrow morning at eight o'clock. The three chosen are: Professor Camus, his roommate, and the municipal councilor, Marchenoir."

"But I don't have to . . . ?"

"Of course you do. You have everything you need. There's no need to disturb anybody or cause a rumpus in town. Consequently you will command the firing squad. As you need to keep some men on guard, six men will be enough. Take good shots. See that everything is arranged this evening, but don't let anyone know about it. Anyway, you'll have another phone call from me tomorrow morning around seven o'clock. Between then and now I'll send you a written order so that everything will be official. The general in command of this district has already given his consent. I'm only waiting for his signature. You'll have the order in two hours at most. You'll sign the receipt, won't you, and fill in the time?"

Walter Kunhardt passed the night praying to every possible God—the God of religious faith, the God of philosophy, the unknown God—to grant him a miracle.

At seven o'clock the telephone rang.

"This is Colonel Struder. All ready? You've chosen a spot? You have a suitable wall? No, nothing new, absolutely nothing. Regulate your watch. I have twelve past seven o'clock. You'll begin on the dot of eight. You start with the professor, don't you? I shall very probably be there. But don't wait for me."

At eight o'clock Struder, standing at one side and a little behind Kunhardt, his eye on his watch, made a little sign. Kunhardt dropped his sword and gave the command: "Fire!"

The men of the firing squad, rather elderly reservists, were repelled by their task. At least four of them fired without looking. Pierre Camus fell, but it was evident that he still lived.

"Finish him off," Struder ordered Kunhardt.

"But . . . Colonel . . . I haven't . . . my revolver."

"Here you are. Take mine."

THE SEVENTH COMMANDMENT

Thou shalt not commit adultery

ANDRÉ MAUROIS

VII

THOU SHALT NOT COMMIT ADULTERY

A STORY BY

ANDRÉ MAUROIS

"I SANG well," she was thinking, "I sang well," and with an agonizing pleasure she remembered that great river of sound flowing through her chest, her throat, her mouth. She did not see the huge hall, a black gulf from which she was separated by a wall of fire, but she knew that three thousand faces were tense, delighted, happy. "Oh, how well I sang! . . . Brünnhilde couldn't be sung better." Her partner Vernet had said it during the intermission: "Brünnhilde couldn't be sung better," and Vernet knew. He had been playing Wotan for twenty-five years. He had sung *Die Walküre* with French, Italian, German, and Swedish sopranos. And Vernet had said, "Brünnhilde couldn't be sung better." How beautiful and perfect life was!

Catherine Albert, wearing her helmet with its broken wings, was stretched out on the stage of the Paris Opéra. Vernet had placed his shield upon her and his spear near by. "Vernet still has a fine voice," she was thinking, "but all the same he gets tired more quickly than he used to." Lying on the papier-mâché rock, she wondered how she looked to the audience. "An authentic Valkyrie," Francis Eric, the young composer whose melodies she liked, had said when he came to see her in her dressing room a little while before.

"An authentic Valkyrie," she thought. Francis, a hard and derisive young fellow, did not pay compliments: it was true that even in street clothes she looked like a Valkyrie. Too tall, repelling a good many men by her aggressive strength, yet splendid with her broad forehead, her thick black hair, her vigorous body, she was born a Wagnerian goddess. The quick, burning notes of the incantation enveloped her. Ridiculous artificial flames, too regularly lined up, were covering the stage. "O God! What a lack of dignity in all this!" she thought. "If only someday I could sing at Bayreuth! . . ."

For her Wagner's dramas were the rituals of a religion, with Bayreuth its Mecca. She had made the pilgrimage and returned a convert. Many of her friends reproached her for this. "Wagner," they said, "yes, in a certain sense it's beautiful. But it's a pagan art. It's contrary to all French civilization. For a thousand years France has tried to contribute clarity and directness to human thought, a heroic simplicity in the Greek manner. Wagner is obscurity, instinct, the primitive forest and malignant divinities. Wagner is the potion with which Germany intoxicates herself before setting fire to the world. . . ." Catherine refused to judge this kind of theater in nationalist terms. A profound and secret need within her responded to it: to the proud chastity of Brünnhilde, to Isolde's tragic certainty that true love could only be consummated in death.

The "slumber" theme, five fluid notes in a descending scale, was breaking into the fire music. Careful not to breathe because the slightest movement would make the scales of her cuirass glint with reflections a statue walled within a sonorous cathedral, Catherine mused, "Accursed. Like Brünnhilde, I too am accursed. A Valkyrie on the stage, I go through life like a warrior, unresponsive to men's advances. Incapable of desire or pleasure. . . . Aimery, you strange boy. You roused such a thirst in me and never knew how to quench it—Aimery, dear Aimery, what has become of you?"

Wotan bent majestically to kiss the forehead of the condemned maiden. Leaning over Catherine, Vernet whispered, "When you get up to take your bow, look out for the stage brace. You can sprain your ankle in that thing."

Catherine thanked him with a barely perceptible movement of her eyelids. The heavy shield resting on her chest crushed her somewhat, but she liked the discomfort. The jets of vapor spreading over the stage sounded like water pouring from the taps in a bathroom.

"Thank God it's over!" said a stage hand under the flooring.

"The greatness and ignominy of the theater!" she thought. "Sublime texts with ridiculous little drawings on the margin."

She closed her eyes. From the orchestra, emerging for a second from Brünnhilde's slumber music and Loge's magic fire music, the Siegfried theme continued to rise up. How often she had awaited it as a young girl, in the shadow of the box with an iron grille, her fingers linked with Aimery's. In those days a mad hope tingled along her spine each time that "annunciation" came to her from the brasses. Now Aimery was living far from her, married to someone else, and Catherine was famous. "What hero," she thought, "will dare to cross the circle of fire from now on? . . ." But did she still long for one? Did she not have her art? "Sorrow bursting into happiness. . . ." And what happiness, she was thinking, could surpass this? Recalling with delight the sense of being entirely possessed by that great river of sound flowing through her chest, she opened her eyes again. Wotan climbed to the top of the rock. The jets of vapor died down. It was over.

Curtain. In the audience a touching silence. Then the applause. Vernet lifted the shield, helped Catherine to her feet. One had to bow. How she preferred the end of a Bayreuth presentation, with applause forbidden. She sensed the audience as wild with pleasure as she herself after an almost perfect performance. Five curtain calls. Six curtain calls. People were on their feet, crying "Bravo!" They refused to leave their seats. The sixth time, Vernet said to her:

"Go out alone, Catherine! It's you they want."

She protested, but knew it was true. The audience was interested in the others only as they supported her, acted as a frame for her.

"We'll all go," she said to the eight Valkyries hiding behind the scenery. But her comrades pushed her on the stage and then retreated into the wings. Here she stood alone before this great structure of red and gold. Then the enthusiasm increased. A long ovation rose up from the orchestra, descended from the balconies. A great French singer was born.

2

When she returned to her dressing room, Catherine Albert found a crowd of admirers waiting in front of her door. For more than one reason her triumph was received with sympathy and enthusiasm. Catherine Albert was the only daughter of a great actor, Frédéric-Albert, who for forty years had held a position in the French theater equal to that of such women as Rachel or Sarah Bernhardt or such men as Talma or Mounet Sully. Thanks to him, the Comédie Française had known new seasons of success after a rather dull interval. Frenchmen took fresh interest in the roles of Rodrigue, Horace, Ruy Blas, Hernani, and even Œdipus. Frédéric-Albert's most admirable quality was his ability to be noble and natural at the same time.

"In this sublime tragedian there is material to make the greatest of comedians," the critic Émile Faguet wrote one day.

The following day, tempted by this opinion and also spurred on by his artistic instincts, Frédéric-Albert, much to the surprise of the administration, asked permission to attempt several comic parts: Alceste, Tartufe, Figaro. The finest French comedies are masked and secret tragedies. When Frédéric-Albert played these roles he highlighted the tragic side, but a powerful, bold, and bitter comic style overlay the sadness.

Then Faguet said: "Frédéric-Albert is the most complete actor I have ever known on the French stage."

The man was perhaps less complete than the actor. Very handsome, like his daughter, and like her a little taller than average, he had the intelligence of his profession, yet his general culture was extremely limited. Nothing existed for him but the theater.

Nevertheless, few men of his generation were more beloved. Around 1900 he had become the ideal Don Juan to thousands of young girls and women. Every actor enhances his own prestige with that of the characters he embodies. Yet, curiously enough, he is often a rather unfeeling person. Accustomed to counterfeiting emotions, he no longer needs to possess them. Born with the ability to change himself into others, he has hardly time to exist. For a long time Frédéric-Albert played the role of seducer, attaching no more importance to it than he did to the stage role. Two women shot themselves for him and one swallowed veronal. All three survived, and he remembered these adventures merely as mediocre melodramas.

Then one day, when he was forty years old, a young girl not connected with the theater tried to fix this wandering star. Marthe de Trene belonged to a family of minor provincial nobility and, being an orphan, lived in Paris with her grandmother. Since she loved the theater passionately, in 1907 she subscribed to a series of poetic matinees given in the Trocadero by the Comédie Française. Each week she admired Frédéric-Albert's incomparable reciting of Villon, Musset, or Baudelaire. She praised his voice and his charm so highly that friends arranged for her to meet him at dinner. He liked her. She had observed in his acting certain intentions, inflections, shadings to which he attached great importance and which no one else had ever noticed. She interested him and when she asked him to give her diction lessons he agreed, although he had long since ceased to take pupils outside of the conservatory where he gave courses. He got into the habit of discussing his roles with her. Not that she was a comedian. He had to tell her almost immediately that she was not meant for the theater: "You feel strong emotions but you can't express them," he said. "The actress' art is just the reverse." Marthe's beauty, however, her evident purity and the fineness of her judgment, touched the famous comedian. He had seduced many women but no young girl harder to conquer or more worthy of being conquered than this one.

When, three years later, she spoke of marrying him, her grandmother and her uncles began to shriek:

"An actor! Where did he come from? Who ever heard of his family?"

It was true, but Marthe *knew* he was a genius and that she loved him.

"A libertine who's had dozens of mistresses. Does a leopard ever change his spots?"

"He's promised me," she said. "Anyway, even if he doesn't change, I will be faithful and he will come back to me."

"He's twenty years older than you are!"

"That will be to my advantage."

Since she was of age and controlled her own fortune, she became Madame Frédéric-Albert. The marriage was a happy one. Paris watched the transformation of Frédéric-Albert with affectionate amusement. Don Juan had been turned into a faithful husband and did not even seem to find faithfulness painful. One daughter, Catherine, was born in 1912, and the unfeeling Frédéric-Albert, to the surprise of all his friends, turned out to be an excellent and even enthusiastic father. When the little girl grew up and he discovered she possessed a strikingly beautiful figure, and that her voice, gestures, and inflections were effective, he had great hopes for her.

Despite his age, he was still successfully playing parts written for very young men.

"Youth," he said, "is only a question of composition."

An admirable sentence.

3

"Do you remember me, Mr. Eric?" said a voice with a German accent.

"Who wouldn't remember you, Herr Riesenberger, after seeing you conduct at Bayreuth?"

The old German conductor and the young composer were both waiting outside Catherine Albert's dressing room until the door should open.

"You were satisfied?" Eric asked.

The German drew himself up. "Art is long and life is short," he said. "How can one ever be satisfied? Your orchestra doesn't rehearse enough . . . the tempo is too slow . . . the Wotan lacks fire . . . but this Catherine Albert! She is Brünnhilde herself. . . . We have better voices in Germany. Unfortunately, the singers who have them have grown stout. They have Brünnhilde's voice but not her presence. This one is . . ."

For a long time he searched for a word, then said: "Sculptural. And even more. I've seen her work; I admire her discipline. . . . I didn't know Frenchwomen were capable of being so hard on themselves."

"Why not?" Eric asked. "When French people love their art intensely, as Catherine does, they can impose the most severe discipline upon themselves. I've rehearsed Catherine in songs I've written myself. . . . I've always been impressed by her conscientiousness."

At that moment there was an eddy in the ranks of people as they moved aside to let a superb old man, draped in a romantic cape, pass through.

The German leaned toward Eric.

"Who is that man?"

"Catherine's father—Frédéric-Albert, one of our greatest actors. Don't you know him?"

"Oh, her father's an actor? . . . He ought to be proud of such a daughter."

"Tremendously proud," said Eric. "In the beginning he expected to make a tragedian out of her. He took a lot of trouble—in vain. She couldn't read lines. And, anyway, she doesn't like that sort of thing. On the other hand, the singing lessons she took with Vernet filled her with enthusiasm. She felt herself born to be a singer; she learned entire roles. She waited for a miracle. Her father didn't believe in it. And then the miracle happened."

"Where there's a will the miracle always happens," said Hans Riesenberger, raising his head. "The true miracle is never a miracle."

"One evening at the Opéra-Comique," Eric went on, "Marcelle Denya, the leading Manon, had a sudden attack of appendicitis. Her understudy was away on a tour in the provinces. The other possible Manon had the grippe or was pregnant or something. They telephoned Vernet, who was teaching at the conservatory, to ask for a student from his class in singing. He suggested Catherine Albert, who made her debut without even an orchestra rehearsal."

"The usual story!" Riesenberger said. "And of course she created a sensation?"

"No, not right away, but she had a critical success. To tell the truth, there were mixed reasons. Catherine was beautiful. The public adored her father. The romantic marriage of her parents kindled the imagination of the Parisians. And then Paris loves families of actors: Mounet Sully and Paul Mounet; Albert Lambert, father and son; the two Brasseurs, the two Coquelins, the two Guitrys, Frédéric-Albert and his daughter. . . ."

"Is her mother also of the theater?"

"Oh, no! Her mother is a self-effacing woman, timid but charming. Among these superhuman creatures, come down from Valhalla, she is a little crushed. . . . Wait, there she is."

Madame Frédéric-Albert, a woman in a gray veil with a slender figure and still very pretty, had just opened the door of the dressing room.

"You can come in now," she said.

The Valkyrie had removed her white robe, her heavy red mantle, and put on a negligee which left her splendid neck bare. Panting a little, happy, triumphant, she reminded one of a beautiful thoroughbred after winning a race.

"Catherine," said Eric, "I had prepared a thousand very nice things to say to you, but . . . just imagine whom I'm bringing you?

Herr Riesenberger! . . . Did you know he was in the audience?"

"No," said Catherine as the German bowed. "If I had known I would have been paralyzed with fear."

"Heil dir, Walküre! . . . You would have been wrong," said Riesenberger, stressing each syllable. "You would have been wrong because I like, I liked what you accomplished this evening very much. . . . And I even propose to ask you a question which will doubtless please you."

Her heart skipped a beat, for she knew that what she longed for most was about to happen.

"I propose to ask you," Riesenberger continued, "if, in case—I say, in case—you should be invited to sing at Bayreuth, you would be free?"

"But I should die of happiness," she said.

Frédéric-Albert, who was listening, said with some irritation: "Catherine!"

She glanced reproachfully at him and then introduced him: "My father . . ."

Riesenberger bowed very low. "I don't offer you anything," he continued, "I haven't the authority to make an offer. But I have the right to make the suggestion and I shall do so. The decision depends upon those whose authority is greater than mine and whose decisions are not always made on musical grounds. However, just now, I know that *someone* wishes a rapprochement with France. . . . Music, like the exchange of students and the Olympic games, can contribute to this. . . . You know that our Leader goes to Bayreuth every summer. I have reason to believe that he would not be displeased to see a French singer. Our Leader, you know, is a Wagner enthusiast and his patronage . . ."

The sound of glass breaking and water spilling cut short his words. An awkward gesture by Frédéric-Albert had just upset a vase of flowers.

"Oh, Papa!" said Catherine.

"It is natural," said Riesenberger smoothly, "quite natural that your father should be excited by a success that is truly . . ."

He sought for the precise word a moment and then, not finding it in French, said: *"Fabelhaft."*

4

Bayreuth intoxicated Catherine Albert. To practice a religion and suddenly find oneself its priestess is an extraordinary happiness. At Bayreuth, a performance was a piously conducted ceremony. No apprentice looked for personal success. The dignitaries of the cult officiated. Like Norns, the daughters of Cosima Wagner spoke oracles. Nothing could be modified in the staging of a scene, once directed by the Master, the god. Catherine went to kneel on the proudly modest stone, without a name upon it, under which Wagner and his wife rested. She was grateful to the intimates of Wahnfried for treating her as an initiate, for showing her the Wagner manuscripts, Cosima's intimate diary. One of the young girls took her to the tomb of Liszt and said proudly:

"Isn't it remarkable, Fräulein Albert? . . . Liszt, a Hungarian, Cosima, half French, Houston Chamberlain, an Englishman, and Winifred Wagner, an Englishwoman, have all been annexed by the German genius. . . . And even you, Fräulein Albert, you who are so French, haven't you, too, learned our language out of love for Wagner?"

Catherine was received in a friendly way by the family of Count Jahrenberg, who lived in a château near Bayreuth. He had married a very beautiful Belgian, with whom he always spoke French. The couple were very cordial to Catherine. When she returned to France she expressed her enthusiasm very loudly. Several of her friends criticized her.

"You are wrong, Catherine," Eric said to her, "to form connections of this kind with Germans. I don't mind your singing among them. I even approve of it: it's your profession. But you say this Count Jahrenberg and his family have become your friends. . . . Tomorrow we shall be at war with these people. Then you'll be sorry."

"But why, Francis? France was at war with Prussia in the eighteenth century and Voltaire continued to be the friend of Frederick. . . . France has had ten wars with England and private friendships have never been affected by them for long."

"Well, I'm no historian, Catherine darling, but it seems to me that it was different. In those days it wasn't war to the death. . . . These Nazis hate us. What they want is to destroy France. Yes, indeed! Don't be so full of illusions. Even your dear Wagner, that precursor of Nazism, hated us."

"Wagner? Yes, of course. We treated him so badly! Each one of his visits to Paris was associated with terribly humiliating experiences. You remember the incredible *Tannhäuser* intrigue!"

"A fine reason to hate France! French people who counted were very fair to him. Gounod said: 'I pray God to give me a failure like that!' And God knows how spiteful Wagner was about Gounod. He never even wanted to hear *Faust*."

"Do you blame him?"

"I certainly do. A great deal of this summary criticism of Gounod is merely a fad. In any case, the failure of *Tannhäuser* doesn't justify Wagner's hatred for France, his ferocious joy at the bombardment of Paris, or his ignoble *Capitulation*."

"These are old stories, Francis! The Germans receive the French at Bayreuth splendidly now. Believe me, it's a friendship that shouldn't be despised."

"I embrace my rival, but it's only to strangle him. . . . They want to lull us to sleep. They'd like us perhaps as slaves. That's possible. Captive Greece. But I have no desire to play second fiddle. And what credit do they deserve for giving you a good reception—you, who sing their music, who sing it beautifully, and spread it all over Europe?"

"Artistic jealousy, Francis?"

"No, Catherine, advice from a friend who doesn't like to see you following a path he feels dangerous."

Some days later Madame Frédéric-Albert, in her turn, interfered in the matter, for this gentle woman could sometimes be very firm.

"Catherine," she said, "I wish you would be careful what you say in front of your father. You hurt him the other evening when you spoke with such a shocking leniency about Hitler and his friends."

Catherine resisted. "Why do you say 'with leniency'? I simply told how, at a performance of the *Meistersinger,* I met Hitler, who was there with Winifred Wagner in the *Fürsten Galerie,* and he said a few complimentary things to me. That's all. A fact is a fact. I can't say that he insulted me."

"No, my dear, but you ought to remember that your father is Jewish and if he were in Germany today he would be horribly persecuted. It's naturally disagreeable for him to hear you talk about meeting that man. I'm surprised that you don't feel it yourself."

"That business again!" Catherine said crossly. "Yes, yes, I know. Papa's parents were Jews from Avignon who became Catholics during the Second Empire. . . . It's possible, but what does it matter. Papa was born a Christian. Why dig up the buried past?"

"Because prying into family histories is exactly what your Germans do. You know perfectly well that they don't care about religion but about what they call race."

Catherine shrugged her shoulders. "Race! No one is less Semitic than Father. He's a hundred per cent French, and southern French, which is all to the good."

"Of course he's a hundred per cent French, but that's not the point. . . . Catherine, don't deceive yourself. Whether he has any Jewish traits or not, in the eyes of the Germans your father would be a Jew. You yourself, if the Germans knew you were half Jewish, wouldn't sing in Germany."

"And how is it they don't know it?"

"Because in order to look up the origin of your father's family, it would be necessary to consult the archives of Avignon. No one has thought of doing it. Your father is a Catholic, he goes to church every Sunday, his name isn't Jewish. Even I would certainly never have guessed it if he hadn't told me."

"Has he told many other people?"

"He does every time the conversation lights upon this subject. He doesn't hide it, and he's right. But his friends never think of it. In our whole life I've never known a quarrel or an unpleasant discussion about the subject. I had you brought up in a convent. Your father approved of it. He's as good a Catholic as I. Only, the persecution of the Jews has horrified him and he detests the Nazi doctrines—as is natural."

"All that has nothing to do with Wagner."

"With Wagner? Perhaps not. But it has a great deal to do with Hitler."

"Just where is all this leading, Mama? What are you asking me to do?"

"I am asking you to make your contacts with the Germans strictly musical and to talk about it as little as possible before your father, that's all."

Catherine shook her head in exasperation, sighed, and did not answer. When she was irritated, her pretty face could wear an expression of uncompromising hardness.

5

The first eight months of the war, from 1939 to 1940, changed the life of Paris very little. The enemy propaganda endeavored to spread through France the hope that the conflict would simply fizzle out without any real fighting, and it succeeded. Badly informed, lulled by false rumors, the public succumbed to a dangerous inertia. The theater followed the example of everything else. Except for a few benefit performances for war activities, the same peacetime routine continued. In 1914 the presentations had reacted strongly to the war spirit, sometimes all for the better and sometimes not. Camille Saint-Saëns had promoted an absurd campaign against foreign music. Nothing like that in 1939. Everyone prided himself on artistic tolerance. Catherine could sing her favorite Wagnerian roles all winter and was always well received.

She led a secluded life. Her dresser, Melanie, a woman friend from the Opéra, Cazenotte, and two old retired actors, the Remonds, formed a sort of court, lived at her expense, and never left her. Poor Cazenotte was a mediocre singer to whom, thanks to Catherine's influence, the administration of the Opéra gave small roles. She was *a* Valkyrie, *a* Flower Maiden. Cazenotte unstintedly praised everything that Catherine said and did; she followed her like a faithful dog. Mr. Remond, who was good with figures, kept Catherine's accounts and looked after her contracts. Mrs. Remond acted as her secretary, took charge of furnishing the house, and supervised the housekeeping. There had never been a man in Catherine Albert's life. Although many had tried to win her, she was born chaste. The episode with Aimery had left her only the memory of having been unbearably deceived. When an enterprising Lohengrin or some sentimental Tristan took advantage of a duet to press her tightly in his arms, Catherine pushed the tenor away with a melancholy smile. Sometimes the man, moved by her beauty, dared to persist. Then Catherine admitted her mysterious inhibitions, her complete indifference. "But you'll see! It won't be like that with me," more than one obstinate aspirant said. But Catherine, haughty and frozen, did not wish to be convinced.

In May, 1940, when the German offensive was unleashed and suddenly pierced the French lines, Catherine Albert was not surprised. She had expected some apocalyptic event. At the beginning of June many people began to leave Paris. Frédéric-Albert refused. He had retired two years before, but he wanted to end his days beside the Théâtre Français in the apartment in the Rue de Richelieu where he had lived for thirty years.

"No, no," he said, "I owe everything to Paris. I shall not desert her."

In vain Catherine insisted: "But, Papa, it's absurd. A time may come when you'll be in danger. And what's the use of your staying here?"

"Et s'il n'en reste qu'un, je serai celui-là," the old actor declaimed.

Catherine could make no headway with him. Moreover, she also wanted to stay. But she thought her position different. Was she not, in the eyes of the Germans, a famous singer? The only Frenchwoman whom they admired without reservation? She knew they would treat her with respect. Who could tell but, thanks to her, Paris might not be more honorably treated? She imagined unbelievably beautiful presentations in the course of which the French and the Germans would be reconciled because of her genius.

Through the streets under her windows millions of men and women passed, seeking escape. From her balcony, Catherine watched them pass and thought proudly: "I remain."

At the end of three days the flood subsided to a mere trickle, and finally stopped. A surprising silence followed, heavy with menace. Tuesday, the eleventh of June, Paris was declared an open city; the walls were covered with notices urging the population to be calm. An opaque, artificial fog covered the city like a shroud. Paris, its attention fixed on the north, awaited the mortal blow. There was a tragic and interminable delay. During the night of the thirteenth to the fourteenth, far off, the dull reverberations of an army could be heard. When, toward seven o'clock, it began to march through the deserted streets, all the shutters remained closed.

Soon meetings with the Germans could not be avoided. They could be seen in the Champs-Élysées, on the quays, going about in groups, admiring the beauty of the city they had violated. This was the time when people said the Germans were very "correct" and that they had detoured the Arc de Triomphe in order not to march over the tomb of the Unknown Soldier. These were, in fact, their orders, and in these early days their behavior was severe, formal, but polite.

Catherine went as far as the Opéra. A uniformed German was in the director's office. She gave her name. The German rose, clicked his heels, and saluted.

"I have seen you at Bayreuth, Madame. Seen you and applauded you. I hope we shall hear you soon."

Catherine bowed without saying a word.

"One of your German friends came this morning to ask for your address," he continued. "Herr General Graf von Jahrenberg."

This time Catherine's face lit up.

"Oh, Jahrenberg is here?"

"Yes, Madame. . . . I am sure you will hear from him."

The officer spoke French without an accent.

"You have lived in France?" Catherine asked.

"No, in Belgium. . . . But I like France, French art, pretty Frenchwomen. Madame, why did you declare war on us? Our two countries were meant to understand each other."

That was evidently the "party line."

"Are you a musician?" she asked. "Are you going to manage the Opéra?"

The man laughed loudly.

"Oh, nothing of the kind. We're leaving it under French management. I'm only here to keep order."

When she left the office she had found out that the performances would not be interrupted for long and would even go on all summer.

"Should I play for the enemy?" she thought. "Would it be decent?"

Then she told herself that she would not be playing for the enemy, but for the Parisians and for herself. And, since she wanted to be reassured, she was.

Two weeks later she appeared in *Die Walküre* before an audience composed partly of German officers in gray-green tunics covered with decorations and partly of French civilians. There was no mixing. During the entr'acte the Germans strode about the main lounge; the French gathered in the corridor which ran back of the boxes on the ground floor.

Jahrenberg came to pay his respects to Catherine in her dressing room and recalled old times in Bayreuth. Whereupon all her Parisian friends withdrew, and she was conscious of their silent but deep disapproval.

"All the same, what can I do?" she said to herself. "Send him away? I neither can nor want to do it."

The Comédie Française had also reopened. When in *La Rabouilleuse* the veterans on half pay sang, *sotto voce, "We watch over the safety of the Empire . . ."* the applause broke out simultaneously in the orchestra and the gallery.

In spite of his retirement, Frédéric-Albert went every day to the theater to be present at a rehearsal or to give advice. One evening during an intermission of *Hernani* he stepped in front of the curtain to recite Victor Hugo's hymn:

Praised be our eternal France!
Praised be those who died for her!
And the martyrs, strong and valiant;
Those spurred on by their example
Who seek a place within the temple
And who shall die as they have died.

The whole audience rose in silence. The German officers who were present took no notice, but the next day Frédéric-Albert was requested not to appear again upon the stage of the Théâtre Français.

6

"Why didn't you come to see me yesterday after the concert, Francis? I sang your songs. I expected you to say something."

Francis Eric, seated at the piano, played three notes of an arpeggio. Then he said:

"I did come, Catherine, but I found your Jahrenberg with you and I beat a retreat. I told you that I didn't want to meet any Germans."

"I don't understand you, Francis," Catherine said. "You always seem to be criticizing me. I'm just as sincere a patriot as you. I was terribly anxious that France should win this war. She lost it. We have to accept the situation bravely."

"The war isn't over," Francis Eric said.

"All right. Let's admit that. How does my letting General von Jahrenberg come to see me affect our chances?"

"I'll tell you how: accepting defeat discourages the French and encourages the Germans. If they meet poker faces everywhere, they will have a sense of failure. Let the Parisians ignore their parades, their concerts, their changing of the guard, make them feel depressed."

"But, Francis, thanks to Jahrenberg, who seems all-powerful, I'm able to help many of our unhappy countrymen. And I *do* help. Would Vernet still be singing if I hadn't defended him after he blew up in front of Riesenberger? . . . After all, Jahrenberg does his best to soften . . ."

"Don't for a minute believe it's going to last, Catherine. You can do nothing with a Nazi—do you understand?—*nothing*. In Berlin, back in the days when I was making a score for a film, I met several Englishmen who said like you: 'We must tame them, humanize them, direct them.' It's not possible. Those fellows always take everything they can get. They'll go gently at first so as not to startle the French, but they'll tighten the vise slowly and pitilessly, until there isn't a drop of blood left in the corpse. No, Catherine, I'm sorry to say you won't save anyone. I know very well that your intentions are good, but I see you swept toward a terrible fate."

The twenty-seventh of September, 1940, the day after Catherine Albert and Francis Eric had this conversation, the Militärbefehlshaber in Frankreich decreed that "every Jewish person must present himself or herself at the police station of the district (or at the commissariat of police of the quarter) for special registration. . . . All those being considered as Jews who had at least three grandparents of pure Jewish blood . . . or who at the date of publication of the present regulations belonged to congregations of the Hebrew religion."

Frédéric-Albert went to the police commissariat of his quarter. A special office had been opened. The commissioner of the district was an agreeable man intensely fond of the theater, to whom Frédéric-Albert had often given complimentary tickets for his family. As the commissioner passed the line of men waiting he saw the actor.

"Don't stand there, Mr. Albert," he said. "Come into my office. . . . Here, come right in. Have a seat. . . . Are you really Jewish? I didn't know it."

"I hardly know it myself," Frédéric-Albert said, "but I suppose the Germans will make it their business pretty soon to teach me what it is to be a Jew."

The commissioner closed the door and said in a low voice: "You know, Mr. Albert, if I were in your place, I should forget to register. After all, nobody knows, I can assure you. You have nothing to fear from me. Just keep quiet. It'll save you a lot of trouble. . . . I'll give you a permit as far as the unoccupied zone. Once there, you can easily cross into the free section. With the Germans it's just a question of money."

"Thank you, Commissioner," Frédéric-Albert said, "but I prefer to register."

The commissioner threw up his hands to indicate he could take no further responsibility.

"As you please!" he said. "Anyway, there's no reason why you should stand in line... . . I'll send an officer to register you; he'll bring your card."

"Thank you, Commissioner," said Frédéric-Albert, "but I'd rather stand in line with the others."

"Really? All right. Fine. I understand your point of view. You see, Mr. Albert, I find these laws revolting myself and I am thoroughly disgusted at having my police stations used for such stupidities! But what can I do?"

"Nothing," Frédéric-Albert said.

That evening Catherine, who was visiting her parents, heard the story of what had happened.

"Poor Papa," she said. "How sad all this is."

And she went over and kissed him. She was genuinely sorry for him. And besides, she was asking herself with considerable anxiety whether her father's declaration would have some effect upon her own status. He guessed this, for he had very sure intuitions wherever his daughter was concerned.

"You have nothing to fear for yourself, Catherine," he said tenderly. "I took care to point out that your mother is *one hundred per cent Aryan,* as they say."

"Yes, I know," she said. "But they're terribly severe in the theater. In Germany they didn't allow actors who had a single doubtful grandmother to appear on the stage."

"A doubtful grandmother!" Frédéric-Albert said bitterly.

When Catherine returned home that night she talked about her worries. Fat Cazenotte came and sat beside her and put her arms around her shoulders.

"Oh, Catherine, you certainly don't have to worry. They need you. . . . What would happen to the Opéra without its star? You can't be replaced in some parts."

She sighed: "Oh yes, of course," but she had the look of a wounded animal.

7

Going to the Opéra for a rehearsal with the orchestra never failed to make Catherine happy. She loved the atmosphere, the street clothes of the singers which emphasized the workmanlike character of the profession, the dry rap of the conductor's baton on the music rack stopping the torrent of sound with a gesture, hurling passionate abuse, then unchaining the tempest anew. Today Riesenberger was to conduct a rehearsal of *Parsifal,* and she was glad of it. She had always learned a great deal from him.

"Thank God for work," she thought.

Thanks to her profession alone, she was able to endure this wretched period without suffering too much. Lack of food, lack of heat, lack of news, all this slid off her without leaving any traces in her subjective universe. There she erected immutable marvels, edifices of sound which nothing could destroy. The gods lived there, secure from the twilight. Catherine Albert was a distressed Frenchwoman whose country had been stolen, but Elsa, Brünnhilde, Kundry, Isolde, Eva—who could reach them?

As she went happily up the stairs she sang the ascending notes of the Prelude.

"Kundry," she thought, "tonight I shall be Kundry—the sorceress, the sinner, the saint. . . . And once again Riesenberger will say: 'All right,' in that hard way which means: 'It's perfect.' Let's hope he doesn't abuse Cazenotte the way he did yesterday. It's true she's ridiculous. But who notices her in the crowd?"

When she passed the doorkeeper's room he ran after her.

"Mademoiselle Albert, Mr. Molinie wants you to go to his office before the rehearsal without fail."

Molinie, Assistant to the Director of the Opéra, was Catherine's friend. What could he want? It was doubtless a question of a date. Or perhaps the business of a German tour which she had refused in order to avoid a new disagreement with her parents, but which she could not postpone for very long if the *Kommandantur* insisted.

"Good morning, Molinie. You want to see me?"

"Yes, Catherine. Have a seat."

She noticed he had a serious and troubled look. He pointed toward a red document.

"A very distressing thing has happened, Catherine. The occupying authorities have received an anonymous letter stating that you have Jewish blood. I assure you that I knew nothing about it. But they have made an investigation and discovered, so they say, that it's true your father has registered as a Jew. I don't have to tell you that I consider this kind of prying absurd, do I? That I don't care for it at all; that I admire your father's talent and your own, and that I would admire you both just the same if you were Mohammedans, Brahmins, or Mormons, but that I rejoice that you are French, which is all the greater glory for our country. . . . Only, Catherine . . ."

He saw that she was trembling, got up and put his hand on her shoulder.

"Only, the Nazis are among us with tanks and Stukas, with armored forces and the Gestapo, and we have to pay attention to their orders even if they are idiotic."

"But, Molinie, what are their orders?" she asked in despair.

"Well. Their eternal mania! They allow *only* hundred per cent Aryans in the theater and on the radio! As if *Aryans* existed, without mentioning the *hundred per cent!* As if France wasn't a mixture of twenty races. As if a single Nazi could be certain of not having a drop of Jewish blood himself! You know perfectly well I think exactly as you do about all this. . . . Only, if the Gestapo don't want you to sing, there is nothing I can do about it."

"And Riesenberger?" she asked. "Hasn't he, at least, full authority to insist upon having me? For two years he's been telling me that I am the only possible Kundry in France!"

Molinie went back and sat down and began to play with his paperknife.

"Riesenberger," he said, "is more remarkable for his talent than for his courage. In peacetime he never defended his German Jewish friends. All the more reason why he won't defend a Frenchwoman. . . . I am certain that at the bottom of his heart he thinks your exclusion is scandalous, that he admires you sincerely, but he wouldn't lift his little finger to help you. He would be too afraid of compromising himself!"

She was holding back the tears that came to her eyes, and her warrior's face had lost its composure.

"But it's crazy!" she cried. "My father's family just like my mother's has always been French. And, anyway, what do these things have to do with music? It doesn't make sense—it doesn't make sense at all."

"None at all, my dear, I agree with you. These people are crazy. But they are strong. And when madness has force behind her, reason must run to earth—until she can strike back."

"The Nazis themselves, those of the highest rank, have applauded me. You're my witness."

"Yes, but they are slaves of their own ideology. They don't dare break the rules to which they attribute their success. You've certainly seen how they have pitilessly eliminated Bruno Walter, Einstein, and others in Germany. Genius finds no pity in them. . . . Don't cry, Catherine, please. I'm miserable enough at having to tell you all this without being able to do anything for you. This morning I argued for two hours with these Gestapo creatures. . . . I've even thought of resigning. But what's the use? They'd be only too glad! They'd replace me with one of their people. And that wouldn't help you."

She did not answer, and Molinie was silent for some time. Catherine raised her face at last, covered with tears.

"I suppose," she said, "there's no use my rehearsing this afternoon."

"Riesenberger," he said, "called off the rehearsal a few minutes before you came in."

8

She never knew how she got out of the Opéra, how she went down the waxed staircase from the business offices, how she got to the subway. Her whole universe was in ruins. What was she going to do with herself? Was she born for anything else in the world except singing? Oh, if she could die, if she could sleep!

Kundry's swoon. Brünnhilde's enchanted sleep. Oh! if some god could have put this fallen Valkyrie, this great mute voice, to sleep until the day when a French conqueror should deliver her!

When she returned home, Catherine stretched on her bed and closed her eyes. How could she sleep when wounded pride, a stubborn hope, revolt, and disdain struggled together in her spirit?

Plump Cazenotte entered.

"What has happened, Catherine? You're crying?"

In her voice was a barely perceptible pleasure and Catherine Albert's sensitive ear caught the dissonance immediately.

"Cazenotte wrote the anonymous letter," she thought.

Then she remembered having told the fat girl about Frédéric-Albert's visit to the commissioner. "Oh! Catherine! *You* certainly don't have to worry. . . . They need you!" She remembered even the inflections of the voice and perceived the hidden resentment in the tone.

"I'm certain," she thought. "It's Cazenotte! How could I have failed to see it before? . . . This girl hates me."

The discovery made her feel like fighting. No, indeed, she was not going to let this wench triumph without at least trying to defend herself. She jumped from the bed and ran to bathe her face in cold water.

"Everything will be all right, Cazenotte, everything will be quite all right. Just leave me alone."

When the flabby Flower Maiden had gone, Catherine went to the telephone. She was now ready to give battle.

"Invalides 12–43. . . . Fräulein Catherine Albert wunscht mit Herrn General von Jahrenberg zu sprechen. . . . Ja, bitte. . . . Ja. . . . General, it's Catherine Albert. . . . Could I see you for five minutes before this evening? At your home rather than your office. . . . Yes. . . . Yes. . . . Thank you, General, I'll be at your house at seven o'clock."

Catherine's relationship to Count Jahrenberg had been one of friendship from the very beginning. He had never made love to her, for which she had been profoundly grateful. But she knew that he admired her, that he shared her passion for music, and that he enjoyed speaking French with her. He spoke it very well, almost too perfectly, with grammatical niceties that were slightly pedantic.

He received her that evening, as always, with the courtesy of the old order. When she got to her story, the General's face darkened.

"How is this?" he said. "Is it true that your father is Jewish?"

"Yes," Catherine said, and she was surprised at the hardness of her own voice.

"This is a nuisance," he said coldly. "Decidedly a nuisance."

"I don't make myself clear," she said. "My father's family is Jewish, but he is Christian."

"To the Nazis," he said, "religion makes no difference."

She noticed that he said "to the Nazis." It was admitting that he was not one. She regained her hopes to some extent.

"But haven't the Nazis themselves allowed some exceptions?"

The General raised his head, weighing his words.

"It's true," he said, "General Milch is an exception, and there are some others, too. But they always take care to justify them in the eyes of the Party purists, in the eyes of the guardians of orthodoxy, by a pretext of some sort."

She looked at him questioningly.

"What does that mean?"

"I mean to say that they have recourse to witnesses or written testimony under oath to prove that the one they want to save is not really *Jewish.*"

"And how can it be proved?"

"If, for example, as in your case, the father *alone* is Jewish, by having the mother swear that the husband is not the father of the child."

"Oh! . . . And there are women who will swear to such things?"

"Very many, Fräulein Kathe—and even swear falsely."

She kept silent for some time.

"There are remedies worse than the disease," she said. "I can't see myself asking my mother, who is a saint, to swear upon her honor that she has deceived her husband! And, anyway, no one would believe it. She has had only one love in her life, and a very beautiful one."

"People believe what they want to believe," the General said. "And there are some of us in Germany, not without influence, who would like to believe it so that Catherine Albert may continue to sing."

"But the least investigation would show . . ."

"There would be no investigation, Fräulein Kathe," said the General.

9

Long days of solitary wretchedness. The dull sadness of a world empty of all happiness. The need to sing, to act, more lacerating, more an obsession than, in others, the desire to make love. The need of being possessed by the audience, of abandoning herself to the embrace of sound.

She had dismissed Cazenotte after a violent scene. The wretched girl had confessed.

"Forgive me, Catherine! But I've been so unhappy, too. You say you're miserable at being banished from the stage. But you're only banished by the Boches and you can tell yourself it's unjust. But I, I'm kept out by my figure, by my voice. . . . Forgive me. I began to hate you when I saw you triumph over everything, even the war, even the defeat. . . . You've had too much luck, Catherine! And I've had too little."

Now there was silence. Catherine, to avoid comforters, gave out that she was sick. Jahrenberg telephoned. She answered that she was too miserable to see him. She received Francis Eric, however. With him, because he remained so calm, she could speak without hysteria.

"I should like to die, Francis! Don't you know some compassionate doctor who will quietly give me a hypodermic to put me out of misery?"

"Catherine! I certainly don't understand you! Deliverance won't come to us from a hypodermic but from an army. You're unhappy, darling. But the whole world is unhappy now. It won't last forever. The time will come when you shall be able to sing the *Marseillaise* in the Opéra on a day of triumph. . . . And what performances, Catherine! Can't you imagine your reappearance? The audience which has been so sorry to lose you will acclaim you. The ovations will be meant for both you and France, because if there is any good side to this trial it is the fact that our country is enduring it honorably. . . . The French do not accept Hitler's laws. France, the country of reason, refuses to be driven mad. . . . Above all, Catherine: look at Molinie, Remond, or me. Does a single one of your friends love you less during this unjust disgrace?"

"I know that very well, Francis darling. Don't think I'm ungrateful or bitter. But, unfortunately, I don't have your optimism. I know Germany very well. I've seen the strength of those people in their own country. I can assure you nothing can be done against them. The world is helpless against them. The strength of the Niebelungs triumphs through them. And because of their system, I am excluded. You can't understand, Francis, because your art doesn't require success or direct contact with the public. You can compose in retirement, at your piano, and know that someday people will play your tunes and unknown women will sing them. . . . But we of the opera exist only on the stage. We exist while we're alive, feted. For us to be in disgrace is worse than death!"

She hesitated a moment, then added despairingly:

"Some women, when they're deprived of their art, still have reasons for living: for some, passion; for others, love in marriage, children. . . . As for me, Francis, you know very well that I have nothing like that. Love has always remained a closed book to me, inaccessible, a paradise from which I'm exiled. Isolde's cries take the place of those which pleasure never drew from me. And now I have lost that, too. . . . *Mir erkoren, mir verloren.*"

She sang sadly, *sotto voce:*

"*Tod geweihtes Herz!* You remember, Francis? Death-consecrated heart."

During the days that followed, Catherine had so many gloomy ideas that she went to see Mr. Belzeaux, the old lawyer whom the Albert family used, to discuss making her will.

"A will! At your age!" the lawyer said. "It's true that in wartime . . ."

"Oh, the danger doesn't affect me."

She told him her sorrows. When she came to Jahrenberg's advice, the lawyer suddenly came to life.

"But don't you see," he said, "this German is right? It is true that your mother can make this declaration, and the Nazis, if they want to accept it, will let it pass without checking it. I've seen very remarkable examples of this. For instance, the other day it was a question of saving the Mangeot factory. You know it? The big automobile concern. Miss Mangeot, the only daughter and heir to the property, thirty years ago married a Jewish engineer, Roger Meyer, a brilliant fellow, a university man, born with a silver spoon in his mouth. A very happy marriage. Three children. Meyer became the head of the business and managed it to everybody's satisfaction until these stupid racial laws were put through. The Germans demanded that the Jewish head of the business be eliminated: Meyer and even his wife, who was suspected of being under 'Jewish influence.' . . . I am their lawyer. What did we do? We had the eldest son declared illegitimate, therefore Aryan. We made all the nominal gestures and thus avoided the administrator that the Nazis would have put in his place: a notorious rascal who would have ruined the business in six months."

"And Mrs. Meyer-Mangeot didn't find it . . . shameful . . . to make that declaration?"

"Shameful? And why *shameful,* Miss Albert, when the declaration is false, when everybody knows it isn't true, including those who accept it and who have weighty reasons with a metallic sound for not contradicting it. After all, what is it a question of doing? Of enduring a period of unpleasantness, of avoiding an obstacle, and of tricking a dishonest adversary. In such a case you have a right to lie. . . . When France becomes herself again, all such declarations will be annulled and the farce will be over. To evade Nazi laws is a duty, Miss Albert. We do the best we can. Only, we have to be ready to play the game."

Catherine's glance, in the dusty study, traveled over innumerable documents. The pulse in her burning temples pounded heavily.

10

Balls of fire whirling in immense emply blackness. Isolde's cries emerging from waves of orchestral music. Flaming logs into which Catherine's horse leaps with one spring. A sky in which a Valhalla of limestone falls to ruins with the noises of a smithy. Twilight of Catherine's gods. A huge river engulfing the ruins. Prelude to the *Rheingold* and the rocking of waves. The sinuous songs of the three Rhinemaidens.

Catherine grows quiet, opens her eyes. Her mother is seated near her. The gentle face, framed by the gray veils, seems anxious.

"Mama! How is it you're at my house? Have you been here since morning?"

"It's not morning, my dear. It's six o'clock in the evening and you've been very sick."

"I've been sick? For how long?"

"For five days. Don't get upset. You've had an attack of fever. You've been delirious. You must be very weak."

"I don't know. My head aches . . . very badly."

She rubbed her hand over her forehead.

"Oh . . . Ice?"

"Yes. We'll take it off presently. Don't touch it. . . . But first I want to tell your father you're awake. He's downstairs and very worried!"

"Poor Papa!"

When she was alone Catherine tried to reconstruct around her the world which had gone up in flames during her delirium. What had happened? She remembered the conversation with Molinie, the showdown with Cazenotte, the gray-green uniform of Jahrenberg, the sinister study of the lawyer. "Shameful? And why *shameful,* Miss Albert?" The weight of pain on her skull made her wish to rid herself of a burden. Oh, that weight! What was it? The ice-bag? No, it was that ancestral curse which deprived her of her profession, her strength, her life. "Shameful? And why *shameful,* Miss Albert?" She thought: "I'm going to talk to Mama . . ." The door opened. Frédéric-Albert's handsome head crowned with its white hair appeared in the opening.

"I've just come to kiss you," he said. "Don't talk."

"Dear Papa," she said.

The next day Catherine was better. She was able to sit up in bed while her mother combed her long hair. Falling back on the pillow, she thought of the sleep of the Valkyrie, of the songs she would no longer sing, and agony stabbed her anew.

"Mama! . . . Mama! Aren't you there?"

Marthe Albert, who was arranging flowers in the next room, hurried in.

"I was putting the roses Francis Eric sent you in water, dear. Do you want something?"

"Mama, I have something very difficult to tell you. . . . I don't know if I have the courage, and yet . . ."

She caught her breath.

"And yet, Mama, I think it's my only chance of getting well. . . . A horrible chance."

Mrs. Frédéric-Albert placed her cool hand on her daughter's forehead.

"You've still got fever," she said. "This is no time for difficult conversations. However, I *know* what you want to tell me, dear."

"No, Mama, it's impossible; you couldn't know."

"Even if Mr. Belzeaux told me?"

"Oh, if . . . Then you do. But how did he dare? I didn't make a decision. I didn't ask him to do anything. I swear I didn't, Mama!"

"Be quiet, my dear, be quiet. I know you didn't tell him to do anything. But since you kept repeating his name while you were delirious, I asked him to come here, and after some reticence he told me about the conversation."

There was a long silence. In the courtyard the janitor was singing as he watered his kitchen greens. Far off heavy steps could be heard: a German patrol.

"Well, Mama?" Catherine said.

"What would you have me say, dear? I find it impossible, of course. As if renouncing your father, whom I've always admired so, whom all France admires, should be a possible means of curing you! Really, it's too dreadful . . . and too stupid."

"Of course. It's horribly stupid, and I know very well that you wouldn't like to—only——"

She was going to say: "Only, I'm going to die." Then she thought that talking about her death would be a form of blackmail.

"Only, my dear?" her mother asked gently.

"Oh, nothing. . . . Only, it would just be a farce. And everyone would know it: you, I, Papa, the Germans . . ."

"Perhaps. But all the same it would be a farce that *we*, you and I, would have to play our parts in. A farce in which your father would be playing a humiliating role. Of course, when you find yourself among ferocious animals, everything is changed. . . . But that, no, that would be too despicable—your father would be hurt by it—and you, too, in a calmer mood wouldn't be proud of it."

Catherine, lying surrounded by her black hair, closed her eyes. A hope, just glimpsed, was snatched from her. Again whirling balls of fire.

"Please understand, Catherine," Mrs. Albert went on, "I didn't tell Belzeaux that it was impossible. I said we'd think it over. But thinking it over hasn't made it seem desirable. Remember our home life, dear. You're a witness to it. Years of love, never a shadow, passion followed by friendship and passion surviving with friendship. What your father is to me I don't believe you can understand. There isn't a man of your generation to be compared to him. A splendid artist. A person who has never committed the slightest unworthy action. As for me, I have had no life of my own. I have always been in his shadow. And I'm proud of it. Of having been the wife of Frédéric-Albert, of having never even been tempted to look at another, of having been the heroine of a single love, and such a great one! And you want me to sully all this by a dreadful, lying declaration. . . . Really, I can't do it."

"But, Mama, I don't want you to do anything . . . *Schlafen, sterben, ich muss* . . . I only want to die. . . . You know, Mama, I've always wondered why, except for the word *Dienen,* Kundry plays a mute role in the last act. I know now. It's because in the newly created world there's no longer a place for a Kundry. Let her keep silent!"

Mrs. Frédéric-Albert bent down and kissed the hot forehead. "Try to sleep, dear. We'll talk about all this again tomorrow."

But silently, inwardly, she said to herself: "I cannot do it. I will not do it.

11

Dr. Lemay was an old man with a white beard who had had a stroke which had left him with a twisted mouth, but his intelligence was unaffected and he was still a great authority in his profession. Mrs. Frédéric-Albert, alone with him in his office, felt the weight of his experience and his objective wisdom.

"I've visited your daughter several times, Mrs. Albert. There is no organic lesion. She could be easily cured. But she is affected by dangerous obsessions. At all cost her mind should be occupied, she should be engaged in some congenial activity."

"I have no doubt, Doctor—but the *only* activity congenial to her is the theater. Nothing else in the world interests her. Catherine has never wanted to marry. Society life bores her. She hates the idea of being alone in the country. Her profession is her only reason for living. And you know the obstacle there."

Dr. Lemay didn't answer, but fixed Mrs. Albert with his glassy stare. As he said nothing, she went on timidly:

"Did Catherine speak to you of a possibility . . ."

"Yes, Mrs. Albert. I finally got this idea, which is at the bottom of her breakdown, out of her. It is really a tragic problem."

"And do you think, Doctor, that it would be my duty to lend myself to this abominable deception?"

He thought it over, caressing his half-paralyzed left hand with his sound right one.

"Mrs. Albert, a doctor can't give that kind of advice. . . . It is certain that your daughter will be saved if she reappears in the theater. That will be the 'safety valve,' the solution she needs so badly. In a few days she will be herself. . . . But, on the other hand, there is your husband. He is no longer young. In these times there are reasons why he, too, is sensitive and unhappy. How would he endure this blow? Would he see it as a slight, an indication of a lack of affection and respect? Or would he generously pretend to look at it as merely an administrative formality? You are better qualified than a doctor, Mrs. Albert, to answer these questions."

When she found herself in the street, at Dr. Lemay's door, she felt so undecided that she very nearly went up again to ask for more definite directions. What was she to do? Which was her duty? She no longer knew. Unconsciously, she started toward the Place de l'Étoile, talking to herself:

"What must I do, O Lord, what must I do? We have been so

happy, Frédéric and I. . . . Should we sully our memories in order to placate these monsters? The beasts! the beasts!"

People looked at her and seemed surprised. Had she spoken aloud? She hurried her steps.

"What can I do, God, what can I do? Say nothing to Frédéric? But if Catherine died, or should kill herself, he would never forgive me. . . . Poor Frédéric! He is so proud of his daughter! And she is proud, too. But we are all caught in the meshes of an abominable net of circumstances."

She was now going down the Champs-Élysées. But for a few cyclists, the wide avenue was empty.

"Frédéric! Frédéric! We've been so happy!"

A German officer passed her. She looked at him with such hatred that he started slightly.

"The brutes! the brutes! Why are they here, in our country? . . . We were so happy!"

When at last she entered the Rue de Richelieu, where she lived, she had made up her mind to speak to her husband. To tell him the truth. But not to urge him to give his consent.

"I have no right," she thought, "to hide anything from him. I hope he will refuse. And yet . . . Oh! I do not know what I want!"

When she had finished, all he said was: "Catherine wishes it?"

"She doesn't say so. But I *know* she wishes it. . . . And still she loves you very dearly."

"I believe it. I don't hold it against her. After all, if anyone in the world can understand Catherine's suffering, I can. For there was a time when I, too, had to play in order to breathe. . . . Only, in spite of everything, it's hard. I would never have believed that my life would end this way and that my own daughter . . . Because, Marthe, after all, she *is* my daughter, isn't she?"

"Oh! Frédéric! How can you ask such a thing? You *know* I've never loved anyone but you, that I've never looked at another man, have never *seen* another man."

"Who knows?" he murmured dreamily. "One sees such strange things nowadays."

"Frédéric, are you mad?"

"No, dearest. But I am very unhappy . . . terribly unhappy."

"Then just say *you* do not want me to do it. I shall obey you. And gladly. I can tell you that this is much more painful for me than for you. You, after all, are the victim; it's a sympathetic part. But Catherine and I, we are monsters. . . . Or, at least, we're going to act like two monsters."

"Not you, my poor Marthe. You're trying to do the least possible harm. Catherine is different. It seems to me she could have overcome her unhappiness, have made it a credit to herself, and that would have been more—shall we say, if you like, more dignified? . . . After all, the war will be over one day; all these German laws will be annulled. Catherine is still young enough to have the future before her. . . . But since she feels this so badly, since she has more than she can bear, and my sacrifice can save her, I'll do it with all my heart."

"You're always the same, Frédéric, the most generous person in the world."

He listened with a sort of bitter happiness.

"It's strange," he was thinking, "there's an intense and intoxicating pleasure in self-sacrifice."

Marthe went over to sit beside him and laid her head on his shoulder.

"The Germans can take everything from you," she said, "our country, your fortune, your name, your daughter. . . . There is one thing they can never take from you: my love."

He caressed her white hair.

"Yes, even that love," he said; "they're going to force you to soil it, to deny it."

"Frédéric, if it hurts you too deeply, we shall refuse. . . . I will explain to Catherine. What you said just now is true. If she could rise superior to this cruel farce and endure her unhappiness proudly, she would have everyone worth while in France on her side."

"Of course. But how can we expect so much courage from Catherine, if we aren't capable of showing it ourselves? No, no. It's not for her, when she's so young, to make the sacrifice. It's up to me, for I have only a few years in which to suffer. And why suffer? I feel the defeat; I don't feel the persecution. Why should I feel hurt because you are going to pull the wool over a German's eyes in order to save my daughter? . . . No, Marthe, I shan't feel it at all, not at all—quite the contrary."

He thought a minute.

"Do you remember, Marthe? I have always dreamed of playing King Lear. Neither Claretie nor Fabre wanted to stage it. And now Hitler gives me the part. . . . It all turns out right in the end."

12

"Mach' die Thur zu," said General Count von Jahrenberg to the orderly. *"Ich will niemand sehen."*

Then he turned to Catherine Albert.

"Just to make sure," he said, "that they will leave us in peace."

She thought sadly that on the lips of a German, in Paris in 1940, the word peace took on a sinister sound. And yet Jahrenberg among "these gentlemen" was one of the elite.

"And so your mother is ready," he went on, "to make a declaration of illegitimacy? Then everything will be easy. I am glad of it. I shall arrange an appointment with Herr Gerichtsgeheimrat Glockenthal, who takes care of such matters. After registering the declaration it should still take perhaps three or four weeks to lift the ban. . . . But there's no doubt about the result."

"Of course," said Catherine, "if there were any other way, we would like to avoid it. My poor mother is brokenhearted at what she has to do. My father is being brave, but to him it's a very unjust humiliation. It's painful to me to have to inflict it upon him."

Count von Jahrenberg bent to offer Catherine a cigarette. She made a gesture of refusal. He took one and lit it gracefully.

"Fräulein Kathe, we mustn't exaggerate the importance of these things. . . . Look, you came to Bayreuth several times. You knew the Wagner family well. You've seen the almost religious venera-marriage. But, Fräulein Kathe, there weie *four* daughters by the Wagner family? Cosima Liszt, by her first marriage, was the legitimate wife of Hans von Bülow."

"Yes, of course. I met the two daughters born of the first marriage, Frau Thode and Countess Gravina."

"You put it exactly right: the *two* daughters born of the first marriage. But, Fräulein Kathe, there were *four* daughters by the first marriage; the two younger ones were Isolde and Eva, both born at a time when Wagner was already Cosima's lover."

Catherine interrupted impatiently: "I know . . . I know!"

"Do you know that they wanted to become the daughters of Wagner *legally,* thirty years after his death?"

"No," said Catherine. "That I didn't know."

"Well, you can easily imagine, as the years rolled on, that it was extremely profitable to be a daughter of Wagner. The royalties came to several million marks each year—and quite a respectable number of millions. Isolde and her husband, Dr. Beidler, claimed a share of this giant cake. Isolde went to the courts and asked to be officially recognized as a bastard daughter."

"Everybody knew she was, and nobody better than Bülow."

"Yes, but she was born five years before the divorce and consequently the law was against her. . . . *Is pater est, quem nuptiae demonstrant*. . . . And neither Wagner nor Cosima wanted a scandalous lawsuit. But when the Beidlers demanded their portion of the inheritance, Cosima saw she had to give in. This woman of seventy-seven, always in deep mourning, not merely respectable but sacred, almost divine, had, like your mother, to make a declaration before a judge. . . . They read her the statement of a former chambermaid, dug up by the Beidlers, affirming that at the time of the birth of Isolde and Eva, Baroness von Bülow had already for several years left her husband's bed. And Cosima, with incomparable dignity, without moving a muscle of her pale face, declared under oath that she, during the last five years of her marriage with Bülow, 'had only had sexual relations with Richard Wagner.' . . . Actually this courageously accepted humiliation was all in vain. For an octogenarian housekeeper who had worked for them inconsiderately stated that, the Wagner villa being always full of guests, Hans von Bülow had several times shared a room with his wife there. Isolde lost her case, but what concerns us is this: the great Cosima agreed to do what your mother is obliged to do today. Exactly the same thing."

Catherine shook her head.

"No . . . not quite the same. In fact, not at all. Cosima had to admit an adultery which was real, even celebrated—a publicly advertised deception. It was unpleasant, but it wasn't shameful. . . . Here am I asking a mother who is justly proud of the purity of her life to invent an adultery which she has never committed, which she was incapable of committing, and to renounce a man who is still alive and whom she loves deeply. . . . It's much more dreadful."

Jahrenberg phlegmatically knocked the ashes from his cigarette.

"What can one do?" he said. "All this isn't very pretty, it's true, but that's how life is. The Devil has more to do with running the world than the forces of good. 'There is no nonsense,' the Devil says, 'that can't be hammered into men's heads if it is repeated often enough in a very solemn style.' "

He got up.

"I shall then ask *Herr Gerichtsrat* to receive Mrs. Frédéric-Albert. I'll let you know the day and the hour. . . . And once more we shall see our favorite Brünnhilde in the Opéra. None of her admirers will be more pleased than I. . . . *Leben Sie wohl, seeliges, herrliches Kind!*"

She dared to say: "But why must life be made so difficult? Why these persecutions, these injustices?"

"The Devil!" said General Count von Jahrenberg. "The Devil, Fräulein Kätchen. . . . In Faust's time the Devil was a gentleman. Today, to make certain of his power over the masses, Lord Mephistopheles has to stoop to some very vulgar ideas."

He opened the door, bowed very low, and said: "A pretty foot is a gift of God."

13

Even though General von Jahrenberg had arranged the appointment and she was armed with a permit, Marthe Frédéric-Albert had some difficulty in reaching the office to which she was called. The street was closed off. A guard allowed some visitors to pass. Arriving at the hotel where Counsellor of Justice Glockenthal was exercising his authority, she still had to get through barriers and orderlies. In the corridors men and women with desperate faces were waiting. The attitude of the German occupation toward the French was one of rigorous formal politeness and extreme factual cruelty. Everything was refused, but with a curious civility. It was a form of torture by letting hope exist. Affable phrases encouraged the applicants. But they never got any further, and whenever it was a question of a Jew this politeness gave place to the most offensive insolence. Mrs. Frédéric-Albert, "wife of a Jew," even though recommended by high authority, was treated without courtesy by Counsellor of Justice Glockenthal. He was ordered to grant the favor which she asked: he had decided to make her pay as dearly as possible in the form of humiliation.

"Frau Friedrich Albert, geboren von Trene?"

The ironical and cutting tone of voice wounded the Frenchwoman. She disliked the man. He was young, with handsome enough features, but his shaved head gave him the look of a Nazi in a film melodrama. He wore spectacles. He seemed arrogant and cynical. At the end of the long table before which he was seated there was a freckled stenographer, a very ugly, mousy sort of girl. In her turn, Mrs. Albert asked:

"Counsellor of Justice Glockenthal? I believe an appointment has been made for me."

"General Count von Jahrenberg," he said dryly, "has notified me."

He rang for an orderly and spoke a few words in German of which Marthe Albert only understood her name. The orderly returned with a yellow document. The Counsellor flicked the pages, then turned his spectacles toward Marthe Albert.

"Your name is," he said in French, "Marthe-Aude-Marie de Trene?"

"Yes, Counsellor."

"You were born at Villeneuve-les-Avignon, May 10, 1883? . . . You belong to an old Aryan family?"

"French," she corrected him.

"We're not talking about that," he cut her off sharply. "You have no Jewish ancestors?"

"No, none."

"But you married a Jew! How could you commit that . . . let us say, youthful *mistake?*"

"It was not a mistake. I loved him."

"And nevertheless you deceived him immediately after the marriage, in 1911?"

She realized with bitterness that she had come here to lie, and for a few minutes it was her duty to lie. The aggressive manner of the man with the polished skull, his evident scorn, had awakened a sharp emotion in her which had shaped her first answers. She thought, "I cannot do it. . . . No, I cannot do it." But she must not go on this way. Frédéric himself had ordered her to go through with it. So she said:

"Yes, in 1911."

"With whom?"

She had not expected any such question and had prepared no reply.

"With one of his friends."

"What was his name?"

Marthe winced.

"Is it really necessary? . . ."

"Madame, it is necessary to have a little common sense. If you are trying to prove that Catherine Albert doesn't have a drop of Jewish blood in her veins because she is not related to her alleged father, we must be absolutely certain that her true father was not a Jew. . . . I didn't think I should have to explain such a simple matter."

Marthe looked about her with despair, seeking a plausible name.

"Madame, I'm waiting. . . . The name?"

She thought suddenly of a cousin who had formerly courted her and who had died with a ball through his head in the battle of the Marne.

"The same name as mine," she said. "Trene . . . Paul de Trene."

"Hundred per cent Aryan?"

"Of course."

"And what were the circumstances of this love affair? What proof can you give?"

"The certificate of baptism of my daughter. Paul de Trene was her godfather."

"Oh . . . Well, perhaps we do have the beginning of proof. But haven't you kept your correspondence with him, too? No? For lack of written documents, have you anyone you confided in who would testify before me? . . . Servants?"

Marthe sighed deeply.

"Couldn't you have the kindness, sir, to spare me all this. . . . I feel faint and I am ashamed."

He looked at her even more severely.

"Shame, Madame? Shame? Shame at having safeguarded the Aryan race in the person of your child! On the contrary, you ought to be proud! Save your shame for that unworthy union with a Jewish actor, not for the purifying adultery which has atoned for your fault."

"Excuse me," she said, "I was always taught that adultery is a capital sin."

"There are," said Glockenthal sententiously, "degrees in crime. The most serious is soiling a pure race. When adultery has been committed to avoid a more serious transgression, then adultery is wholesome, courageous, a matter of expiation. . . . Anyway, we German National Socialists don't attach the same importance to adultery as the obsolete Judeo-Christian civilizations. What matters to us is the offspring, the purity of its blood, the certainty that it will have Nordic reactions. If we are assured of that we ask nothing more about it. We allow, we even encourage sexual relations outside marriage, between selected parents, because these fecund Germanic unions give German soldiers to the Reich and result in German families. The eugenic services of young girls have the same sacred and patriotic importance as military service has for our young men."

He spoke very loudly, hammering each word in. "Is he sincere?" Marthe wondered. "Or is he trying to compensate for the weakness of his convictions by the violence of his tone?" She had a feeling that the second hypothesis was the true one and that this young man was acting a part for other people's benefit in order to keep his job.

"I don't know," she said. "That was the way I was brought up. You can't get rid of your background by an effort of will."

"But it's only by freeing ourselves from the past that the New Order can be brought about," he shouted.

She felt tired. She did not wish any further discussion and hoped that since he was busy catechizing her he would forget to ask her questions. He spoke interminably, inexhaustibly. . . . The orderly entered and announced another visitor. Glockenthal looked at his watch.

"Mein Gott!" he said. *"Es ist schon fünf Uhr.* How time flies! Let us sum up, Madame. You are ready to swear on your honor

that Miss Catherine-Paule Albert is not the daughter of your Jewish husband?"

"Yes, Counsellor."

"And that she was born of your liaison with Paul de Trene, which makes her one hundred per cent Aryan?"

"Yes, Counsellor."

"Fine. Dictate your answers to the printed questionnaire to Miss Emma Sturm, take the oath, and sign two copies. . . . I shall inform General Count von Jahrenberg that all is in order."

Marthe left in a daze, very agitated.

"Perjurer!" she thought. "Adulteress and perjurer. . . . Adulteress and perjurer."

Once more passing through the corridors carpeted with papers on which there was writing in Gothic characters, she remembered how, when in school, she had read with emotion that Joan of Arc was condemned to the stake as "heretic, relapser, apostate, idolater."

14

Before the war Hitler had several times made public his theory on the art of oppressing a people. According to him one must work slowly, carefully, and not impose the greatest humiliations until after successive surrenders which would end by impressing the idea of impotence and submission upon the people's mind. That was the method which he and his agents and representatives used in France in connection with the Jews. In September, 1940, it was only a question of an apparently inoffensive registration. After October, public services and all liberal professions were closed to Jews. Soon an inventory of their property was required, after which they were "invited" to open their safe-deposit boxes "on an entirely voluntary basis."

In May, 1941, they found themselves excluded from the commercial professions and forced to withdraw from all positions which might bring them in direct contact with the public. During the summer the execution of hostages began, kidnapings at the entrance of the subway, internment without cause in concentration camps. Each time a German was mysteriously struck down at night in an empty street, a reward of several millions was offered to whoever would report the assassin. Not a single genuine murderer was ever identified, but after each incident a certain number of Frenchmen, described as "terrorists" or "Judeo-Masons," were lined up against the wall. After July, 1942, many Jews were deported to Poland and, about the same time, wearing the Yellow Star became obligatory. And so, by careful stages, a maniacal ideology drove the victims toward ever more limited regions of the Nazi hell.

Catherine Albert during these two deadly years kept her place in the Opéra, but she felt a wordless criticism growing all around her.

"How did you manage to get the ban lifted?" Molinie asked immediately with a certain distrust.

"I used influence," she replied vaguely.

But her friends were not satisfied. Even their praise of her performances now lacked warmth. Catherine Albert still knew moments of perfectly unadulterated happiness when she sang a role that she loved. She had great success in *Ariadne and Blue-Beard,* in Gluck's *Alceste,* in Massenet's *Thaïs,* in Fauré's *Penelope.* Riesenberger came from Berlin to direct the *Ring* and, for Catherine Albert, these evenings were hours of deliverance.

She needed them. She was anxious about her parents. Frédéric-Albert, who, at first, had so courageously accepted the situation, now looked dejected and broken in spirit. Was it age? Lack of food? Or the effect of the persecution? His eyes were always full of tears and he kept harping on his wife's declaration to the Germans.

"Who knows?" he sometimes said. "Who knows? Maybe it was true after all. . . . Maybe Catherine *is* Paul's daughter. I remember you were very fond of Paul. He was obviously in love with you. He had been brought up with you."

"Frédéric! Please don't say such things," his wife cried. "You're breaking my heart."

"I'm only repeating what you told the whole world . . . What people are whispering when they see me now."

He had the strange delusion that everybody in Paris knew the painful story and that his own friends were laughing at him. He was mistaken. On the contrary, his friends did their best to alleviate the painful effect of the German measures. Not only had the Nazis failed to arouse a violent anti-Semitism in France, but they had killed the superficial anti-Semitism which might have existed previously in the mind of certain French bourgeois. Shielding persecuted Jews became a form of passive resistance to Germany. The Cardinal Archbishop of Lyon and the Bishop of Montauban spoke publicly in favor of the Jews. If an old woman wearing the Star of David wished to cross a slippery street, young Frenchmen hastened to offer her their arms. The Germans forbade the Jews to travel in any except the last car of a railway train. Immediately this became a car of honor and non-Jewish Frenchmen took care to keep it filled. In the beginning the French police officers refused to assist the German police with the house-to-house search during which unhappy Jews were arrested and sent to concentration camps in Poland. Then the Germans shot several policemen and the rest were obliged to submit, inwardly furious.

Frédéric-Albert suffered perhaps even more than most people from these indignities because all his life he had been accustomed to acclaim. His admirers continued to be faithful to him. Many clubs and underground organizations invited him to recite verses for them. His bank account had been frozen, and he would have been poverty-stricken had not Catherine given him half of what she earned at the Opéra. She and her father had never mentioned the declaration made before Glockenthal. She found him always very tender, but she was dismayed by the look of despair which his face, ever before calm and serene, now wore. Frédéric-Albert was no longer the superb old man so admired in public places.

He had let his beard grow; his back was bent. Catherine had once said: "No one is less Semitic than Father." This was no longer so. He now looked like the old patriarchs of the Bible, but an afflicted patriarch, abandoned by his God. He spoke of nothing but death.

"My poor papa," Catherine thought. "I want so much to save him. But what shall I do? I've tried a hundred times to make him move to the unoccupied zone. He didn't wish to. . . ."

Never before had she been so solicitous toward her parents. Almost every day, after the rehearsal, she hastened to the Rue de Richelieu. One day her mother took her aside.

"I'm worried," she said. "The Gestapo agents are certainly investigating your father. They went to the janitor, who immediately told me all about it. They asked hundreds of questions about the hours when he leaves the house, about his friends. Yesterday when we were out, they came to our home and terrified my poor Julie, who is good as gold, but stupid and cowardly. They wanted to make her admit that your father acted secretly and belonged to underground organizations. Julie said stupid things, not very serious perhaps, but how do we ever know? They confiscated our address book and carried off the scraps from the wastebasket. . . . Oh, of course, they found nothing against Papa, but I'm frightened."

"So am I," said Catherine.

With an effort her mother asked: "Do you still see this General? What is his name, now?"

"Jahrenberg? . . . Yes, I've seen him recently. He had to spend a whole year on the Russian front. He isn't well. He limps. When he comes to the Opéra he has great difficulty getting up to my dressing room. . . . Why do you ask?"

"You ought to speak to him and try to find out why the Gestapo is concerned with your father. Could this General stop the investigation?"

"I don't know, Mama. . . . I shall try. I'll do everything I can."

"I want you to do it, Catherine. Please. If you knew how

frightened I am . . . Your father is so rash. It looks as though he were courting disaster. Since that awful day, he has never been the same. He keeps talking about suicide."

"But surely, Mama, he would never think of leaving you . . . alone."

"He's not the same any more toward me, Catherine. Something is broken between us."

"You mean, by your declaration? Really, Mama, I cannot see why. Papa knows it was all a put-up job."

"Yes, of course. . . . And yet, sometimes he doesn't seem to know. Poor Frédéric! He isn't himself any more. . . . And then he keeps repeating that his death would free both of us. That's why I'm so frightened."

"I understand, Mother," Catherine said tenderly. "I'll do my best."

She, too, felt a bitter pain and a foreboding that the wheels of time were moving slowly toward some dreadful moment.

15

Catherine was dressing for the last scene of *The Twilight of the Gods* when someone knocked on the door of her dressing room. The maid went to see who it was and then came back.

"It's Mr. Eric, Miss Albert."

"Put up a screen and let him come in. I'm not in the first tableau. I have time."

Over the screen, she said: "Good evening, Francis darling! I saw you from a distance yesterday, at the Fauré concert. How lovely it was, wasn't it?"

"Yes," he said, "and so French! I had tears in my eyes. Just the same, Catherine, even defeated, we represent something in the world. Something which is Fauré and Valéry and Poulenc . . . and which is also some young student . . ."

"Of course. And it has also been Racine, La Fontaine . . ."

"It's the same thing. Are you coming to the Ravel concert next week, Catherine? . . . He, too . . ."

There were several heavy knocks on the locked door.

"Who is making all that noise?" Catherine said from behind the screen. "It's absurd!"

The dresser went to open it, and a haggard woman rushed in.

"Now, look here," the dresser protested. "What's the idea of shoving people like that?"

"Miss Catherine! Miss Catherine!" cried the woman. "It's me, Julie. Oh, Miss Catherine, you must come right away. . . . They're at our house!"

Catherine appeared with her shoulders bare.

"What are you saying, Julie? What's going on?"

"The Gestapo, the cops, Miss Catherine. They're at our house! They've shut Madame and the master up in the bedroom. They say that the master has to leave tonight, alone. . . . Yesterday the master said to Madame that if they came he'd jump out of the window. Yes, he said that, Miss Catherine. He said: 'Why should I hesitate to die? I have no wife, no daughter.' Yes, Miss Catherine, he said: 'No daughter.' You must come right away, Miss Catherine, without changing. . . . I ran out through the garage."

A buzzer sounded in the corridor.

"O God! I've got to be on stage in ten minutes! Francis! Francis! What should I do?"

"You mustn't hold up the performance."

"But why not? . . . If I were sick . . . or dead?"

"No, Catherine. No! It would create a scandal which would make things worse. I'll run to the Rue de Richelieu and tell them you'll be there in an hour. That you will certainly bring a suspension of the order. Meanwhile phone Jahrenberg. Right away. You must hurry. Come, let's go." He said to Julie: "Can you run?"

Catherine, while Melanie draped the tunic of Brünnhilde around her shoulders, called Jahrenberg at his home and at his office. The General was out.

"Might he be in the audience?" she thought. "No. . . . He would have come to see me. . . . How can I reach him?"

"Miss Albert!" the call boy cried. "On stage!"

"To sing!" she thought. "Shall I be able to sing?"

But she *knew* that she could and that an actress at such a moment always finds sufficient strength. From the moment she stepped on the stage, pensive and hieratic, the great river of sound flowed through her.

"Brünnhilde," Gutrun was saying. *"Du brachtest uns diese Noth! Weh! dass dem Haus du genah't. . . ."* Yes, she had brought sorrow to her people, to her house. Siegfried lay dead at her feet. She removed the fatal ring from the hero's finger. The funeral pyre rose up. She seized a torch: *"Flieght heim, ihr Raben!"* Two young equerries brought a horse. Suddenly, as she went on singing, she was struck by the extraordinary coincidence of the words of the role with her own thoughts: "Neither traitorous pacts, nor transient contracts, nor ferocious decrees have an eternal meaning or enduring value. Pure, in rapture as in suffering, only an immortal love transcends all things."

Ah, to leap upon such a pyre on horseback! To blot out a hateful universe with her own death. . . . To die, to sleep. . . . The curtain was falling. She rushed off stage.

"I won't change, Melanie. . . . No! Just throw a cloak over my shoulders. Hurry! The cloak I just wore! Anything will do!"

"But the costume, Miss Albert . . ."

"Never mind the costume! Don't you understand it's a matter of life and death?"

Going from her lighted dressing room into the wholly dark city mournfully depressed her. It had rained and the still gleaming streets were almost empty. There was no cab in sight. Catherine walked toward the Rue de Richelieu. The few people who passed her noticed with surprise the long white robe, gleaming under the gray mantle in the muddy street.

"My poor papa! I must save him . . . I must . . . I must. I'll talk to these Gestapo men. I'll threaten them."

Then she realized how powerless she was.

"Who are they afraid of? They're even stronger than the army itself. But I must save him . . . I must."

Running through the night, she made out a compact group of people in front of her parents' house. . . . Once more balls of fire began to whirl. What had happened? Suddenly Eric was in front of her, an Eric with a shaking voice.

"Catherine. . . . My poor Catherine. . . . Don't come any nearer!"

As she pushed him away, he took her in his arms to prevent her from going on.

"But what are they doing there—all those people? Why? I must see them. I'm going to save him. Does my father? . . . I must talk to them."

"No, Catherine! Don't come any nearer!"

Out of the depths, with a pitiless gentleness, a German voice said: "Too late, Madame, they are both dead."

"Yes, both of them, Catherine," Eric said. "Both. . . . Don't come any nearer. . . . It's too terrible."

She fainted. He caught the beautiful helpless body. The policeman's lantern, pointed at them, made the whiteness of her robe gleam. Suddenly she opened her eyes, stood up, freed herself from Eric's arms, and rushed at the group of Germans.

"He *was* my father!" she shouted. "He *was* my father! . . . I'm proud of him! He was my father! Tell everybody: he *was* my father!"

THE EIGHTH COMMANDMENT

Thou shalt not steal

SIGRID UNDSET

VIII

THOU SHALT NOT STEAL

A STORY BY

SIGRID UNDSET

THE stretcher-bearers were flushed and perspiring when they reached the summer stable on the mountainside. The afternoon sun struck full on crusted snow, casting pale-blue shadows on the billowing tablelands. The glare blinded their eyes, which still smarted from the smoke of the battle in the valley. Billowing murky clouds of this smoke filled the winding cleft and veiled the mountains on the eastern side. From below came the sustained boom of artillery and a smattering of rifle and machine-gun fire.

One of the wounded soldiers, leaning against the sun-baked west wall of the stable, turned his bandaged neck a little when the boys with the stretcher passed him: "Why—it's Halvor Bjørge."

The snow around the stable door was trampled and blood-spattered. A tall, slim girl with a soiled apron over her ski dress opened the door. She threw out another pailful of steaming, bloody water beside the steps. Then she beckoned and led them down the dark passage that divided the main part of the stable from the dairy: "In there."

"How is it going, Siri?"

"Like hell. We've got the bad cases over in the hayloft. And, Dad—well, we must use what instruments we have." Her soft baby face hardened.

The stable room seemed very dark after the golden sunshine outside. An elderly woman tended kettles of boiling water over a little stove. At a sign from the doctor she lifted the old kerosene lamp that hung above the table, giving him light to remove the windbreakers and sweaters from the man on the stretcher. The two young stretcher-bearers turned white.

"We carried him as gently as we could. But we could give him nothing except two tablets of aspirin."

"But how could he swallow?"

"Don't know. He sucked at them, anyhow."

Siri changed into another apron and dipped her hands into the flowered milk basin that held some solution. Then she spread over the long table a gray crumpled sheet that had received a make-shift laundering.

The elderly woman gasped. "It's Halvor Bjørge!"

The man on the stretcher opened his eyes. His grimy, yellow, pain-racked face still suggested, in a ghostly way, uncommon handsomeness. A week's growth of blond hair obscured the fine molding of his chin. "You know my wife, Arne?" he managed to whisper.

"Sure," the tallest of the stretcher-bearers murmured. "She taught me in her class at Kringsja for four years." Suddenly he stopped. This was no time to say a word more than necessary.

The doctor looked down on the mangled body. "Leave him on the stretcher. Here, boys, shove those two benches under the stretcher, as carefully as you can—easy now."

While the two women eased the stretcher on to the benches, Halvor Bjørge opened his eyes again. "Doctor, I know it's no use trying to do anything for me. You have so little of everything—you can use it better on so many others."

"Nonsense, don't say that. We'll pull you through."

"No, I know I'm done for, Dr. Holm."

"Hush now, save your breath."

"Well, if you really mean it. Thank you, Doctor. It's awfully kind of you."

The doctor nodded. The two women drew nearer. "You boys—I don't think there's anything you can do here. Go over to the hayloft and see what you can do for the boys in there. Get some of the lighter casualties to help you. And when the sledges come, go down with them to the field hospital on Haugen. I hope to God they'll be here soon."

Halvor Bjørge whispered: "One moment, Arne. Tell my wife. But don't tell her too much. Say I did not feel too bad about it. Tell her—and the little girls. Tell her I've heard about the boy, too. I'm glad. There's still a Halvor Bjørge."

Outside the shadows lengthened. The rising smoke cloud over the valley grew darker. Guns boomed. Red sparks of fire kept flashing in the wooded hillside across the valley.

2

One afternoon late in the fall of the year Arne Høyer checked himself on his skis down the slopes above Bjørge.

The main building stood out black against the dark-red sunset. It had empty, gaping windows and half the roof sagged. Evidently, the Bjørges were still living in the old washhouse, where he had seen Inga when he brought her husband's last words to her that spring.

Arne stepped out of his skis and walked along the row of barns and byres. Somebody was in the cowhouse. A light glimmered faintly through a small paper-patched window. From the old washhouse, which nestled under a steep cliff, a wisp of smoke curled darkly over the mountains to the north. Inside a woman's voice was singing softly a tune that country people everywhere were singing or humming now:

God bless our precious fatherland,
And make it bloom like a garden.

Norway blooming like a garden, of course it would—some time. But it seemed such a long way off, with the stink of *Deutschtum* everywhere. He knocked softly on the door.

Inga Bjørge, her baby at her breast, opened it. When she saw the stranger she hurriedly gathered her blouse and started rocking young Halvor, softly patting his bottom. He protested loudly against the interruption of his meal. "Oh—I thought it was Mother—but it's you, Arne. Come right in."

Inside it was very dark. The faint glow from the door of the cooking stove made a patch of ruddy light on the floor where the two small girls sat with their toys.

"How nice of you to look in." Inga dropped the howling baby on a bed, struck a match to light the old kerosene lamp. "We haven't got the electricity back yet—but sit down, please."

The old room was crowded with furniture that they must have salvaged from the main building. Pretty handmade rugs were spread on the flagstone floor. The good paintings and family portraits looked a little out of place on the dark timbered walls, peeping from among clotheslines hung with diapers and tiny shirts. In the corner by the bed stood a small bookcase flanked with stacks of books.

Inga Bjørge laughed. "We couldn't leave the things we needed most over in the house for the snow to spoil. It's impossible to buy window glass, you know." She swung the copper coffeepot on to the stove. "All the same, we're lucky to have this still standing. Lots of the people up and down the valley were burnt out completely. Bjørge is as full of holes as a sieve, but we'll patch it up some time—at any rate, before Halvor takes over. My, how he's bawling—you cannot hear your own words."

"He seems like a husky youngster," Arne volunteered. "Nothing the matter with his lungs."

"Thank God for that. But he's spoiled, you know." She picked up the roaring, kicking baby and draped a white crocheted shawl about her thin shoulders. Then she sat down and hid the child underneath. A sound of smacking and happy grunts was followed by silence.

A bit embarrassed, the lad held out his hand to the little girls who looked at him solemnly. "Good evening, Ragnhild; good evening, Tone." Immediately they turned their backs and retired into the corner by the bookcase.

"Never you mind them, Arne, they're a little shy with strangers." The mother gave a sweet, wistful smile.

Inga Bjørge was a small, slight woman, with a thin, dark face shadowed by heavy black hair. Her large gray eyes seemed radiant under long dark lashes.

She had never been exactly pretty, but she had always looked rather distinguished. Of course, she came from a good old family in the north of the valley, but people had wondered a bit when the dashing Halvor Bjørge had married the young schoolteacher. People said his mother had been none too pleased.

Inga appeared very tired and worn, but Arne decided she had looked that way ever since her marriage. Probably she had found it none too easy becoming the mistress of this big farm, with her mother-in-law in the house too, for Margit Bjørge was not easy to please.

"Well, Arne, it certainly was thoughtful of you to look in."

"I've been staying up at the Ramstads' cottage over the holidays. I just happened to run down this way, and I thought I might drop in and find out how things are here."

"Oh, we're all right, thank you." Inga looked seriously into his face. "We're in good health, all of us. And we're living in our own home. When you think of all the people who have had to stay with strangers after they lost everything when the fighting was here in our valley—— But how are your people, Arne?"

"Very well, thank you. But you know it gets on your nerves, living in town now, with all those Germans. You hear their boots tramping, tramping—and their terrible singing and band-playing. And now they've brought in a lot of their womenfolk who are even worse than the men, if that's possible. The other day Siri Holat went into Miss Øhre's shop and in came one of their Brown Nurses; she wanted to buy all the knitting wool Miss Øhre had left on her shelves. She ranted about the wonderful new country Hitler had given them, and how she looked forward to its winter sports."

For a moment Inga Bjørge's eyes flashed with fury. "Is that so?" Then she looked Arne full in the face. "So they're going in for winter sports, are they? Our friends might pay you a surprise visit then, someday, up at the Ramstad place."

Arne returned her look squarely. "I know. We won't be surprised." He turned to little Tone, who had cautiously approached him. "Want a ride?" and he swung the child on to his knee.

She struggled for a moment. Then: "Stand me on your foot, and then whisk me high, high in the air. That's the way my daddy used to do."

Inga hurriedly rose and carried the sleeping boy over to the bed. She returned with cups and plates and started laying the table. "We'll just wait for Mother—she'll be here any moment now. Then we'll have a nice cup of coffee. I have some really good cookies. Do you know," she laughed, "I couldn't have said that before—it would have been such bad manners not to make a lot of apologies about anything you put before a guest—as if it couldn't possibly be good enough for him. That, I suppose, is one of the things we'll never get back to."

Ragnhild had joined her sister. She, too, perched herself on Arne's foot and piped up eagerly: "Boy, when the Jemmen were here, do you know what they did? They smashed my doll's house that Daddy built for me, and the bench and the bedclothes and all the things Mummy had put into it. And Daddy's fiddle and—oh, a lot of our stuff. They were so rude. And do you know"—here she whispered—"they made a mess on the floors all over the rooms. Can you imagine? Even Tone doesn't do that, she's getting to be a big girl now."

Inga laughed scornfully. "They were afraid to go to the outhouse after dark. Can you imagine? They have plenty of courage when they fight in a body. But they were so afraid of snipers, and of the dark, we thought they were quite hysterical. They did the thing Ragnhild told you everywhere they had night quarters. Nils on North Bjørge says it's just as well they burned down the house—the stink of *Deutschtum* could never have been cleaned out of it."

"I know. We saw some of the places they had stayed in. So they destroyed your furniture, did they?"

"Some of it. They used books for fires in the stoves."

"Well, I suppose that's natural. It's the only use they can think of for books."

"That's right. But don't you think, Arne," she said wistfully, "it's strange I should still grieve about the loss of—possessions? Yet when I think of Halvor's violin and my piano, I can't help it. You see, I used to accompany Halvor, and he played very well. I suppose they think peasants have no business to own libraries and pianos and all that. They're always talking about how our living standard here in Norway must be cut down to the German level."

Margit Bjørge swung in sidewise through the door, carrying the milk pails from a wooden yoke over her shoulders. She stopped short, peered at the guest. Then she came forward and shook hands, ceremoniously. "Thank you for calling, Arne, you are welcome here."

It was easy to see that Halvor Bjørge had inherited his good looks from his mother. Her wrinkled old face, framed by the black kerchief and crowned with white hair, was still handsome. The delicate bone structure stood out under the yellowish skin. She had piercing blue eyes and she still held her tall, slim body as straight as an arrow.

She poured the milk through the sieve and filled the separator while Inga put food on the table. The older woman whispered something to her daughter-in-law, who flushed and began to take her washing off the clotheslines around the cooking stove. When she had finished her chores, Margit removed her kerchief and overalls and put them outside the door. "I still smell of the byre, but it can't be helped. We have to live in this single room and make the best of it."

"Of course. How many cows have you now, Margit?"

"Only nine. The Germans helped themselves to eleven. They paid with those *Reichskassenscheine* or whatever they call them. We call them rogues' checks. Well, we have so little fodder we couldn't have kept many more—even though we have only one horse and the mare and the colt in the stable."

"The mare?" Arne made conversation. "Which mare—the red

one that took the blue ribbon at the show last year? I remember her, she was a beauty."

"No, not Gyda. She's gone. This is her sister, Bella. We haven't shown her, but Halvor thought she was promising."

Inga was working the separator. The droning made it unnecessary for Arne to overexert himself by making conversation with the old woman, who rather scared him. Margit sat down and poured coffee. "Now please, Arne, help yourself. I know it's not much to set before a guest, but it's the best we can do, things being what they are."

Arne kept a straight face, but he felt sure Inga had smiled off in her corner.

"You see, we have to send most of the cream into town," Margit continued. "They want all they can gorge for themselves, but they prevent us from rebuilding our co-operative dairy down at Amot. Then there are lots of people we have to help, one way or another. So many of our men were killed in action we must do all we can for their families. Aren't you going to return to the university this semester, Arne?"

"No. I'm helping Father in his office. I have to stay with the old folks at least until they've got over the loss of my brothers a little. Not that they show it, but I know they feel it terribly."

"Aye. It's all the harder on them, since none of the boys were married. We, at least, have Halvor's children. And we have the boy."

"I know that's what Mother thinks. That's why it would be so difficult to leave home. And yet, I might leave someday—and they'd understand. I've never been able to get over it, Margit—all I could do during the war was serve with the ambulances and act as a dispatch-runner. Think of all the bloody nonsense we believed—pacifism, inevitable progress, and the rest. Now, at least, we've learned that nobody will have peace unless his neighbor is willing. So I may try to go away some time, to a place where I can learn the one craft we Norwegians had neglected."

Inga came over and sat down, with Tone in her lap.

"What delicious cookies, Inga—and sandwiches with rolled meat."

"Well, they ought to have been better," Margit said again politely. Inga looked stolid and passed Arne the plate. "Now you must eat, Arne—you have a long run home tonight."

Inga Bjørge followed him out to the corner of the house, where his skis stood in the snowdrift. A faint afterglow still lingered behind the gutted home. Overhead, cold starlight sparkled in the deep-blue sky.

"But, Inga—my knapsack weighs twice what it did. What have you done to it?"

"Oh, just a trifle. I know there are lots of things you can't buy in town any more. So Mother thought we might put in a few—if your mother will please accept them—it's nothing much."

"Thanks a lot—but do you know, you're at it again just as you used to be."

Inga laughed merrily. "Force of habit, I guess." Her small cold hand grasped his. "Do you remember, Arne—no, I don't think you do. When I had you in my class at Kringsja long ago? I tried so hard to get you children interested in botany. I know I didn't have much success. Linnaeus was my hero then. I had just read about his travels in Sweden. I often think of him these days. His book on *Nemesis Divina* was one of those the Germans happened not to burn. He wrote it for his only son, to impress upon him that never in his long life had he seen evil and injustice escape punishment. And he concludes: 'The vanquished still have weapons left—they appeal to God.' "

3

The tall, lean old man strode up the winding path from the valley toward Bjørge in an easy, swinging gait. His young fawn-colored harehound bitch rushed in and out of the thickets along the path, nosing the ground, barking joyously at something up a spruce. Then she returned to her master, wagging her tail. "Yeah, Lassie, you're glad to be at liberty, too. Now, Lassie, back."

On the wooden footbridge across the Bjørge brook the man stopped and looked toward the place where he had been born. From here it seemed very much the same: the brook rushed down the narrow gorge; its brown bog water broke in creamy swirls of foam among the rocks. The wet summer had not done so much damage to the crops up here as down in the open country. Dark, leafy elderbushes lined the stream. White autumn daisies dotted the lush, green hayfield. But farther on he could see an unripe field of oats, struck down in patches by the rain.

Professor Bjørge walked slowly along the path across the fields toward the cluster of buildings. The first snow of the year covered the peaks of the far-off mountains.

He saw the old home now. The light blotches where the gaping window holes had been boarded up reminded him of sticking plaster on a scarred face.

Three men were hoisting the sheaves of rye on to the drying poles in the sloping field by the farm buildings. The old man stopped and shouted: "Good afternoon, Magnus." His dog frantically chased the chickens that were picking among the stubble.

Magnus turned, recognized the stranger, and ran toward him, grinning. He was lean and springy, about the same age as the professor. "I say, it's really you, Matthias—welcome home." They shook hands. "So you're out of the hospital again—well, that's fine. Margit thought they wouldn't release you unless you were willing to give in and go back to work under the new managers."

"Got out four days ago, and haven't taken back my resignation. Of course, they may swoop down on me again any time—they frequently do. Meanwhile I thought I'd come home. Maybe Margit and Inga can find something for me to do here during the harvest. I tried to telephone, but couldn't get a long-distance call through."

"Well, it's fine to see you, Matthias. How was the hospital?"

"Not too bad," Matthias Bjørge said grimly. "They didn't do

much to me. But what I've seen and heard—you wouldn't believe such things could happen unless you'd seen them with your own eyes. They suspected my brother-in-law, Henrik, of knowing things they wanted to hear. They made him go down on all fours, crawl, get up and jump, then down again and crawl. They call it punitive gymnastics. He was kicked and beaten until he fainted. We Norwegians have no words to tell how we feel about such things. Even in the Middle Ages we might sentence a man to death, but never to physical indignities. Remember, in the Sagas, how the men who tortured a prisoner were branded with infamy and held up to the scorn of the ages? Those Germans are utterly degraded—yet they fancy themselves to be blood relations to us Nordics."

"Here in the valley we'll never believe that nonsense any more. You know, some of the farmers were quite pro-Nazi before the war. They swallowed that tripe Hitler dished out about the peasants being the real nobility of the nation. Of course, they had no use for Communism, and Hitler hadn't let on yet that he might make some use of the Russians after all. Most of them were cured the very day the Germans sneaked in and attacked us."

Magnus and his childhood friend wandered toward the houses.

"Speaking of thieves—you remember old Nick, as they used to call him? Your brother caught him at it time and time again. Late one winter evening he met him over by the storehouse. Nick had a sledge with a big crate on it, and he had just covered his load with some gunnysacks. Anders went over and felt underneath the sacks. 'Now, Nick,' he says, 'we know you are used to helping yourself, and you're welcome, only, you must not overdo it. So I think I'll ask you to return one of those sacks of flour and two of the hams. One sack of flour and one ham will last you and your old woman quite a while.' 'That's right,' says Nick, 'but you see, Anders, I planned to sell the others in the town to get a little hard cash for Christmas.' Anders was adamant. He took away one sack and two hams, but gave Nick a fiver and a wad of tobacco for a Christmas gift. You know, Nick always was a queer fellow, and we never used to be strict with people who were funny or different from others.

"But here's what I was going to tell you. Old Nick is just the same as ever. One day this summer he went down to the station where the trains were standing loaded with foodstuffs for the Germans. Nick managed to filch some tinned goods and coffee and things, and when he called here on his way home he showed it to Margit, quite proud of having been clever enough to fool the Germans. Margit says: 'But you mustn't do that, Nick, it's too dangerous. The Germans don't understand our way of life. They'd punish you if they discovered you had helped yourself to anything they had stolen from other people.' Nick pooh-poohs the idea. 'They'd never do such a thing. Didn't you ever hear of honor among thieves?' 'Sure,' says Margit, 'but I never heard of honor among Germans.' "

Outside the door of the old washhouse the three children were playing in the sunshine. Matthias Bjørge picked up young Halvor, who promptly started howling and pommeling the chest of the stranger. "Good afternoon, Ragnhild, don't you recognize me? Good afternoon, Tone."

Ragnhild wiped her hands on her stomach and held them out. "Better let me take Halvor, he doesn't like strangers. Yes, I recognize you," she observed sagely. "You are Uncle Matthias. We thought you were in prison."

"So I was, my girl—only we call it a hospital. But I can tell you, it's fine to be back here again. Well, I see Halvor isn't afraid of dogs." Lassie had started romping with the children and upset the little boy, setting him down on his fat behind.

"No, Halvor is not afraid, but he dislikes strangers. All of us do—because of these people who come here and order us to sell them whatever they want. And we cannot buy anything we want for the money they pay. Anyhow, Mother says the money they pay us with they have stolen from ourselves."

"What a sensible girl you have become." Matthias Bjørge chuckled. "And so big."

"Yes, I'm a big girl now," Ragnhild said complacently. "I'll start going to school soon now. Mother and Granny are down by the spring. They're doing the laundry because Birgit went up to the stable with the mowers, and Eli has to cook for the harvesters. I have to mind the little ones."

Hugging her fat little brother so that he rode on her pushed-out stomach, Ragnhild walked with the guest toward the copse, making grown-up conversation. Tone danced behind with the dog. Thank God, they looked healthy—and they were pretty youngsters, Matthias thought. Ragnhild looked like her mother, but the two younger ones inherited their father's golden fairness.

Down by the pool a spring welled forth from beneath an overhanging moss-grown cliff, a big iron pan rested on the fire. Margit fished out the boiled garments with a long pole; Inga knelt by the brook, rinsing. Margit looked up first when Matthias shouted and hurried to meet him. "I say—it's you, Matthias," she called out excitedly. Then she shook hands, calm and polite. "Welcome home, Matthias, and thank you for coming. It will be fun to have a man about, to take charge."

"I supposed Magnus did that very efficiently, but I'm out of work too."

"I know." Margit looked grim. "Well, you'll be in time for the elk hunting. You missed it last year, and that's the only time you didn't stalk the elk, except the years when you were abroad."

"No hunting for us Norwegians this year, Margit—not for the duration, I guess. They tried to put some of their stooges on the board of our Hunters' Association, and we all walked out on them. They won't make us ask their permission to use our own guns in our own woods—no. So I've killed old Bamse now. I'm afraid he'd have been too old, anyhow, when the time comes for us to go after the elk again. This little bitch is the only dog I have now. And I wanted to ask if you would mind keeping her here for the winter. The Germans have brought in their pets, which have all the animal diseases. The veterinaries advise us to keep some of our most valuable breeding specimens in safety, if we can. And this little one is really a beauty, don't you think so?"

"She's fine-looking; we'll be glad to keep her." Margit fondled the dog. "But, Matthias—you know our mountains are wide, and the others aren't much good at finding their way off the beaten tracks. So the other day some of the old fellows said they meant to get their elk steaks this fall same as usual. And you know, they have their stuff stowed away where nobody but themselves would ever find it."

"But they mustn't do that. We can't afford to lose even one old fowling piece for something no more important than a hunting trip. I must try and see some of the boys about that."

"Do. Well, come in—you see, we are prepared to stay here for the duration. But if you don't mind sleeping in a boarded-up room, I thought of fixing up your old place in the main building, at least until the nights get colder. We eat our meals in the kitchen anyhow these days, with the harvesters."

He had thought he must be hardened by now. First there had been the things he had seen in Oslo and then the sights and the sounds of the prison. Yesterday, he returned to find their peaceful district center made over into a German garrison town. The old military camp on the outskirts where he had spent so many happy summers, first as a raw recruit and then as an officer of the reserves, had been debased into a concentration camp. Walking along the road up here today he had noticed the chimneys of burnt-down farms still standing—so many of the beautiful old places destroyed. And when he entered the front door of his old home, the same choking feeling rose in his throat. The lovely pilastered frame had been battered, the transom with the delicate pattern of laurel sprigs was smashed and empty of glass.

The men seated along the big table came over and shook hands with Professor Bjørge. Only the young girl by the kitchen range remained with her back toward him. Matthias went over to greet her. She was a nice-looking, plump young thing, but she flushed scarlet when he took her hand. "Good evening, Eli—but sure, I know you, you're one of Roald Storhaug's girls," and then he too flushed. Now he remembered: her brother was the new Quisling sheriff.

Everybody looked embarrassed, and Eli's face was still very red when she carried the steaming dish of new potatoes to the table. The men helped themselves silently and began peeling and dipping the potatoes in butter and salt. There were also platters of cold cured beef and pork, and a dish of herrings—but the herrings were vile. For once Margit's excuses had nothing to do with the old-time ritual.

Matthias laughed: "They are the same brand we get everywhere. But there's one consolation, the herrings the Germans get may be even worse. They grabbed the best for their own use, and they stored it so carefully that most of it became completely spoiled."

"Their storehouses in the town stink to heaven," said one of the men. "If anything could make us madder than we are now that would do the trick. We have to sell what they want, accept their fake money, and then they let what they buy rot and ruin through sheer ignorance and arrogance. Meanwhile our city folks have to do without all kinds of things. I'm sure the Germans have tons and tons of butter down there, but it's so rancid that it's good for nothing but greasing their boots."

"They can use it for explosives," Matthias pointed out, harshly.

"All those shacks will burn down before they get around to that," the youngest of the farm hands gloated. "The railway service gets slower all the time. You know, they've taken more than half of our locomotives and cars out of the country and what they've left is falling apart. Then they've started drinking too, and they're getting careless."

Magnus shook his head. "We always heard how damned efficient the Germans were. You used to think so, Matthias, remember? But it seems they're only efficient at killing and looting and destroying. As for the German civilians, their brains are chicken turds and their hearts are cherry pits. But their bellies are bottomless beer barrels."

Professor Bjørge nodded. "That's right—this generation seems incredibly stupid and knows nothing except soldiering. Why"—he laughed—"some time ago a member of the German administration appeared at the office of our administration and ordered us to start the big fisheries at once. When we tried to explain to him that the fisheries operated only during the annual migrations of the cod he refused to believe us. But then, you never can make them believe that anything anybody says is true."

"I suppose that's because they know their own people tell nothing but lies."

"You're right there, Magnus. They know it, subconsciously. But then, it's a funny thing about all Germans—even the decent Germans I used to know in the old times—when they've said something they imagine that makes it true, even when they know, in a way, that it is not. I suppose that was what made them a nation of poets and thinkers, as they once loved to call themselves. They believed their fictions and unreal philosophies themselves. It's really a kind of primitive faith in word magic—the uttered words have a kind of power to sway fate. I shouldn't be surprised if even Hitler believes that the lies he utters magically turn into truths."

Magnus snorted: "They can't be as crazy as all that. And they don't rely on that kind of magic, Matthias, when it comes to invading and looting other people's countries. They rely on big armies, heavy bombers, machine guns, terror, treason, and lies. All their magic boils down to thinking up something that nobody with a shred of human decency or honor would ever do—and then doing it."

Matthias nodded. "Of course, I always knew they were utterly unlike us. But we didn't pay much attention. Now, of course, we can all see that we never understood them. It's also clear that they'll never understand any other people but themselves. There was my old friend, Professor Weissmantel, in Germany—the man I used to work with in the laboratory. The last time he was here, in 1937, I saw a lot of him. He always wanted to talk about my work, and

I'm afraid I was not so cautious as I ought to have been. This time, when he arrived at my office, he rushed upon me with open arms—and when I clasped my hands behind my back, quite involuntarily, he looked hurt and miserable: 'But, Matthias, my dear old *Herzensbruder*.' He did not understand a thing. He gabbled on. In 1937 he insisted that he detested Nazism, and said there were still lots of things he disagreed about with the Nazis. But when it came to stealing our institutions and ordering us to hand over our patents, our secrets, and everything—he thought he had a perfect right to do as he pleased. Since our country had been conquered by his country we must surrender everything that was ours. And then he finally said: 'But, Matthias, I just can't understand why you Norwegian's have come to dislike us so much all of a sudden.' Well, I could only reply if he could not understand it for himself certainly no Norwegian would be able to explain it."

4

One sweet, sunny September day followed another. The morning air was ice-cold; the fields were gray with dew. It was a joy to drive the mowing machine over the hayfields—the second crop was fine this year. Before noon, as the sun gained strength, the valley became a dream of green and blue—its lower reaches veiled in haze, the mountain slopes dark with spruce and flecked with golden, russet birches and rowans. Shining white clouds came sailing up from behind the ridges, and against the deep blue of the sky the snow on the peaks toward the north shone like lightning in the sunshine.

The women planned to go berrying one morning. A neighbor of the Bjørges, coming down from the uplands, said that the ground around the stumps where the forest had burnt ten years ago was scarlet with *tyttebaer*. *Tyttebaer* can be preserved without sugar, and plenty of *tyttebaer* juice would be nice now that coffee and tea were so scarce.

Matthias, who had gone with the berrypickers, stretched out in the heather after climbing to the higher ground. In spite of his three weeks on the farm he still felt the strain of those months in prison. Carrying little Halvor on his back most of the way up the slopes had been quite a job—the youngster had clasped his throat like a halter, and he was heavy for his age. Matthias felt tired.

Under him, at the foot of the bluff, three little tarns lay strung out among the rolling lichen-gray country, blinking sky blue and rimmed with brown sedge and bog cotton. The white trunks and golden autumn foliage of the little birches looked like candles. The wind felt quite mild and soft on his damp forehead. Up from the wood beyond the tarns he could hear the voices of the girls as they were picking berries.

There were other parties of berrypickers on the moor too—some women up at the other end of the burnt-out clearing where the path skirted the tarns. There was no mistaking their broad German rumps and their short stocky legs as they bent over, picking the berries. All the small tourist homes the farmers had built on their mountain holdings were full of German women and children. People said they had come from the bombed areas to rest their nerves and fatten up on the dairy produce of Norway. The men, officers and civilians, had preferred the more modern hotels and played around with fishing tackle and shotguns, imagining themselves great sportsmen, like the old Junker officers. The Norwegians had lots of good laughs at their expense, yet they were furious too; these hunters maimed more animals than they killed, and occasionally they hit the cattle on the moors too. Even during the fighting here in the valley the peasants had expressed astonishment at what bad marksmen most of the Germans were. Specialists in mechanized mass murdering, they were not much good as individuals with shotguns.

Well, they would certainly leave the mountains as soon as frost and snow and storms began in earnest, Matthias thought. And then he would go up and stay for some days in the uplands.

But right now maybe he had better get up and find some berries. Those German women were down by the northernmost tarn. Matthias rose, picked up his tin pail, and started down the slope farthest from the German women.

He had almost reached the foot of the bluff when he saw Inga and Margit with Ragnhild hurrying along the path by the tarns; Eli and the two little ones followed in their wake. And then he took in what had happened.

The Norwegian women had put their baskets down by the blackened stump of a burnt tree, already more than half full of *tyttebaer*. And then three of the foreign women had bent over, scooped berries out of the baskets, and filled their own rucksacks.

Inga called out in German: "Excuse—but you are mistaken—those are our baskets. We picked those berries."

The other women looked up; they seemed just a trifle embarrassed. Then one of those in the rear pushed forward and said something to her companions in an angry, guttural voice. As they still seemed undecided, she elbowed her way to the front and started to fill the big pail she carried, spilling the berries all over the ground.

"Don't you understand me? I'm sorry. But I told you, we picked these berries. These are our baskets, you understand."

The energetic lady scooped and scooped; two of the other women, evidently bullied by their enterprising friend, half reluctantly dipped their tin cans into Margit's basket.

Matthias hurried toward the tarn, jumping from tussock to tussock in the bog along a little brook. Inga spoke in loud, icy tones:

"Well, I must say—I didn't know you were licensed to steal from private persons."

"This country is ours now." The ringleader, purple in the face, confronted the Norwegian women. Her voice rose to a high pitch: "It's ours. We have conquered it, and we have a right to do as we like here, and take whatever we want."

By now the other women perceived the tall man hurrying along, stepping from boulder to boulder in the brook. They nudged each other. But before they had decided what to do, Margit hit the ringleader smack in the face. And, while the others started milling around, too astonished to meet the assault, Margit's long arm shot out. Placing one foot on the stump, she whisked the offender off her feet and laid her across her knee. The German kicked and screamed madly, but Margit pinned the woman's legs between her own, and with her long, bony hand belabored the creature's wide expanse of bottom.

The other German women at first cackled and fell over each other. Then, seeing Matthias approach at full speed, they turned tail and ran up the path. Margit's victim struggled, kicked, and howled. The worst of it, Matthias thought, was the way Ragnhild's little face radiated savage joy. Inga stood as if she had been turned to stone, and Eli and the two small children whimpered with fear.

"Mother!" Inga cried.

"Margit!" Matthias called out.

Margit suddenly let go, sending the other sprawling on all fours.

"Get up now, quick!" The German seemed to understand that much and picked herself up, looking thoroughly scared. Margit pointed to the rucksacks and the strangers' baskets. "And don't leave your things all over the place—take them, and get the hell out of here."

The woman did as she was told, ran, turned at a safe distance, screamed threats and dirty names, then turned and ran some more. Matthias could not help noticing how ridiculous short-legged, broad-rumped women look when they try to spring.

Margit Bjørge brushed off the front of her skirt. Deliberately she went down to the water's edge and rinsed her hands. She was trembling all over—like a blood mare, Matthias thought. Slowly her white, lined face was suffused with blood. Then she undid her kerchief, smoothed her white hair, and rearranged the kerchief.

Matthias opened his mouth, once, twice, but discovered he did not know what to say. He had heard of Margit Bjørge's terrible fury on the rare occasions when her iron self-control gave way. But he had never seen it before. He was scared.

Margit picked up her tin can. "Well, we had better try to get our baskets filled"—but she turned, and walked down the hill.

Inga had taken Halvor on her arm. She looked up in Matthias' face. "Uncle Matthias—O God, what do you think is going to happen to Mother now? I am so afraid, Uncle Matthias." A shadow of a smile flitted over her dark, sensitive face. "But she was grand all the same—wasn't she?"

Matthias and Inga trooped silently down the mountain path and found Margit, in a little dell among the bearded old spruce trees, picking *tyttebaer* as if nothing had happened.

Halfway down the mountainside the path crossed a small clearing in the woods through which flowed a turbulent little brook. Potato patches and barren little fields spread out on either side. Stone walls, wire netting, and wooden rails fenced them in. There were also several tiny huts built of old timber, flattened-out gasoline drums, and other odds and ends, roofed over with sod and corrugated iron.

Margit sat on a log by the brook, unpacking their provisions. Eli divided the remaining milk among the children.

"Nobody home," Margit said. "God knows what he is up to now."

"I hope to God he won't run into trouble," Inga sighed. "You know, all of us have a soft spot in our hearts for Old Nick. But I'm afraid he's poaching again. Not that we care. As long as it doesn't get him in trouble with the new authorities. You know, he was an inveterate poacher. Halvor had to tackle him once, when he was chairman of the West Side Hunting Association. They worked hard to preserve the game and he had to enforce the rules in his own woods. So he said to Nick: 'At any rate, let the game birds alone during the season when they are protected. After all, these are my woods, not yours.' But Nick replied: 'Maybe the woods do not belong to me. But I belong to the woods.' Halvor liked that reply so much I don't think he ever did much about Nick's poaching again." Inga smiled tenderly.

Matthias Bjørge nodded. "Yes. That's the way we are. Law is

what we think about our rights and our duties toward our fellow men. We chose the men to write these thoughts into laws, and when they did that they had to submit the laws to the people to sanction or reject them. It's been that way ever since the old days when the king made the laws and the men of the Thyng decided whether to accept them. And whenever our kind of self-government was suspended or interrupted, we disregarded—at least as far as we could—any laws imposed upon us against our will. But the laws we had given ourselves, in accordance with our own ideas of justice and injustice, remained sacred to us as our own word of honor. That's why we were always easy on those who were queer or unlike other people; they were not the sort of folks the laws were intended for, and they couldn't be expected to understand why the laws should be obeyed. As long as they were not crazy in a way that made them so dangerous they had to be put in asylums, we made reasonable allowances for their behavior.

"The Germans were never like that. Law to them meant a body of do's and don't's that some ruler laid down for them. They were an honest people in the old days, at least at home among themselves. My God, I remember when I studied at Heidelberg, we used to walk out on Sundays to those charming little country inns. Our way took us through lovely chestnut woods and country lanes lined with fruit trees. One of the first times I stopped to pick up a couple of chestnuts. My German friends cried out in horror—I mustn't do that. It was *verboten* to touch as much as a single chestnut or cherry lying in the road. Everything belonged to the state or the prince or something, and the crops belonged to the farmers who had leased them. Well, that was their way. But it's no wonder they go wrong when they come to countries where their own rulers aim to destroy law and order. No inner voice said to them, 'Thou shalt not steal!' If they had any voice it was their master's barking: '*Diebstahl verboten*.' So when the same voice hollers that *Diebstahl* is the order of the day, the average German believes it's all right to grab all he can in the occupied countries."

"You mean, you see an excuse for those females up at the tarn?"

"In a way, yes. I mean, there is one single excuse for the obscenities the whole German people commit wherever they go. It is their bottomless degradation. Few Germans ever had any personal moral sense. The bulk of the nation had the morals they were ordered to have. So with an amoral or criminal set of rulers they become amoral or criminal with perfect complacency."

"But such people"—Margit breathed hard—"such people—why, they aren't human."

"No," Matthias said wearily. "They're subhuman. And in a way they're aware of it. That's why they insist they are supermen —*Herrenvolk*. They're like the people you see in nuthouses who insist they are Christ or Jack the Ripper or King Olav Tryggvesson."

"I don't care." Margit clenched her narrow, bony hands so the knuckles whitened. "I'm glad I gave that woman what she deserved. I feel ever so much better for it—no matter what they do to me I don't care.

"Don't look so sad, Inga dear. You are quite capable of managing everything on Bjørge without me. Everything—the children too." For a moment she let her hand rest on Inga's knee. "You are a clever girl. And a good one, too."

A week passed and nothing happened. When they were alone Matthias and Inga talked things over. Maybe the *tyttebaer* stealers had felt a little ashamed, or reluctant to talk about the ignominious punishment the old woman had administered to their leader. Or, maybe the local Quislings still retained a kind of awe for Margit Bjørge. For forty years she had been the mistress of Bjørge, and the whole community had always feared her indomitable will, and respected her for her sense of justice and her unsentimental, efficient helpfulness toward her neighbors.

Eli went home to Storhaug, hoping to find out something, but she could not learn a thing. Her father and her brothers refused to have anything to do with the son who had turned traitor. They forbade his name to be mentioned at home. But the mother had always loved Alf the best of all her children; he had been an ailing child, difficult to raise, backward at school, and so queer he had often scared her. She still met him secretly, and Roald always knew where she had been when she came home red-eyed and went on crying all night. But he did not have the heart to talk to her. When this business was over Alf might be sentenced to death; if not, somebody from the village would surely polish him off. And Roald Storhaug knew that would kill his wife Laura.

The only news Eli brought back was that the Germans would requisition horses for their Russian campaign. It had been immensely cheering to all of them to listen to the secret radio and hear about the difficulties the enemy had run into in Russia. It still was, of course. But the horses—the horses——

Margit paced up and down the floor of the big kitchen, her eyes stony, her whole body trembling with rage. All of a sudden she turned on her heels and went out.

"Matthias, we'd better keep an eye on Mother—I'm scared. The horses are like her own children."

Outside, a cold green sky brooded over the darkening mountains. The first stars pierced the velvet dusk. Hoarfrost crunched under their feet. Matthias and Inga peered into the darkness, shivering with cold and excitement.

At last they heard the noise of rolling stones in the scree above the brook. Then the tall old woman glided through the darkness like a shadow. Matthias stepped out to meet her. He clasped her right wrist, touching the Colt she had gripped in her hand.

"Margit, you must not do that."

"They're not going to get Bella. Do you think I would let them take my Bella to Russia, to perish in pain and misery, serving those swine? Let go my hand, Matthias."

"Listen, Margit. If you do this, it will lead them to search for hidden arms all over the countryside. We cannot have that. My God, I'm sure there is not one farmer who would not much rather shoot his horses himself than surrender them. But we cannot afford the consequences. Not yet. Now less than ever—when we glimpse the daybreak—the day of reckoning with that spawn of hell."

Margit Bjørge gritted her teeth. Then she turned and walked away into the night without a word.

Matthias and Inga huddled up to the kitchen range, waiting. An hour passed, then two.

"Do you know where the cache is?" Matthias could not help speaking in whispers.

"Yes. It should take her about an hour and a half to come back."

"It didn't take her an hour to find that gun of Halvor's."

"She must have moved very fast. I suppose she made up her mind before we could know anything about it."

They sat in silence, listening for a sound from the outside.

"How people are going to finish the fall plowing now——" Matthias shrugged his shoulders.

"And they'll requisition so much hay that we probably won't be able to feed even the livestock we have left, through the winter. Unless something happens."

"I'm afraid the happenings we wait for will not come off before spring," Matthias said seriously. "We were not the only nation unprepared for war."

"No. But if this is going to go on for years, I can't see how we'll rebuild our ravaged land, our industries, our mines, our railways, our livestock, our merchant fleet, our whole economy. Then think of the health of our nation—undernourished children in the cities lack the stamina to fight off the epidemics they have foisted on us."

"And yet they have not been able to make us yield an inch, Inga dear. We have no reason to feel downhearted. For every Norwegian they clap in prison or murder, ten more stand ready to take over and carry on his work. According to their creed, they had only to kill off the intelligentsia, kill off the leaders, and the masses would prove utterly incapable of resistance. Well, they have discovered that creed doesn't work outside Germany. Everywhere the resistance is as fierce as it ever was. That's a fine thing! After all, Inga, we are the same people who made this harsh, beautiful country of ours a good land to live in. We are the same, only more so."

After a while Inga rose to her feet. "I'm afraid, Uncle Matthias. Where can Mother be? What if something has happened to her?"

"Margit would not do such a thing." He lit the lantern. "I have an idea."

They found her in the stable, sitting bolt upright on an old chest. When they appeared in the doorway she scarcely turned her head. "I'll be with you in a moment. Just go in again."

The day the troop of German soldiers came for the horses Matthias Bjørge had to follow them around the farm. Margit stood motionless in the door of the washhouse. After a few attempts to talk to her and some gibes the Germans let her alone; they even seemed a bit uncomfortable under her icy stare.

They really ought to be scared to death, Matthias reflected, if they knew anything about the old Nordic beliefs, other than the Wagnerian operas with fat men and loud-voiced women dressed in hardware-store equipment. Our forefathers knew that a mother's curse and a mother's hatred had a power to be feared, and with good reason.

Then came the order for the Norwegians to turn over their blankets to the German army in Russia. Sheriff Storhaug called up to remind all householders to surrender their blankets by October 3. Failure to comply cost three years' imprisonment or a fine of 100,000 kroner.

Margit kept calm. "As a chemist, Matthias, don't you know something to put on the blankets, something that wouldn't show but that would make them fall apart?"

"My chemistry isn't much good up here, Margit. I haven't got the necessary materials."

But Margit kept asking questions just the same, and when the day came to turn in the blankets she washed them before handing them over.

"They'll be washed at the depot," Inga reminded her.

"That so? Well, I never sent anything out of my house that wasn't perfectly clean. I always was a stickler on cleanliness, you know. Now, keep your hands away from the tub, Inga, I want to do this job all by myself." And Inga noticed that she did not rinse her laundry before hanging it on the clotheslines.

Margit's hands looked like a leper's—dead-white and strangely puffed. She rinsed them again and again and then rubbed them in melted tallow, chuckling all the time. For days afterwards she kept breaking out in that ungodly chuckle as she sat nursing her hands, hiding them from sight in the folds of her apron.

Then came the demand for all privately owned windproof jackets and trousers, all ski pants and thick sweaters. Failure to obey this order carried the same penalty as failure to turn over the blankets.

"I cannot believe it," Inga said. "Stealing the pants off people's bottoms—you'd think even Germans would be ashamed to do that."

"Don't pretend you're dumb, Inga, because you're not," her mother-in-law retorted angrily. "Didn't you hear what Terboven said: 'It is a matter of complete indifference to Germany if a thousand or ten thousand of Norwegian men and women and children starve or freeze to death.' Maybe you think the Germans cannot tell the truth? But they can when they make threats, even if everything else they say is lies."

Nobody had thought it would be possible for the Germans to be hated more than they were already, but the Germans themselves took pains to convince the Norwegians on that point.

Margit went into action. She took Halvor's clothes down from the storehouse. His working outfit, his old soiled windproof overalls, his sweater—let them have it all. Something had to be sent. But his good sports clothes—"We'll tear them up and have Tora Elvestad help us make them over for the children. His best navy blue will make good warm suits for Tone and Halvor. His gray lounge suit—we'll make a coat and pants for Ragnhild from that. And here is his tuxedo. You can get a really smart tailor-made suit out of it, Inga, you are so small and slight."

"But, Mother," Inga protested between laughter and tears, "they haven't requisitioned that yet. Even the Germans wouldn't fight their war in Russia in tuxedos."

"You think so? Don't be a fool." But her voice was soft as she lightly touched Inga's hand that caressed the black broadcloth. "You won't forget anyhow, the way Halvor looked when you stood before the altar with him. I should think it might even brace you up a little, my child, to have a dress made over from his wedding finery."

Margit evidently had decided to save as much as she could before they clamored for more. The same night she carried down from the store loft her scarf of stone marten and Inga's set of silver fox—Halvor's Christmas gifts to them some years ago. She sewed them up in oilcloth, mothballs and all, and early next morning Magnus went uphill, destination unknown, with the furs in his rucksack.

At noon, when Matthias returned from an errand down in the village, he found Margit out by the woodpile chopping wood, and as he drew nearer discovered she was splitting a pair of skis. Two more lay on the ground, all of them Halvor's.

"Let me do this for you, Margit."

"No. I want to do it myself—thank you just the same. If you want to help, you might go down and make a fire in the old fireplace by the pool where we used to do our laundry during the summer."

She carried the strip of split wood in her arms, almost as if it were a baby. Inga and Ragnhild followed with smaller ski splinters in their aprons.

"I've taken his boots down to the kitchen. There's a pair of new ones I believe would fit you, Matthias. They're too narrow for Magnus, but I hope he may be able to use the old ones and a brown pair of Halvor's."

Margit had decided the Germans should get nothing if she could help it.

Early one morning Matthias Bjørge lay dozing and shivering in his draughty room when he heard the sound of motorcycles tearing up the drive. He jumped up and leaped to the window. Pushing aside the old plush tablecloth Inga had put up instead of the blanket, he tried to peer out between the cracks in the boarding. He could not see a thing in the darkness. Then came a flash of light, another and another. The motorcycles shot past the bend in the drive. He wondered whether they had come for him, for Margit, or for both of them. He dressed hurriedly and started throwing his toilet articles in his handbag.

Violent banging on the door of the kitchen—it sounded like the butts of rifles or revolvers. Matthias looked disgusted. Those hired hooligans never outgrew the thrill they got out of carrying firearms. "Coming," he called out, putting on his topcoat.

The headlights showed six of them outside. There was also a small car with a uniformed German at the wheel. Another German in uniform stood directly behind Alf Storhaug. He seemed to be the real leader, although Alf stepped forward, looking very self-important.

"Well, Matthias, my man, we're here to invite you to come with us for a trip to town. What do you think of that?" In a way he looked like Eli, fair and snub-nosed, except that his face was not plump. Instead it was puffy and at the same time covered with lumps—a bulging forehead, protruding cheekbones, and sagging fat around the jowls.

"You see, we know what you've been up to. We know all about it. But just the same we're going to make you tell us some more about what you've been doing up here. And that may be really unpleasant, you know—these interrogations sometimes are. But for old acquaintances' sake I don't mind telling you, you better not try to deny a thing, we know all about it already."

Inga came running up from the washhouse. Margit walked leisurely behind.

"Good morning, Inga. Good morning, Margit—yes, here we are again." He grinned. "Beginning to get used to seeing the sheriff, aren't you? It's a pity that the police should have to keep an eye on a distinguished old family like yours. But you see, times are different now, we have done away with all that deference we used to pay to the powerful old bosses and fine families of the countryside."

"Don't we know it," Margit said coolly. "You've proved that you have no respect even for the distinguished old family on Storhaug, Alf."

"How in hell did you learn—did Father send you word—no, he couldn't—how the hell did you get to know—well, well, we'll look into that too." His face was contorted with rage. Suddenly he struck Matthias Bjørge in the face. "Get into the car now, and quick. Yes," he sneered, "you may get my brother Rasmus as a traveling companion."

Somebody shrieked—Eli had joined the group. "Oh, Mother, Mother," she moaned.

"That's news to me," Margit said quietly. "I meant the fact that a boy from Storhaug has turned traitor."

The second German had got into the car. It started down the drive. Inga turned with a gasp and began to run after them, calling Matthias by name.

"Stop it," the sheriff yelled, "stop it—you come here, Inga. We're going to check up on your stores while we're at it, and this time we mean to do a thorough job." He grinned. "So maybe that sister of mine will oblige us and fetch the keys of the storehouse. Didn't you hear?" he roared, as Eli did not move.

"Hear? Nobody spoke to me," Eli said haughtily.

Margit shrugged her shoulders. "I'll fetch the keys."

5

The doctor's wife had pulled out her dining table full length, and still the children sat crowded around it. Some of the older ones had to sit in the corners or perch on the window sills.

It was nice to have the windows open—it was a sultry day outside, gorgeous with autumn colors. When the windows had to be kept shut the smell of the children's bodies and their clothes became quite nauseating. Sometimes, Inga thought, the worst hardship they had to put up with was the lack of soap—and what little they could get nowadays was so bad it was almost impossible to use it on the children. It irritated the skin diseases they already suffered from—diseases that no one in Norway had ever seen before.

Her mother-in-law had shrugged her shoulders: yes, it was nasty that the Germans had brought back every kind of lice and pest that we had almost eliminated from our country. But Margit remembered when it used to be quite common for poor people's children to be lousy, but they lived and thrived just the same. "Of course, it was a good thing to get rid of the lice, and it was mostly thanks to you teachers. But I'm sure you'll be able to do the delousing job over again all right, once we're rid of their big brothers, those two-legged lice that are eating us all up."

Inga Bjørge had become a schoolteacher again. The headmaster, Mr. Haramb, was doing forced labor somewhere on the Finnish frontier; they might never see him again, he had suffered from kidney trouble for years. It was strange and heartbreaking to remember how unpopular he had been, how the children had made a point of teasing and tricking him. But it was wonderful too, the way a man nobody had trusted because of his pompousness and petty, self-important ways had defended the souls of the children about whom he used to be so irritatingly sentimental. Haramb proved he had meant every word he ever said; he stood firm as a rock in the face of bullying, torture, certain death. And he was just one of many who had risen to heroism, quite unexpectedly.

Eirik Brekkan, the young teacher the farmers had been so set against because of his radical views, his scoffing at religion, and his "warmongering," was imprisoned in Germany as a "Communist."

Miss Erlandsen of the preparatory school was still so crippled by her attack of infantile paralysis she might be able to resume her work someday, or she might not.

So Inga Bjørge taught school again, together with old Dr. Hakonssen, who had been pensioned off eleven years ago. The doctor lectured on natural history, biology, and health, and the doctor's wife taught religion, since her brother, the minister, had been evicted from the parish. The new schoolhouse, a fine modern building of their native green sandstone, had been taken over by the Germans and the Quislings. The old schoolhouse used as preparatory and as a health center had burned down in the war. So now the children were taught in private homes—the youngest ones at Jelstad, the four senior classes at the doctor's.

Some of the children looked very thin and pale, especially the youngsters from laborers' homes down by the station. Their fathers had had to leave and take work in the town, in German-managed industries and building activities. Of course, the advantages the Germans had promised their families never materialized. And when the youngsters disbelieved anything, they would ask: "Is it true, or is it German?"

True, everybody did as much as possible to help everybody else. Inga's own children too were not so robust as they had been—except Halvor, of course; his grandmother saw to that. But when she trudged uphill all the way to Bjørge with her two little girls, Inga saw how quickly they got tired and out of breath. Ragnhild was the stronger of the two, as slight, thin children often are. But she was worried about Tone. Her gold-and-rose-colored little girl looked faded and listless now. . . .

"That's right, Elna. Now, Petter Evensen, can you tell us something more about Erling Skjalgsson? Do you remember how he treated his thralls, for instance?"

"Erling always had a great many thralls on his manor. And he used to stake out for each man the work he had to finish each day. When they were through with it they were free to work for themselves. So they cleared the moors around Sola and raised grain and cattle, and they used the money they made to buy their liberty. A clever man could win his freedom in three years; many took five or seven, but the thrall who had not managed to become a free man in ten years was looked down on as being shiftless and dumb."

Inga looked out over the children. "You know, one of our poets says: 'The greatest heritage is for a man to be born of good lineage.' When we sang those words, we used to think of our forefathers who had been chieftains, or of our peasant ancestors who had tilled their own soil since time immemorial, and who had never been anybody's serfs, or of our sailors who had been the lords of the North Sea in Viking ages and now sail the seven seas in steel ships and tankers, carrying the war materials that the United Nations need in this war of liberation. But do you know that of all the ancestors we have a right to look back upon with pride and to invoke in our fight today, I think those old thralls are among the finest. They broke ground on Jaeren, by the ocean that mirrored the white sky of our light summer nights, making those nights lighter still for the man who dug out the roots of oak and pine trees and carried stones from the fields he was making until his back ached and his body bent double with toil. That man had a will to die free and give freedom as an inheritance to his sons.

"Many of the farms the Germans have destroyed must be the very same homesteads those thralls first cleared. And that shows us the meaning of everything you have seen happen in Norway since April 9, 1940. Erling Skjalgsson made free men and Norsemen of thralls. The Germans came here to try to make thralls of Norsemen."

I'll have to tell them these things while I may, Inga thought, as she trudged homeward with Ragnhild and Tone. The next time I shall tell them about our old laws, the things Matthias said to us once, about the difference between the Germans and the Nordics. They regard the law as a body of commands and prohibitions imposed by powers outside themselves. To us law is an expression of our creative urge toward a just and equitable society, as sacred to us as our honor. But our poor children are growing up under a rule of lawlessness and iniquity that we all have a duty to resist and fight to the death. It will be a big job to teach them authority should be obeyed, when authority in Norway again means the voice of our own conscience. But don't you think, Uncle Matthias, that this is what our martyred teachers and clergy, what all our fallen soldiers, all our sailors braving death on oceans infested with submarines and bombers, want us to do? The Germans may steal everything they can carry off; they may rob us of everything brute force can take away, but they must not be able to steal the souls of our children or take away from us that which makes us Norwegians.

Uncle Matthias, she wondered—shall we ever see him again? They took him off to Germany to serve fifteen years' imprisonment. He is an old man; he may not live to see the day of liberation. Many will not be with us on that day. Even here in our valley —poor old Nick, kicked and beaten to death because he defied the Gestapo when he was taken away for stealing food—food stolen by the Germans themselves. Rasmus Storhaug, too, died in the hands of those unutterable perverts.

"Oh, Mother," Tone panted, "you run so fast."

"Sorry, darling. Let's sit here and rest a little."

High above them the old brown buildings on Bjørge glowed in the afternoon sun. The spruce-clad hillside behind rose steeply, a rich dark green dotted with the gold of the birches and the red of the rowans, with the deep blue of the autumn sky above and behind.

My little son will live here and carry on the work of his father and his father's fathers someday. Sometimes it seems as if the worst was the destruction of the tilled soil, the fouling of our country with their barracks and defenses put up against the nation it belongs to with right and honor. But then, there is so much that seems the worst—and every day they start new worse things. And before the end comes they will do things we are unable to imagine. And yet, if it occurred to them to fortify that mountain bastion up there dominating the valley north and south . . .

When German troops poured into the village, when the outworn railway ran day and night in spite of breakdowns and derailings and disgorged machinery and building materials, when labor gangs put up barracks down on the river flats and foremen and German engineers were quartered everywhere in the crowded houses down by the station, Inga felt she had known all the time that this was going to happen.

They received eight days' notice, and were permitted to take with them their most necessary belongings, provided they could find a horse and cart to move them. This meant very humane treatment—according to German standards. But then there were stories, carried by the secret whispering service that seemed to know everything, telling how the Germans had returned to their old game and were being "nice" to the common people. From the town came tales of German soldiers secretly going to workingmen's homes after dark, trying to press bits of chocolate upon the children or sausage upon the housewife: "My name is Fritz Berger. Remember it? I am a good German." And then they seemed hurt and frightened when so very few fell for their simple ruse. Secret instructions passed among the Quislings prepared them for the day when the Germans might be driven out of Norway. Go into hiding. Surrender as soon as possible to an Allied military post or to the Norwegian police, and claim protection against the fury of the people.

Margit went about her packing, stony calm. Inga dared not speak to her mother-in-law. The work of destruction had been started, and Inga, afraid to have the two little girls about, with the men swarming all over the place, had already left the children at the doctor's.

Margit Bjørge had kept indoors, but the day before they were to leave she went out and stood by the corner of the washhouse.

A sudden spell of mild weather had freed the spruce on the mountains of their burden of snow. The dark wooded slope above Bjørge shone golden green in the sunlight that filtered fitfully through bluish-gray and silvery clouds. A mild wind breathed on the fields, where the upturned black soil looked like wounds torn in the snowy expanses. Parts of the old houses had already gone down; even now, Inga knew, Bjørge existed only in their own minds. But when a lull came in the shrieking and groaning of machinery and the discord of alien voices barking orders, the soft sighing of the wind in the woods seemed like a promise of spring—the spring that was still so far away.

Margit, making her way along the rut that carriages had dug past the site of the cowhouse, went beyond the men in uniform and the ragged and dirty workers, bent, and plucked something from the soggy field. Returning, she showed her daughter-in-law what she carried in her bony old hand: some young plants from their field of winter rye, the threadlike leaves still green, the broken black grain clinging between the white neck and the root fibers. Three she picked out and gave to Inga, and three she kept for herself. Then she went indoors and put them inside her old Bible—the uppermost of the miscellaneous objects in her well-worn handbag—with the reflection: "The last grain grown on Bjørge—at least, for a long time."

For the last time the two women of Bjørge sat by the stove in the dark old washhouse. Inga had hung her coat and skirt over the small window to keep out the glare of the floodlights that had been put up all over the place. From without came the sounds of rumbling and groaning machinery.

Pouring the tea that she had made from dried leaves of fireweed and mixing it with the last of the milk, Inga offered: "Well, Mother, it's nice and hot at least.

"Mother"—in an agonized whisper—"do you think it will ever be possible to make this bit of land come to life again—to make living things grow here?"

"How should I know?" Margit spoke calmly. "It depends on what they're going to do with it. Some of it may be redeemed—or it may not. But they'll be made to pay for it, Inga, never fear. They'll be made to pay for every evil and cruel and obscene thing they have committed wherever they have made a hell on earth for people to live in. Their way will take them through the same hell, never you fear."

She soaked her lump of heavy black bread in the lukewarm mixture and started eating it with a spoon. "Let us be thankful for our good luck in getting that room up in Hjertasen. It's so far off we shan't be able to see what they're doing up here. I don't know if I could look at it for long without doing something . . . killing somebody," she said softly.

Snowflakes were sifting down in the glare of the floodlights when Margit and Inga stepped out into the darkness of the winter morning. They lugged their sacks of bedding to the sledge waiting for them well out of the driveway, so as not to obstruct the traffic to the fortifications. The old man who was to drive them said, apologetically, that anything might happen to the property of Torstein Hjertasen if he left the horse and sledge. "But if you, Margit, will hold the horse, I'll go and help Inga carry out the rest of your things."

The driver—the hired man from Hjertasen—was a small, wiry old fellow, the vehicle a small, old flat sledge with a crate for the driver to sit on. The horse was a tall, raw-boned, red-roan animal, not much more than a skeleton of a horse covered with hide. Wherever a harness could possibly break his skin, patches of gray hair showed it had been broken.

Margit stroked the miserable animal's neck and cupped her hand over his lips. From her coat pocket she took a chunk of the soggy dark bread and fed him, crooning low and tenderly.

"He's as deaf as a post," the driver volunteered. "Deaf and mute, poor boy. The Germans did something to him—they did something to most of the horses they took away, when we were fighting in Norway, to keep them from whinnying. Their veterinaries did, God damn them. It's a bloody shame, isn't it?"

Margit looked at him, taut and white-faced. "I have heard of it. But I didn't believe it could be true," she whispered.

"Oh, yes, it's true, all right. Not to all of them. I suppose they had no time for that, but down south by the lake they did it to many. Well, Torstein was glad he was able to buy this poor old critter, even so. He lost all his horses, you know."

They had to drive down across the steep fields toward the valley to avoid the traffic. The two women sat huddled on their luggage. It was daylight before they got as far as the station.

From there the going was still slower. The promontory of Bjørge had been blasted to make room for the main road and the railway, and on the other side of the road the river roared in green and white rapids below the gorge. There was scarcely room for the sledge to pull out to the roadside to avoid the trucks and cars coming and going, and when they had the road to themselves for a little while the old horse was just able to plod along. The snow was coming down heavily now in big wet flakes.

It was past noon when they finally turned in the old dirt road that led up the east side toward Hjertasen. All three got off the sledge and walked to ease the load for the horse.

From behind them sounded the roar of rapidly approaching motorcycles and in a moment they were overtaken. With lamps burning palely through the snowy daylight, and splattering mud, three motorcycles pulled up beside them. Uniformed Germans and Quisling hooligans roared something at them.

The man from Hjertasen shook his head, pretending to be as deaf as his horse. A burly, thick-set German pushed a Quisling aside. He was armed like a walking fortress; in fact, all the men were armed even more heavily than usual.

"Answer at once," the German rasped in Norwegian. "You heard what we asked you. Did you see any Russians running this way?"

"The Russians?" Margit blinked down into the face of the German, a picture of senile innocence. "Are they here already? Aye, they advance quickly."

The German struck her in the face. The sight of blood running from her nose and mouth apparently made him still angrier, and he brought the butt of his rifle down with a crash on her shoulder. Another blow, and she crumpled up in the snowdrift. They kicked her and then jerked her to her feet. When Inga, shoved into the snow by the roadside, got to her feet and tried to run to Margit, a man slapped her face viciously.

Two of the motorcycles roared on. By now Inga had caught on to what they had been saying. When a train had stopped with engine trouble down in the pass, some Russian prisoners had managed to get out and had disappeared in the snowstorm. They were supposed to have made their way eastward. If they did not succeed in getting away over the mountains and perhaps ultimately reaching the Swedish frontier, it would not be for lack of support from the Norwegians.

Roaring at the three of them, the Germans from the third motorcycle took down their names and address. At the moment they could not be bothered with taking them away. "You wait—you'll hear from us soon."

Inga bathed Margit's face with snow and tried to make her as comfortable as possible among their sacks of bedding. With a trembling hand Margit felt in her bleeding mouth—her dental plate had been broken and it hurt her. With Inga's help she succeeded in getting it out. Spasms of pain contorted her face, but in between the spasms she chuckled. It was ghastly, this chuckling half drowned in blood.

It was dark before they arrived at Hjertasen and Inga could

put her to bed. Her right collarbone had been fractured and some ribs too, Inga was afraid. Late at night she got a call through to the doctor. He promised to come as soon as he could, but that might not be until the next night.

And before the doctor arrived, Sheriff Storhaug's henchmen had taken Margit Bjørge away.

Inga was kept busy. When the doctor's villa was requisitioned, the children were returned to her and had to be taught their lessons wherever room could be found. Hjertasen was rather out of the way, but some of the big boys and girls who could not get to a higher school managed to come rather regularly to her classes.

Margit's niece, Borghild Marstein, managed to send her news from town about her mother-in-law. She had had to be taken to a private home where some rooms were used as a hospital for Norwegians—the great district hospital, the Red Cross Hospital, the nursing home for t.b.'s, and all the private sanitariums were full of Germans. The niece had been permitted to visit Margit once while she was there. But after ten days she was moved to the old Police Station. There she was crowded with five other women in a man's single cell. Borghild Marstein had not been able to see her there, but she knew that one of her cellmates was Siri Holm, who had been arrested for "contempt of the German Wehrmacht." Siri, Dr. Holm's daughter, was quite a good nurse, though she had not admitted to having had any training, as she was afraid of being taken to nurse Germans. Borghild had learned that, considering the circumstances, Margit's condition was not too bad.

Then, eight weeks after she had been arrested, Inga got news that Margit Bjørge had been released and was staying with her niece. Borghild Marstein did not think Margit would be fit to travel for a long while. It would be fine if Inga could get permission to come to town and see her. And if she could possibly bring Halvor.

It was Alf Storhaug who somehow learned about the matter

and got her a permission to buy a railway ticket. Eli brought it up to Hjertasen.

"He's trying hard as hell to curry favor with people," she said contemptuously. "He's frightened out of his wits, now that everyone believes the Germans are in for a licking like nothing in the world. He stops me to talk whenever he sees me in the village, wanting to know what they say about him at home. I tell him I've never heard them mention his name since I moved back to Father. He thinks Lars will shoot him dead at the first opportunity. However, that's no reason why you shouldn't benefit from his cowardice when you may."

Inga had not been in town since the war had started. Before she got there she noticed the changes: farms on the outskirts had disappeared, and all kinds of new buildings—barracks, workshops, factories, and houses, and plots fenced in for she knew not what—had spoiled the lovely environs past recognition. From a fellow traveler she learned that many of the buildings the Germans had put up stood empty. They preferred to live squeezed in among the population and to billet their men in private homes as a protection against air raids. Two Gestapo families, for instance, lived in the villa of Judge Høyer, where Mrs. Marstein had worked. Then the Marsteins were evicted, and now they had a room in a workman's cottage that housed four other families. Oh, they were quite well, the talkative little man told her, and their baby was a fine youngster, but of course, it was trying for Borghild to live in close quarters with so many strangers and to have to share a kitchen with four other women.

The streets were hateful, Inga decided, with Germans in uniform or without, and broad-bottomed, big-bellied, stocky-legged German women in furs everywhere. With some difficulty Inga found the place where the Marsteins lived. It was the usual five-room workingman's cottage. Once, obviously, it had been a neat, white-painted home in a garden plot; now it was sadly dilapidated.

She found Margit in bed in a sort of cubbyhole behind the

Marsteins' room. It was so narrow, with the bed under the slanting roof, a chair under the dormer window, a washstand, and Margit's clothes hanging from pegs on the wall, that one had scarcely room to turn.

She tried hard not to show how shocked she was at the sight of her mother-in-law lying so yellow and wrinkled among the grayish pillows. Margit's face was strangely different, with the toothless mouth looking as if an ax had ripped a gap across the beautifully molded oval of her face. And her white hair had thinned so that the skull gleamed like ivory underneath.

But her eyes were as keen as ever, and she tried to smile when she saw Inga. Only when Halvor held back, staring in wonder at the old woman in the bed, did Margit look troubled. Then, when the little boy held out his hand and said, "Good afternoon, Granny, are you sick?" she laughed, relieved. He had recognized her.

Her left shoulder was bandaged and the arm was in a sling. She was terribly emaciated. Inga had always thought of her as a lean old woman. Now, she saw, it must have been her tallness and slenderness of frame that gave one that impression: she had really been a well-muscled woman, but now she was reduced to bones and tendons.

"And how are you, my child—and how are the girls?" She spoke indistinctly, but calmly. "Sit down, dear, and tell me all the news about you and everything at home. I'm very glad you could come."

Margit would say very little about her experience in prison, except to tell how nice Siri Holm and the other women had been to her. "She won't talk about it," Borghild Marstein confirmed. But she knew that her aunt had never been questioned. They just kept her for eight weeks and then sent her away with the warning that they would keep an eye on her. "I wonder if they'll have to do that for any length of time," Borghild said. "She's very frail. The collarbone hasn't set—maybe it never will, at her age."

Inga stayed in town for three days.

The last afternoon, when Inga was to leave with Halvor on an early train, Mrs. Marstein had made potato scones spread with jam. They were going to have a nice little meal, with the last of Inga's gifts and her fireweed tea. The door to Margit's alcove was open.

Suddenly there was an imperious rap at the door. "Germans," Borghild Marstein whispered uneasily. "Damn them, they can't even knock at a door in a decent way." But she called out: "Come in."

A big blonde woman, draped lavishly with silver foxes, sailed into the untidy little room. "Mrs. Marstein living here? Any of you speak German?"

Inga intimated that she did at least understand it. The guest looked around for a chair, but, seeing none vacant, slouched down on the Marsteins' bed. Then she started unwrapping a large parcel she had carried under her arm.

"Now, listen, this is important. I'm here on a friendly errand, Mrs. Marstein. I am Frau Oberleutnant Egon Malzahn. We're living in the villa that once belonged to Judge Høyer. Now, listen —I have learned that you were for many years in service in the Høyer family. So the other day, when I had the usual house-cleaning done, it occurred to me that you might be interested in these —they seem to be family pictures of the Høyers."

Borghild Marstein looked. In the parcel were several albums of snapshots—the three Høyer boys as children, Mrs. Høyer with Nils as a baby at her breast, Nils naked on a white bearskin, Johan and Nils as Boy Scouts, Johan in his ensign's uniform, Arne in a white sailor suit with his seventeenth-of-May flag, the boys on skis, the boys with girls, Arne dressed up for private theatricals.

"They were in Mrs. Høyer's desk and in her dresser. I gathered all I could find. Now, I'm sure Mrs. Høyer would give a good deal to be able to retrieve these pictures of her sons. Two of them were killed in action during the war, I know."

Borghild Marstein's face softened. "I say, *gnädige Frau,* this is awfully kind of you," she began in an uncertain voice.

"Of course, the Høyers will never be permitted to return to

Norway. But we know they're in America now, and no doubt they'll be earning a lot of money. So I'm willing, Mrs. Marstein, to let you have all these family pictures for five hundred kronen. You know, someday when we have won this war, peace will come. And then you'll be able to contact your former mistress in America. I'm sure she'll gladly pay you as much as a thousand dollars for these pictures of her children."

The two Norwegian women looked at her, gaping. Then from the back room came a horrible, choking sound, and a chuckle. Margit was laughing, with the tea spurting from her mouth—coughing and chuckling and coughing and laughing.

The Frau Oberleutnant looked astonished—and a bit suspicious. "Well?"

Borghild Marstein collapsed on her chair, mutely shaking her head.

"Thank you so much"—Inga tried to speak quietly, though choked with irrepressible, half-hysterical laughter. "But no. Nothing doing. We don't care for that kind of bargain."

The German lady scowled angrily at the women who sat rocking with laughter, tears streaming down their faces. Then she got to her feet, shrieked something they did not listen to, her face purple with rage, and sailed out, her merchandise clutched among her dangling silver foxes, dwarfing the door.

"Can you imagine. Can you imagine," moaned Borghild Marstein, while from the bedroom came peals of high, fierce laughter. Unable to stop, they laughed and laughed and laughed.

But it is too horrible, Inga thought, her sides aching with laughter. They are brutes, sadists, thieves, shameless liars, obscene criminals—they have maimed and broken and destroyed millions of innocent men and women and children. And at the same time, they are so utterly ridiculous.

THE NINTH COMMANDMENT

Thou shalt not bear
false witness against
thy neighbor

HENDRIK WILLEM VAN LOON

people that they were unable to rid themselves of these nightmares long after there was the slightest risk or possibility of such another massacre of the faithful. Even when I was young, we were still being sent to bed with the threat that if we were not good, the Spaniards would get us.

Born into this community and bred in this atmosphere of suspicion and hatred for everything popish, young Samuel had never known a day when he could really call his soul his own. When, during his tenth year, the Catholics had at last been sufficient in number to ask most humbly that they be permitted to build a house of worship of their own, he had eagerly joined the other urchins who every evening after dark used to gather around the fence that hid the new structure, to pelt it with stones and, if possible, break the windows. Even after the edifice had been completed (for safety's sake, it had been made to look like a Greek temple rather than a church), young Samuel would never pass through that street if he could possibly find another route to carry him to his destination. Someday, he felt sure, he would see the Devil sunning himself behind one of the pillars of the façade and he would never survive the encounter.

For the rest, Samuel had lived an exceedingly quiet and uneventful existence. He had attended the public schools (for although the agitation for "denominational schools" was already in full swing, they had not yet been established) and had most carefully abstained from all sports, from dancing, from theatergoing, and from every other kind of worldly distraction, that he might not be led into those temptations which twice every Sunday he heard denounced from the pulpit as vivid remnants of the wicked old popish days.

He had never greatly bothered about the future. Someday, he knew, he would succeed his father in the old man's frame-making business. People in this remote part of the country still believed in sound craftsmanship, and there was a lot that had to be learned in that low, back room with its overhead load of endless meters of lath, its tables covered with pots of paste, and its piles of "religious objects" which were kept in stock for the customers who used to patronize the Templum Solomonis, or Temple of Solomon, as the grandfather, the founder of the business, had called his establishment.

Of course, there was a certain demand for jobs of a somewhat different nature. Some of the landed gentry who had clung to their ancestral estates in the heart of the island would bring Samuel pictures of race horses or hunting scenes and bid him ensconce them in his gayest frames, that they might preserve those mementos of happy days in the field for the benefit of their children and grandchildren whom they hoped to train in a love of these manly pastimes. Samuel would do their bidding, but his heart was not in that kind of work and he therefore thought it only fair to charge such customers a little more than the job was worth, so as to compensate himself for the damage done to his soul by letting himself be contaminated by these labors of the Devil.

Occasionally, however, he would draw the line, and then he would explain his refusal with a magnificent flow of words which left no doubt as to his views upon the wickedness in which this world once more found itself engulfed and that the football field had taken the place of the Church.

He had one secret ambition. Someday he hoped an unsuspecting Catholic would bring him an idolatrous picture of a saint or perhaps the Mother of God. The speech he intended to deliver on that occasion he had most carefully prepared, but alas, he had never had a chance to indulge in this indignant declamation. The wily Catholics patronized a frame-maker of their own faith and never so much as set foot in the shop of this aggressive heretic.

In the meantime, to recoup himself for the financial losses that came from taking business quite so seriously, Samuel had added Bibles to his stock in trade. These had proved so profitable that he sometimes dreamed of the day when he would be able to withdraw entirely from the frame-making business and devote himself exclusively to his Bibles and to certain volumes of sermons, prepared by the accredited preachers of his particular faith. For, shortly after his twentieth birthday, Samuel had completely broken away from the official Dutch Reformed faith to which his ancestors had belonged. He had come to regard it as altogether lacking in ardor and having a tendency toward what he contemptuously called "the sin of compromise."

In this he was, I regret to say, quite right. The younger members of the clergy had gone in quite heavily for those more ethical conceptions of the last twenty years of the nineteenth century which had nothing to do with that God-given "letter of the law" for which good Samuel would most willingly have gone to the scaffold. For that law was God's law, and God's law to him was the beginning and the end of all things. He therefore, in a bitter letter of denunciation, had resigned as a member of the Great Church (old Bishop Ludger's former Cathedral), and had joined an obscure sect, founded eighty years before by a peasant in a remote Frisian village.

This honest rustic had got into a terrific quarrel with his local dominie anent a certain passage in the eleventh chapter of Leviticus, where the coney is declared an unclean animal because it "cheweth the cud but divideth not the hoof." The ruminating coney had led to other hairsplittings of an even more questionable nature, and all this had led to an open break between the followers of the Dutch Reformed faith and the Coneyites (as they were popularly known). This, in turn, had caused wholesale emigration of Coneyites, who, rather than submit to the dictates of the synod of the state Church, had pulled up stakes and had migrated to distant lands, where their descendants may still be found, enjoying life, liberty, and the pursuit of their own notions about the cud-chewing coney.

As for those who had remained at home, their schism had proved a veritable godsend. Since they obstinately refused to take any active part in the politics of a government which oppressed them (it refused to pay the salaries of their ministers), they could devote themselves entirely to their own pursuits, and being hard-working and thrifty citizens, they were rapidly accumulating more wealth than their neighbors who dwelled in the darkness of worldly ambition. Missionaries from Friesland soon visited every other part of the country, and Nieuwstad, with its tradition of six hundred years of piety, became a seething center of this new heresy. Soon the Coneyites, who used to meet in an old brewery (known to the scoffers of the community as the Rabbit Warren), were able to allow themselves the luxury of a half-time preacher, a worthy cobbler who spent the hours he was not preparing his sermons half-soling the shoes of the members of his congregation.

As this amateur cleric suffered from the legendary ailment of his real profession (gastric trouble), there were many Sundays when he was unable to attend to his duties, and on such occasions Samuel was usually requested to officiate and to deliver the customary two-hour sermon. He loved those mornings when he could wrestle openly with the Prince of Evil, whom he detested with a personal hatred which not infrequently outstripped his eloquence.

Now, though Samuel knew his Old Testament by heart (the New appealed to him but moderately), he had an instinctive fear of passages that might be capable of a number of different explanations. For he knew his congregation and realized that any statement of his not fully endorsed by one of his listeners would lead to days and often weeks of disputes and wranglings. Therefore, in his sermons he preferred to stick to the Ten Commandments. They were the real thing. They said exactly what they meant and, best of all, allowed simple-minded but ambitious Samuel to play the role of another Moses. How he loved it! He could see himself standing perilously balanced among the boulders and the shafts of lightning on Mount Sinai and shielding his eyes while the Lord guided his hand as it wrote down the different "thou shalt not's."

Of course, there was the difficulty of the language, but Samuel, way down deep in his heart, felt convinced that on this famous occasion the great Jahweh had spoken in Dutch rather than in

Hebrew. And therefore, whenever he chose his text from the twentieth chapter of Exodus, he could (as he used to express it) put his teeth into something hard, like the rod of iron which the Psalmist had praised so eloquently as the most trustworthy of all instruments of chastisement.

Needless to stress the fact that Samuel was primarily a moralist. He was a Dutchman and he felt it his duty to call to the truth of the Book of God whosoever came within hailing distance of his far-carrying voice. Let it be said to his everlasting honor, however, that Samuel never showed any signs of that "pride of spirit" which was so apt to occur among his fellow Hollanders who felt that God had chosen them among his elect. Such a thought had never entered his mind and never would, for in spite of his rigid and uncompromising attitude toward what he called his "convictions," he was at heart a very simple and very friendly little fellow who meant to do well by his fellow men, provided they gave him just the tiniest little chance to bring unto them his own vision of the everlasting verities. And his faults, or rather his shortcomings, were not so much of his own making as the result of circumstances over which he himself had no control whatsoever.

Born into a small city with a noble past but without either a present or a future, he had spent all his days so far removed from what he shudderingly called "the world" that he felt completely at a loss whenever he was obliged to leave his own little bailiwick or was thrown into contact with people who took that world pretty much as they found it and asked no questions as long as the company was pleasant, the beer was good, and the girls were obliging. Had he been born in Amsterdam or Brussels or some other big city, he would undoubtedly have been different. But his cradle had awaited him in a small house on a small side street of a very small town where nothing had happened for almost three entire centuries. And so he had become what he was—an honest and honorable and God-fearing subject of an equally honest and honorable and God-fearing Queen, doing the best he knew according to the dictates of his uncompromising conscience, paying his taxes on the dot, and never being late at divine service. If he himself happened to be preaching, he was usually an hour and a half early.

I knew the poor fellow well (God keep his soul!) and had a sincere affection for him in spite of his terrible habit of inveigling me into theological discussions whenever I brought him an old etching or some ancient map that needed framing. I have no love whatsoever for those kinds of religious disputations and I avoid them like the plague or the writings of Gertrude Stein. But I liked old Samuel in spite of his fiercely burning eyes and his equally fiercely burning arguments whenever he felt it necessary —most humbly and politely—to point a reproving finger at the scandalous levity of my own way of life. And I often dropped in, whenever business called me from Veere to Nieuwstad, for I liked to share a cup of coffee with him and his excellent wife, a most worthy mate to a man of his caliber, a most efficient *huisvrouw,* a most devoted mother to her small son and daughter, and as rabid a follower of the only true faith as her husband. Therefore, as soon as I could return to our beloved island after the last war, I made it a point to pay my respects to the "Temple of Solomon: Frames Neatly and Cheaply Fixed and Bibles for Sale," where everything looked very much as it had before.

I had not seen either Samuel or his wife for five years, and I found them but little changed. Both he and his wife had of course grown a little older, but like their faith they were fashioned of such rock-ribbed substance that it took more than a world war to affect them, either physically or psychologically. They had the correct answers to all the questions life might possibly ask, and therefore nothing could happen to them.

I noticed, however, that there was a look of worry in Samuel's eyes which I had never noticed before. I knew him too well to risk any direct questions. He was much too much "buttoned up on himself," as they call it in our native language, ever to reveal anything about his own affairs unless they were directly connected with his church, and his church seemed to be doing better than ever. He was even contemplating building a new and larger house of prayer, as he told me before I had been five minutes underneath his roof. His neighbors, however, after the fashion of neighbors all over the world, were not at all unwilling to talk with me about what had happened to the owner of the frame shop. And so, without any urging on my part, I gradually got all the details of a story which would not have very deeply affected an ordinary and normal human being but which had almost killed our poor frame-maker. He was not like ordinary human beings: his every thought and deed were dominated by the terrific consciousness of being a sinful creature in the eyes of a stern God and whose faith in belonging to the Elect had been most severely shaken by the little incident I shall now relate.

As soon as the war was over there had been a terrific hue and cry about the starved children within the borders of the former German Empire. And indeed, those poor infants were in a sore plight. Conceived, so to speak, in the original kohlrabi, nursed on potato peels and *ersatz* milk, they had been the victims of every conceivable malady resulting from malnutrition. The stupidity of the Allies in continuing the German blockade for more than a year after the conclusion of the armistice had caused the death of tens of thousands of them. The survivors, bleary-eyed and with grotesque tummies and a tendency to lose their hair at a very early age, were far from attractive, but the Dutch and the Danish people, as well as the ever hospitable Swiss and Swedes and Norwegians, had not bothered about their looks. All they knew was that millions of children were starving through no fault of their own, and spontaneously they had opened their homes and their hearts to these unfortunate victims of this last great outbreak of human folly. And endlessly the trains from Germany, Austria, and Hungary had begun to roll toward the so-called neutral countries, each of these trains carrying its heartbreaking load of little boys and girls who never in all their lives had known what it was to eat their fill or even their half fill.

At every station, these poor creatures, on their weak and malformed legs, had anxiously scanned the faces of these strange women (most of them in tears) who, in a language of which they did not understand a word, had told them how happy they were to see them and how they would now feed them platefuls of rich cream and give them money to buy as many bars of chocolate as they cared to eat. The little mites might have heard the magic word chocolate, but they had never seen the substance, and now they found themselves in a wonderland where chocolate grew on trees, so to speak.

Of course, there had been a few difficulties. These good women at the stations meant well, but it took the combined efforts of all the Dutch medicos to prevent them from killing their little charges by their sudden display of generosity, for it was discovered that (during the first weeks, at least) a breakfast consisting of a single egg and a solitary slice of bread would cause gastric disturbances which often, alas, proved fatal.

The method the authorities followed to park out their charges to the best advantage was a very simple one. The first trains were dispatched to the more remote parts of the country, exactly as had been done in the fall of the year 1914, when half a million Belgian refugees had invaded the country. As soon as these distant villages and towns had been filled up, the trains had begun to stop at stations a little closer to the German frontier and had there delivered as much of their cargoes as those communities could hold. In this way it came about that five days after this charitable enterprise had been started, the Samuel family found itself augmented by one very blond, very thin, very much frightened, and very hungry male child of North German extraction.

Mrs. Samuel had picked him out at random, for in the matter of dividing these children among the different households, it was a question of "first come, first served." It was not necessary to investigate the prospective foster parents, for in a small Dutch town everybody knew everybody else, and the Samuel family was beyond reproach. Therefore, when Mrs. Samuel put her hand on the boy's shoulder and with as much tenderness as she could put into her stern voice announced, "Child, you come with me," the urchin obediently picked up the handkerchief which contained all his worldly belongings and did as he was told.

Being of about the same age as the Samuels' son, he was given a cot (homemade by the master of the frames) in the room of Samuel, Jr., and there he immediately cried himself into so deep a sleep that for a while his hosts feared he might have passed out altogether. However, after twenty-four hours, he suddenly returned to life, ate an astonishingly large meal for one who was supposed to be fed pap by the spoonful, and quietly announced that he was ready for whatever new adventures might befall him.

Within the next twenty-four hours he found himself completely at home among his new surroundings. He was taken to a Dutch school, but at his age a difference of language offered no difficulties. By the end of a single week he could follow his lessons with perfect ease and, after a month, had so completely mastered the new tongue that often he was mistaken for a Dutch boy—an error of judgment to which he invariably reacted with so fierce a resentment that he soon became known as the *Mofje,* or "the Little Muff," that strange appellation having since time immemorial been the name by which the Germans have been known to their Dutch neighbors. It was not exactly a flattering term, bearing a close resemblance to certain unfortunate expressions with which, before the beginning of the present war, we used to refer to our neighbors of the Southern Hemisphere.

Little Johann, however (for that was the child's real name), was not a very sensitive boy. As a matter of fact, he took immense delight in hearing himself called the *Mofje,* and when well-meaning strangers, attracted by his blue eyes and blond curls, asked him who he was, he invariably answered, "Why, don't you know? I am a little Muff and these other children are just plain Dutchmen."

But aside from a certain tendency toward placing himself as far apart from his comrades as possible and considering himself superior to the native breed, he was a pleasant and docile infant who caused no trouble whatsoever and, with an efficiency that was rather surprising in one quite so young, was soon helping old Samuel in his workshop. He also ran errands for his foster mother, having discovered that many of the Dutch shopkeepers to whom he went for a loaf of bread or ten cents' worth of treacle would say, "Ah, there is the *Mofje*. Poor child, he must be hungry," and would reward him with a piece of candy or a small bat of chocolate. Then he would hasten to find a quiet spot where he would devour this unexpected delicacy with the indecent haste of a starved wolf—which, indeed, he was. He had never had enough sweet things during his short and miserable existence on this planet and he felt as if he would never be able to get his share of the honey cake and lollipops of his adopted country. Truth to tell, his new home did not exactly spoil him with such delicacies, for sugar cost money and good Dutch Calvinists are greatly opposed to the idea of wasting valuable pennies upon the mere superficialities of life.

Neither Mr. nor Mrs. Samuel was exactly a student of the modern science of nutrition. They fed their children what their own great-great-grandparents ten generations removed had fed their offspring, and sweets were considered something very rare and very extra which should be preserved for such high occasions as marriages or birthdays.

The father and mother allowed themselves exactly three spoonfuls of sugar for their daily ration of two cups of tea and their one cup of coffee. After they had helped themselves from the silver sugar bowl, which was one of their few purely "worldly" possessions, the box was once more locked and the key was placed underneath the family Bible, which lay on a small mahogany table in the corner of their living room.

The chance that anybody in the family outside of the parents themselves would ever dare to touch that sacred key was about as great as that of hearing the name of the Lord being used in vain in this God-fearing household. But the morning came when Samuel had to make up his mind that the impossible had happened.

Somebody had taken the key and had helped himself to the contents of the sugar bowl.

It had been petty theft, but the very idea of such a thing—the possibility of a theft having been committed in his house—struck the soul of Samuel with a horror he had never experienced before. His own children, of course, were out of the question. They not only lived in fear of the Lord, but they also trembled before the sight of their father. Little Johann was the only possible culprit.

Samuel called the German boy into his bedroom, a dark and solemn-looking room situated in a part of the house enjoying a minimum of fresh air and light. He sat down before the table at which every evening, just before retiring, he read a chapter of the Gospels. Little Johann was kept standing.

"My boy," Samuel said kindly, "did you steal sugar? I want you to be honest, for you are confessing not only to me but also to your God."

"Ja, mein Herr," little Johann answered, in the strange admixture of Dutch and German which he used whenever he had to speak to a Hollander he did not quite like, and by now he had come to hate, with a venomous if carefully concealed contempt, the man who was supposed to be his "well-doer."

"Why did you steal this sugar?"

"Because I was hungry and wanted sugar."

Samuel, who by this time had learned something about the effect of hunger upon underfed children, did his best to look at the case from a practical angle, for he wanted to be a man of his time and he knew what the absence of sweets over a period of years could do to the constitution of a starving child.

"If you wanted more sugar than you got, then why did you not ask me or your mother for more?"

"I don't know, *mein Herr."*

"You are not afraid of us?"

"Oh, no, *mein Herr."*

"Was it the sinful wickedness of your character that made you commit this sin?"

"I did not think, *mein Herr,* that it was a sin. I took only a little."

"In the eyes of God, it did not matter whether you took much or little. The idea of taking that which does not belong to you is what is so abhorrent in His eyes."

"Ja, mein Herr."

Samuel reached for the Bible on the little table with its blue-and-white checkered cloth. He found the right spot as easily as a trained prestidigitator will find an ace of hearts in a pack of cards.

"Listen to this, my child," he said, his voice trembling with emotion. "Here the Lord speaketh through his servant Moses and he sayeth: 'Thou shalt not steal.' That is the way it stands writ in the nineteenth verse of the fifth chapter of Deuteronomy: 'Neither shalt thou steal.' Fortunately, my boy, you have not sinned against the next commandment, which tells you not to bear false witness. You have not lied, but have confessed to the truth. Therefore, I shall be lenient and shall not chastise you as I should have done if you had borne false witness. But you shall not leave this house before you have copied these verses from Deuteronomy a hundredfold."

The little boy gave a quick glance at the page in Deuteronomy which Samuel's finger indicated. He realized that it would take him the greater part of a week to perform this task, and it was the end of July and the great vacation of six weeks had only ten more days to run.

"Please, *mein Herr,"* he whimpered, "tomorrow all the boys and girls of our school are going on a picnic in the dunes. And they had asked me to recite them a poem in my own language. The Master told me I did it so well, it would be an example to these Dutch children. Please, Herr Samuel, let me go tomorrow at least!"

"You have heard what I told you. I am not only supposed to look after your physical well-being, but, for the moment at least, your immortal soul has also been entrusted to my care. You shall therefore stay in this house until your task is finished and you shall have copied these verses a hundred times. And now you may go to bed. Good night."

It took little Johann four days to finish his task. He missed out on the picnic but he managed to hide his disappointment underneath a cloak of cheerful indifference. Another boy—a Dutch one—had been appointed in his place to recite a poem. He had done it very badly and had got so hopelessly stuck in the middle of the second stanza that he had been obliged to stop and the whole thing had been a sad failure, with everybody saying how much better their "Little Muff" would have done if his chances had not been spoiled by that silly psalm-singing frame-maker.

After that, peace and quiet returned to the Samuel household. But a month later, it became apparent once more that someone had helped himself to the contents of the sugar bowl. This time, Samuel decided to act with greater circumspection than before. One evening he hid himself in the corridor that led from the living room to the kitchen and waited there until long after everybody else had gone to bed. Half an hour after the last light had been turned out, he heard soft footsteps. It was little Johann, sneaking into the living room. He gave the boy ample time to commit his crime and then went upstairs before the culprit could find out that he had been observed and detected. Even at breakfast, Samuel did not betray that he knew what a dreadful crime had been committed underneath his roof. But after the porridge had been removed from the table, he bade his wife and children leave the room, and little Johann stay.

"Johann," said Samuel, fiercely clasping both arms of his chair, "answer me truthfully. Did you once more sin against one of God's holy commandments and steal what does not belong to you?"

Johann, remembering what had happened before, decided to make the best of his predicament by a flat denial of the charge.

"Johann," Samuel asked once more, "did you steal sugar?"

"Nee, mein Herr," said Johann in his worst jargon.

"Johann, for the last time I ask you. Did you steal sugar last night from the sugar bowl? Did you, after all of us had gone to bed, take the key from underneath the Bible and help yourself to the contents of that locked box?"

Little Johann looked at him with eyes of complete innocence. *"Nee, mein Herr,"* he repeated, "I did not."

"Johann, you lie."

"Nee, mein Herr, I speak the truth."

"Johann, I saw you opening the box and taking the sugar."

"Nee, mein Herr."

"Johann, sit down while I read you another of God's holy commandments." And after putting on his spectacles, old Samuel read him from the Bible which he had already opened at the right place, the twentieth verse from the twentieth chapter of Exodus. He did not, however, read the whole of it. He left out the last three words, which he feared might weaken his case with the quick-witted youth, who would have claimed that he had not borne false witness against his neighbor but had merely lied about himself.

If he had expected that the simple words, "Thou shalt not bear false witness," would have made any sort of impression upon the obstinate brat, he was to be sadly disappointed, for little Johann merely shook his head and repeated his former denial: "I did not do it."

"And who, then, may have done it?"

"I don't know. Why don't you ask your son? He lives in this house, too."

Now Samuel had him at his mercy. "Johann," he shouted, giving the boy a terrific box on the ear, "it stands writ, 'Thou shalt not bear false witness against thy neighbor.' I caught you in the act. I saw you take the key and steal the sugar, and now you bear false witness against your own brother. God would never forgive me if I spared you now!" and, picking up a piece of a heavy frame which for some reason had been left lying on the table the night before, he gave the boy such a merciless beating that he himself felt exhausted, for he was by nature a mild sort of person who had never before lifted a finger against anyone.

Overcome by his own physical weakness, he threw the boy away from him with a final effort of his fast-waning strength, and that is where he made his mistake. For Johann, an accomplished actor, let himself fall in such a way that his head struck the side of the door, whereupon he passed out altogether and lay on the floor, a pathetic heap of clothes, his face very white and his eyes tightly closed.

At that moment, Mrs. Samuel rushed into the room. She was indignant. "How could you be such a brute?" she said reproachfully. "The boy did wrong, but that was no reason to kill him, as I think you have done."

"In that case," Samuel answered, "he will go forth to meet his Lord with a clear conscience. I shall now leave him to thee. A bit of water will bring him back soon enough, and afterward he can go to school."

But little Johann did not go to school that day. Instead, he spent the greater part of the morning moaning in his bed. He had not really been badly hurt. Samuel had not been strong enough to do him any serious physical damage. The contact of Johann's head with the door had, it is true, caused quite a lump, but no worse than any child might have suffered while playing with his comrades and taking the experience as a lark.

Johann, however, knew exactly what he was doing. His pride had been hurt beyond endurance. This old fool, this psalm-singing, shortsighted Dutchman, with his little growth of whiskers and his steel-rimmed glasses, had dared to lift his hand against a member of a race which had (so some of his compatriots had informed him) just won the greatest of all wars. Such an act had to be avenged, and while Mrs. Samuel was patiently applying cold compresses to his brow, he was carefully laying his plans and was figuring out how he could best avenge himself.

He knew that he was supposed to be a ward of some sort of society which had undertaken the responsibility for his well-being. From time to time, a lady of the Committee for Refugee Children had paid an unexpected visit to the Samuel home to find out how the boy was getting along, whether he was properly clothed and sufficiently nourished and whether he had anything to complain of. These visits had been rather perfunctory. Both Samuel and his wife were so generally and so favorably known that it seemed a waste of time to worry about the happiness and well-being of one of their small charges. Little Johann's first impulse had been to slip out of the house and carry his complaint about the brutal treatment he had received to the lady of the Committee, but on second thought he decided against such a step. For all that would happen was this: some other kind lady of the Committee would visit Samuel and admonish him to be a little more careful in the future. He would then tell his side of the story, and they would answer that of course he had acted under great provocation and that the boy should not have told him a lie, and there the matter would be dropped.

That was the last thing little Johann wanted. He should have his full pound of flesh and his revenge should mean public humiliation for his detested foster father. From his days in the old country he had remembered the name of an organization that was closely associated with the idea of trouble for all those who came in contact with it. That was the *Polizei.* He himself, of course, had never had anything to do with the police. But he had seen a great many policemen during his time, and all of them were ferocious-looking fellows, heavily armed with pistols and swords and bludgeons and forever frowning at anybody who passed their way.

He knew that there was a *Polizei* in Nieuwstad, for one day he and a lot of his little friends had followed two policemen who were conducting a drunken man to the station house. And that station house, as he had then discovered, was situated in the basement of the Town Hall, right around the corner on the Big Market and only a few minutes away from the Temple of Solomon.

Having made up his mind that he would place his case in the

hands of the police, Johann now had to await a chance to escape from his sickroom. He accomplished this very neatly by pretending to fall asleep. For a while, Mrs. Samuel remained sitting by his side. She was worried about his condition, for he gave a marvelous imitation of a very sick boy, sighed and groaned at regular intervals and whimpered as if he were in an agony of unbearable pain. Finally, however, the good woman noticed that he was growing quieter and, a little while later, seemed to fall asleep. It seemed safe to leave him alone while she went about some of her neglected household chores.

That was the moment little Johann had hoped for. He quickly got into his clothes, being careful to assume the air of a small boy who has just been cruelly maltreated. He even went as far as to tear off part of the collar of his jacket and to brush his hair in such a way that the bump on his head showed to the best advantage. Finally, putting on a pair of sneakers (which otherwise he wore only on Wednesdays, when he had his one weekly class in gymnastics), he ventured downstairs.

He did not leave through the front door, but crept out of the cellar window (a mode of exit which he had often used for secret nocturnal expeditions to a near-by strawberry patch) and, while passing through this narrow aperture, managed to get himself so thoroughly covered with dust that he looked like the incarnation of woe when he finally emerged into the side street that led directly to the market place.

As soon as he felt himself out of sight of the Samuel family, he made a beeline for the entrance of the Town Hall, where he had seen the policemen take their drunken prisoner. Once inside the high, dark hall of this noble old Gothic structure, he was somewhat at a loss where to go next, for there were quite a number of doors and he did not quite understand what was written on most of them. So, for safety's sake (for you never knew what next could happen to a small boy caught snooping around in a Dutch city hall), he started to cry. And, behold! a distinguished old gentleman who wore a high hat and carried an ebony cane, and who had just left one of the rooms, stopped in his tracks and, when he beheld this unhappy child, asked him most kindly why he should be so unhappy and what he might be looking for in the Town Hall at an hour when he should be in school?

Feeling even sorrier for himself than before, little Johann now burst forth into such a paroxysm of tears that another door opened and another gentleman in a military-looking coat stepped into the hall. When he beheld the other gentleman with the high hat and the cane, he hastily buttoned his collar (which, on account of the day's heat, he had somewhat loosened), straightened himself up, saluted stiffly, and barked, "I beg Your Honor's pardon, but I thought that I heard a child crying out here and I came to see what it was all about."

"And you heard correctly, my dear Captain," the gentleman with the high hat answered. "It looks like one of those German refugee children, but he seems so upset that I can't make out what he wants. Suppose we take him into my room and find out."

Johann was thereupon taken into the burgomaster's room (for it was no one less than His Honor himself who had rescued him), and bidding the captain be seated, the burgomaster hastened to fill a glass that stood on his table with water from a shining tin container that hung from the wall, told little Johann to drink it, wiped his eyes, and then asked him what might have brought him to the Town Hall.

His Honor was rather upset. So far his city had always been praised as a model of perfection for the way it had handled its refugee problem. A scandal was about the last thing he wanted, but the small child (most evidently one of his charges) looked very much the worse for wear, and if there had been any maltreatment, he meant to find out and take the necessary measures to prevent the repetition of so regrettable an incident. He therefore spoke with uncustomary kindness to his unexpected guest. Probably this boy had got into some kind of trouble with his foster parents. Several of these children were very difficult to handle, and this might be a case where an overbearing youngster (that was the chief complaint on the part of the foster parents—the overbearing arrogance of their wards) had so exasperated his host that he finally had had recourse to that corporal punishment against which all those who had been entrusted with these children had been warned in at least a dozen circulars. It was a tickish problem.

Most Dutch parents still believed that if you spared the rod, you would eventually spoil the child. It had therefore been hammered into their heads that no matter how great the provocation, they must under no circumstances allow themselves to lose their temper and touch as much as a single hair of one of their young housemates. Up to then, this rule had been carefully observed. How great therefore was the astonishment of both His Honor and the chief of police when a few moments of questioning revealed the fact that this badly battered infant was the child that had been entrusted to the care of no one less than Samuel, the frame-maker of the Temple of Solomon and the lay preacher of the church of the Vegetable Market.

The burgomaster looked at the chief of police and the chief of police looked at the burgomaster and then they both shook their heads. His Honor was the first to break the silence and, using the local dialect, so that the German boy should not understand him, he said, "It seems incredible! Why, Samuel is one of our most deserving citizens. Of course, he is perhaps a bit too—let me say—rectitudinous—if there is such a word—in his religious attitude toward life, and I can imagine him quite severe if he caught this boy in an act which he considered sinful, but such a brutal beating! Look at the child! No, a brutal beating like this—I would never have thought it possible!" and turning to the boy he said, in that careless German which even Hollanders of the higher classes are apt to affect when speaking the language of their eastern neighbors, *"Nun, mein Junge, verzählen sie mir wass eigentlich allemaal passiert ist."*

This was the moment for which little Johann had waited. He felt a deep contempt for any person so ignorant of his noble native tongue that he said *verzählen* instead of *erzählen,* but this old dunderhead must be no one less than the head of the city of Nieuwstad and that was the man to whom he wanted to talk. He therefore gave him a detailed and circumstantial description of the neglect and abuse he had suffered in Samuel's home, ending up with the incident of that morning, during which he had been thrown against a door with such violence that it might have killed him, as His Honor might observe for himself by looking at the ugly bump right there on his forehead.

His Honor duly observed. So did the chief of police, but the whole incident still failed to make sense. That Samuel, the proprietor of the Temple of Solomon, should suddenly have turned executioner was an idea so far removed from the realm of possibility that neither of the two men was willing to believe it without further corroboration.

"I'll tell you what we'll do," the burgomaster finally said to his chief of police. "Tell one of your men to drop in on Samuel, just casually, when he happens to pass that way, and ask him whether some time at his leisure—let us say tomorrow morning after eleven —he will call on me for a few minutes' personal conversation."

"Yes, sir," said the chief of police, rising to his feet and saluting himself out of his superior's room.

For a moment, Johann was at a loss what to do next, but the burgomaster saved him. "Here, my boy," he said, giving him a quarter, "that is for you. Now go home and wash up. You look much worse than you should, and I am rather afraid you have done your best to impress us with the way you look. I am sorry if anything should have happened between you and your foster father. Mr. Samuel is known to all of us as a most exemplary citizen. Maybe you were a bit troublesome and gave him provocation until he finally lost his temper. How does he treat you otherwise? I am sure his wife feeds you well. You are as fat as a little pig. Why, you are bursting out of your coat! That button hardly holds it together."

Little Johann, charming young liar that he was, at once fell back into his role of injured innocence. "No, sir," he answered. "That coat belonged to my younger brother, the one who died from hunger, and we had no money to buy another."

"Well," said the burgomaster, who was beginning to feel an intense dislike for this child, "suppose we forget all about it. I can assure you that nothing of the sort will ever happen again. Here is another quarter to buy yourself chocolate. Now run home and be a good boy and don't mention any of this to anybody. Promise?"

"Yes, Your Honor," answered little Johann, who had a quick ear for titles and a native gift for flattery. "I thank Your Honor for his kindness and I promise Your Honor that I shall never speak about this with anybody."

Then he rushed out of the Town Hall and made for the nearest candy store. "Give me fifty cents' worth of caramels," he ordered, "the big ones with lots of chocolate, the two for a nickel. The burgomaster gave me two quarters to make me forget the beating Mein Herr Samuel gave me. See!" (pointing to the bump on his forehead), "there is where he struck me, and all over my body I am black and blue. I am so lame I can hardly walk."

Having collected his chocolate caramels and having delivered his message, he galloped back to the Temple of Solomon, crept in through the cellar window, and, sensing that his absence had been unnoticed and beginning to feel hungry, he resumed his moaning until Mrs. Samuel came up with a bowl of cold sour cream and half a dozen rusks and an extra dish of sugar and told him, "Now you must get up, my little Johann. The master has forgiven you, and here is something extra for you, so that you will forget all about what happened this morning and all of us will forget, won't we? And we will be happy and praise the Lord, who is a Father unto us all and who will forgive us our trespasses if we truly repent."

The good woman was undoubtedly sincere in her hope that now everybody would forget everything about everything, but a small Dutch town is not an ideal spot for such an appeal to charity and understanding. Later in the morning, one of the town policemen had casually walked down the street in which Samuel lived. For a while he had contemplated the Bibles and the pictures of ladies in voluminous white draperies, clinging desperately to crosses that arose from mid-ocean, and had thereupon entered the store as if he were intent upon making a purchase. But since he was known as a stanch Social Democrat (a political party which Samuel hated and detested almost as much as he did scoffers) and as the town's leading agnostic to boot (a breed which Samuel hated and detested almost as much as he did all Social Democrats), his visit had at once been observed by the old milliner who, on the other side of the street, was engaged in selling very elegant hats to the more conservative members of Nieuwstad's social elite.

The hat-store proprietress knew perfectly well that this Bolshevist of the police force would never under any circumstances have any private business with that hairsplitting Pharisee of the Temple of Solomon. Her curiosity therefore was greatly piqued and it received a further shock when a few minutes after the policeman had departed, Samuel, in his Sunday going-to-church clothes, had been seen to close his door behind him and in an agitated sort of manner had moved in the general direction of the Big Market and the Town Hall.

The lady of the hats felt that she could not stand any further uncertainty and, taking her shawl (for she still belonged to the shawl-bearing generation), she hastily followed Samuel until he was swallowed up by the entrance of the Town Hall. Finding herself in front of her pet candy shop, she decided that she must celebrate the occasion by buying an ounce of her favorite cookies, though it was only Tuesday and she made Friday the day on which to indulge in her one weekly extravagance—an ounce of cookies covered with a most alluring, pinkish-looking sugary paste.

The baker, of course, did not fail to observe that this regular customer was not calling on her regular day and he felt in duty bound to draw attention to the fact. "Well, of all things," he said, weighing his culinary product in his copper scales. "When will wonders cease! First the little German boy from Samuel comes in here with fifty cents, given him by our burgomaster, and now here you are on Tuesday instead of Friday!"

"The little German boy from the Samuels with fifty cents, given him by the burgomaster! And why, if I may ask, had the burgomaster given him fifty cents? I did not know His Honor parted with his money quite so easily. It surely was not his habit when you and I were young!"

As she was twice as old as the mayor, this statement did not quite make sense, but she was much too excited to notice her calendrian error and the *Cuisinier et Patissier,* as he announced himself to the public on his shop sign, was too intent upon ferreting out whatever scandal might lie concealed in these queer transactions to pay any attention to this detail.

"Well," the confectioner said, gently pushing a recalcitrant cookie back into the box in which it belonged, "the burgomaster gave him fifty cents to make him forget a certain bump on his head."

"A bump on his head? How did he get it? Tell me, how did he get it?"

"It seems that our pious friend Samuel had lost his temper with the child for something or other he had done, and having lost his temper, he had given him such a beating that it almost killed him."

"That it almost killed him? You don't say! Almost killed him? But that is terrible! And Samuel, too, who is usually such a kind man!"

"I suppose some people would call him kind," said the baker, who belonged to a different denomination from Samuel's and who therefore detested him and all his followers with a deep-seated hatred. "But some of us happen to know how he treated his little daughter when he heard that she had danced at last year's school picnic. He made her stay at home for a whole month! That would teach her the sinfulness of dancing. And this

German boy is so small and so weak and so defenseless that the old fraud probably felt he could go as far as he liked."

"Well, he's inside the Town Hall now. He was sent for by the burgomaster and will have a chance to explain to our civic father what he has done." At which the Nieuwstad representative of the *haute couture* hastily departed to spread the happy tidings that old Samuel, the frame-maker and Bible vendor, had almost beaten his little German refugee to death and now you should see the lump on his head and now Samuel had been taken to the Town Hall by a policeman and he is with the mayor and supposed to explain to His Honor how it all had happened and what he might have to say for himself.

Meanwhile, inside the burgomaster's private room, the frame-maker and the civic father were getting along much better than those outside had any reason to expect. His Honor, in the matter of faith, was rather in sympathy with the creed professed by Samuel. His official position made it necessary for him to attend divine service at the Dutch Reformed Church, but way down deep in his heart he considered the doctrines preached by the ministers of the Big Church as much too advanced for an era in which the radical tendencies of the Socialists and Communists had so dangerously undermined the authority of the Crown that one might just as well live in a republic.

The stricter ordinances taught by the followers of Samuel's creed would prove a much sounder bulwark for the defense of Church and altar than the sociological lectures delivered twice every Sunday by the bright-looking occupants of the Big Church's richly carved pulpit. The burgomaster therefore hastened to put Samuel at rest with an amiable gesture of welcome and an invitation to make himself entirely comfortable in one of the chairs usually reserved for visitors of much greater distinction than shopkeepers and small tradespeople. And when he spoke, it was not in the tone of a stern judge but of an old friend who has only one desire—to set straight whatever has gone awry.

"Well, my good Samuel," he began, "and what is all this I hear?

A little German refugee comes trembling into my office with a fanciful tale of how you almost killed him because he had taken just one little piece of sugar. Of course, he undoubtedly exaggerated everything, but you know how careful I must be. I have four Social Democrats on my town council. These German children were most specially recommended to my care. I am responsible for their well-being. Should these Socialist rowdies get hold of this story, the Amsterdam papers might take it up and that might mean the end of my official career. So please tell me what really happened."

Samuel had grown red in the face. "What is that I hear, Your Honor?" he stammered. "The boy told you I had whipped him because he had stolen a few pieces of sugar? Why, there is not a word of truth in it! He had taken sugar before out of our sugar bowl, but I realized that he needed a little extra sweet and all I did was to make him write out the Decalogue a hundred times, and that surely is not too heavy a punishment for breaking the eighth commandment. And ever since, Your Honor, my wife has given him four spoonfuls of sugar on his pap instead of two, which my own children get. No, Your Honor, this time he did something much worse than stealing. He lied. He lied to me, and that is something I shall never countenance in a member of my family and I consider this child a member of my own family. Yes, he lied to me," and Samuel gave the burgomaster a detailed account of the incident of that morning.

His Honor listened most attentively, but soon felt sufficiently reassured to relax somewhat and suggest that a cigar might not be out of place. He took his long, silver cigar case out of his pocket and offered it to Samuel. Overcome with pride by this token of condescension, Samuel hastened to take one, though he had not smoked for years, as cigars made him ill. After that, the two men got along marvelously and found themselves in complete accord upon all the principles involved in the case.

But the Socialists in the town council were facts—harsh and brutal facts—and so His Honor begged the frame-maker to be very, very careful in the future how he dealt with this boy. "I realize your position," he told his visitor. "He had sadly fallen into sin when he lied to you. But please remember the committee that looks after these children and also remember my Socialists in my town council. Wrath, as Job so truly said, killeth the foolish man. So let us drop the matter right here and now, and the next time this damnable child provokes you, cease from anger and forsake wrath. These children, as I have heard, are going to leave us very soon, anyway, and in the meantime make the best of your uncomfortable bargain and thank you for calling on me, and when you leave this office I shall have forgotten all about it."

The burgomaster was as good as his word, but the community at large did not in the least intend to forget such a juicy bit of gossip. It was a hot and dull summer and the people were bored. That same evening, everybody was thoroughly familiar with the gory details of this attempt at manslaughter. A week later it had become a nation-wide scandal. Little Johann could claim that he was not in any way responsible for this development. After his first rather hasty remarks to the baker, he had never again mentioned the incident to anybody. When people stopped him in the street and, with offers of candy (for his weakness was well known), hinted at a few more details about the encounter in Samuel's living room, he invariably assumed a look of complete innocence and denied violently that anything had been amiss between him and his foster parent. It was all a misunderstanding. Nothing of any importance had happened. Mr. and Mrs. Samuel had been real parents to him. He loved them devotedly and he loved the whole of Holland, the country that had been so good to him and to his little German comrades, who all of them loved Holland and would never cease to love it, as they owed their lives to the generous-hearted Dutch people. But he looked so utterly woebegone whenever anyone spoke to him—he continued for weeks afterward to walk with such a bad limp—that everybody knew what had really happened as well as if they had been present. And they praised this brave and loyal little foreign boy and held him up to their own children as an example of a fine young Spartan who knew how to suffer without showing his feelings.

One day little Johann noticed that he was being followed by two men with cameras. His dramatic instinct told him what to do. He increased his limp and let both his shoulders sag, as if his back hurt him. Next morning at school, the offspring of the three Social Democrat members of the town council gleefully shouted, "Hey, little Muff, come and look! Your picture is in the paper!"

But not little Johann! He deliberately turned his back and refused to look at the photographs which showed this latest victim of "religious bigotry," and which carried a story that this poor German boy, the son of liberal-minded and freethinking German parents, had been brutally beaten when he had refused to take part in the religious hocus-pocus which his foster father had tried to force upon him. But that afternoon he stole ten pennies out of Mrs. Samuel's purse and ran (forgetting to limp this time) to the railroad station, where he knew he could buy copies of those two leading Socialist dailies. He was careful not to take them back home but he tore the pictures out and hid them until he could put them away with quite a collection of other literature, all of it derogatory to the Dutch character and carefully gathered together ever since this charming guest had arrived in the country of his hospitality.

He eagerly hoped for further developments, but there were none. The coming fall elections took all the available space in these newssheets, and nothing came therefore of that "investigation" which had been demanded by the Socialist members of the Nieuwstad town council. One of the older members of the party, a representative in the States-General of many years standing and a man of vast political experience, had successfully squelched the idea as soon as it had been mentioned to him.

"Whatever you do, be careful not to play into the hands of the Germans," he had warned, puffing heavily at his inevitable cigar. "A scandal of this sort would be grist to their mill. They have only one idea—how much brighter and how much honester and how much nobler and decenter and everything else they are than other people. It is an obsession with them.

"Now, I don't know what happened in the house of that absurd religious fanatic, but I am familiar with his type, too. If he licked the stuffing out of that boy, he probably had a perfectly good reason. I saw the young fellow's pictures in the papers. He looks like a sneak and a nasty little liar. So I suggest that you drop this business. There is nothing in it but a lot of headaches for everybody concerned, and we will never get anywhere at all if we waste our time on that sort of nonsense. Let us first get our own children out of the factories where they should not be working and then let us get excited about these brats from across the line, who eat us out of house and home and will come back someday to murder us in our own beds."

When the old gentleman spoke that way, his orders were usually obeyed, and so little Johann, much to his regret, had no chance to add further documentary evidence to his dossier of abuse. He spent his last three weeks with his benefactors being the golden-haired angel child of before, and his foster parents decided that by the righteousness of his behavior he was now trying to atone for the unhappiness he had brought upon their household.

Mrs. Samuel was the one who suffered most of all. Samuel was so adamant in his faith that nothing could affect his feeling of righteousness. He never gave the slightest evidence of being aware of the loneliness which now surrounded him, nor did he pretend to notice a considerable falling off in his daily business, for people were afraid to patronize a store where the door and the walls bore the legend "Murderer," scratched into the woodwork and into the paint by the hands of Johann's little German playmates.

His wife, on the other hand, took all these insults greatly to heart. She now rarely left her home. She continued to be as kind to her little charge as before. Indeed, she fed him much better than her own children, for he was to return to his native land very soon and she wanted to be proud of her handiwork when she took him back to the station. But her natural tendency toward melancholia had been seriously affected by the unpleasant gossip started by the incident of the beating, and Samuel often looked at her with profound misgivings. He told himself, however, that she would undoubtedly recover as soon as little Johann should have returned to his beloved fatherland, and his departure was now merely a question of days.

On the night before he left, Samuel asked him to remain in the living room after the others had gone to bed.

"My son," he said, "for I have always considered you one of my own children, I am sorry this—let me call it this 'thing'—happened between us. As far as I am concerned, it has been forgotten, and I hope you feel the same way. But I noticed certain tendencies in you which fill my heart with anxiety about your future happiness. When you came to our house, I hoped that you might find your Saviour while you were underneath our roof. I am afraid that you have failed to do so and I blame myself. I should have loved you more, and never did I love you more dearly than when God showed it to be my duty to chastise you. Tomorrow you will leave us. I want you to take this book and to keep it always as a memento of the days you spent with those strangers who found you suffering by the roadside and who took you in and fed you and nursed you and cherished you. I know they were Samaritans, they were not of your own race, but they did their best according to their lights. Take this copy of God's divine word and keep it always and may the Lord let His face shine upon thee. Good night and heaven bless you."

The next morning, he helped carry little Johann's belongings (considerably more voluminous, however, than when he had arrived) to the railroad station, presented the boy with a paper bundle containing dozens of extra sandwiches which his good wife had prepared, and bade him farewell. He even waited until the train had pulled out of the station. From every window, small boys and girls were wildly waving to the people they left behind and many of them were loudly wailing. Samuel hoped to catch a final glimpse of his little Johann but failed to do so.

That was only natural, for as soon as he knew himself to be out of sight of his hated host and foster father, little Johann hastened to open the package Samuel had given him the night before and found it to be the expensive Bible from Samuel's store. He knew what he was looking for and he was not disappointed, for a certain chapter in Deuteronomy had been duly marked with a blue pencil. His fingers trembled with excitement, and he started to read the unfamiliar Dutch: *"En gij zult geen valsche getuigenis afleggen,"* and then stopped abruptly.

"Bah!" he said, "the silly old fool!" and, tearing the page out of the book, he stuck it into his mouth and chewed it into a spitball, which next he took in his hand and threw at the back of one of the women who were supposed to look after the children until they should have reached the frontier. Then he picked up the Bible itself and shouted, "Hey, boys, let's have a little football," and gave Samuel's parting present a violent kick which sent it all the way to the other end of the compartment. The other children, grateful for a little diversion after the emotions of the last moment, joined in most heartily.

In less than five minutes, God's holy word had been reduced to a rag. Then it was rescued by one of the supervisors. The old lady was deeply indignant. "This is a shameful thing to do," she stuttered, while her face turned first red and then deadly white. "Who started this? I insist upon knowing!"

She looked directly at little Johann. He stared back at her in his most insolent manner and, "I don't know, *Juffrouw,*" he said. "I did not do it."

And so, true to himself until the last, this promising young German patriot bade farewell to his old life and began the new one.

The years that followed were not very happy ones for the Samuel family. The little Johann incident had soon enough been forgotten by the community at large but it continued to prey upon Mrs. Samuel and finally afflicted her mind. She sickened, and no doctor seemed able to help her. She took to her bed and after "a long lingering illness borne with the fortitude of a true Christian" (as the death announcement in the Nieuwstad *Courant* expressed it), she passed into a better life with the fullest confidence in her Lord and Saviour.

After she was gone, her daughter had to take charge of the household. Little Rebecca at that time was still a child, but on such occasions, children can often adapt themselves to their new duties with an almost uncanny ability, and outwardly, therefore, everything in Solomon's Temple remained as it had always been.

The son of the house, as soon as he had left school, had become his father's apprentice. He was a mild and docile boy and did as he was told. The Samuels had been frame-makers for so many generations, it was only natural that the boy should succeed his father. He would have to do his year's military service. After that, he would settle down, get married, and continue where his father left off.

As for little Johann, he had now been forgotten. He had sent one postal card after his return home. There had been a picture on it—a picture of a Greek goddess, showing the lady in an advanced state of nudity, but since it was a "classical" picture, it could pass through the mail. In the space marked "for correspondence," little Johann had scribbled: "I am so grateful that you can be sure I shall never forget anything. Your loving Johann."

Old Samuel had wondered why the boy had underscored the word *anything,* but still felt so ashamed that the letter carrier had seen this dreadfully obscene female figure that he had paid no further attention. Regularly thereafter, on Christmas morning, a similar kind of postal card arrived from their former guest. It always bore the same kind of message and it invariably ended with a promise that the sender would never forget anything, and that *anything* was always heavily underscored.

After the death of Mrs. Samuel, the daughter informed Johann of their loss. He wrote her a letter full of sympathy and affection and grief at the death of someone who had always been so good to him and added that he would always remember *her* kindness to him, and this time he had underscored the word *her*.

A few years later, shortly after her twenty-fourth birthday, the daughter was married to a young clergyman of her father's faith. He "stood" (as they so quaintly express it in the Dutch language) in a small village in that part of the province which lay on the other side of the river Scheldt. An old cousin—a pious but well-meaning woman—was thereupon engaged to run the household, and everything remained as it had always been. In the spring of that same year, the son was drafted for the army and was sent to the city of Bergen-op-Zoom, a small, fortified place on the mainland which was vaguely supposed to guard the causeway which connected the two principal islands of Zeeland with the province of Brabant. Since the Netherlands had not known the meaning of the word "war" for over a century, nobody took the business of "playing soldiers" very seriously. There was a little drilling and a little marching, but the son could spend all his Sundays and holidays at home. This greatly pleased the father, who had been sadly affected by the death of his wife, and who was drawing more and more within himself and who now never went out any more, except, of course, twice on Sundays to go to church.

And then one fine afternoon in the month of July (and as lovely a month of July as the Low Countries had ever seen) there suddenly was a ting-a-ling-ling of the store bell, and who should walk in but little Johann. At first Samuel, who was attending to his accounts, failed to recognize him, the boy had grown so tall and so broad and so fine-looking. But when Johann threw his arms around him and called out, *"Lieber Papa!"* he knew that it could be none other than his former foster child. He at once took Johann into the living room (right behind the store), where nothing had changed since the day of his departure.

"My boy," he said, "it is good to see you! And looking so fine and prosperous, too! We no longer will be able to call you our little Johann."

"But I still am," the young Teuton insisted. "For nothing has changed, and I love you just as much as ever."

"And what brings you here so unexpectedly? Are you here on business?"

"No, not at all. I have found a splendid job. In our wonderful new Germany, we all have jobs. But I had worked very hard and my employer insisted on my taking a short furlough—I mean a little holiday—and I thought why not do now what I have always wanted to do and visit the dear old home in Nieuwstad and have a look at the old market and the old streets and all those old places where I was so happy when I was here as a child."

"That thought, my boy, does you credit and I hope you will stay with us. Your old room still awaits you."

"I appreciate your hospitality but I don't want to be a bother. I have already taken a room at the Abbey."

"Our best and most expensive hotel. I must say you have done well for yourself!"

"Oh, I can't complain, but of course I shall see a lot of you. I shall try and get a good deal of exercise while I am here, but in the evenings, if you will allow me, I will always drop in for my *kopje thee*—do I still pronounce that correctly?—and then you can tell me all about everything. Where is my little sister?"

"She's married and lives in Breskens, just across the Scheldt."

"And my brother?"

"He's with the army, doing his year's service."

"That's interesting, and where is he?"

"In Bergen-op-Zoom. You remember the town where the railroad leaves the mainland."

"How wonderful! Then I can visit him."

"That is not necessary as he comes home every Sunday."

"Oh, but that's not enough. I loved him dearly. I must go to Bergen-op-Zoom and look him up."

"That may not be quite so easy. They have been rather strict with foreigners since there has been all this talk of war."

"But you forget, *mein lieber Vater,* I am not really a foreigner. At heart, I am still the same little Dutch boy who left you sixteen or seventeen years ago—or was it eighteen? How time does fly. But I still speak the language perfectly, so much so that in the train, everybody took me for a Dutchman."

"That is fine. Of course you will stay for dinner. I have got to finish my accounts, but that won't take me more than half an hour. In the meantime, is there anything else I can do for you?"

"Yes, there is! I would very much like to buy a bicycle. It's fine exercise, and I can then visit all the dear old places I remember so well from the time I lived with you."

"You need not buy one. I have one here for you for nothing, my son's old bike. All it needs probably is a little oiling, but you can have it and welcome. A bit of exercise will do that bicycle as much good as it will you, though I must say that to me you look in the pink of perfection."

"I know, but that is the excitement of seeing you again. And then one more thing before I forget it. I want to take a lot of pictures. The island is changing so fast and all these lovely old villages everywhere—why, a few more years and there won't be anything left of them. I want to remember them as they are today and I want to buy myself a good camera."

"You remember that place on the Big Market where they used to sell glasses? Ever since we got so many tourists, they have gone in for cameras and all that sort of thing. I noticed a whole window full the other day. Many of them were those complicated machines they make in your country."

"Yes," Johann agreed most heartily. "When it comes to first-rate work, nobody in the world can beat us. And now I must go to my hotel, for I promised my employer that I would telephone as soon as I arrived."

"You must mean a lot to them when they are so interested in you. Tell me what kind of work are you engaged in?"

"Oh, that's rather difficult, for we are a very big organization, but I will tell you some evening. And now may I look at that bicycle, for I have not ridden one for so long, I may have lost the knack."

"That's curious. Have you no bicycles in Germany?"

"Millions of them, but they are a little slow and we must work very hard and can't afford to waste time. We therefore use automobiles."

The old man looked at him with unbelieving eyes. "Automobiles!" he said. "Why, only the richest people in Holland can afford to have an automobile."

"But ours are different. They don't use gas, or very little. We don't believe in having things only for the rich and the Jews. We want everybody to be happy and to enjoy the good things of life and not only the Jews and the rich."

This tirade made very little sense to Samuel. He had vaguely read such things in his little newspaper about the younger Germans hating all Jews, but he had never paid much attention. Little Johann's talk seemed silly to him, and he suggested that his visitor come into the cellar and have a look at the bicycle.

The vehicle was found to be in an excellent state of repair; only the tires needed a little attention. Old Samuel said that he would look for the pump, which his son must have left behind somewhere, but Johann told him not to bother. "I will attend to that after I have gone and looked for that photographic store on the Market," he announced, as if he were laying down the law, "and then perhaps you will dine with me tonight at the Abbey."

Samuel shook his head. "No, my boy, such luxurious places are not for me. I would not feel at home there," he answered, "but you come here for dinner tomorrow and then we will talk of the olden days."

Thereafter, Johann dropped in for dinner every second night. In the meantime, he visited every part of the island, but on several occasions, he traveled a little farther to go and see his foster brother in Bergen-op-Zoom. "He must be lonely in that dull little hole," he told Samuel, "and we can take long walks together and he can show me everything of interest, though it is a pretty dull part of the country and there is not much to see."

Then he asked whether he could sometimes use the old man's workshop to do a little developing. "I'm getting a wonderful collection of pictures," he boasted, "and I want to be sure that all of them come out all right."

Samuel, of course, gave him permission to do so. A few days later, he asked Johann to show him a few of his snapshots.

"Oh, they would hardly interest you. They mean a lot to me, because I don't know whether I will ever be able to come back, but you have all that with you every day."

However, the next evening, quite unexpectedly, he showed Samuel several dozen of the pictures he had taken. They were all commonplace representations of roads and bridges and farmhouses in some of the most isolated spots of the island. "These will hardly interest you," Johann said, "but to me who has been away so long, they mean a lot."

Still a few days later, the telegraph office called Samuel up to inquire whether he perhaps knew the whereabouts of a certain Johann so-and-so who was said to be stopping with him. "No, he does not stay here," Samuel answered, "but he is coming to me for dinner. If you will deliver the message here, I will see that he gets it."

When the telegram arrived, Samuel wondered what he should do. To him, a man of old-fashioned habits, a telegram still meant an important event, usually something connected with sudden death. He did not want the boy to be shocked by whatever serious tidings might lie hidden within that bright green envelope. "I had better open it," he told himself, "and then I can prepare him." But the telegram contained nothing that could have frightened anybody. All it said was, "Thank you for those lovely snapshots, which were just what I wanted. Please send me a lot more of the same kind and meanwhile take good care of yourself. All my love." And it was signed, "Aunt Amelia."

When Johann came in for dinner, he asked whether any message had arrived for him. He had inquired at the telegraph office and had been told there it had been delivered at Samuel's address.

"Yes," his host said, "here it is."

Johann's face grew white with rage. He slammed the table and shouted, "Someone has dared to tamper with my private property!"

"It was I, my boy, who opened it. I am still a bit old-fashioned and I always expect telegrams to bring us bad news. But as soon as I noticed that it was nothing of the sort, I closed it up again without reading any further."

"Oh, well," Johann answered, falling back into the mood of good-natured hilarity which had been so characteristic of him since he had arrived, "it's really nothing of any importance, and I am sorry that for a moment I lost my temper. It's from my Aunt Amelia, my mother's sister, who is forever worrying about me. I had sent her some of my snapshots and she thanked me but warned me not to do too much and to take care of myself."

Early the next morning, Samuel had a brief note from Johann. It was written on the stationery of the Abbey. "Dear Father," it read. "I had another telegram and was told they needed me and that I had to come right home. There is a lot of extra work at the factory, for we expect a very busy year. Sorry I had to leave without saying good-by, but 'duty is duty,' as you yourself always taught me. My love to all of you, and I am more indebted to you than you can possibly know. Your loving little Johann."

Two hours later, Samuel had a visitor. This man of mystery asked to see him alone and then showed him his credentials. He was an agent of the Dutch secret police.

"Mr. Samuel," he began, "I am sorry to bother you, but have you had a visitor recently—someone from Germany?"

"Yes, of course. When he was a little boy, right after the Great War, he spent half a year with us to get fed up again. Now he had been given a vacation and he had decided to spend it with us to refresh the memories of his childhood days. He was a lovely youngster and always so grateful for everything we did for him. I am sorry he had to leave in such a hurry that he was not even able to say good-by to me."

"How did he spend his time?"

"Oh, like any other ordinary tourist. I had given him my son's bicycle and he used to ride all over the island, taking snapshots."

"Did you ever see any of his pictures?

"Yes, I did. He showed them all to me."

"What sort of pictures were they?"

"The usual ones. Country roads and bridges and a few of those isolated farmhouses along the coast. I remember that he had photographed those farmhouses, for I always loved them, with the trees all around them—those trees that seemed to protect them as God's love protects his children."

The man from the secret police offered no other comment than a soft whistling sound. Then he asked whether Samuel had a telephone and whether he could use it.

"Of course," Samuel told him. "What is the number you want? I know most of them by heart."

"I want the Abbey Hotel."

Samuel dialed Nieuwstad 50 and handed the receiver to his visitor.

"Hello! Is this the proprietor of the Abbey Hotel? Yes? Tell me, please, I am speaking for the police, did you have a young German visitor these last few days and is he still with you? What is that you say? He left last night? And he did not go by train, you say, but he took his bicycle and said that he was going for a ride—wait until I write all this down—and then he did not come back and did not pay his bill, either? Thank you very much. Yes, we had a little bill against him too, but I suppose we'll both be left holding the bag. Thank you very much.

"Well," the secret agent said, looking at Samuel, "that settles that!"

"You might telephone to the frontier and have him stopped there."

"Much too late. That fellow was as strong as an ox. He must have reached the Belgian frontier in less than four hours. In Essen he could have taken an early train for Brussels and from there he could have taken a plane for Cologne. No, he's gone and we will never catch him. Of course, no blame attaches to you. But I had better go and get busy on a few of the others."

"The Lord have mercy upon us!" Samuel exclaimed. "The others! Are there any others?"

"The country is full of them."

"Why didn't you arrest them all and get rid of them?"

"We can't. There is nothing against them. They're all here as bona-fide tourists. This one just happened to be less intelligent than the others and so he gave himself away."

"How?"

"By that telegram that you read."

"But I saw that telegram. It was absolutely innocent. It wished him a pleasant vacation and told him to be careful and watch his health."

"Do you remember how it was signed?"

"He told me. It was signed by an aunt of his, his Aunt Amelia, or some such name, and he said she was a sister of his mother who had always taken a great interest in him."

"Mr. Samuel, you are an honest fellow and undoubtedly you can keep a secret. Do you happen to know who that Aunt Amelia is?"

"Yes, I just told you. It is his mother's oldest sister."

"Unfortunately it is not. Aunt Amelia is the signature the General Staff in Berlin uses when it wants to warn one of its agents that he has probably been detected and had better get out of the way before it is too late. Thank you, my dear sir, for your co-operation, but I am afraid it is too late. As usual, we have been much too generous with our dear German neighbors. But thank you, just the same. Sorry to have bothered you, and good night."

After he was gone, Samuel sank to his knees and asked God to look deep into the wicked heart of this unrepentant sinner whom he had tried to love as his own son, and if possible to bring him to a realization of the fate that awaited him unless he changed his ways.

This time there were no post cards. Little Johann had passed for good out of the life of his former benefactor. Meanwhile it was getting very lonely in Nieuwstad. All the young men had been called to their regiments and the women were taking courses in first aid and nursing. Everybody, however, felt convinced that the Netherlands would never be dragged into the turmoil that threatened the whole world with destruction. The good Queen stood firm on the ramparts of her realm. Her ministers worked day and night to see that a most careful state of neutrality was observed by the Dutch authorities. And there was Adolf Hitler himself, the Führer of the Third Reich, who never ceased to reaffirm in the most solemn of words that come what might, Germany would not draw the sword against a nation which in the hour of Germany's greatest need had stood by her side and had saved her children from extermination.

One evening Samuel read this pronunciamento in the local paper and he read it with great satisfaction. "I always said so," he told his housekeeper, pouring out his third cup of tea. "That little German Führer is not as bad as he has been painted. Now he has once more given us his solemn word and that is enough for me. Once more we can sleep in peace. Adolf Hitler himself has told us so."

Then he went upstairs and knelt before his bed and prayed for the safety of his son, the soldier, who was lying dead with a bullet through his heart, the last of half a dozen men who had died trying to defend the dyke that led from the mainland to

Zeeland. All of them had been shot in the back. A battalion of German soldiers, dressed in Dutch uniforms, had attacked them from the rear. How had they been able to pass through the lines? Nothing easier! These soldiers were the children of charity of twenty years before and they had been careful to keep up their Dutch. They could now speak it while sticking their bayonets into the hearts of those they used to call their "little brothers."

At five o'clock next morning, Samuel was awakened by a heavy knocking at his door. He put on his carpet slippers and went into the store. His daughter stood outside.

"Father," she told him, "you must come at once! Your life is in danger. Nieuwstad is sure to be attacked and you might be killed. One of my husband's parishioners, a fisherman, ferried us across the Scheldt. In Flushing, we got the help of another one of the faithful—and how good they are to their dominie! This man lent us his horse and carriage. That is how I came here. I shall take you to Flushing and from there, the fisherman has promised to sail us to England. You must come. It is your only chance of saving your life."

"But my child! I am an innocent man. I have never done aught against the will of the Lord. To run away now would be a confession of guilt when there is no guilt. No, I shall stay here and await what the Lord has in store for me."

"Father, you must come and right away, too! My children are in that carriage. I cannot risk their lives by waiting for you. You must come!"

"I shall stay here."

"Father, if I were alone, I would remain with you, but now my first duty is toward my children. Father, I beg you on my knees! Come!"

"Daughter of my heart, I shall stay, but you go before it is too late and may God bless you and keep you."

The daughter returned to her carriage and went back to Flushing. Together with her husband and her children and some sixty other refugees they made for the open sea. The next afternoon, they were discovered by a German flying boat. The pilot leisurely dropped his plane to about thirty feet above the small craft. Then he opened up with his machine gun and passed back and forth over the unfortunate little vessel until he had reason to suspect that everyone on board was dead.

As a matter of fact, two children escaped with their lives and when, a few hours later, a Dutch torpedo boat came to their rescue, these small survivors were brought back to England. One of them, a boy of six, was Samuel's grandson. His line therefore was not wiped out.

Samuel's daughter had been right. Surprised by the enemy near the railroad dyke, the two main islands of the province of Zeeland had fallen an easy prey to the onrushing Nazis. A final struggle had taken place just outside the old moats of Nieuwstad. By that time, the last of the Dutch airplanes had been shot down and it had been quite easy for the Luftwaffe to let Nieuwstad share the fate of Rotterdam. For three days the city was a roaring hell. Then the flames had subsided. Nothing had been left that would burn.

Samuel had spent these three terrible days with friends in a near-by village. Together they had watched the blood-red sky. Together they had prayed. Together they had found solace in singing the Psalms of King David and together they had slept in the straw of the hayloft. On the fourth day, the fire seemed to have sufficiently subsided to make it safe to visit the ruins of their former homes. Nothing remained of the Temple of Solomon but the four blackened walls. Half of his old sign announcing the sale of Bibles still remained dangling above the door, but of the interior of the shop, not a vestige remained.

Samuel looked at this scene of devastation and thought of God's wonderous ways. For though everything else was gone, that part of the sign which mentioned the holy book remained. At that moment, a heavy hand descended upon his shoulder. A Nazi soldier stood behind him.

"I knew you would come here," a gruff voice said, "and I am

delighted, for what was to have prevented you from escaping after you had betrayed me to your own secret service?"

"I never betrayed you, my son. I even tried to protect you."

"Fiddlesticks and lies and you can tell that to the judge if you live long enough. You tried to protect me! You did not betray me! I suppose that next you will tell me you never hit me! But this time I've got you. This time you are at my mercy. You are under arrest and you are under arrest by me, you old, psalm-singing bastard!"

"Please do not use such a word, and you need not fear that I shall try to run away. I have nothing to be afraid of."

"Nothing to be afraid of? Wait until you see the judge! He'll tell you."

"Where are you taking me?"

"Where they should have taken you when you gave me that beating. You, a thieving, close-fisted old Dutchman, daring to lift your hand against a German child!"

"You had lied to me. You had borne false witness . . ."

"Oh, shut up, and forget that Bible stuff! It made me sick twenty years ago. It still does. Come along and save your talk."

Little Johann, now in the full regalia of a Nazi sergeant, led his prisoner to the old town jail. There he signed a few papers and left with a cheerful, "Happy prayers to you! God knows, you'll need them."

Samuel remained alone in his cold, forlorn cell for ten whole days and then had his first hearing. He spent that time as little Johann had bade him do. He prayed. He also asked for a Bible, but was told that he had done enough Bible reading and had now better devote his few remaining days to the contemplation of some of his sins.

"But how can I?" he protested. "I never harmed anyone in all my life."

"How about that time you almost murdered an innocent German child?"

"I did not murder him. I merely chastised him. He had broken one of God's holy commandments—he had borne false witness . . ."

"Yes, we know all about it. But you will have your day in court and then you will receive justice. We Germans are the most justice-loving people on earth."

Meanwhile, his case had received some attention. The member of the court-martial who was to decide his fate (for the courts were very busy and one judge was supposed to be enough for the simpler cases) happened to belong to an old Prussian Junker family. War had always been his people's profession and so he had quite naturally hastened to offer his services to Adolf Hitler when the little Austrian had decided to continue where the Empire had left off. His fellow tribesmen had no love for their new commander in chief. Indeed, they despised him. But anyone who gave them a chance to return to their former sphere of influence was their friend and ally, and they had hastened to make common cause with the "lousy Bohemian corporal," as old Marshal von Hindenburg had called him.

The captain (for his doubtful political antecedents made it impossible for him to reach any higher rank) who was to try Samuel had quite accidentally come across his dossier. He was really looking for something else when it fell into his hands. "That is a queer story," he told himself. "It goes all the way back to 1920. This is, of course, a matter of personal revenge. But that is the way these Nazi swine are. They are vindictive as the devil. They never forget or forgive. Let me see what it is all about."

After he had finished, he pushed the papers away from him with a gesture of disgust. "God help us all," he told himself, "if we are going to make the world safe for that sort of vermin." Then he rang his bell and told his orderly to go and find him a certain Sergeant Johann So-and-so, who must be somewhere in Nieuwstad. An hour later, the orderly appeared with little Johann.

"Zu Befehl, Herr Hauptmann."

The captain inspected Johann carefully. He did not like his looks. "Sergeant, did you bring charges against an old Dutch frame-maker by the name of Samuel? In those charges, you seem to accuse him of almost having murdered you when you were here as his guest, just after the first war."

"It is true, *Herr Hauptmann.*"

"Why did he almost kill you? What had you done?"

"It was right after the war, *Herr Hauptmann.* We children were starved. We needed food. He never gave me enough to eat. One evening I took a lump of sugar which the old scoundrel kept for himself and his wife."

"You mean to say you stole a piece of sugar."

"I took it, *Herr Hauptmann!*"

"You were his guest and you lived in his home as part of his family. Wouldn't he have thrashed his own children if they had stolen sugar?"

"I did not steal, *Herr Hauptmann,* I only took."

"Makes no difference, and if you give me another answer like that, I shall have you locked up. I want no impudence from you!"

"Zu Befehl, Herr Hauptmann."

"You disgust me. I suspect you of being a liar."

"I would like to remind you, *Herr Hauptmann,* that I am one of the Führer's soldiers."

"I know. Unfortunately, it does not make you one of nature's gentlemen. Orderly!"

The orderly appeared. *"Zu Befehl, Herr Hauptmann."*

"Go to the cells and try and find me a Dutchman by the name of Samuel, and hurry up. As for you" (this to little Johann), "stand there and wait."

"Zu Befehl, Herr Hauptmann."

Five minutes later, Samuel was pushed into the room. His eyes were painfully blinking after his many days in a dark cell. His hair and beard were uncombed. He looked a sorry sight.

"You sent for me, *Mijn Heer?*"

"I did, but don't speak until you are spoken to."

"No, *Mijn Heer.*"

"Do you know this fellow?" pointing at Johann.

"Yes, *Mijn Heer.*"

"Once upon a time he enjoyed the hospitality of your house?"

"Yes, *Mijn Heer,* after the last war. He lived with us for almost half a year and I treated him like my own son."

"Would you have given such a terrible beating to your own son because he had stolen one little lump of sugar?"

"But, *Mijn Heer,* I did not need the sugar. I chastised him because he had broken one of God's holy commandments."

The captain looked puzzled. These pious Dutchmen were a curious breed. "Since when," he asked, "is the taking of a piece of sugar a breach of the ten commandments? I thought I knew them all, for we Lutherans too are taught our ten commandments, but I do not remember a commandment which tells you not to pilfer a little sugar when you are badly in need of a bit of sweet."

"There is a commandment, *Mijn Heer,* which warns us against giving false witness."

"Against our neighbors."

"In such matters, *Mijn Heer,* the Lord does not draw the line between self and others. This boy (for he was only a child then, though he should have known better) lied to me. Yes, *Mijn Heer,* he denied having been near the sugar bowl, though with my own eyes I had seen him take the key from underneath our family Bible, open the box, and stuff his mouth full of something that did not belong to him. And then he lied and hinted that my own son might have done it."

The captain unexpectedly looked at the sergeant. "Sergeant," he warned him, "keep that grin off your face."

"Zu Befehl, Herr Hauptmann."

"Well, that seems about all for the moment. You can both of you go." Then to old Samuel, "I shall hurry your case along. It will come up tomorrow morning. Be prepared for anything. The charge is a serious one."

As a matter of fact, the charge did not seem to him in the least bit serious. But he had to be on his guard. That damnable sergeant, for all he knew, might be a stool-pigeon the Nazis had smuggled into his regiment to watch those who, like himself, had a *von* before their name and who therefore were suspected of being lukewarm in their loyalty to the all-highest Führer.

He sat alone in his room until late that night and then decided that he had found a way out. A very simple way at that. It was preposterous that a harmless old religious fanatic, who had opened his home and heart to a starving German child, should be punished for an act he had committed twenty years before and for something to boot in which he had been entirely right.

"That sergeant," so he told himself, "is bad news. He's a liar and a hypocrite. I hate to think what he must have been like when he was young. But I have found a way out and I will save the old fellow. All this happened a long time ago, and it will be impossible to find witnesses."

When in the morning of the next day Samuel woke up, he saw the prison-keeper standing in his cell. "I have a visitor for you," he announced. "By the captain's orders, the barber will attend to you. In the meantime, I shall take your clothes and have them brushed and here is a clean shirt."

"As the captain pleases," Samuel answered, getting up from his couch.

Looking like a different person, Samuel, shortly after eleven o'clock, was ushered into his judge's presence.

"Sit down, Samuel," the captain said, "and be at your ease. I have most carefully looked through this bundle of accusations. I see that our young friend also has denounced you as the man who betrayed his presence in Nieuwstad just before the outbreak of the war."

"But, *Mijn Heer* the Captain," Samuel remonstrated, "I had no idea what he was doing. Otherwise would I, as a good Hollander, have given him my son's bicycle?"

"Of course not. But don't let that worry you. I have telephoned

Berlin. The fool had given himself away in a taproom in Flushing by bragging about his important mission. That part of the case therefore has been disposed of. There remains the other part, the part where he accuses you of having almost killed him as a child because he had helped himself to a single lump of sugar (he is very specific about the amount he stole), and that, of course, is something we cannot allow to pass by without the most severe form of punishment. German children are sacred and they must be protected now as in the past and in the future. What have you to say for yourself?"

"Nothing, *Mijn Heer* the Captain. I punished him because he lied to me."

"Are you sure?"

"Yes, *Mijn Heer.*"

"Very well, then. Now suppose you have forgotten all about the incident. You are an old man and old people are apt to forget. There are no witnesses today who will remember the affair. Suppose you tell me that you have forgotten what happened."

"But I have not forgotten, *Mijn Heer* the Captain. It was the most horrible thing that ever happened to me. I hated to chastise a child that had been entrusted to my care. But it was my duty. It was my duty before God."

The captain picked up a cigarette (those Dutch cigarettes were still pretty good, if a bit expensive) and lit it. This, apparently, was going to be a very difficult case. The old man was as obstinate as a mule, and when he started talking about his principles, you felt as if you were listening to old Martin Luther himself.

"Listen, Samuel," he said, "your people and mine are at war, but I and many of my fellow countrymen will never forget what you did for our people in their hour of need. I have got to obey the laws of our Third Reich. I have sworn a holy oath to be faithful to those laws, just as you have sworn an oath to be faithful to those of your God. However, between friends (and I am now speaking to you as a friend), we may be able to arrange things so that they will be satisfactory to everybody concerned. Now, here I have a slip of paper and it reads—listen while I read it to you: 'Deponent under oath declares that the incident of his attack on the German child entrusted to his care never took place.' You sign this and then it will be his word against yours. He won't be able to testify against you. I had him ordered to the Polish front this morning, and so he will never again cross your path. You are therefore perfectly safe. Of course, all this will not be quite true, or perhaps it will be, but that is no concern of ours. You can afterward figure that out with the good Lord Himself, and I am sure He will pardon you for just one little white lie, probably the only one of your whole life. That unspeakable sergeant, that miserable little Johann, as you used to call him, is not really worth the death of a good and honest Dutchman. Now, take my fountain pen and sign. You need not even reread the paper. Just sign and you walk out of here a free man."

Samuel looked at the captain in silence, but only for a moment, and then he pushed away the hand holding the pen.

"I am sorry, *Mijn Heer* the Captain," he said, "but I could not do that. I punished the boy for bearing false witness. I could not now bear false witness myself, merely to save my life."

"But listen to reason, you old fool, you hopeless old idiot! Do you know what it means if you do not sign? Do you realize what our laws are? Do you realize that a foreigner who has dared to lift a hand against a German child will be shot?"

"Yes, *Mijn Heer* the Captain."

"Then, for God's sake, sign!"

"I cannot, *Mijn Heer*. I cannot bear false witness."

"Not even to save your life?"

"It stands writ, 'Thou shalt not bear false witness.' "

"For heaven's sake, shut up!" the captain shouted. "You are driving me crazy with your 'it stands writ.' "

"Nevertheless, *Mijn Heer,* it so stands writ."

"And that is your last word?"

"It is, *Mijn Heer.*"

The captain started to sign another paper. Halfway through with his name, he stopped. "I give you one more chance."

"I cannot take it, *Mijn Heer.* It stands writ."

"That will be enough," the captain interrupted him. "God knows, I did my best." Then looking old Samuel straight into his eyes, he said, "I would like to shake hands with you."

"Gladly, *Mijn Heer.*"

"No hard feelings?"

"None at all, *Mijn Heer.* You are merely doing your duty, and I hope that God will forgive you, as I hope he will forgive me for doing mine."

"I wonder," said the captain, but this time he spoke only to himself, for old Samuel had been taken away.

An hour later he was stood up against the wall of the prison yard of Nieuwstad and was shot to death.

THE TENTH COMMANDMENT

Thou shalt not covet thy neighbor's house,
thou shalt not covet thy neighbor's wife,
nor his manservant, nor his maidservant,
nor his ox, nor his ass,
nor anything
that is thy neighbor's

LOUIS BROMFIELD

X

THOU SHALT NOT COVET

A STORY BY

LOUIS BROMFIELD

SAINT-FIRMIN is a remote Swiss village that lies just beneath the Pic du Diable. It was never a fashionable winter resort with the Americans, English, or French—not a place like Gstaad or Saint-Moritz or Davos or Villiers. It was frequented almost entirely by Germans or by expert skiers who knew that it had some of the finest ski slopes in the world and that the village was the home of a whole tribe called Zupper who had produced from among its members a dozen of the finest skiers in the world.

The village lay sprawled across a kind of saddle between two mountains, the Pic du Diable and Mont Noir, and there were long, sweeping, sometimes savage runs from the peaks of both mountains down into the town itself. One ended near the railroad station, another just at the door of the Kulm Hotel, which had once been a huge sanitarium for sufferers from tuberculosis, and a third came to an abrupt stop just outside the Kurhaus. Swooping down these long runs one had the feeling of surveying the whole of the world, a white world, sometimes glittering in sunlight with blue shadows along the glaciers and the projecting cliffs, sometimes clouded and veiled in falling snow and mist, sometimes warm and damp, when the warm foehn blew up from Italy, with the thunderous sound of avalanches everywhere in the still air.

You had to climb for your skiing. There were no ski lifts and no funiculars. Perhaps that was why it was never frequented by the fashionable international world. Also it was difficult of access. One went to Zurich and changed trains twice, climbing up and up along frozen chasms and waterfalls and winter glaciers, through mist and snow, to arrive at the little old-fashioned station covered with tiny gables ornamented with jigsaw ornaments and carving. On the long journey up, especially if you left Coire at dusk and started as the day faded into darkness, you had a terrifying sense of having died, of making a journey into another world. And when you wakened the following morning and looked out of your window into a white and glittering creation, the sense of having gone overnight into another world still persisted. The little village with its scattered houses, its two hotels, the gay Beau-Site and the vast Kulm, the boardinghouses and the Kurhaus, seemed to hang in some remote part of the skies with only the two great mountains above it.

We came there because an Austrian in New York, a crack skier, had recommended it. "It is a dull place," he said. "But you'll find the finest skiing in the world. The people aren't very interesting —at least those who don't ski are not."

It was the kind of place we were looking for—not Saint-Moritz with its bars and international glitter, not Davos with its hordes of young Englishmen and sporting, husky, rosy-cheeked girls—but a kind of lost place where we shouldn't know anyone, where the company was neither glittering nor interesting, where I could work and the dogs could run and the children could spend the whole day out-of-doors.

It was a long journey from New York, dully long with a caravan including nurse, children, dogs, and even a canary bird. We landed at Genoa, and went from there to Zurich and from Zurich to Coire and then to Saint-Firmin. There was an endless tangle of passports and visas, frontiers and changes, so that the last stage of the journey came as a relief. Yet there was something frightening and primeval about it, despite the wild, unreal beauty, which was spiritually more exhausting than all the nightmare of baggage and complications which preceded it. On the last stage of the long journey there was a full moon, obscured from time to time by wild scudding white clouds, lighting up the glittering waterfalls and throwing the deep gorges and the wild, wind-torn pines into black shadows. The tiny mountain train skirted gorges that dropped away two or three thousand feet into the obscurity of eternity. I do not like great heights and whenever the moon flashed out to reveal the great depths below us, my heart stopped for a moment and there was a sudden sickness at the pit of my stomach.

It was a wild journey through country which did not exist outside the imagination of Wagner or Gustave Doré. Halfway there, I wished that we had never embarked for this lost place.

A little before midnight the train came suddenly into a high wide valley where a half-frozen stream ran between forests of stunted pine. Above the valley the glittering snow swept away in the moonlight up and up to join at last the milky colorlessness of the frozen moonlit sky. And then quite suddenly we were in a village and the train stopped and the train guard, a short, thin, sallow man with a limp, called out, "Saint-Firmin! Last stop! All out!"

The little station, with its gimcrack gables fringed with icicles and all the signs in both French and German, was a cheery place, like a toy. There was a buffet with all sorts of rolls displayed and piles of fruit and bottles of Swiss wines. The sleigh from the hotel was waiting and the driver, in his blue cap with Hôtel Beau-Site in gold letters on it, stood by while we had cups of hot Swiss chocolate. After that we drove in the big sleigh behind four steaming horses up the steep streets to the hotel. It was late, but in the little chalets and the pensions an occasional light gleamed yellow against the blue white of the moonlit snow. The terror and exhaustion of that final lap of the journey wore off a little but a kind of dread, indefinable and uneasy, remained. Perhaps foreboding was a better word. It was as if unknowingly I had brought myself and my family into a strange world where we did not belong, a Gothic world, disordered and grotesque as a German folk tale.

The proprietor of the Hôtel was a tall, heavy German-Swiss by the name of Turnbaum. He had sloping shoulders, a potbelly, and a long nose, with blond hair cropped short above pale-blue eyes set too near together. His coat hung on him like a tent and when he shook hands, the palms were damp. The hotel appeared neat and new and well kept, but that night we saw little of it but the entrance hall. We fell asleep, exhausted, almost without being aware of the rooms we were given. They seemed pleasant enough with bright chintz curtains and big bay windows.

I was awakened by a brilliant light in my eyes, a light so violent that it came through the drawn curtains, as if a powerful searchlight had been turned full upon the windows. Putting on a dressing gown, I pushed back the curtains and was forced to close my eyes against the brilliance of the light. There was nothing supernatural about it—only the reflection of the brilliant morning sun against the snow-covered mountain directly opposite. When my eyes became accustomed to the glare, the whole immense landscape appeared—snow, snow, mountains of snow, without a tree or a house or a break in the whiteness and glare. I thought at once, "The Austrian is right. It is God's own skiing country." The excitement which only a skier can know rose up in my heart. This was paradise. I hurried through bath and dressing.

Downstairs I found the hotel empty, with only two other people in the dining room, a dark woman and a blond man of about forty. The odd thing was that I knew them. They were not married. It was clever of them to have come to this forgotten place, and only the strangest of circumstances had brought here someone who knew them. We shall call them Herbert and Maggie. Herbert was in business of some sort—a businessman with the businessman's air of omniscience. Maggie was a rather ugly but a clever, smartly dressed worldly woman of thirty-two or -three. That is good enough. They play little part in the story. Neither was romantic, and I did not believe their escapade had anything to do with romance. It was—as you might say—practical, almost utilitarian.

It was idiotic to pretend that I did not recognize them. Perhaps if I had been French I should have gone through the formality of pretending that I was blind and did not see them. But all three of us were Americans. Neither my wife nor myself had strong feeling about people enjoying themselves. We believed that sexual morality was people's own affair, so long as it did not corrupt the decency of their relationship with outsiders. That point has a certain bearing on the rest of the story.

They saw me and grinned, and the woman, Maggie, said, "Dr. Livingstone, I presume."

We had breakfast together and presently my wife joined us. It was a gay breakfast, for, oddly enough, we were all glad to see each other. I felt a curious pleasure in their company, as if it relieved a little the feeling of loneliness and dread in this wild, beautiful place. It was a little like coming across old friends in purgatory.

Very quickly they explained the emptiness of the hotel, "Old Uriah Heep Turnbaum tells us it's because the season hasn't begun. He says, 'Wait until the fifteenth,' and the whole place will be teeming. That's when we clear out."

"How did you ever hear of Saint-Firmin?" my wife asked.

Herbert beamed at us through his clear, shining glasses. "I heard about it in Germany," he said, "from a manufacturer named Hagen in Stuttgart. He says it's a place that is very popular with Germans—rich Germans."

"I didn't know there were any rich Germans."

He laughed. "Boy," he said, "you'd be surprised. I've just come from there."

Maggie added, "They're not very popular anywhere just now.

It's too soon after the war. They all huddle together wherever they can find a resort where they aren't treated as pariahs. When they appear, I'm clearing out. Herbert doesn't mind them, but I can't stand them. One or two Germans are supportable, but in crowds, nothing doing—I suffocate!"

"You talk about them," I said, "the way some people talk about Jews."

It was the time of the ghastly inflation in Germany, when no money had any value, when people were starving and it needed ten million marks to buy a newspaper. I simply did not believe we would be overrun by Germans once the season began. How could there be Germans with enough money to come to Switzerland, a country on the gold standard with a terrifically high rate of exchange?

I had not been in Germany since the fall of the first postwar government. I had never liked it very much. I am not much of a mystic and have no special belief in reincarnation save in the strong intuitive reaction which I feel for countries and people, as if I had known them before in some previous existence. I always felt when I was in Germany that it was a country I knew very well but that something dreadful had happened to me there in some previous existence. I did not, like many people, find even Munich a warm, gay, and fascinating place; to me it always seemed a liver-colored false Florence dominated by the memory of an insane king, where one grew surfeited with heavy rich food and beer. For me the Black Forest, with the mists drifting through the tops of the black pines, seemed a place fit only for Fafnirs and Alberichs. For me Germany was always the same, under any government, a place where the sinister lay just beneath a façade of medieval towns and gaily painted cottages. Berlin was a horror. I was always glad to cross its frontiers and go into France, into Austria, into Holland, even into poor wretched Poland.

I didn't say much of this. Herbert was an intelligent fellow, a very smart businessman, and he was inclined to see things only in terms of business, a point of view which can be very short-sighted and limiting and at times even disastrous. There are so many elements besides columns of figures or records of profit and loss—things like human emotions and character, famines and fanaticism, things like Hitler. But at that time the world hadn't even heard of Hitler.

Sometimes in the evening the four of us played bridge by the fire in the big empty hall of the Beau-Site, but more often we talked. There was always a pleasant drowsiness after a day spent out-of-doors in the magnificent snow and sunshine which kept the conversation from being as violent as it might have become under more normal circumstances. Herbert and Maggie weren't much as skiers. They were learning and they stuck to the nursery slopes along with the children. My wife isn't an athlete, so for company I hired a guide called David Zupper. I hired him too because it was dangerous to go out alone into all that gigantic expanse of snow.

Zupper belonged to that great tribe of skiers, all called Zupper, like most of the inbred inhabitants of the village. He was everything that Herbert was not, and vice versa. David was built like a panther and for him skis were wings. He did not think or concern himself with problems. He lived by instinct, knowing the signs of an impending avalanche or a blizzard, or the sudden softness which preceded the coming of the foehn. For him there was no sense of dread over Saint-Firmin. The great mountains were his home as they were the home of the shy wild ibex.

With David and sometimes one or two other boys from the village we would climb up and up from eight in the morning until noon, through clouds and blizzards, until at last we reached the hut at the top of Mont Noir. Then, after eating the lunch we carried, we would set out down the mountainside, swinging back and forth across the endless expanses of clean, powdery snow, down, down, down, coming at last to the tree line, just above the railway station. Then a final dangerous swoop in and out among the trunks of the trees and we ended up in front of the Friedl Bar to have a hot grog with lemon in it and a big sausage sandwich. It was a wonderful life and David was a good guide and companion. He was clear-eyed and untouched by what was happening in Germany or Austria or Russia.

So the days were spent in the glittering white wilderness with David and the evenings, after a hot bath and a good dinner, with Herbert and Maggie beside the fire.

Herbert, in his expensive tweeds and his shining gold-rimmed glasses, confided in us that he had been spending much time in Germany on a mission that was a secret one. It concerned a complicated deal which on one end involved the Farbenindustrie, a combine of chemical interests, and on the other two of the biggest German and one of the greatest of heavy German industrial units—the Hagen Iron Works of Stuttgart. It was the period before it was discovered that all bankers and industrialists were not minor incarnations of God, and I was impressed by the grandiose schemes and plans which Herbert discussed. Neither my wife nor myself was much at business and so we believed not only all that he presented as facts but a great deal which time showed was sheer fancy. Maggie, who was a buyer and had to deal with some pretty crooked, shrewd people, was nobody's fool and seemed to take some of Herbert's more grandiose world schemes with a whole shakerful of salt.

Idiotic or not, the schemes and theories had a melodramatic and rather terrifying quality, like so many of the stories, true but surpassing belief, that were typical of that mad period between the two wars—like the stories of Rasputin and Kreuger and Stavisky and Daladier and Reynaud and their mistresses and many others—stories that one dared not to write as fiction because people would only say they were trashy and sensational and untrue.

Herbert said, "Things are not so badly off in Germany as you think. We must help Germany to her feet because she is valuable. We must do business with her big men in order to make money. Germany is an enormous market. If we let her sink down she will only go Bolshevik and infect Europe and the rest of the world.

Some of the ablest financiers and industrialists in the world are in Germany. We must work with them."

I know that all this sounds rather stale now, but at that moment, high up in the wilderness, it sounded interesting and new and persuasive. If I had lived by my instinct as David Zupper did, I should have said, "I don't believe this. It is rubbish. It can only lead to disaster." But I only listened and was impressed as most of the world was at that time by men like Herbert.

For certain men in Germany he had a kind of worship. They had managed somehow to keep great organizations intact through inflationary chaos. They had managed to place great assets through strange and intricate deals in countries outside Germany.

Maggie asked flatly, "Do you like these men?"

"Yes, certainly," said Herbert. "They are fine fellows, most of them, and very clever. Now, you take Hagen himself—the Baron, the older one . . . the one who told me about this place."

He was always "taking Hagen." There seemed to be something about Hagen which fascinated him. Herbert was very good with words when it came to describing grandiose plans but he wasn't very good about people, and so the only picture I got of Hagen was that he was tall and thin and had a big house in Stuttgart, a kind of palace in Berlin, and a huge estate with a medieval castle on it in Bavaria. And he was "awfully smart" as a businessman. That was about all I could get out of Herbert as an impression of the Baron Hagen.

In those quiet evenings before the "season" began, Uriah Heep Turnbaum, the proprietor of the Beau-Site, was about a great deal. He was always coming in, rubbing his moist hands together, to ask if we had everything we wanted or to poke the fire. Two or three times, he himself appeared behind the little oak bar in the place of the bartender, to mix our cocktails before dinner. He was always respectful, although oily, and rarely joined in the conversation. He appeared to enjoy listening to what we were saying. He was not an agreeable companion even on the other side of the bar, and his interruptions were always annoying. He was at once groveling and arrogant in the most peculiar fashion. It was this combination of qualities which made me suspect his Germanic origin.

Maggie said, "I don't believe he's Swiss at all. I've never seen or heard of a Swiss like him. The Swiss may be tiresome and disagreeable at times but they are independent always. The Swiss are by nature a free people."

The bright days and the pleasant nights went by quickly and then one night by chance, Maggie and I found each other alone at the bar just before dinner.

She said, "I'm going away tomorrow."

"So soon?"

"The Germans are due to arrive on Monday. I can't take them. I'll just get mad and make a scene or something." She drank her Martini and then said, "And I've had enough of Herbert. I'll go nuts if I have to spend another forty-eight hours with him."

I smiled, and she went on, "He couldn't be nicer and I ought to be ashamed of myself, but that's how it is. He's so damned nice he's driving me crazy. I can't cope with that child's mind any longer. I can't hear him say once more 'now take Hagen' when my instinct tells me that Hagen is a crook and a son-of-a-bitch."

I couldn't help asking, "How did you ever take up with him in the first place?"

She made a curious answer. "He was so nice and clean and simple. I'd just had a goings-on of the other kind—fascinating, subtle, devilish, etc, etc. Herbert seemed so nice and simple and American. But, brother, I just can't take any more simplicity. It's driving me nuts."

"I get what you mean."

"Herbert wants to stay on. We had a row tonight while I was dressing—as much of a row as you can have with Herbert. I said I was going to leave and he said I didn't care for him and didn't show him any consideration and when I didn't deny either thing he got mad. He wanted to stay on until his rich German friends turned up. They're due to begin arriving on Monday, so Maggie's out of here with the larks tomorrow. I don't want any part of them."

"He's going to take it hard. He thinks you're fascinating."

"He thinks I'm fast and wicked. But living in sin isn't any fun unless you get a laugh once in a while and Herbert hasn't a laugh in a carload."

"Where are you going?"

"Straight for Paris and the Ritz Bar. I feel as if I'd been living for a month in that country that lies backstage in the last act of *Walküre,* way up behind Brünnhilde's rock. When the *Walküre* begin to arrive it's time for Violetta to get out."

"Funny—I have the same feeling about this place. It's all unreal."

"It's that old Wagnerian aura. The Boches have left it behind them here. I wish you luck with them."

Then Herbert appeared looking pink and clean and innocent and sulking a little. He looked so clean he seemed almost shiny.

We said good-by that night and when we came down in the morning Herbert and Maggie were gone, but in their place had arrived the first of the German contingent. Oddly enough, I took a liking to them on sight. They were both past middle age and both had a look of distinction. The man was small and dark and rather finely built with a hawklike nose and a strong, wide mouth and high, intelligent brow. He was dressed quietly in dark rather shabby clothing. He might have been of any nationality. One might have encountered him in London or Paris or New York or even India.

The woman was unmistakably German or Swedish, taller than the man and very blonde. She, like the man, must have been in her fifties, and there was something in her carriage and splendid figure which made me think at once that she must be a singer. She was beautiful in a fine Junoesque fashion.

At breakfast they sat at a window quite a distance away from us.

The man was reading the German newspapers he had brought with him from Zurich, and now and then he read her something of interest or put down the paper altogether to discuss something with her. The woman kept watching us and turning away whenever I glanced in their direction.

I thought, "They appear charming and intelligent. If the others are like them Maggie is quite wrong about the invasion."

That evening when I came in I found the two of them talking to Nannie and the children. Dogs and children have the most astonishing way of picking up strangers and making introductions. I think half the interest, half the people in my life have come into it through my having had children and dogs. They are able to break down all reserves, to cross barriers of race, creed, and color.

When I came up, Nannie said, "These are the newcomers." And turning to them, she said, "I'm afraid I don't know your names."

The man brought his heels together and said, "Herr and Frau Oberregierungsrat Moll."

And from that moment we were friends. They had the simplicity and assurance of intelligent people who have accomplished something in life, who knew the world. There are people in the world whom one might call "the elect"—people who are decent and dignified, warm and human, who have a sense of values which never permits them to be rude or avaricious or vulgar, but whose greatest characteristics are generosity and the simplicity born of experience; and that, my friends, is something quite different from Herbert's kind of simplicity. One learns to know them almost at sight, for all these things are written in their faces. One finds such people anywhere in the world. They are confined to no country or civilization. Herr and Frau Oberregierungsrat Moll were like this.

I noticed that the dress of Frau Moll was *démodé* and just a trifle shabby and that Herr Moll's tweeds were worn beyond the point of shabbiness which the Englishman cultivates deliberately. I wanted to see more of them and asked them to meet us in the bar at seven-thirty. They accepted so quickly that I got the impression that they were very lonely, not only in Saint-Firmin but at home in Germany as well.

When my wife and I entered the bar, the Molls were already there waiting for us and rose as we came into the room.

They did not have cocktails but each took a glass of sherry. We talked of the skiing, of the wild beauty of Saint-Firmin. They had known it for many years. They both spoke excellent English; Herr Moll, without any accent at all. When I asked for the check, a strange thing happened.

Herr Moll said to the barman, "Please, may I have the check for the sherry?"

"But I invited you for a drink," I protested.

"Please," said Herr Moll, "I will explain later."

I allowed him to pay for their sherry and when the barman had gone, Herr Moll said, "I was not being ungracious. I must explain to you." A curious look of pain came into the dark, intelligent face. "You see, we cannot afford to buy drinks for people and so we cannot accept them. You see, the money I earn in Germany has no value outside Germany and almost none inside. We are only here because my wife has a little money which comes from what she had saved and invested in London. It is very little but enough to bring us here if we are very careful for ten days or two weeks. We stay as long as it lasts and then go back to Germany." Then he said a curious thing, "It makes the rest of the year possible. You see, we have to get out of Germany for a little while each year."

He spoke perfectly simply, as people do who look upon money as a convenience and a means to personal liberty but as no more than that.

"I understand," I said, "if you like it that way."

We dined together and slowly bits of their two lives came out casually to form at the end a kind of beautiful mosaic. They lived in Cologne, where Herr Moll was a judge of the Supreme Court. They had a house there and a small place in the Palatinate where they went in summer. The Oberregierungsrat collected old editions and fine bindings, although lately, because of the inflation, little had been added to the collection. He said quite simply, "If ever you come to Cologne, you must come to see us."

I was right about Frau Moll. She had been a singer and still sang two or three recitals a year, mostly for her own pleasure. She had sung in Vienna, in London, in Paris, and of course nearly every German opera house—no big roles except in the smaller opera houses like Hanover or Württemberg, where she had sung Brünnhilde and Sieglinde.

With a smile she said, "I was never a great singer but I have always been a fine musician. One can lose one's voice but not one's musicianship."

They were unhappy and there was sadness in the dark eyes of the Judge and the blue ones of Frau Moll, even when they smiled or laughed. For the first two or three evenings they were reticent, but slowly they began to open up. They had come early, they said, before Saint-Firmin became crowded. It was not so nice then. They liked the villagers, gnarled, ugly, and inbred as they were. And it was a change. They always kept coming back to that without, I think, realizing how much they talked about a change.

In the meantime, a few more Germans arrived with each train, morning and evening, now four or five, now as many as ten a day, and slowly I began to see what it was Maggie meant about clearing out before they arrived. They were not what you might call nice types. Physically they had a look of coarseness, like a breed apart. One had a dim impression of a herd of cattle. They were noisy. Of all ages, from children to grandparents, they trooped in and out. They were rude to the servants and quarreled over the food and the service at the table. And they had a way of staking out preserves in this or that corner of the hotel public rooms. If you entered their preserves even by accident, they glared at you or made rude remarks. Worst of all, the older women had a way of taking possession of all the best chairs and the most comfortable corners and keeping possession of them by depositing a book or a knitting bag in a chair. This was supposed to stake out a permanent claim. If you moved the book or bag and sat in the chair, sooner or later you were told rudely that the chair was engaged and were asked to get out. This was a curious convention I had never before observed. It seemed to be a German custom.

Gradually, the Molls and ourselves were thrust into a corner, the most obscure and uncomfortable corner of the room, away from the fire, away from everything. It became apparent that in such a world we simply did not know how to take care of ourselves. Once I heard one buxom, masculine woman say, "Well, at least this is one place where Germans have some rights. If only the whole world were like this." And her male companion, a tall, heavy man with a thick neck, answered, "One day it will be. One day we'll have everything the French and English have and more too."

I am a good-tempered fellow, but I felt the blood rushing into my face with apoplectic force. I suddenly knew exactly what Maggie meant.

In the streets and the shops, the same behavior prevailed. The bus became impossible. After each run down the mountain I came to prefer walking up the long steep slope from the station to the hotel to losing my temper over the struggle and the rudeness one had to encounter to find a place or even get aboard the vehicle. Again and again I heard talk about "the rights of Germans." It seemed to be very nearly an obsession.

In the meantime our friends the Molls grew more and more depressed. They had neither the coarseness of their countrymen nor the will to combat their methods, and like ourselves they were pushed into a corner. They rarely spoke to their compatriots and never held any conversation with them, but they never betrayed to us their dislike of the other Germans in Saint-Firmin. Because we had grown very fond of them, we never discussed the question with them except on the basis of individuals, as if they were not all of the same nationality. We came to have special names for certain particularly obnoxious ones. There was the Old Sow, the

Wolf, the Chambermaid, the Prussian, and so on. To the Molls, the Prussians were a race of foreigners who had nothing to do with southern Germany. More and more the Molls disappeared in the daytime, going for long walks, each armed with a walking stick, down the mountain below the timber line. They even took to carrying a lunch packed for them.

As each train came in with new Germans, I became aware of an increase in the unhappiness of our friends. I knew suddenly that one day it would reach a point where they could no longer stand it and would go away, and that filled me with regret, for then we should be left alone among the wolves. Once or twice I considered moving all of us to some other part of Switzerland where we would find British and French, Americans and Austrians, but my wife objected.

"After the New Year," she said, "it will be better. They will thin out. I can't face moving dogs, children, and luggage all over again. Anyway, we couldn't get in anywhere at this time of year."

It was the argument about moving dogs and children which won me over to her point of view. I could not face another trek before the final one homeward to France at the end of the winter. It was clear that we were trapped. It was extraordinary how members of the human race could befoul a corner as wild and beautiful and clean as Saint-Firmin.

Then one night, two days before Christmas, as we sat in an obscure corner, huddled into the only chairs which had been left us, Herr Oberregierungsrat Moll said, "We are going away tomorrow. This afternoon we went down the mountain to Flensdorf. It is a tiny place. We found a room there in an inn. It is quieter. We could not bear to spend Christmas here."

What he was saying very clearly was, "We could not bear to spend a German Christmas here among these Germans."

We expressed our sorrow at having them leave. My wife said, "We shall be very lonely without you"—lonely in a crowded hotel, in a crowded village.

We talked then of other things for a time, but you could see that all the time Herr Moll was troubled by something. At last, when it was nearly midnight, he suddenly sighed as if the effort was great, stiffened his thin body, and said, "There is something I have wanted to say for a long time. I feel that we owe you an apology for our own country people. I hope you won't think they are all like this. There are civilized, nice Germans but you don't see them outside Germany now. They haven't the money. They're starving to death at home. We were lucky—Anna's having a little money placed in London. We have nice friends at home I should like to have you meet. It would give you a little different idea. Also, they are imprisoned inside Germany—all of them ruined because they believed in their government and its banks and currency." A look of utter contempt came over the lean, dark face. "These people here are all connivers and speculators. They have speculated in the currency of their own country. They have made fortunes out of the misfortunes and tragedies of Europe. That is why they have money outside of Germany."

Frau Moll said, "Yes, you must come to Cologne just to see for yourself. We aren't all industrial people and bankers and shopkeepers there. Some of us are quite civilized."

It was the first hint I had had of how the industrial and banking people really linked up with Herbert and his giant projects, with his deals with the Farbenindustrie and Baron Hagen, the steel king. But it was not quite clear to me then. It only fitted into the pattern later on as events became history and history in time clarified the interlocking pattern.

Judge Moll said, "Most of the industrialists and bankers have taken care of themselves. They've made deals with Schneider and Vickers and the big American oil companies, and the speculators are all right for the moment. And a lot of political adventurers are getting on. There are some of them here now—take Heintzlemann, that big fat brute with the red face. He's here for some reason, to see someone, to plot about something. He's no more than a gangster." He sighed and pressed his thin hands against his temples for relief. "I don't know what is happening in Germany. No one does. But it appears that all the wrong people are coming out on top."

Frau Moll said cozily, "If only you could have known Cologne before the war. You must at least come and meet some of our friends."

Then suddenly Oberregierungsrat Moll began to talk, passionately, intelligently, with a curious and scholarly objectivity, about the German people. He said many things that I was to remember long afterwards, perhaps for as long as I lived. What he said made me understand many things I would never have understood otherwise.

He said, "There is a curious fundamental curse of envy in so many Germans. And there is much self-pity. They envy Britain her power, America her wealth, France her civilization. They want all these things but they are not willing to earn them. They want to take them by force—things which can only be earned since force only weakens everyone and destroys the very power, wealth, and civilization they covet. The trouble is that Germany got started too late in the race. Their leaders, the demagogues, play upon the natural envy and the covetousness of the people. They always preach force and unscrupulousness. And they play upon German self-pity, which is very strong. They are always talking about German rights and the great debts owed to Germany. We are, alas, inclined at times to whine."

A little later he said, "The German and his country are both handicapped by being provincial. You rarely meet a German who is cosmopolitan, really interested in his mind. He is nearly always rigidly German—harping on German *Kultur*. Science to him is not an abstract thing belonging to all the world. There is only German science, only German music, German art. Even socially he is provincial. You'll see that in the diplomatic world. There is always something especially German about German diplomats. They are always asserting their Germanism, always putting a wall around themselves." He sighed again and pressed his temples. "The demagogues have all these things to play upon, to exploit.

That is what is so frightening now with the worst people in Germany coming into power. There is a kind of innocence, a kind of bucolic ignorance about so many Germans. Above all people in the world they are material for the demagogues to work upon."

Before we retired, he said only one more thing I remembered long afterward, "Sometimes I think the German people are under a curse which works only for their destruction. It is as if they were a people bent perpetually upon suicide."

He might have said more but for the fact that the door from the bar was suddenly flung open and into the room came the red-faced Heintzlemann. He was roaring drunk and was leaning upon a younger man with a round face with pale-blue eyes and straw-colored hair. Heintzlemann kept bellowing something in German which I could not understand because he spoke in a low Silesian dialect.

The pair swept through the room, treading on the feet of the Old Sow, who rose indignantly and began to berate them in the coarse language of a fishwife. She followed them, cursing at them until they reached the door at the far end of the sitting room. There Heintzlemann turned and spat at her. He called out, "You think you're better than I am, do you, you old swine? Well, just wait! You'll see! You'll see!" Then he bent down, kissed the young man with the pink face and straw-colored hair on the cheek, and, still bellowing, turned and continued on his way.

The scene had a paralyzing effect, even upon the coarse Germans who filled the sitting room. There was something animal and inhuman about the spectacle. Oddly enough, it was the kind of scene you would expect to see only in Germany. It could never have happened among Frenchmen or Englishmen or Russians or Americans or Austrians. It could have happened only among the people in that room. There was something sickening about it.

Anna Moll rose and said quietly, "I think we had better go off to bed."

We rose to join them and I said, "We will come to the station to see you off in the morning."

They did not protest. They only said, "That will be very kind of you."

It meant that I would lose nearly a whole day of precious skiing because the climbing was easiest and the snow best in the morning. But it did not matter. I felt their loneliness very keenly. They suddenly appeared to have turned very old, older than their years. I was aware that, in their shame, they wanted to run away now, out into the night, anywhere at all. I thought, "If Germany is like this, I see why they talk so much about getting a change."

My wife and I went to bed without talking at all, and for a long time I lay awake thinking about the gentle Molls and the other Germans in the place, so brutal, so incredible, so frightening. I was filled with a sense of dread for the future, vague and indefinable. What it was I feared, I did not know, but the scene was filled with potential, explosive terror.

Long afterward, looking back, I understood what it was. All the people in that room, save the Molls and ourselves, were Nazis—the coarse ones, the speculators, the conniving money-makers who had saved themselves and built up their own selfish interests with the brutality and envy and coarseness of potential Nazis. Only at that time there was no such word as Nazi and Hitler was a name unknown but to a few outside of Germany.

I had forgotten even that Herbert had talked casually about a new political party called the National Socialists in which Baron Hagen was interested as a possible instrument for "saving Germany."

The next morning, accompanied by the dogs, we walked to the little station to see the Molls on their way. The sun was shining on new powdery snow. The pines below the station looked like Christmas trees with the snow still lying on their flat, outspread branches.

It was a gay morning, but there was no gaiety in the hearts of any of us. The Molls looked tired and pale, as if they had not slept at all. When we talked, the conversation was stiff and forced. I was aware that they were still ashamed.

Mercifully the little train appeared, late, sneaking up through the snow-covered pines. As it drew into the station I saw that it was crowded with more Germans arriving for Christmas. They were peering out of the windows and crowding the platforms. There seemed to be hordes of them, and the sight did not raise our spirits. The moment the train stopped they began crowding off, many of them already in ski costumes, all of them wearing too many things, too many scarfs and badges and fancy jackets and furs, in the way Germans have. They shouted and quarreled and all tried to get their skis out of the baggage van at once.

When they had all descended, Herr Moll said, "We'll go now. There's no use in your standing about until the train leaves."

"Yes," said Frau Moll, "go along. Get your day's skiing before the crowd gets started."

You could see that they wanted to be on their way down to the peace and quiet of the obscure little inn in Flensdorf. I shook hands with them both and then Anna Moll did a curious thing, she kissed my wife on the cheek and said, "Forgive the familiarity. We shall miss you." There were tears in her eyes.

They climbed aboard the train and looked back once and smiled.

Then we turned away and as we came round the station the two dogs, Hustler and Dinah, began to bark wildly and strain at the leash. What they saw was another dog, a Scotty like themselves.

The stranger belonged to a young woman standing on the edge of the platform with a middle-aged man. They were a remarkable-looking pair. The girl was pretty in a rather buxom fashion and very young, not more perhaps than twenty or twenty-one. She was dressed in a shabby coat of some unnamable dyed fur and on her head was the German's idea of a chic French hat—a kind of "Dorothy Vernon of Haddon Hall" contraption in brown velvet with a brown ostrich plume trailing down the back. The fur coat was short and from beneath it hung the brown velvet of the suit she wore.

The man gave the impression of a prosperous provincial French undertaker—one of the sort with a clientele which demands only funerals of the first class. He was tall, with a long, narrow face. The complexion had a waxy pallor darkened where the heavy black beard showed through the skin. His eyes were a yellow brown and he wore an absurd overcoat, very long, of black material with a collar of expensive black mink. Topping it all was a stiff bowler hat. Against all the panorama of snow and mountains and forest and in the midst of all the crowd in skiing clothes, the pair looked absolutely preposterous.

The three dogs kept up their barking, and once again my pair performed their service of introducing me to remarkable and unlikely people. This time not only were they encountering another dog; this dog they encountered was of the same breed.

The girl looked toward us and smiled. It was a frank, simple, warm smile which made you like her at once. Then in very good English she said, "Let them get acquainted."

So still on the leash, the three dogs were introduced. Oddly enough, Hustler, my male Scotty, instead of attacking the newcomer according to his habit, wagged his tail. It was evident that he liked the stranger.

"What are they called?" asked the girl.

"Hustler and Dinah"

"Mine is called Runty. He was so little when I got him. I love Scotties. They're so little and so brave."

I laughed, and my wife said, "Our two run away every time they get a chance. Yesterday they turned up at a village six miles away. How they got there through four feet of snow, I don't know."

The dogs kept on sniffing and wagging their tails, and the man simply remained standing there watching us without saying anything.

"We're waiting for the big sleigh from the Beau-Site," said the girl. "It was full before I got my luggage out of the van." Then she said, "Excuse me, my name is Baroness von Schildsen." Then the color came into her face. She was shy and what she said next appeared to cost her great effort. She turned and said, "This is Baron von Hagen." And after a second she said as if to explain the situation, "He is a friend of my husband. We came across each other on the train."

It took me a moment to recover from the shock. From all Herbert's talk about him I had formed a picture of the powerful Baron Hagen which was quite different. I hadn't expected this rather dank undertaker. He didn't at all fit the idea of a powerful king of heavy industry. We shook hands, and his face for the first time showed any expression. It relaxed into a smile which had a certain charm. Then the big sleigh appeared and was at once rushed by an army of Germans.

Out of experience my wife and I drew back rather than be trampled and gave up the whole idea of the sleigh. But the girl and von Hagen were able to hold their own. Something about the Baron's appearance and manner or the mink-collared coat struck awe in the other Germans. Coldly he said, *"Bitte!"* and stepped forward, looking formal and imposing, to take the best seat. He put the girl in beside him, but she did not keep her dignity. She snatched up her dog Runty and shouted a long string of indignant German words at the jostling, elbowing mob. It was in coarse, slangy German which I cannot remember and did not wholly understand. But it was something like this, "What goes on here? What a bunch of bums! You ought to be ashamed to call yourselves Germans! Get out of the way!"

As the sleigh drove off she turned and, smiling quickly, waved to us. The Baron sat looking straight ahead.

The sleigh, with much jangling of bells and cracking of the whip, dashed off up the hill toward the hotel, and I thought, "It is very odd that a man with all that power and money didn't hire a private sleigh but waited for the hotel conveyance."

The next night was Christmas Eve. There was a big Christmas tree and much singing. Three of the younger Germans brought out guitars and sang old German folk songs. Several barrels of beer were drunk and everything turned *gemütlich* and sentimental and all the Germans suddenly loved each other. They even relaxed their rudeness toward the non-Germans in the hotel. The Old Sow and the Wolf and all the others became close friends. It was all overdone and hysterical, as overdone as the rudeness and ruthlessness which had preceded it. There was an unbalanced quality about the whole thing. It became a kind of sloppy, indecent orgy of sentimentality, as if they were saying, "Christmas is a German festival. It belongs to us alone. Only we know how to celebrate it." For once there was something they need not envy others.

Before going to bed I noticed one remarkable thing—that for the first time, the red-faced, odious Heintzlemann was not drunk, and the younger man with the straw-colored hair, the pale-blue eyes, and the pink cheeks was not with him. Early in the evening we had a drink with Baron von Hagen in the bar. After that he joined the singers and was as well behaved as any small-town German shopkeeper on Christmas Eve.

For a little while after dinner we stayed downstairs, fascinated by the exotic quality of the medieval love feast which had overtaken our fellow lodgers, and about ten o'clock we went to our own rooms to decorate the Christmas tree for the children and arrange the gifts for Christmas morning. A little while later, one of the maids knocked at the door and said that David, the guide, was waiting downstairs to see me.

I found him standing in the hallway, very tanned and wiry and straight, with his cap in his hand. He was watching the orgy of *Gemütlichkeit* through the doorway, so absorbed that I had to speak twice before he noticed that I was there. He grinned and the blue eyes twinkled with mockery.

Then he said, "I just came to tell you that we can't go out in the morning. A storm is blowing up—a bad one—the kind nobody could go out in and return alive."

We went into the bar and had a drink, finding a corner for ourselves where we hoped to be unmolested. We both had

Schnaps, I think as a kind of protest because all the others were drinking beer. It was difficult to hold a conversation in the face of all the singing and uproar, so we just sat there watching. There was a kind of grossness in the spectacle, of the kind you see in the pictures of Breughel. David's rather cold, clear blue eyes were very steady. Once he turned and said in his very bad Swiss French, "*Ces ne sont vraiment que des cochons!*" And suddenly I understood for the first time how he really felt, along with all the other guides and all the villagers. Each year they tolerated the invasion because it meant prosperity for them for the rest of the year. There was a kind of hatred in his voice that tied in with the curious aura of Saint-Firmin itself and that sense of dread which I had felt from the very first. I began to believe that it was the presence of the Germans in the place rather than the wild scenery which brought the sense of wild, Gothic unreality. I do believe that fierce and concentrated hatred and contempt can create a kind of intangible intensity in an atmosphere, like electricity.

Then I saw Uriah Heep Turnbaum coming toward us, washing his hands like Lady Macbeth. He was always bad news, but I hardly expected what was coming. He bent down and whispered in my ear. At first I did not catch what he was saying and, despite the menace of his bad breath, I was forced to ask him to repeat it.

This is what he said, "I am sorry but there is a rule against bringing guides into the bar of the Beau-Site. Someone has just complained."

I am usually a quiet, peaceful man, but certain things are likely to bring up sudden almost apoplectic attacks of temper. I felt one coming now. I could feel the blood rushing into my face. It was incredible that any of the coarse people in this room should object to the presence of a sportsman, a swell fellow, a gentleman like David. Such an issue was never raised among people in other skiing resorts where skiers looked upon men like David as a race of aristocrats.

I said, "Who objected?"

"That I cannot tell you," said Turnbaum.

"You will tell me or I will stay right here and if there's any more trouble I'll smash the whole place to hell."

This appeared to awe Turnbaum, who seemed to think I was drunk.

"I will tell you if you don't make trouble."

"I only want to know. I don't want to be mixed up with these swine if it can be helped."

At the word "swine" his face changed color. He said, "It was Herr Heintzlemann."

"That pederast! That perverted hog!"

Turnbaum shrugged his bottle-shaped shoulders. "He is with the Baron Hagen, a very important man. What can I do?"

David was still watching. Fortunately he appeared to believe that our conversation was a private one and none of his business.

I said, "Very well. We'll go up to our rooms and drink. I'd prefer not to mix with this company."

"Thank you," said Turnbaum. "It is not my fault, you understand." But I could see that he hated me, and I was more certain than ever that he was no genuine Swiss at all but one of them.

He went away and I said to David, "Let's get out of here. Come up to the sitting room and have a Christmas drink with my wife."

We left the noisy room and upstairs found my wife decorating the Christmas tree. It was pleasant up there, away from the obscene celebrations going on belowstairs, celebrations which seemed to me to have very little to do with the spirit of the Christ child.

Following up his remark, I led him to talking about the Germans downstairs. The *Schnaps* rather loosened his tongue and he talked more easily than I had ever heard him talk. Out of his heart came all sorts of things. When I asked about the people belowstairs, he said, "They are a new kind of German. In the old days they were mostly young and came here only for the skiing. They weren't so bad. These are mostly little people who have got rich somehow. I don't know how. But they hate and envy everybody who is not German. Why should they hate and envy us poor mountain villagers? They are *bad* Germans. Not all Germans are like them, but most Germans have something of that in them. They are a resentful and envious people who want the whole world!"

Later on, he said, "Something bad is going on in Germany. I don't know what it is, but my grandfather who lives in Zurich says all Swiss know the signs. They have lived through them before. He says it's a kind of deviltry that gets into them—that it comes out of the swamps and forests, out of the blood and soil, just as it did in Roman times."

I was interested in the speech but I did not remark at the time a curious phrase which later became a kind of slogan of great significance. I only remembered it years afterward when it became the favorite phrase of Alfred Rosenberg, the philosopher of all these people belowstairs. The phrase was "blood and soil."

Outside the rising wind howled louder and louder. Once I pushed open the window to see if it were snowing. The gale threw the sash back into my face, almost knocking me down. Before the window closed, the snow swept into the room, carried across the floor as far as the Christmas tree by the wild fury of the storm. Certainly there would be no skiing in the morning, perhaps not for many days.

Then David suddenly rose and bade us "good night" and "merry Christmas."

After we had gone to bed and the lights were out, I lay in the darkness for a long time, unable to sleep, listening to the howling of the storm. It was an odd, unnatural Christmas. Here in our own rooms, it was peaceful and secure enough, but all around that sense of dread kept creeping in. As I lay there awake, the memory of the scene belowstairs became fantastically important and rather terrifying, like a nightmare in which the overdone *Gemütlichkeit,* the Old Sow, the Wolf, the unspeakable Heintzlemann, and the Baron all played roles.

In the morning, the wind still howled and the snow beat against the windows, but in the sitting room it was warm and the children and the dogs played and barked about the Christmas tree while we drank chocolate and ate hot Swiss rolls covered with butter and mountain honey. I had the feeling that we were in a kind of warm and cozy pocket in the very midst of a wild and hostile universe.

After breakfast I dressed lazily and went downstairs to let the dogs out for a run. When I opened the door they ran barking to disappear into the driving snow. Waiting for them, I stood in the doorway. Evidently our German friends were sleeping off the effects of the Christmas Eve celebration, for the lower part of the hotel was completely empty. There was not even a servant in sight and the great hall was a picture of desolation with torn paper streamers, confetti, stale stains of champagne and beer on tables and floor. The whole place had a curious dead, acrid smell.

I was glad of the cold, clean, snow-filled air. The Scotties stayed away for a long time. I whistled, but still they did not appear. Dogs are likely to become intoxicated by a snowstorm. I gave up whistling and waited and then out of the snowstorm I saw a figure coming up the drive. As it came near I realized that it was the Baroness, the girl we had seen briefly at the station. I recognized the pretentious, shabby fur coat. She came out of the falling snow on to the portico and I saw that she was crying and upset at finding me there.

I felt like apologizing for my presence and said, "Is there anything I can do for you?"

She blew her nose and said, "It's my dog, Runty. I let him out and he ran off into the storm. I called and called but he didn't come back. I've been looking for him for the last hour. I've been all the way to the station. I can't whistle very well and in the storm, it's no good calling. He can't hear my voice. I'm afraid he'll lose his way and not be able to get back. He has such short legs and the snow is so deep."

I smiled, "Mine have done the same trick." Then to reassure her I told her again of the escapades of Dinah and Hustler, how somehow they made their way through deep snow to the other side of the mountain.

"It looks as if I'd have to go look for them. Would you like to come along? Maybe we'll find Runty at the same time."

She could not answer me at once for sobbing. There was something hysterical about her grief, out of all proportion with the loss of a dog—a loss which was only possible and not probable.

I said, "Perhaps you'd better have a drink first and warm up."

"No! No! I don't want to go in there. I want to find Runty."

She wouldn't even come into the great hall while I went to fetch a hat.

When I returned she had managed to control her sobs and was waiting in a sheltered corner of the portico, the shabby fur coat pulled up about her ears. When she saw me, she said, "I'm ashamed. I won't cry any more."

"That's all right."

I confess that I was worried about our own dogs. The blizzard was like nothing I had ever seen. I did not see how even a hardy Scotty could stay out in it for long and survive.

We set out down the drive toward the town, our bodies thrust forward into the wind. Any conversation was out of the question. Now and then I turned with my back toward the wind, put two fingers into my mouth and whistled shrilly, without any response from the truant dogs.

Thus we continued all the way down the hill through the empty village. Now and then a single figure would emerge from the blowing snow, pass us without looking up, and disappear again like a ghost. When we reached the station I shouted, "We'll go in and have something hot to drink."

Inside the little *buffet de la gare* was warm, like most Swiss interiors, much too warm. We both had hot chocolate and rolls, and as she drank, the girl began to thaw out a little. She was very pretty in a Gretchen sort of way, with her cheeks aflame from the heat after the biting wind.

Shyly she said, "I'm afraid I seem a fool."

"No. Not at all."

"If I lost Runty I don't know what I'd do. You see, I was very lonely. It's the first Christmas I've spent away from home, and it was awful at the hotel last night. I've never seen a Christmas like that. I went up to my room early and went to bed but I didn't sleep all night. That's why I'm so foolish this morning, I suppose."

"You should have joined us," I said.

"I didn't know you well enough."

"We would have been glad to have you."

I was interested to discover that she was not traveling with Hagen as his mistress. That was perfectly clear. There was something innocent about her which made deception out of the question. It did not even seem to occur to her that anyone should suspect that she was traveling *with* Hagen. It still seemed very odd that she was traveling alone, that she should have come to such a place as Saint-Firmin, knowing no one.

"What about having Christmas dinner with us?" I asked.

Her face was suddenly radiant. "That would be wonderful."

Then I fancied suddenly that I heard barking and even went to the window to discover that I was right. Outside in the blizzard were the dogs, not only Hustler and Dinah but the Baroness' Runty. They were playing and barking wildly, obviously enjoying the storm like true Scotsmen. For a second I felt an impulse to wring their necks.

It was Gretl who, in her innocence, brought us together with Heintzlemann and the Baron. It happened like this.

When we returned from the station with the dogs, Gretl had Christmas dinner with us. That, she said, was what she was called —simply Gretl. Her name was Margaret, but Gretl suited much better the fresh, naïve, healthy quality of the girl. We had champagne for lunch, and she was excited and happy and kept giving out fragments of information about herself, small odd pieces unrelated, like a heap of pieces from a picture puzzle. She was already divorced from her husband, who had been a man thirty years older than herself. She occupied a tiny cheap room built for servants' quarters on the very top floor of the hotel. Her father, who had been a Lutheran pastor, was dead. She was not of the nobility but of the solid German middle class. The title had come to her by marriage. She was twenty-three years old. Life was very hard in Germany. Honest people of the solid middle class actually had not enough to eat, nor clothes or shoes. She could not believe her eyes when she came out of Germany and found that other people had fine, warm clothes, and not only food but things such as champagne and caviar and *pâté de fois gras*. She had gone first to Vienna, where she got a job as a chorus girl in a musical show.

"There," she said, "I met my fiancé. He is coming here after the New Year. You will like him. He is an Italian from Milano."

She had saved the money she had earned as a chorus girl. That was what she was living on now.

It was a strange, disconnected, incongruous chain of isolated incidents which she revealed—a picture of a life utterly disrupted and cast adrift on the turbulent sea of that afterwar period. I kept thinking that in normal times she would have been the wife of some solid good citizen and the mother of two or three children by now. But all that had been changed by the ambition and envy of power, by men she had never seen—the Kaiser and a lot of other Germans who wanted to devour the whole world. I don't think any such idea ever occurred to her. In her simplicity she simply accepted what came along without questioning or thought. At any rate, she appeared very happy at our family Christmas dinner. She fitted into it as simply, as naturally as any girl from my home town in Ohio. The tears, the loneliness vanished, for the moment at least.

From then on she became a part of our lives in Saint-Firmin, like the children and the dogs. We were all fond of her. She had no interest in me save as a friend. She was equally fond of my wife and myself.

On the third night after the dog episode she said, "Baron von

Hagen has asked me to have brandy with him after dinner and asked me to ask you both to join us."

I accepted because I wanted to know better what this industrial genius was like. He seemed so unlike what one expected of a "big shot" in America. As I said, he gave the impression of a provincial French undertaker. We saw him about the hotel or in the village street, a sallow, rather dreary fellow always in his mink-collared, black broadcloth overcoat, without flair, without personality. Wherever he went the other Germans treated him with the groveling servility of a nation for which *hochgeboren* is one of the key words. Hagen was not very *hochgeboren* but he represented what was even more important to the Old Sow, the Wolf, Heintzlemann and the other Beau-Site Germans. He was rich and he was powerful and he vindicated their sense of defeat and bafflement among the other peoples of the world.

It was a strange, unreal evening. I discovered that Hagen had a soft voice which had the quality not of velvet but of plush, as if at some time his vocal cords had suffered an injury. At times it was difficult to understand what he was saying. This forced you to listen carefully and give great attention while he was speaking. The hands, rather clammy to touch, were small and rather oily, with heavy blue veins. They inspired a sense of repulsion. His eyes were not, as they appeared from a distance, dark brown or black but of a yellowish-green color.

He addressed Gretl as "Baroness" and it was apparent at once that he was attracted by her. I thought at first that it was the attraction of opposites—that of a perfectly ageless, embalmed man for a healthy, simple, rustically pretty young girl. He spoke English with a heavy accent.

At first the conversation was stiff and slow, not, it seemed to me, because there was any shyness or awkwardness in any of us, but because his mind was elsewhere. Presently I divined that Gretl was the source of his distraction. One had the impression not simply that he was disrobing her mentally; it was something stronger, more intense and complicated than that.

After three glasses of brandy he seemed to relax a little and to grow more human and warm. I observed that we had a mutual acquaintance, Herbert, and at once he brightened a little when I told him that Herbert had been here a little while before, embarked upon a love affair.

"Yes, he is a clever fellow," said Hagen. "We are working on two or three projects together. They promise rather well. German industry needs help from the outside. It will work toward the mutual good. We have great plans. If only industrialists could manage the world, it would be quite a different place and the danger of war and the Bolsheviks would be greatly reduced. The rest of the world has never properly appreciated German genius, especially in industry."

He had barely finished the speech when Heintzlemann joined us. He came up to the table behind the Baron's back so that the Baron did not see him until he had finished speaking. At sight of the newcomer, the Baron frowned. He did not acknowledge Heintzlemann's greeting. It was Gretl who introduced us.

It is almost impossible to give an impression of the animal vitality of Heintzlemann. He was a big man, heavy to the point of obesity, with a round red face and great hands like clusters of sausages. The grossness of the body was redeemed only by the shrewdness of the small blue eyes. He sat down and ordered a round of drinks and a double brandy for himself.

He spoke no English and although my wife and I could speak and understand German, the conversation continued in English at the will of Hagen, who, I think, sought deliberately to snub his companion and exclude him from the conversation. Heintzlemann appeared not to notice the snub but sat leaning forward, straining to understand and now and then when he fancied he understood some remark of the Baron, he would nod his head vehemently and interject some approving remark in guttural German. There was in his manner the same obsequiousness which marked the attitude of most of the other Germans.

Most of the Baron's talk was along the same line—that the

Germans were unappreciated, that they wanted to be friends with the rest of the world, that they were not understood.

Presently, with a certain venom, I asked, "Are all Germans like these in the hotel?"

But the Baron missed the point entirely. He said, "Oh, no. This is the new Germany you see here. This is the coming Germany—the Germany of vitality and force and skill."

He was approving of them. As he spoke, it became apparent that Heintzlemann understood more English than we believed, for again he nodded his head violently and made some guttural remark about *"Verdammte Juden."*

We met with the Baron on two other evenings, partly because he sought the meeting and partly because I was myself fascinated by both Hagen and Heintzlemann. They were unlike any people I had ever met before, outwardly friendly, yet remote and strange and unreal as mad or morosely drunken people can be. Their standards, their reactions, were utterly unexpected, completely incredible. They each had a hate—Heintzlemann's was Jews and the Baron's was the French. He could not seem to forgive them their civilization.

The conversation was no more inspiring than it had been on the first evening and upon much the same level. Once or twice I was tempted to argue, but it seemed only a useless expenditure of energy. My wife, less philosophical, now and then grew angry and made remarks which would have been insulting to any other people in the world. Perhaps Heintzlemann, sitting there all flesh and grossness, did not understand them. The Baron's complacency was so great that they slipped off his pallid, waxy skin like water off tallow. Both men gave the impression of sexual abnormality. In Heintzlemann's case we knew what it was, for before the arrival of the Baron he had made no effort to conceal it. It was the animal kind of homosexuality which one finds often enough in Germany: there was no effeminacy about him, only brutality. With the Baron the analysis was more difficult to achieve, the effect more obscure. There was something definitely wrong, but what it was could not easily be defined. It simply made one uncomfortable.

One thing which became clear was that his inner, sinister passion for Gretl seemed to grow stronger. She appeared to be aware of this and always stayed close to us as if we were protection.

On the last night before his departure, after we had said good-by and accepted vaguely his invitation to visit him if we ever happened to be in Berlin or Munich, Gretl stopped off with us in our sitting room on the way up to her servant's bedroom. As I poured a nightcap she flung herself down in a chair and said, "Pfui! I'm glad he's gone. He wanted me to be his mistress. He has been after me for a long time."

"They're a funny pair. Heintzlemann is easy enough. I can't make out the Baron."

Then Gretl said a surprising thing, perhaps born of harsh experience on the side of her life which she had hinted at but never revealed.

"It is easy. Did you ever notice his eyes? They are the eyes of a man who gets pleasure out of inflicting cruelty. I know—my husband was like that. He and Hagen are friends. They used to go on orgies together. That is how I met Hagen first. My husband had the same kind of eyes. That's why I left him. I couldn't stand it. That is why Hagen goes for me. He knows I understand what he wants. He would not be embarrassed by having to tell me. We understand each other."

As she talked, her gentian-blue eyes grew dark and the color came into her face. Then a kind of hysteria seemed to seize her and she began to talk wildly.

"His wife puts up with him. She is a beautiful girl. She doesn't seem to mind. Maybe she puts up with him because she likes the wonderful jewels and furs he gives her." She laughed. "Maybe because he keeps her tied on a string. Each night when they come home he puts all the jewels in his safe and locks up the furs so she can't run off with them. When he goes away on a trip he locks them up and she has to go about just dressed in ordinary clothes like anyone else." She laughed again. "He is fantastic."

That was all that came out of Gretl that night, except when I said, "Hagen and Heintzlemann seem an odd pair. They don't seem to have anything in common. Why are they so much together?"

Gretl smiled a little tipsily. "Some sort of dirty work. That's why Hagen came up here. There's a lot of that going on today in Germany. In Munich there's a funny little fellow called Hitler who's got some sort of movement. He goes about preaching. Heintzlemann is always with him."

The name of the "funny little fellow" struck some faint chord of memory, but I didn't think any more about it. At the moment Gretl seemed to me far more interesting. In her innocence she seemed the clue to a great many things which puzzled me about that strange, foreign people—the Germans. Heaven knows, she was not profound. The world in which she lived was a superficial world, all surface. Her concern was with gossip like that about Hagen and his beautiful wife and the jewels which were locked up when she was not wearing them. Gretl never thought out anything to the end. She never looked beneath the surface. She seemed to accept what came her way without much question or complaint. Yet there was something warm and simple and kindly about her which grew into our hearts. I found myself thinking again and again what a pity it was that the life for which she was meant should have been so completely disrupted by men and forces of which she understood nothing.

The next day Hagen left, after sending flowers to my wife with a message repeating his invitation to let him know if we were ever in Munich or Berlin or near his *Schloss* in Bavaria. The gesture rather astonished me, for there had been no real intimacy between us, but only a kind of veiled, fundamental hostility based upon the striking difference of manners, ideals, and background. I could only think he believed that somehow, someday, in some way, I might be useful to him.

After he had gone, the young man with the straw-colored hair and pale-blue eyes reappeared again in Heintzlemann's company and each night they got drunk and sang and make a rather repulsive spectacle of themselves. The most astonishing thing was the indifference with which the other Germans accepted this behavior. Even the hand-washing Turnbaum did not seem to object. One change, however, was noticeable. This was the change in behavior of the other Germans toward ourselves. It was quite evident that our connection with Baron von Hagen had impressed them. They no longer pushed us about and jostled us out of the best seats. They even said, "Good morning" and "Good evening" very politely.

When I spoke sarcastically of this to Gretl, she said, "Sure, they think you're important since they saw you with Hagen. They think you might be able to do something for them, and they're afraid of you too. They're all afraid of everybody else. It's like that in Germany now."

Then Luigi, Gretl's "fiancé," appeared. Without any pretense he simply shared Gretl's attic bedroom.

Luigi isn't worth more than a paragraph. It was easy to see at the first glance what he was—just another Italian gigolo, a young man, probably of peasant or lower middle-class stock, whom nature had endowed with vigorous black hair, a handsome face, large black eyes, and a magnificent physique. He wasn't the usual sort of night-club *thé dansant* gigolo. That had gone out of fashion three or four years earlier. He was another type altogether. He skied like a demon and had the energy of a horse, and he used the prodigious endowment bestowed on him by a kind nature as a way of making his living and leading an easy life. I know Gretl was in love with him in her curious, easygoing way, and he must have been a little in love with Gretl to have left his easy life in more luxurious, attractive, cosmopolitan winter resorts to come to Saint-Firmin to spend a week with her in an attic bedroom.

He was our first experience with Gretl's extraordinary capacity for always picking the wrong man. He had no more brains than Gretl. He was, like her, just a kind of natural phenomenon. He left without creating any impression stronger than that based upon the fact that he was a remarkable athlete and a hell of a good skier. Gretl said he had to leave to go back to his business in Milano. I really think she believed this. She had a remarkable capacity for deceiving herself when her affections were involved. She really thought, while she washed her stockings and underclothes in that attic room, that they were going to be married.

After he had gone, we saw more of Gretl than ever. As the holiday season passed, the Germans began to leave—the Old Sow, the Wolf, and all the others. Heintzlemann and the straw-haired boy were among the first to go. As they left, the place began to grow more pleasant and that feeling of sinister foreboding, which was like a kind of obscure, lingering, physical pain, disappeared altogether at times.

Slowly, bit by bit, in her casual, disjointed way, Gretl came to reveal more and more of her story, so that by the end of January, when the money she had saved gave out, and she left for Vienna to go back to work as a chorus girl and to "meet Luigi," we knew all about her and the picture became clear.

It was a curious story. She came of a perfectly respectable German family on the edge of being *hochgeboren*. She had a widowed mother, two aunts, and a smaller brother and sister. They were all utterly ruined by the inflation and reduced to that respectable destitution which is the most horrid of all poverty. They did not actually have enough to eat, yet their position, which was all they had left, would not permit them to stand in a soup line or even to apply for the full amount of public relief they might have received.

Not far away from their house in a middle-class Berlin suburb there lived a rich and eccentric older man called Baron von Schildsen. He lived in a great house, surrounded by a walled garden, and since Gretl had been a little girl he had shown an apparently kindly but actually sinister interest in her, giving her apples and pears and candy and arranging to meet her as she came out of the *Hochschule* and walk part-way home with her. Only her childish instinct told her that there was something odd about him and made her always refuse his invitation to come into his garden.

When she was eighteen, her mother fainted one day from hunger in the doorway of a department store. It happened twice more, and then Gretl, in her simple, straightforward way, hit upon a solution. Anything, she concluded, was better than living always with an empty stomach and seeing her mother dying of starvation and her small brother and sister crying themselves to sleep with hunger. So one afternoon she walked into the house of the old Baron and quite simply said she would marry him if he would see to it that her family had enough to eat. It did not occur to her to ask him for a settlement. She simply wanted her family to have enough to eat and that was the way to get it.

The old man was only too delighted to marry her, and she went to live in the great house surrounded by the walled garden. He had only one servant, an old woman, who went home every night.

The life was a nightmare. What happened in the big house must have been terrible, for each time she spoke of it, she looked suddenly pale and ill.

"I stood it for nearly a year," she said, "and then I went to a judge and said I wanted a divorce. When I told him as much of my story as I could, the judge said, 'Of course, my girl. And under the circumstances, he will have to make you a good settlement.' "

She got the divorce and the settlement, but as the inflation increased it didn't mean very much. What had seemed a big fortune dwindled in value to little more than enough to keep her family in the coarse, common kind of food which would keep them alive, and Gretl was very nearly back where she started. It was then she decided that the thing for her to do was to leave Germany and earn money outside. A franc or even a krone or a lira could be translated into thousands of marks.

So she had gone to Vienna, where her healthy good looks and

un-German figure got her a job in the theater. What happened to her did not matter too much so long as her family in Berlin had enough to eat.

The story was just as simple as that. The extraordinary thing was that she seemed so untouched. It was, on the face of it, a horrible story, but Gretl herself seemed to have been unscarred by its horror. Perhaps it was that curious simplicity and superficiality which saved her. The past did not trouble her. The present was good enough. She lived always in the future in a kind of fairy-tale belief that someday there would turn up some fairy-tale prince, good-looking, charming, and rich, who would solve everything.

Our fondness for her increased, and on the day she left we went to the station with her and Runty to see them off. She said, "I'll look you up when I get to Paris. That's where I mean to end up."

As the train pulled out, we walked back up the hill in the belief that very likely we should never see her again. We had a kind of nomad philosophy about such friendships. But it was not to be so. We were to see her again and again. I had a letter from her only the other day, a letter smuggled out of Paris into Geneva and thence by plane to Ohio. It was as if there was something in the stars that drew us together, or it may have been that at times she grew weary and disgusted with her strange, disorderly life and sought the stability which our household and family represented. In any case, the curious, unlikely friendship has survived for nearly fifteen years.

With the coming of the avalanche season, I began to grow tired of the monotony of life in Saint-Firmin, and all of us began to feel a homesickness for the farm in France. We wanted to be home in time for the spring planting and the moment when the whole floor of the forest was covered with daffodils. Even my own passion for skiing waned before that homesickness. I wanted to see the gray walls and red roofs of Senlis blossom with the yellow wallflowers, the poplars turn green and feathery against the blue sky of the Oise. But most of all, after the strained, sinister winter, I was homesick again for my neighbors—the farmers, the simple people one met at the market, the Archiprêtre, the Mayor, the *petite noblesse*—all those French people who were so civilized, even the humblest and poorest of them.

I knew I would never again see Saint-Firmin, with its gorges and glaciers and wild beauty. I felt a little sad. It was not the wildness of the beauty that had ruined the place for me, but the aura of people at the Beau-Site. Somehow they had brought all that was sinister in Germany with them.

A year later from Vienna we had a letter from Gretl. It was written in rather stiff, formal English, completely contradicted by the ending, "Your warmly affectionate Gretl." It contained not very much of interest to us, save that even trivial things which happened to Gretl, such as a quarrel with the laundress or a proposition from the stage manager, had an interest. We had never known anyone quite like her. She had been home for a visit to her mother, who was well. She had not stayed for long as she did not like what was going on in Germany. It was, she wrote, no longer like Germany. She had not married Luigi. "He was no good," she wrote simply and directly, "what you call a bum. I guess I was lucky." The Baron Hagen had turned up in Vienna. "He is still after me," she wrote, "but pfui!" Hagen, she said, was one of the backers of that man Hitler she had told us about. At the end, she wrote, "I have got a job in a musical troupe going to London. If I have time while passing through Paris, I will telephone you."

Apparently she did not have time, for we never heard from her. She disappeared, apparently in the direction of London, leaving no address.

Three years passed before I again saw Hagen. In the meantime much had happened, for "the little man called Hitler" was no longer someone unknown and insignificant. He had become a power in Germany, backed by a gang of cutthroats and sadists and adventurers. The feeble attempt at democracy in Germany had broken down, sabotaged and wrecked on the side of Germany by all the elements which hated democracy, and sabotaged and wrecked from the outside by elements within the democracies themselves, who valued wealth and power above decency and sought to build up in Germany "a bulwark against Bolshevism." They existed in England, in France, even in America. I am afraid my friend Herbert, who so admired Hagen, was one of them. For these elements, "the little man called Hitler" was a wonderful instrument. To a Germany shattered, confused, and in despair, he promised everything. He promised employment, a sound currency, food, the destruction of the Bolshevists and the destruction of the capitalists, the end of the Jews, and the elevation of all true Germans to the wealth, the power, the civilization they coveted. It was a neat but sweeping program for a wrecked and despairing nation, choked with revenge and envy. And in the weakness and confusion of Europe, he had help from the stupid and the avaricious outside Germany.

I came to Munich from the sad loveliness of Vienna and stopped at the Hotel Vierjahreszeiten. Vienna was depressing, but in a nostalgic fashion, like the sound of a waltz associated in one's youth with a love affair, but Munich was aggressively depressing. It was never a very gay city, and its bilious-yellow neo-Florentine squares seemed charged with a kind of desperate vitality. Everywhere there were men and boys in brown shirts saluting each other with outstretched arms, filling the sidewalks in the crowded parts of the city, marching in columns, singing rather fierce, wild songs. The singing and marching went on at intervals all through the night beneath the windows of my room in the Vierjahreszeiten. Once in the street I stopped to listen to a brown-shirted spellbinder haranguing a crowd of brown-shirted boys and a few civilians. It was a familiar harangue, in Germany a very old one. It followed the lines of the talk I had heard in the Beau-Site in Saint-Firmin. Germans were a superior race. They had never had what they deserved. The Führer and the Nazi Party would give it to them. They would have power. They would have wealth.

They would ride other inferior races. The Jews must be exterminated. Germany would be supreme.

And all the familiar and fantastic discourse, punctuated by the *Heils* of the crowd, seemed to be believed by them. Indeed, they were hungry for it.

The same night in the open street before the hotel I saw two men kicked and beaten by twenty men in brown shirts and two or three civilians. I was told that the victims were simply anti-Nazis.

All these things were terrifying, for what I was witnessing was not at that time even the operations of a government, but of a secret government inside the government. Hitler was not yet in power, but only the head of a political party. Munich already belonged to the Nazis. They ruled it.

I had expected to stay only a day, but the brown-shirted spectacle fascinated me, even in its more revolting aspects, and so I stayed on for nearly a week, aware vaguely that somehow what I witnessed concerned me as well as everyone else in the whole world. It was the brutal vitality of the spectacle that made it important.

On the third day as I stepped out of the lift I found the hallway filled with men in brown shirts. They seemed to be gathered about two or three important figures, being received by the manager of the hotel. Discreetly I turned to discover who they were, and succeeded. One was von Hagen, the second was Heintzlemann, and the third was Dr. Goebbels. It was my first sight of him. The face was that of a rat. You might have seen it in any criminal court in New York or Chicago where gangsters were on trial. It was exactly that—the face of a shrewd criminal who fancied he could outsmart the whole world.

Heintzlemann was still gross in appearance, although thinner than he had been in Saint-Firmin. He was dressed in riding breeches and a brown shirt with a leather belt. He carried a heavy riding crop. I looked for the boy with the straw-colored hair, but he was not there.

Von Hagen looked much the same. It was summer, but even without the long black overcoat with the mink collar, he still resembled a prosperous provincial undertaker.

I went up to my room and wrote him a note. It was brief, saying simply that I was in Munich and would like him to dine with me. I scarcely expected an answer. He gave the impression of being immensely important and immensely busy. But in the afternoon I found a note from him, saying he could not dine with me but could I dine with him. It was his habit to see certain people during the dinner hour, he might be interrupted from time to time, but if I did not mind that, he would be delighted to see me.

Of course I accepted. There were so many things I wanted to know.

We dined not in the Walterspiel belowstairs but in his own suite, the suite reserved in the old days for minor members of the Imperial family passing through Munich. It was a dreary set of rooms, with a salon furnished in clumsy furniture made of dark wood, upholstered in dusty-red plush. The walls were hung with second-rate tapestries and adorned with the heads of stags and wild boars. I believe it was called the Hunting Suite. The dining room was done in much the same manner, with immensely heavy, grotesquely carved chairs upholstered in machine-made needlepoint. It was all luxurious in an *echt Deutsch* fashion.

Von Hagen greeted me with as much warmth as his dank nature could summon. His hands were still waxen and damp. It was a great pleasure, he said, to find me in Munich. How were my wife and the children?

Then as the cocktails he ordered were brought in, another door opened and a very beautiful woman came into the room. She could not have been more than thirty, with dark hair and blue eyes and a fine figure. She was dressed with great chic in a simple black gown with wonderful pearls.

"This is my wife," said Hagen, and to her he said, "This is a great American friend of mine. We met in Saint-Firmin."

I remembered all that Gretl had told me of the clothes, the jewels, the cruelty and avarice of von Hagen in relation to this woman, and until we had finished cocktails and were halfway through dinner my interest was almost entirely in her.

It was not only that she was beautiful. She had as well a great air of distinction. She left the conversation to Hagen and me, herself scarcely speaking. Once or twice when she did make an observation, Hagen cut her short with an air of contempt and cruelty. He treated her as I have seen men treat dogs which they value more for breeding and the value as show animals than as friends or objects of affection. She did not appear to resent the rudeness. There was something still and quiet and mysterious about her, as if she were quietly enduring her present position, secure in the knowledge that elsewhere, outside the world of Hagen, there were happiness and satisfaction. I thought, "This woman has a lover somewhere whom she loves passionately."

The conversation of Hagen was obviously made to please me. That, the world learned later, was part of the technique. They believed that if they could make you like them, they could deceive you all the more easily. But there was, too, the pitiful desire of the German to be loved. I was aware of an echo of the speech so often heard among the Germans at Saint-Firmin, "Why does the world dislike us?" Yet Hagen's conversation was cynical, too, as if, I think, to show that he took me into the confidence of the Nazi Party. It was the sort of technique which would have worked admirably with Herbert. For myself, I found something repulsive in it, as if he were betraying the secrets of his side and saying at the same time, "You and I know what they are like. They aren't quite gentlemen or decent." It was a method, a habit, I have encountered in many Germans, even in very different times.

The conversation turned to Saint-Firmin, and when I said, "I saw Heintzlemann today. He seems to be quite important," he answered, "He is. He is head of the special guard of the Führer."

I asked, "What has become of the boy with the straw-colored hair?"

Hagen grinned—the grin of an undertaker taking you into his confidence about some scandal in the family of the bereaved. "He disappeared. I believe it was a matter of jealousy."

"You mean liquidated?" I asked, using a word just then coming into usage in Europe.

"He disappeared," repeated Hagen, and I knew what he meant. "But he has been replaced," he added, "several times over, I understand. It is very difficult to resist a man with Heintzlemann's power."

Then a little later I chanced to remark that an organization like the Führer's must need a lot of money and expressed curiosity as to where it came from. Hagen grinned again. "That is where I come in," he said, "myself and many others."

And then I understood. The remark explained a great deal—that men like Hagen, the big bankers and industrialists, had put their money on Hitler, not only the bankers and industrialists of Germany, but men outside, in other countries. I felt a little sick.

But Hagen was saying, "All this competition in the world is a terrible waste. The cartel idea is the solution. If bankers and industrialists could control the world, there would be no wars, but only prosperity for everyone. There would be no Bolshevism." He paused over his pudding and said, "You know, men like you could do a great service to the world by explaining such things." And then I knew why I had been asked to dinner and been treated so cordially. I understood too why, although he had asked me to dine with him because he had two or three rendezvous, we had never been interrupted.

He said, "I would like to show you about—to take you on the inside of the movement. If you could stay a few days. I shall be going to Nuremberg and then Stuttgart. I would be glad to have you go with me."

My curiosity prompted me to accept the invitations, but a sense of aversion made it impossible. I could not picture myself spending several days in the man's company. I heard myself saying, "I should like nothing better but I must be in Paris on Thursday."

"Another time then. Write me at the Stuttgart office whenever you feel inclined to come. I will arrange it."

"Thank you."

Then he turned to his wife and said, "You may go, Lisa, whenever you like."

She rose and bowed toward me. "It has been a pleasure to meet you," she said. "The evening has been very interesting."

It was a formal speech, spoken mechanically. She obviously had no interest whatever in me or in our conversation. I bowed and said I hoped we should see each other again, and she went out quickly. Hagen watched her with a curious look of obsession in his yellow-brown eyes.

When she had gone, I said, "May I say that your wife is a very handsome woman?"

He grinned, "Yes, she is good-looking, although not very clever. Politics bore her. She has not the mind for it."

There was one more question I wanted to ask. I asked it. "Tell me, what is the Führer like?"

He did not answer me at once. He took a sip of brandy and turned it over on his tongue. Then he looked at me for a moment, as if speculating upon how much he dared to say. When he spoke, he said, "That is a difficult question to answer. He is a little man—a hysterical fellow. He is important only because he expresses something very profound in the German character and because the times are made for him—or for a man exactly like him. In another time, in different circumstances, he would be only a ludicrous figure."

Now, long afterward, I still think that Hagen's description, perhaps sincere at the time, perhaps uttered only to mislead me, was an excellent one.

I had had enough and felt unbearably restless as one does in the company of people whose every speech is calculated and devoid of all sincerity. Conversation with Hagen was difficult because it was like talking to a dead man. There was no warmth in it, nothing to kindle the excitement which is the essence of good conversation. I made the excuse of having work to do and said that I knew he was a very busy man.

As I was leaving, he asked, "Have you seen our friend Gretl?"

I said that we had heard from her but had not seen her—that she was in London.

"I know," he said. "She was in Germany a month ago. I saw her. She was prettier than ever. I don't think she likes me very much. I am trying to make her like me." He smiled as he lighted a second expensive cigar. It was the smile of a man who had been used to having his own way, even if he had to buy it.

From the street, below the window, came the sound of the Horst Wessel song and the sound of marching feet—that heavy tramp! tramp! with which every street in Germany was beginning to echo.

Hagen turned toward the window. "Come," he said. "Look!"

We went to the window and below in the street we saw a column of young men all in brown shirts, marching and singing. They were marching with that rhythm and precision which only German troops manage to achieve. It is a terrifying thing—the utter absorption of the individual into a machine, born of desire of the individual to be absorbed, to lose his own identity utterly in the machine—the *will* to be a cog.

Every other man in the procession carried a torch, and the wildly flickering flames gave the whole scene a barbaric appearance. For a time we watched in silence and I thought, "Exactly like that they came out of the swamps and forests of Germany to fight Caesar—tied together with ropes to be slaughtered by the Roman legions. Perhaps it will happen again." And as I watched them, memories of the war came back to me, memories of German troops advancing arm in arm, shoulder to shoulder, singing as they came, to be mowed down by machine-gun bullets. I thought, "It is going to happen again. There is something in the German nature which finds an ecstasy in suicide."

The column passed, and the singing of the song glorifying a pimp began to die away. Hagen turned toward me, "Impressive, *nicht wahr?*"

"Yes," I said, "and a little frightening." I looked at him. "It will be a nuisance if the world has to defeat you again."

His face did not change expression. "This time," he said, "it will not be defeat. Victory for us will benefit the world. We have so much to give it."

I went away the next day, happy once again to cross the bridge into Alsace.

My wife was in Paris to meet me. "Gretl has turned up," she said. "She is dining with us. Something has happened to her."

"What?" I asked.

"I don't know exactly, but she's different. She looks almost chic. But that's only the outside. There's something inside, too."

We dined at Maxim's, where Gretl met us. The fourth was a young man whom she introduced as "My cousin Eric Nattleman." He was tall, very blond, good-looking, and, as it turned out, rather dull. He had some sort of job in the German Foreign Office.

As soon as Gretl came in, I saw what my wife meant. Gretl was dressed smartly, yet the effect was not of smartness. Her clothes were as good as any of those of the women in the room, yet she did not look chic. Underneath, she was still Gretl, the Lutheran pastor's daughter. She was spontaneously happy to see us and kissed us both. She had been in London, she said, where she had had a small part in a play.

The evening was not remarkable, perhaps because of the presence of the cousin. He was definitely a defeating young man, taciturn, pompous, and, like so many Germans, on the defensive. Conversation with him was impossible. Maxim's that night was filled with spectacular people of every nationality. As a spectacle it was remarkable, but Herr Nattleman regarded the whole scene with a priggish contempt, refusing to become a part of it or even to regard it objectively, as the spectacle it was. Perhaps he was right.

Perhaps that was a part of the Nazi strength. Perhaps it was something the rest of us had to learn through the bitterness of war.

At any rate, we were rid of him by the end of the evening.

When we came in for a night from the country we stayed at an expensive but curious hotel. It was called the Suffolk, and one was as likely to encounter there Kipling or Lady Reading as the Marquesa Casati or a Hollywood actress. It was a small hotel, but many mysterious people came and went. The proprietor was Swiss. His wife was Dutch. It was luxurious and beautifully run. When the Germans entered Paris six years later, the officers went directly to the Suffolk, where they were expected. Everything was in readiness for them. It was all a part of a well-worked-out scheme.

That night Gretl was staying at the hotel and her cousin left us at the door. Inside, she said, "Pfui! What a prig! And I used to be in love with him. I guess my taste for Germans is spoiled."

She came into our room for a nightcap and stayed a long time to talk. It was true that something had happened to her. She was a little wiser and a great deal harder, yet at moments she was the old simple *gemütlich* German pastor's daughter. I had the impression that she was tired. Something about her made you want to weep, and while she talked, I found myself thinking again, "She should never have left Germany. She should have married a nice, middle-class German and had a whole family by now." If things had been different, I kept thinking—if the Kaiser had not coveted the whole world. If the Germans had only been content with all the power and wealth they had. And then I thought of Munich and the Vierjahreszeiten and von Hagen looking down into the street at the Brown Shirts marching past, carrying torches, singing a song that glorified a pimp. And I thought, "It is beginning all over again. And a whole new generation of young people like Gretl will have their lives ruined." No, Gretl was never meant to be a trollop. She was very bad at it.

Then suddenly she said, "I forgot to tell you something very interesting. You remember, I told you about von Hagen's wife?"

"Yes," I said, "I met her in Munich. I dined with them. She is very beautiful. I can't see how she puts up with him."

"Oh!" said Gretl, with something of the old innocence. "She doesn't love him. My cousin Eric is her lover. That's what I meant to tell you."

I thought, "So I was right when I saw her in Munich." I asked, "Does von Hagen know it?"

"No," said Gretl. "If he did, he would kill one or both of them—in some way nobody would ever discover. It would be an accident or a strange illness. He told me once that is what he would do if any woman was unfaithful to him."

"He doesn't seem the jealous type," I said.

Then Gretl made an observation of great wisdom. "He's not jealous," she said. "It's different. It's vanity with him. He can't bear to think that any woman he had could find any other man more attractive. There are lots of men like that—most men are, I think. It comes because they know they're inferior. That's why von Hagen thinks of nothing but money and power. It's because he isn't much good as a man or a lover. Nobody in Germany likes him. They only show him respect because he's rich and powerful."

Presently, about four in the morning, my wife yawned and went to bed, but Gretl said she couldn't sleep, so we had another drink and went on talking, and then Gretl came to the point.

She said, blushing a little, "Could you lend me some money? I'm absolutely broke. I got here from London with nothing but my clothes and a few hundred francs."

Being in the money at the moment, I said that of course I'd lend her any reasonable amount, but I expressed surprise that she was broke since she looked so well and expensively dressed.

She laughed and in the laugh was the first bitterness I had ever heard in Gretl. She said, "The clothes are all right, but my boy friend walked out on me. He just went off to Australia and left me cold, without a cent but what I had in my purse."

"Who was he?"

"A stockbroker, about fifty-five. He was nice and kind of dumb but he certainly squeezed every farthing."

So she had picked wrong again.

In the hour that followed until daylight came up over the chestnut trees in the gardens behind the Suffolk, I gave Gretl a lecture, a wholly unmoral but realistic lecture. It might have come out of *L'École de Cocottes.*

"First of all," I said, "you're no good at this kind of life. You weren't meant for it. You ought to go back to Germany and marry and settle down and have a family. That's what you were meant for. Terrible things happen when people willfully distort their own destinies."

She frowned, and after a moment she said, "I know you're right. But it wasn't my fault. Everything got started off wrong. And it's too late to turn back now. I couldn't do that now. I wouldn't know how to live quietly." Then a hardness came into her voice. "Anyway, I could never live in Germany again. I'd suffocate. I'd go crazy. I couldn't go back there after I've tasted what it's like outside. No, it's no good talking to me about that—telling me to go back and be one of Hitler's brood sows."

She was perfectly firm about it, and I confess that I saw her point. It was too late for Gretl to turn back to nursing children and washing diapers. Her destiny was hopelessly twisted.

So I said, "Well, if you're going to lead this kind of life, at least use some brains about it. Get yourself a rich man who is generous too and get a settlement out of him. Get some jewels. Get something to show for it."

"The trouble is," said Gretl, "I always fall in love. I'm just a fool, maybe, but that's how it is."

"Even with the stockbroker?"

"Yes. Even with him. He was so dumb and he had such nice manners. And he didn't know anything about women at all. The only woman he'd ever known until he met me was his wife—one of those long-footed Englishwomen. He didn't go away because he was tired of me. He went away because he was ashamed. He was getting old, you see."

I did see. Gretl's simplicity never left you any doubts about things.

"Well," I said, "get yourself fixed with money and jewels and then you can afford to fall in love with somebody like Luigi."

At the mention of Luigi she blushed. "I know you didn't like Luigi," she said, "but you didn't understand him. He was a child." Then she said an astonishing thing, "Two whores couldn't marry each other. We both knew that always. I always felt sorry for Luigi."

Brutally, I said, "You've got to get over being sentimental. You're too damned nice for your job."

We had finished talking by daylight. I told her I would pay the hotel bill and gave her a check for ten thousand francs. "You can pay me back," I said, "when you strike it rich. Someday you'll come to your senses and get in the money."

She began to cry. She was a little tipsy. "You've both been good to me—so good to me. I don't know why you should."

"Forget it. I guess it's because we like you."

Then she went to her room, and as I closed the door, it seemed to me that Gretl was hopelessly German—nice German. She was a part of an extraordinarily confused picture of which von Hagen was a part, and Heintzlemann and even Herr Oberregierungsrat Moll and his wife were a part. Gretl and the Molls were the reason why so many stupid English and a few Americans were always saying, "The Germans are very much like us. They are so kind and homelike and solid." The same people were always overlooking von Hagen and Heintzlemann and the others, and the fact that people like Gretl and the Molls inevitably and periodically became their victims.

Later, as I fell asleep, it occurred to me that it was odd that Gretl had never mentioned having seen von Hagen on her visit to Germany.

A few days later Gretl left for Vienna. It was as if Vienna and not Germany was her spiritual home. Whenever she came to the end of her tether she went back to Vienna. She said she was going to the Festival in Salzburg. There would be a lot of rich foreigners there. We did not see her again for nearly two years, although we had letters quite regularly. She had fallen in love with a rich Czech from Prague. He was married and had five children, so it was not convenient to live in Prague. Instead, she stayed in Vienna, a city which she loved.

During this period she returned again to Germany to see her mother. Back again in Vienna, she wrote, "I did not stay as long as I expected. Germany is horrible. I shall never go there again. I was insulted and called bad names in the street because I wore good clothes and lacquer on my nails. My younger brother has joined the Brown Shirts and he would not speak to me much of the time. He called me *Ausländer* and worse things. It seems he forgot that he is alive today instead of starved to death because I went among *Ausländers* to make money to feed him. One night he called me all sorts of vile names. If my mother ever wants to see me again she will have to leave Germany. I hate it the way it is now—worse than I hated it when we were starving." Then she added, "I am very well and happy. I love Hansl [the Czech] very much. He is a very serious and respectable man." But she neglected to say anything about a settlement or any jewels. I said to my wife, "It's the same old story. She'll get nothing out of it."

Meanwhile, in Paris, you became aware on every side of the Nazi octopus. Its tentacles emerged now and then in the most unexpected way above the rubbish which coated the whole confused maelstrom of French and international life. Wherever they appeared, they corrupted. Among the rich you heard people saying, "I think this man Hitler must have the answer. There are no strikes, no popular fronts, in Germany. He has found the cure for Bolshevism." Even while the Church and the Jews were being persecuted in Germany, you heard rich Catholics and Jews in Paris defending the Nazis. "Oh," they would say, "the persecution is not real. It's merely political and made for effect. Hitler is really protecting them secretly. One of the secretaries at the German Embassy told me so himself." Or, "Herr Abetz told me confidentially that what Hitler wants most is a close alliance with Germany and France. We have never been able to count on England. We could count on Germany to help us put an end to Bolshevism." You heard the same kind of talk among high officers of the French army. Among English and American diplomats you heard quite often words of praise for the order that the Nazis were bringing about in Germany. I heard one military attaché say, "We need something of the sort in America."

Wherever the tentacles reached among the so-called "upper classes," they emitted a cloud of poison.

Von Hagen came and went from Paris. His name was always in the paper. He was conferring with Georges Bonnet or Flandin or Laval or the big industrialists. Once or twice I encountered him in the corridors of the Ritz, where he always stayed nowadays, abandoning Claridge's, which was the hotel usually frequented by rich Germans. On these occasions we had brief conversations and always he mentioned Gretl and asked if we had news of her. It was not merely the casual mention of a mutual friend to fill in gaps in conversation. He spoke of her admiringly. "She is the good German type," he would say. "I wish we had more of them." I had the impression that Gretl was almost an obsession with him. He mentioned the fact that he had seen her on her last visit to Germany, and again it occurred to me that it was odd she never mentioned having seen him, either in her conversation or her letters.

Once I mentioned Heintzlemann, saying that I understood that he had become very powerful in Germany.

"Oh, yes," von Hagen said, "very powerful. He is the head of all the Brown Shirts, but he is a stupid fellow. All egotist and ambitions. He will come a cropper. He has too many enemies. Lately he has been insufferable."

From the speech and manner I gathered that he and Heintzlemann were no longer having those little secret, intimate meetings at which they had cooked up so many things.

Then suddenly our old friend Herbert appeared in Paris from New York. He was just as clean and shiny as ever, and just as stupid in his intuitions and judgment of people. But he had put on a little weight and definitely had jowls. This time his wife was with him, a nice, pleasant-looking woman who was president of her garden club in Long Island. There was a suffocating sense of innocence about them both, especially in comparison with von Hagen and some of the French and German politicians with whom he was dealing as the purpose of his visit. It was not the pious, smug stupidity of so many Englishmen who contributed to bringing on the disaster, but just plain innocence, of that American kind which cannot believe that there are people as villainous as von Hagen or as fanatic as Hitler or as depraved as Heintzlemann.

Herbert was excited during most of the visit about the details of a gigantic deal he was putting over. In his innocence, he liked to surround everything he did with mystery. He liked to use the expression "big deal," with a comical look of mystery in his clear blue eyes. It never occurred to him, I think, that every newspaper correspondent in Paris knew pretty well what was going on and that he was in Paris to help bring about a gigantic cartel of industrialists, German, American, British, and French, which was to rule the world.

Before he left, he gave a dinner party to which he invited me. None but men were present, some of whom I knew, some I did not. They were big industrialists. The Frenchmen all represented the *deux cents familles* hated by the men of the Popular Front.

It was an extraordinary gathering, held to celebrate the conclusion of the cartel agreement and paid for, of course, by the American. I heard frightening things that night, partly, I think, because of two assumptions on the part of the French—that I too was in the racket, and that being an American I could not understand very well what they were saying. I heard their willingness to sell out France as a nation. I heard them talk not at all as Frenchmen but as creatures who were above nationality, to whom money and power and property were the only values in life. It was the first time I remember having heard the name of Admiral Darlan. It was clear that he was working with them.

Of course, von Hagen was there, looking more than ever like a provincial undertaker in his tails and white tie. He was in a gleeful mood, making bad German jokes, and telling disgustingly filthy stories, his opaque cat's eyes shrewd and cold with watching the effect upon the others. One had the impression that he was faintly hysterical now that the whole coveted world was almost in his grasp and the grasp of Nazi Germany. At end of the dinner, von Hagen, another German, a Frenchman, and an Englishman went off to a brothel—described by von Hagen as a very special sort of place, very discreet, where very special entertainment was provided.

Once in bed I could not sleep for thinking of the things I had heard and divined during the course of the evening. I felt a little sick and filled again with that dreadful sense of foreboding I had known long ago among the white peaks of Saint-Firmin. I wanted suddenly to return to America and escape from this sick, corrupt, dying Europe.

I wakened late and when I telephoned for breakfast, my wife came into the room holding a copy of the Paris *Herald*. She said simply, "It has happened."

"What?" I asked.

"What Gretl said would happen. Von Hagen's wife and Gretl's cousin have been killed in an accident in Germany. The *Herald* simply says their car ran into an obstruction on the road. The *Daily Mail* says it was a steel cable stretched across the road."

I read both accounts of the "accident." The *Daily Mail* reported that Baroness von Hagen, accompanied by Freiherr Eric Nattleman, were on their way in a high-powered sports car from Munich to the Baron von Hagen's *Schloss* at Titelsee when the car struck a steel cable stretched across the road. Both bodies were very nearly decapitated. Confidential sources in Berlin reported that very likely the "accident" was a plot on the life of von Hagen himself, who had many bitter enemies in Germany. The murderers had killed Baroness von Hagen and Freiherr Nattleman by mistake.

Then slowly over the *café au lait* I began to understand the full horror of the story. If Gretl was right and von Hagen himself was the murderer, he had known what was happening as he sat at last night's dinner to celebrate his triumph. He had known it when he went off to the luxurious brothel to continue the evening's entertainment. It may have been the reason for his air of hysteria. To my wife I said, "It couldn't be true."

She was more skeptical. "Remember what Gretl said. Remember those people at Saint-Firmin. Any of them could have been guilty of such a crime."

But it was difficult to believe. No one, not even myself, believed a man at the top of the Nazi party could be such an utter criminal.

A week later there was a letter from Gretl. Hansl, the Czech, had died suddenly of a stroke. There was no provision made for her. It was the old story again. Another love affair was ended and she was broke. She would, she wrote, see us in Paris as soon as she could get her affairs in order. At the very end she wrote, "You see, what I told you about von Hagen is true. He must have found out about his wife and Eric."

It was altogether a sickening world.

The third thing to happen was the death of Heintzlemann. We wakened one morning to find the newspapers filled with news of "the purge." It had happened swiftly, with a primitive and savage barbarity. Heintzlemann was one of the first victims. Hitler himself had gone to Heintzlemann's villa, where he found him with a boy. The boy, Hitler murdered himself, screaming with rage as he pulled the trigger. Heintzlemann, said the paper, was given a revolver and the choice of shooting himself or being shot. He was dead, although the press did not know whether as a suicide

She hurried away and in a few minutes came out again and joined the *hochgeboren Dame* in the car.

A little after six she reappeared in the bar. She had changed her clothes and looked very smart and was wearing a ruby bracelet that cost plenty and a big emerald on her left hand. Over Martinis, I said, "What's all the mystery? Are you marrying Hitler?" And she answered me with a touch of the old Gretl's naïveté. "No," she said quite sincerely, "not him."

"Göring?"

"He's just gotten married."

"Goebbels?"

"He has a wife."

And then partly as a guess, partly by intuition, I said, "I know."

"You couldn't."

"It's von Hagen."

The color came into her face and she did not answer at once.

"Why can't you tell me?"

"I promised not to tell anyone. It's to be a secret until after the ceremony. I promised not to tell as part of the bargain. I promised I wouldn't see any of my old friends. In exchange I don't have to live in Germany. I don't even have to go there. He's very peculiar, but that's how it is."

For a moment I was silent, puzzled and thoughtful. Then I said, "Of course, you know you're marrying Blue Beard. Remember the first wife?"

"Yes. I know all that. I think I can manage that."

"And you know the other unpleasant things about him."

"Yes. I'm not a young virgin getting married. But I think I can manage that too. I've been through a lot of things—a lot more than I've ever told you."

I became relentless, partly through curiosity. "Why are you marrying him?"

"He is the richest man in Germany and one of the most powerful."

"You remember what happened to Heintzlemann?"

"It won't happen to him. Even if it did, it wouldn't matter."

"I still don't get it."

"He has been mad for me always, even when his wife was alive, even when I was married to my first husband."

"But you?"

"I'm tired of being a victim. I'm tired of falling in love." She looked at me with a hard expression about the eyes and mouth. "I'm taking the advice you gave me. This time I'm going to clean up."

I laughed. "The more you clean him, the better it will suit me. You ought to cut the pictures out of the frames and sell them."

She only said, "Watch me!" A curious silence fell between us. I think she was embarrassed at having suddenly revealed so much and I think we were both regretting the simple, warmhearted Gretl who wasn't there any more, whom neither of us would ever find again.

"Well, I wish you luck."

"I'll be all right," she said.

"Why didn't you tell me you had seen von Hagen each time you went to Germany?" She didn't answer at once, and I added, "I knew it. He told me himself."

"I was ashamed."

"Is that why you told me the cock-and-bull story just now about promising not to tell whom you were marrying?"

"Yes." And quietly she added, "I must go now. The old dragon is waiting upstairs to chaperon me at dinner. The future Baroness von Hagen has got to be respectable now."

She rose from her chair. I got up too. "If you ever get into trouble, let us know. We'll always be interested."

She said, "I haven't forgotten the money you loaned me. I haven't had enough to pay you since then. I haven't even got it now, but as soon as I have, I'll pay you back."

"O.K. I haven't worried about it."

"Kiss Alice for me. I love her. I've never known any woman like her. To put up all these years with a tart like me."

"You're not a tart. You were never meant to be one."

The mouth turned suddenly hard again. "Watch me this time, baby."

She went away to join the *hochgeboren* dragon.

A fortnight later we received an overopulent engraved announcement with a coronet at the top telling of the marriage of Baroness von Schildsen and Baron von Hagen.

A little while later the Molls reappeared in the story in the form of a letter from Frau Moll. It contained only a line or two saying that Herr Oberregierungsrat Moll was dead in Cologne. Frau Moll wrote, "I know it may seem strange to hear from me after so many years, but my husband and I were always very fond of you both. In those trying days at Saint-Firmin you did much to make it bearable for us. We have thought of you often in the long years in between, and spoke of you often. Only a little time before he died my husband was talking of you. He said, 'I always like Americans. There is something bright and young and generous about them.' I thought you would like to know of his death and that he thought of you frequently."

I was sorry then that we had never taken the trouble to go a little out of the way and pay them a visit in Cologne.

But the letter did not end the story. A little while later a second letter arrived, this time bearing the postmark of Luxembourg. In it Frau Moll wrote, "A friend of mine is posting this outside Germany. There were many things I wanted to tell you in the earlier letter but could not, as everything I write and do is watched.

"My husband died, I think, of a broken heart. When Hitler came into power, they took away his judgeship because he opposed them. We were very nearly ruined and they continued to persecute and humiliate him in a thousand small ways. They took away his precious library of which he was so proud and worst of all they burned his books in the streets of Cologne. They had a special pile of rare editions with a sign on them, 'From the collection of former Herr Oberregierungsrat Moll, corrupted by foreign ways.'

"We could have gone away to England perhaps and have gotten along somehow, but my husband was born in the Rhineland and he loved it. He preferred to die there rather than as a stranger in a foreign country.

"I would like to see you both again but I am afraid it would be a shock to both of you. I am an old woman now. I live as quietly as possible, going out very rarely. It has been a long time since I have done any singing. Six years ago the Nazis forbade me to appear in public as a singer. I do not know what has become of our old Germany. It is not here any longer. I doubt that it will ever come back, for when we old ones are dead there will be no one who remembers it. It is not only that the Nazis have destroyed other people, they have destroyed the good Germans as well.

"I know you will be interested to hear that the one they used to call the Wolf is *Gauleiter* of our region now and that the Old Sow is called, 'Mother of the Woman's Youth Movement.' They were all there that winter in Saint-Firmin for a purpose.

"I would like to have news of you. Occasionally a friend goes into Belgium or Luxembourg and I am able to post a letter from there. You don't know how much a letter from the outside can mean to us here in Germany. But you must write carefully—just news of yourself without any comment on politics. My pitifully few letters are all opened before they reach me, and it would be very bad for me."

We wrote, of course, simple newsy letters about ourselves and the children, the garden and the dogs. Very discreetly we suggested that she join us for "a long visit" but we only got an answer that she was too tired and ill to leave Cologne. She was too old to make the change. That was the last we ever heard of Frau Moll. I think she must have died or perhaps she was killed in the raids on Cologne.

The nightmare was closing in.

Austria was invaded and Czechoslovakia threatened, and then Mr. Chamberlain took his umbrella and galoshes to Munich and there was no longer any doubt.

For months we had no news either of the Baron or the Baroness von Hagen and then one morning the papers announced that the Baron von Hagen had fled to Switzerland. He had, it seemed, encountered the disfavor of the Führer and those about him. How he escaped was unknown, but he had been deprived of all his property, all the vast holdings in banks and industry. This was divided between the Nazi Party and the Hermann Göring Works. But more than this, there was an order for his arrest for the murder of his first wife and a man called Eric Nattleman.

Once more there swept over me the sense of living in a bad melodrama in which there was no sense of reality whatever. These were people we knew—von Hagen, Gretl, the Molls, all those people in the hotel at Saint-Firmin and at the banquet von Hagen had given in Paris. They were made of flesh, of blood. The strange things which had happened to them had really happened.

That afternoon I went into Paris and booked passage for my wife and children. I was aware that when people in Europe came to accept the fantastic things that were happening as simply the course of events, the jig was up. The Europe which I had loved for so long was doomed. It would continue a little longer and then suddenly go down into the abyss. The Europe I had known and loved for nearly half my life would never again exist.

I went to Le Havre with the family, depressed at their departure. The children were excited and the dogs barked a great deal. From the deck of the *Normandie* I looked down on the port and the many-windowed, dreary Hôtel Frascati, thinking what a splendid smash a bomb would make of its brick and glass. A little later as the ship slipped out of the harbor, I felt a sense of relief and a great satisfaction in being an American. My family was going home, out of an insane world dominated by a madman. I think home never meant so much to me before.

I took the evening train back to Paris and on arrival went straight to a small but expensive little restaurant called Tout Paris. At that time it was filled with Austrian refugees, mostly from Vienna—not as guests but as entertainers. It was run by an Austrian, the band and the waiters were Viennese, and among the clientele were many Viennese refugees who could not afford to pay their checks but who sang or danced for their supper. They were good singers and dancers, with all the nostalgic charm of Vienna. I went there, instinctively seeking a last remembrance of things past, in Sachers and the Bristol and the Café de l'Europe, of the Festival at Salzburg and the Mirabelgarten—all the good civilized things which had been destroyed forever by the covetousness of men like von Hagen and Heintzlemann and all the others. Well, I reflected, as I took a table alone in a corner, Heintzlemann is dead, murdered, and von Hagen is in disgrace. Maybe the others will go in the same way. Perhaps, after all, there is a law rewarding good and punishing evil. Perhaps, after all, there is in the end a universal decency.

Feeling depressed, I ordered champagne, and as the waiter brought it, I heard a familiar voice—the voice of Gretl.

She was standing by the table and with her was a white-blonde Belgian trollop who looked a little like one of Frans Hals' women. I knew her slightly. I had seen her plying her trade in a dozen resorts and capitals. I was a little shocked to see Gretl in her company.

Yet Gretl did not look down-and-out. She wore a short coat of sable and three or four bracelets worth plenty of money. She looked extremely well and seemed gay and excited.

The two girls joined me and sat drinking champagne while I ate. We listened a good deal to the music, which was good, and especially to the singing of a Viennese girl who had been a star in Vienna. Gretl told me her story. She was in Paris without money or home, bound nowhere. Her mother was a Jewess, so there was no longer any place for her in any Germanic country.

She sang all the nostalgic songs, *Ein kleines Hotel, In Grinzing,* and, of course, *Vilia.*

Between the songs, Gretl talked in an odd, strained fashion. Once or twice I looked at her suspecting that she was taking drugs, but I think it was only a kind of overwrought excitement. The Belgian tart didn't say much. Her talents were not for conversation.

When I asked, "Where's Hagen?" she said, "In Switzerland. He's scared to come to Paris."

"Why?"

"He's afraid somebody will bump him off. He just stays in the villa at Lugano. It has a wall around it. He has five guards and a lot of big dogs."

"How did he let you out?"

"I didn't ask him. I just came. He didn't know I was coming. Anyway, it's all finished."

"You've got a sable coat and some mighty fine jewelry. Didn't he lock it up?"

"I just went to his room and took it while he was out driving. It's only small stuff. The rest is locked up."

I thought, "She's learning." But now there wasn't even a trace of the old Gretl.

"There's a lot more stuff—ten times this much. I'll get that later."

"How?"

She giggled and looked at the Belgian girl. "Never mind. We've got it figured out." The girl laughed too. She was obviously as much born to be a tart as Gretl had been born to be a good housewife and mother.

Then a dark, heavy little man came over to ask the Belgian girl to dance, and she left us alone.

"Now," I said, "what's the inside story of Hagen? Why did he scram from Germany?"

"They started cleaning him, and he got mad and fought them. Bit by bit they were taking away everything he had, his banks, his factories. . . . They were turning up under the control of Göring and some of the other boys."

"Sooner or later it seems to happen to all of them. Remember Heintzlemann?"

"That's what they'd have done to Hagen. It was all planned. He heard about it and pretended to go to the *Schloss* at Titelsee, and in the night he slipped over the border." It was odd that even now she always referred to him coldly as "Hagen." She never said "my husband" or called him by his Christian name.

"They never learn," I said.

"Who?"

"The people who think Fascism will protect them. They're always the first victims."

"I think he's gone nuts."

"How?"

"He saves wrapping paper and bits of string, and he has got uniforms for the hired guards and reviews them every morning."

"Is he broke?"

"No. He has plenty salted away outside. He is in a lot of deals in America and England that bring him in a big income. They're all like that—all the big shots in Germany. They don't even trust each other."

"I shouldn't think they would."

She wanted more champagne, which I got for her. Then she said, "Hagen thinks he's got all kinds of diseases, too. Sometimes he thinks he has syphilis and sometimes it's tuberculosis and sometimes cancer. There's nothing the matter with him but his imagination. He looks like a ghost. There are always doctors in the place. He thinks about himself so much he doesn't worry much about me any more."

I was silent for a time, thinking again that all these stories, all these people, were monstrous unrealities. I thought, "I've got to get out of here or I'll go nuts too."

The old sense of pollution, almost physical, swept over me to the accompaniment of Viennese music. It was extraordinary how easily people seemed to lose all decency and perspective in that insane prewar world. In a way they followed the pattern of Gretl's metamorphosis, changing imperceptibly without being aware of it. The corruption and despair, the cynicism, spread everywhere like a malignant disease. Perhaps, I thought, war and revolution are the only cures.

I asked suddenly, "Where did you pick up this tart?"

Gretl said, "She's all right. She's my adviser and manager. She's got a lot of smart ideas. We haven't finished yet with Hagen. He'll do anything I want except give me money and jewelry. I had to sell a ring to get the money to come to Paris. But he's got a lot of loot left."

"Well, you've earned it, I guess."

"I hope to tell you."

She talked just like that, using American slang she had picked up in the bars and cafés and restaurants—American slang was very fashionable then—American slang and cigarettes and cars and movie stars, from one end of Europe to the other.

The Belgian girl brought her friend back to the table and with him a middle-aged, shifty-looking man of undiscernible nationality who was introduced as Mr. Hoffstein. I didn't like either of them.

A little later I left them. It was the last time I saw Gretl.

The rest of the story which began in Saint-Firmin is brief enough.

Came the fall of France, which found von Hagen in Monte Carlo, where he had gone for his health. Once there in a rented villa surrounded by his dogs and uniformed guards, he was terrified to leave, even to return to Lugano. Then one day he was induced to go for a drive with his wife, and as they crossed the border on the road to Nice, the car was suddenly forced off the road by another car containing five men. They shot and wounded the one guard with him and dragged him into their car. That was the last ever heard of him.

Not quite a year ago I met Gregory Williams, an old newspaper-correspondent friend of mine, in "21." He was one of the last of the Americans to leave Paris, and we sat until two in the morning talking about all the people we had known in Paris, in Vienna, in London, in Berlin, and what had become of them. And presently the name of von Hagen came up.

"Certainly he is dead," said Gregory. "And they probably gave him the works before he died. I can't say I'm sorry. He was a rat if ever there was one. If they'd only kill each other off, the world would be a lot better place. I must say they've done pretty well and I guess they'll do a lot better before the thing is over."

"Did you ever know his wife?" I asked.

Gregory Williams grinned. "Sure I did."

"How is she doing?"

"She's doing all right. She's the queen of Paris now, living with the military governor in one of the Rothschild houses. They say she cleaned Hagen and took him for a ride and turned him over to the Nazis. She has cars and jewels and everything." He grinned again. "People over here won't believe some of the stories that happened in Europe. They just think you make them up. They say, 'Gee. You ought to write novels.' "

It was a queer end for a Lutheran pastor's daughter. But the end of von Hagen's story rather cheered me. It almost made me believe there was such a thing as Nemesis. I said, "Let's drink to the end of the rest of the bloody bastards."

We raised our glasses. "It won't be long now," said Gregory.

A month ago I received a letter postmarked Lisbon, bearing no return address. When I tore it open there fell out of it a letter and two one-hundred-pound British bank notes. The letter was in Gretl's handwriting. It read: "I took your advice. I'm doing fine. Here is the money you lent me long ago in Paris. It ought to cover the loan and the hotel bill and a little over. Good luck to you and Alice. See you after the war. Your affectionate friend—Gretl."